STARSHIP REPO

TOR BOOKS BY **PATRICK S. TOMLINSON**

Gate Crashers

Starship Repo

STARSHIP REPO

PATRICK S. **TOMLINSON**

TOR

A TOM DOHERTY ASSOCIATES BOOK

NEW YORK

This is a work of fiction. All of the characters, organizations, and events portrayed in this novel are either products of the author's imagination or are used fictitiously.

STARSHIP REPO

Diagram by Rhys Davies

A Tor Book
Published by Tom Doherty Associates
175 Fifth Avenue
New York, NY 10010

www.tor-forge.com

Tor® is a registered trademark of Macmillan Publishing Group, LLC.

Library of Congress Cataloging-in-Publication Data

Names: Tomlinson, Patrick S, author.
Title: Starship repo / Patrick S. Tomlinson.
Description: First edition. | New York : A Tom Doherty Associates Book, 2019. | "A Tor Book."
Identifiers: LCCN 2018055234 | ISBN 9781250302717 (trade pbk.) | ISBN 9781250302700 (ebook)
Subjects: | GSAFD: Science fiction.
Classification: LCC PS3620.O5806 S73 2019 | DDC 813/.6—dc23
LC record available at https://lccn.loc.gov/2018055234

Our books may be purchased in bulk for promotional, educational, or business use. Please contact your local bookseller or the Macmillan Corporate and Premium Sales Department at 1-800-221-7945, extension 5442, or by email at MacmillanSpecialMarkets@macmillan.com.

First Edition: May 2019

Printed in the United States of America

0 9 8 7 6 5 4 3 2 1

GOES WHERE I'M TOWED

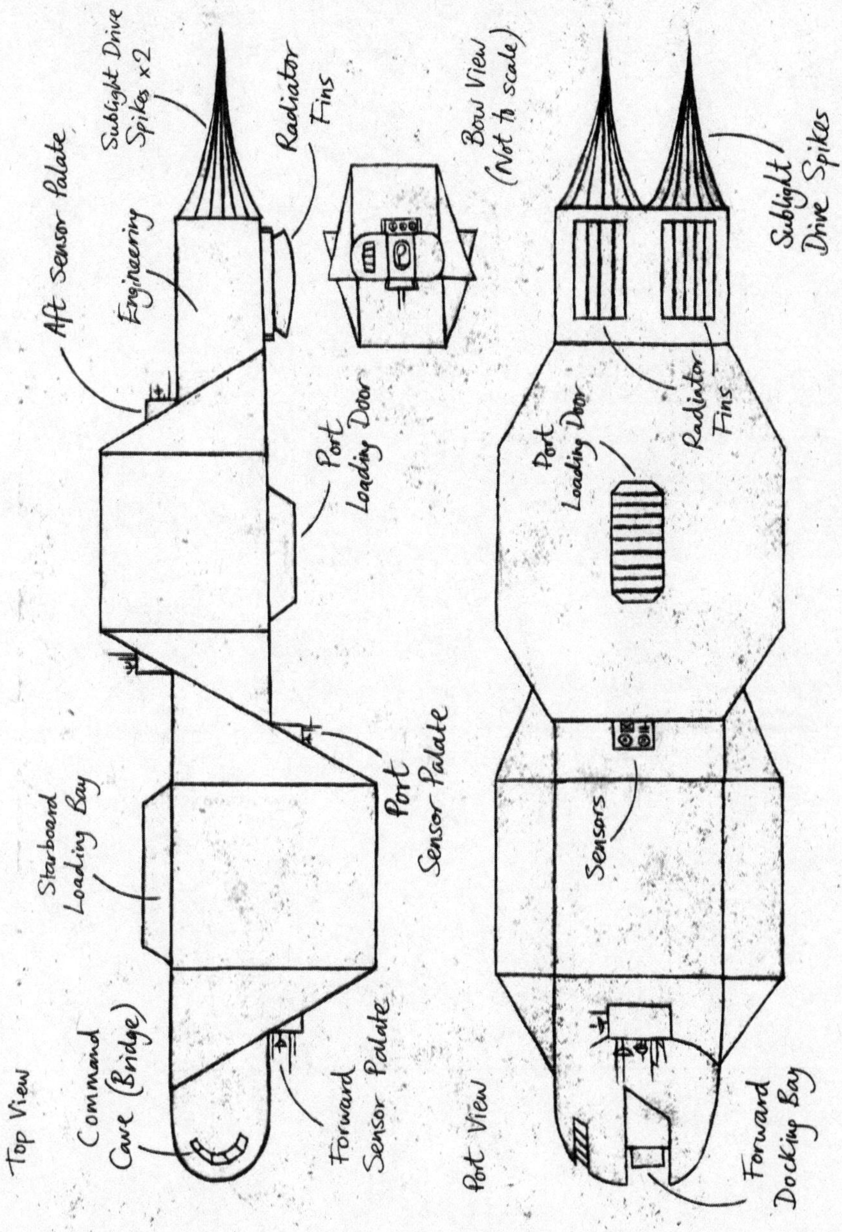

STARSHIP REPO

CHAPTER 1

It was the first human ever to come through Junktion's customs portal, at least so far as Pelax knew. He spotted the frail creature standing several beings deep in the queue, right behind an Ish mother with a brood of a dozen hatchlings playing on top of her carapace. The human reached out to try to pet one, only to get her finger pinched by a suspicious claw.

Pelax suppressed a chuckle. In the five years since their escape from containment, humans had quickly developed a reputation for sticking their digits where they didn't belong. At least this time, a lesson was dispensed quickly. Being a professional, Pelax sat on his curiosity and dealt with the more mundane citizens quickly and efficiently until the human girl was next in line.

At least he was pretty sure she was a girl. He was hardly an expert. He waved her forward with a flipper. "ID and travel chit, please."

The girl reached into a cheap cloth pouch slung over her shoulder and produced the required documents. Pelax took them and ran them through the authenticator. Orange meant they were genuine or such high-quality forgeries that she deserved to pass anyway. Then, Pelax looked at the name column.

"Firstname Lastname?"

"Yeah, I know," the girl said. "It was a data-entry error. They keep saying it'll get sorted out any day now. My real name is—"

Pelax held up a flipper. "For the duration of your visit to Junktion, your 'real' name is Firstname Lastname. It's fitting, really. After all, you're the first human I've met." Pelax was not versed in human facial expressions, thus he was unsure if the complete rigidity was a sign of good humor.

"I'm not the first one to say that, am I?"

"*Everyone* says that. I almost said it before you just so I didn't have to hear it again."

"Okay, I get the point."

Firstname bowed her head. "Sorry, I didn't mean to bite your, er, head off. It's been a long couple of months. That is your head, right?"

Pelax rolled a flipper. "Port of origin?"

"PCB. Sorry, Proxima Centauri B. Earth space."

"I meant the last Assembly spaceport you departed from."

"Oh, um . . . Lacora, maybe? I was there long enough to pee and change transports." She put her hands on the desk, then pointed with a finger. "What's that box?"

Pelax glanced over along her line of inquiry. "It's an authenticator. Please remove your hands and stand behind the yellow line."

Firstname lifted her hands and stepped back. "Sorry, sorry. Can we move this along? I'm starving."

Pelax ignored her plea and cross-referenced her travel chit's internal log against Space Traffic Control's flight records. Lacora was correct.

"And what is the nature of your visit to Junktion—business or pleasure?"

"I'm a refugee. We can't afford much pleasure. I heard there's work to be had on the docks. So I'm going to try to get some."

"How old are you?" Pelax asked, even though the information was on her ID.

"Seventeen awake plus four frozen."

Pelax grimaced. "What's that in Assembly Standard Cycles?"

"Oh, um, I don't know the conversion, sorry."

The line behind them grew restless with the delay. Pelax knew he had to get the queue moving again or the rest of his shift would be spent with grumpy clients venting their frustrations and slowing the line further.

"Temporary visa granted for two weeks. That's seventeen days." Pelax stamped the approval into her ID and travel chit.

"That's an odd number. How can it be two of anything?" First asked.

"Oh, you don't know about Hole Day? Well, that's something to look forward to. If you've found a job by the end of that time, bring proof of employment up to the immigration office and they'll get you set up with a resident visa. Enjoy your stay at Junktion. Next!"

The human smiled at Pelax and grabbed her documents. It wouldn't be until he closed his terminal and headed home he'd realize his wallet was missing.

Firstname left the customs portal behind and let herself get swept into the river of sentients moving through the arteries of the space station known as Junktion. Hyperspace station, actually, or the "upper" half of it was. The facility sat smack at the intersection of several of Assembly space's busiest trade routes, both in normal space and hyperspace, bottlenecked by a cluster of pulsars and black holes that forced ships to reroute against these threats to navigation.

Junktion was like an iceberg, with half the station floating in normal space, while the other half bobbed through a hyperspace window kept permanently open to allow cargo and passengers traveling through hyper to dock, disembark, and reload, all without their ships ever having to transition between the two universes and put cycles on their hyperspace generators, which made it very valuable to the captains and their transport companies.

It was also truly massive. The ceilings in the main passageways were tall enough to fly through, with several winged species doing exactly that, flitting about their business like man-sized dragonflies. Junktion supplemented its artificial gravity systems with a gentle spin, but from where she walked inside the outermost layers, the curvature was barely perceptible.

From where she stood among the crowd, another thing was becoming inescapably obvious. First really was the first human most of them had ever seen. All around her, curious eyes, set inside skulls or mounted on stalks, turned to steal a glance at her before darting away again like the cantina scene in *Star Wars* if it had been filmed on Fifth Avenue. Blending in here would be . . . challenging.

Her stomach had been barren since the travel rations she'd traded for on Lacora ran out a day and a half earlier. First tried to push her way toward the far wall. Eventually, through sheer Brownian motion, she reached it and found a small alcove that would afford her a measure of privacy to take stock of her resources. She had thirty-six PCB dollars, which she might as well use for toilet paper, a few coins of unknown denominations from some backwater world on the fringe of Assembly territory she might be able to use or exchange for local currency, and the standard personal data handheld she'd been given upon achieving refugee status.

First continued to hope no one at the Assembly refugee processing center looked too deeply into her application, lest they ask what "Cleveland Browns" were and why they qualified as a natural disaster.

She had one new item to add to the inventory, however. Turning her back to the crowds, First pulled the slim wallet out of the drop pocket she'd sewn into the lining of her vest, hidden right in one of the seams, just like Helga at juvenile detention had showed her. There wasn't much in it. A couple of scripts that were probably low-value paper credits, not that she could read them yet, a couple of pictures of what looked like manatee porn, and . . .

First whistled softly to herself as the overhead lights played off the holographic security access card, worth thousands to an interested buyer. All she had to do was find them.

"Jackpot."

She left the wallet and pictures on the ground, then tucked the access card into her drop pocket. The script she kept in hand as she reentered the crowd in search of a place to eat. She spent the better part of an hour surveying the promenade and markets, looking for something that her empty, growling stomach might accept as penance after almost two days of neglect.

As it happened, while she may have been the first human physically present on Junktion, human presence had already taken root. Impossibly, inevitably, First found herself staring at a sign known to all humans for going on four hundred years.

"Welcome to McDonald's," said a giant brain floating in a jar, with tentacles where a spinal cord should be. "My name is Fenax. May I take your order?"

"Uhhh," First stammered. She didn't even know which part of the creature's . . . face, she was supposed to address. "Sorry. This is embarrassing, but I can't read this language yet, and I don't know how much I have here." She opened her hand and uncrumpled the local script, then held it up to the disembodied cashier.

The creature inspected the notes however an eyeless floating brain did such things. "You have a dry-cleaning ticket and an expired one-month-free gym membership coupon."

"Oh. I'm really sorry. I'm just very hungry. I just got off a refugee ship."

"Do you have any other forms of currency? We accept script from across Assembly space."

First dug into her purse and pulled out the coins and PCB bills. "All I've got is a few loose coins and some bathroom tissue."

"Those are Cimini dulos. Not enough for anything on our menu, I'm afraid."

"Right." First deposited the little plastic chips into the Ronald McDonald House container at the base of the register anyway.

"Wait, is that . . . human currency?" the floating horror asked.

"What, the bills? They're Proxima Centauri B dollars."

"How much?"

"Thirty-six bucks."

The brain shivered in its jar. "Forgive my emotional outburst. I grew excited. I collect strange or rare currencies, you see. It's a hobby. I'll give you one hundred standard credits for the bills in your hand."

"Is that a good exchange rate?"

"Honestly, I have no idea."

"Will it get me a value meal?"

"With room to spare."

First slapped the PCB dollars down on the counter. "Deal. I want a Big Mac with fries, a large Coke, and an apple pie."

"A what pie?"

"Of course not. Forget the pie."

"Coming right up, sir."

"Miss."

"What did I miss?"

First sighed. "Nothing. Forget it."

Three minutes later, First set her tray triumphantly down at a small two-seat table at the edge of the dining area and surveyed her conquest. Her first meal as deep inside alien territory as she, or perhaps any human, had ever come consisted of a Big Mac, what looked and smelled like french fries, and what most definitely tasted like a Coke Classic with whatever extra ingredient McDonald's had been adding for centuries.

And to top it all off, she had eighty-three standard credits in her bag. Enough for days if she needed to stretch it. Victorious, First lifted the five-layered abomination and opened her mouth wide to accept her bounty.

"Well, now I've seen it all," came a voice like bagpipes being recycled. "A human eating McDonald's."

First spun around with the burger still clenched in one hand, ready to point a finger straight through whoever had interrupted her first delectable bite of food in days, only to stop short. Standing next to her, if the word applied, was a slug, six meters long, and somehow smiling at her despite not possessing any obvious mouth orifice.

"Big Mac, huh? Good choice, although a little predictable, isn't it? A little cliché, even?"

First's arm went slack against her side. "Guilty as charged, I guess. I just got here, and I don't know if anything else is even edible for me yet."

"I'm only joking, young human. Giving you a tug, if you know what I mean. I enjoy them myself, maybe a little too much." Four limbs, for lack of a better term, erupted from the giant slug's sides and rubbed its midsection. "Two all-bleef patties, special sauce, lettuce, cheese, pickles, onions on a sesame seed bun."

First nodded along to the familiar ditty. "Yes, that's right. I'm surprised you know . . . wait, did you say *bleef*?"

"Yeah?"

"What the hell is bleef?"

"I'm Bleef!" the slug's four arms hugged its torso proudly. "My species reproduces asexually, you see, with buds. But I'm not ready to be a family man, not in this economy, so just before they hit the point of sentience, I hack 'em off and sell the meat to the local franchise here. I'm sure it's not that different where you come from."

First looked at the Big Mac in her hand, then gently set it back down in its box.

"You know, I'm suddenly not very hungry."

"You're not going to throw that away, are you?" Bleef asked, rubbing two limbs together.

"No." First handed it over. "Help yourself. To yourself."

"Much obliged, young human. Enjoy your stay."

First grabbed her Coke and strode away, sticky fingers reaching into Bleef's coin purse while he distracted himself with a stomach-churning display of autoerotic cannibalism that put more than one nonhuman patron unfortunate enough to be seated in the dining area off their lunch.

First returned to the counter to the same floating brain cashier and recovered a ten-credit note from her purse.

"Give me a spicy chicken sandwich, and I'll pay double if you promise not to tell me what's in it."

Her hunger finally sated, First left the food court behind and reviewed the newest additions to her drop pocket, unwittingly donated by Bleef. Two cryptocurrency crystal disks. She wouldn't know how much was on them until she found a cracker to break the encryption, but it was never a petty amount. Given a few hours to get her bearings and meet the wrong sort of people, and she'd sleep in a real bed in a private room for the rest of the week.

"Yes, I think I will enjoy my stay."

CHAPTER 2

"Sorry, boss," the Turemok said, her red electronic eye implants dimming in embarrassment. "Soolie the Fin's squad beat us to the punch. Karkers already had their feet up on the bridge by the time we got to the gangway plank."

Every piece of Loritt Chessel twitched his annoyance at the newest setback. "Jrill, this is the third contract we've had pulled out from under our feet in as many weeks. Our expenses on failed jobs don't just disappear, you know."

Jrill straightened up and looked intently at the wall above Loritt's head. "I'm aware, boss."

Loritt's jaw clenched involuntarily. But he was a professional and a gentleman. His crew was among the best in the sector, and their frustrations at this recent run of bad luck were, if anything, even more obvious than his own. "Relax. I mean, 'at ease.' It's not your fault. You're all doing your jobs, I know that. But something's making us miss a step. What's wrong?"

"Permission to speak openly, si—boss?"

Loritt chuckled. He'd picked Jrill up after the culling of Turemok military officers who'd been in any way involved in the disastrous campaign against Earth five years prior, which had not only seen the "backward savages" destroy the *Xecoron* and the sitting Kumer-Vel with it but landed the entire Turemok leadership under official censure from the Assembly for their attempts to frame the humans for geocide in the first place.

The resulting face-saving purge went to extremes, ensnaring even Jrill, who, as far as Loritt had been able to tell, was guilty only of overseeing logistics at the port the *Xecoron* launched from. "Without the fuel *you* authorized," the logic of her hearing went, "our flagship would still be in its berth!"

"Jrill, how many times do I have to tell you I'm not your commanding officer? This isn't the military. It's a job. You do it well. I value your discipline, but I don't need you to be a slave to it. As long as you're respectful, you're always free to speak your mind. I insist on it."

Jrill shifted uncomfortably. It had taken almost two cycles to get her to say *boss* instead of *sir.* Hatchling steps. "We're taking on more and bigger contracts. They've grown in complexity while the interval to prepare for each has shrunk. We're being asked to do more with the same man power and less time."

"Which means bigger shares at the end of the day for everyone."

"Not if we keep missing the targets, boss. We need to replace our hacker. Zero doesn't divide by five any better than it does six or seven."

Several parts of Loritt inhaled and let out a sigh. "As I said earlier, it's not zero, it's negative numbers in my account, but I take your point. You've all grown so much and met every challenge. Maybe I assumed we'd all just keep leveling up forever. But that's not how real life works, is it?"

"Not in my experience, boss."

"You've talked to the others about this? They're okay with it?"

"Not directly, but I don't believe anyone would object too strenuously. And even if they did, you're the boss."

"I am the boss," Loritt repeated. "Short term, you know this makes things worse, yes? Training and integrating a recruit into a tight-knit group is always problematic. Getting them up to speed saps resources and man-hours and stresses morale."

"We're investing in the future, boss. And if all else fails, I can smack heads together to straighten them out."

"Not Fenax."

"Well, no, obviously not Fenax, except metaphorically."

"And Sheer's head is technically located inside her carapace . . ."

"I think you're deliberately pushing the limits of a common turn of phrase, boss."

Loritt smiled. "All right, Jrill, you win. Got any potentials in mind?"

Jrill tapped her beak. "Come to think of it, I just might."

It had been, in First's estimation, the most productive six months of her life. A line, an actual *line* was queued up for the little card table she'd set up in the promenade. But where back on Proxima she would've been selling lemonade for two bucks a plastic cup, these people were paying for a very different cup-based experience.

Somehow, against all odds, no one in the history of the Assembly had come up with a shell game con. It had been the very first con generations of street hustlers on Earth had been taught, practiced, and mastered. It required one to spot marks, learn sleight of hand, and employ misdirection. It was a springboard to every other kind of petty crime one could employ.

But here, no one was wise to it. The aliens were befuddled by it, mystified even. First didn't need to identify marks because they were *all* marks. She heard them in line, arguing over how she did it. A phase-shifting ball? Cups with built-in high-space portals? A matter reorganizer tabletop?

She patiently let her "customers" inspect every element of her performance until they were satisfied all the objects were mundane, which they were, before taking their bets and, invariably, keeping them.

The only real trouble she'd encountered had been from a Percepilion, whose species had evolved in a binary system with a normal sun and a neutron star companion and could see straight into the x-ray part of the spectrum. But a day's worth of earnings as a carrot and a promise to hire muscle to escort them out the nearest airlock as a stick had secured their silence.

But while the hustle was effective, it was chump change. There was a limit to how much people were willing to risk, and how many games she could play in a day. Multiply X and Y together and you had the self-imposed ceiling on First's earning potential. It was enough to get by, but it wasn't enough to really live. And she hadn't run away from her doleful rat parents and preachy parole officer to just get by. She could do that on Proxima B without lifting a finger or a cup.

Which had led to her night job.

"Okay, folks, that's enough for one day." First stood up and stacked the cups, then started folding the table over a chorus of objections from those already in line.

"We've been waiting a larim!" the next in line demanded.

"Then just set down your currencies and walk away like the last hundred people," First said. "It'll be virtually the same experience. Sorry, everyone, but humans have to sleep a third of the day."

"A third?" a Turemok several slots back in the queue asked incredulously.

"Yeah. A full eight hours, I mean larims. Miracle you people didn't finish us off in one go."

"Careful what you wish for, naked monkey."

"Bring it, shitbird. Tomorrow. After I get my beauty rest. You might try some yourself."

"My people don't take 'beauty rest.'"

"Yeah, it shows," First quipped.

The Turemok braced to make a move, but the rest of the line and onlookers were laughing too hard, costing them initiative. First took the momentary reprieve to duck between a pair of something or others and get lost in the evening rush.

After six months living among the transient throngs of beings that came and went on board Junktion, First still couldn't identify more than a third of them on sight.

Her parents had taken a vacation to Earth once when she was ten. They'd scrimped and saved almost since the moment she'd been born. They'd told her it might be the only time she'd ever be off world, and they wanted her to see their original home.

They'd docked at the space elevator terminal over Dubai, then took the lift down. First had never seen such diversity of colors, features, cultures, and languages in her life.

How naïve she'd been, even there with her eyes opened for the first time in an Arabian bazaar.

That trip had taken two years, each way. They were all in cryosleep for the boring parts of the trip, save for a week in the middle when they'd been woken to keep their brains from going stale. Those years didn't count toward her legal age. On her old PCB ID, her official age was notated as *21-4cs = 17.*

That was before the whiz kids of the ARTist program had cracked hyperspace tech from a stolen buoy. Now, nobody slept. At least not any more than normal.

Still, First hated to sleep. She knew how much she missed in the meantime.

She flashed her transit card at the scanner mounted in the tube entrance and caught a pod hubward three levels and spinward two sections to her neighborhood. She stopped at the local bodega and threw a few credit chits at the Lividite behind the counter in exchange for her usual bag of minerals and deadly heavy metals.

"What does a human do with that much quartz and mercury?" he asked as he did twice a week.

"School project," she answered as she did twice a week. First petted the velvety red qualax sleeping by the door as she left. She still couldn't pronounce its name.

A block, skip, and a jump later and she was home. First ran her key card through the reader and waited for the door to authenticate. Back in the slums of New Kiev in PCB, she'd have to hold her eye up to the door for a retina scan. The problem with universal biometrics in the Assembly was not everyone had eyes, or fingerprints, or a voice, or in some extreme cases, any combination of the three.

The door slid open and spat her card out on the inside wall of her apartment.

"I'm home," First announced out of old habit. She set her folding table down in its usual spot by the entry and walked out into her living room. The spinward wall was taken up by what looked like an oversized, four-pedestal, industrial art installation made of marble and concrete, while the entire opposite wall seemed to be filled with a shallow holographic painting of two of the same.

But so deep into space, appearances could be deceiving.

First set down the bag of chemicals on the floor near the art installation, then picked up a small box with a single large button and a blinking red light. She pushed the button.

"Hello, First," the low, earthy voice said, filling the room. "I got your message. Thank you for scraping the moss off my leg. It was beginning to itch. I'll handle your share of the rent this week."

The message ended as the light stopped. First pushed it again, and the light blinked green.

"Hello, Quarried Themselves, that's generous of you. I brought your usual snack. Stay hydrated, or whatever you call it. I hope you feel better soon. And don't delete this season of *Rocks in Hard Places.* I want to watch it sped up. Season 1 ended on a real cliffhanger."

She pressed the button again, and the flashing green light turned red. Message saved, ready for playback, only at one five-hundredth the speed. First set the box down next to Quarried's leg, where they'd retrieve and review it by morning. Probably.

Dark outer cloak, baggy, plenty of pockets. A set of street clothes underneath in case she needed a quick change of appearance. Fashionable wide-brimmed hat that also obscured her face from overhead surveillance. A large purse for her deck and hand tools, all of which were illegal to even possess, much less use. Enough paper currency to bribe her way into or out of most situations.

Now, First was ready. She took another pod up to the haughtier levels near the inner surface of Junktion's spinning drum. Here, artificial ground, landscaping, lakes, and the most expensive rent districts were found. The best shops, theaters, and restaurants sat ready to relieve the idle wealthy or the visiting working class of their money without discrimination. It was also where an enterprising young lady could find parking hangars and landing pads full of private aircars waiting to be plucked like foie gras ducks.

She wanted a basement garage, out of public view where she could work hidden from too many prying eyes. Close to the outskirts, but not one she'd shopped at before. That narrowed the search; she'd had a pretty good run over the last three weeks.

First pulled out her handheld and perused listings for eateries near her location, looking like any of a thousand other beings trying to pick out a place to eat. But while they were looking at ratings and reading reviews, First was looking at how expensive they were. Too cheap and the customers' aircars wouldn't be worth her time to boost. Too expensive and the security systems protecting the garage would be too formidable.

She needed something low on the high end. And she found it in the Whistling Tormogoth, serving traditional Nelihexu small-plate fare. First memorized the address and tucked the handset back into her purse. It was a short walk to the eatery that First had to force herself to take at a leisurely pace so not to attract attention. In the months since First's arrival, other humans had begun to turn up on Junktion, removing much of her novelty and restoring a measure of the anonymity she relied on.

The Whistle had a bit of a line at the door. Perfect. The garage would be full, and patrons would be delayed returning to their air-cars.

"Excuse me," First asked of a Lividite at the end of the line, "but is this the wait line for the Tormogoth?"

"Why, yes. They're filming an episode of *Grease Traps and Gut Bombs* inside."

"How exciting. How long's the wait?"

"I've been here a larim already."

"I see," First said. "Maybe next time. I don't think my stomach can wait that long."

Just then, what First could only describe as a furry, man-sized pterodactyl in a spandex unitard stumbled out of the Whistle's front door and unsteadily walked by them like a badger trying to balance on top of four pencils.

"He looks stuffed," the Lividite said. "You might want to step back before—"

The ungainly beast crouched low against the ground and then, with surprising speed, launched itself several meters into the air before spreading its impressively large wings. As it did so, it also dropped two liters of a viscous, mottled, foul-smelling fluid that splashed everywhere like a popped water balloon. With a single powerful downward beat of its wings, the beast lifted off into the night air.

"Ah, not fast enough," the Lividite said mournfully as he looked at the splash damage to First's cloak.

"Did," she stammered, "did that thing just poop on me?"

"He's a Condrite. They usually, ah, evacuate themselves at takeoff to reduce mass, especially after a big meal. Best to give them a wide berth if you see one readying for flight."

"He could do it inside! There's bathrooms and everything!"

"You want him to poop in your bath?"

"No! I, ugh, never mind. Excuse me. I have to throw away a cloak."

"When you've cleaned up, you might try Horloth's House one section over. Good food and likely to be less busy."

"Thanks for the tip," First said. "At least your timing is improving."

First stormed off and chucked the soiled cloak in the nearest recycler. She could have had it cleaned, but she decided it was worth the difference to buy one free of the foul memory. Unfortunately, it would also link her to the crime scene if she went through with a hit on the Whistle's garage, so she needed a new hunting ground.

Horloth's it was.

CHAPTER 3

Horloth's turned out to be a prime spot. The garage was located across the block from the restaurant, giving First ample time to duck out of sight if she spotted anyone returning from dinner. It was, as the intermittently helpful Lividite predicted, less busy, but the garage was still reasonably full.

The garage was a little worn, but clean and well maintained. The outer walls were free of the graffiti that plagued the neighborhoods she usually hung around in. An advertising board lit up with tour information for a "human" band called the Wolverines that was apparently doing shows in this arm of the galaxy.

The garage door was locked, but the access key she'd nicked from the customs officer miraculously still worked. Someone in station security had really dropped the ball on that one. The only drawback to this new location First noticed as she stalked through the rows of aircars was Horloth's clientele trended a little less affluent.

It was good and bad. Cheaper aircars meant cheap security systems. But they also meant a cheap payday once she delivered the unit to Soolie the Fin's goons in the docks for shipment off station. She didn't particularly like the Fin or his associates, but she'd stumbled into him when she tried to light-finger his wallet, and he hadn't offered her another choice. Besides, reselling hot aircars on Junktion was effectively impossible, so his distribution network made working with him and accepting his predatory payment rates a necessary evil.

Still, she'd make enough even on a . . . Racola . . . to . . .

A hole in the shape of an aircar stared back at First from across the garage. Its black paint polished to such a shine and depth it drank what light fell on it like finely aged brandy. Its profile was unmistakable.

A Proteus Infinite.

She'd only ever seen one on a showroom floor as she pressed her nose against the glass of the dealership's window. No reason to feel bad about boosting this beauty; the owner could afford it.

First caught the line of drool running down the corner of her mouth before it reached her chin, but only just. She moved on the car like a lady, quickly but respectfully, knowing full well its suite of security sensors already watched. Instead of coming at the Proteus directly, she slipped behind a beige, entry-level Guff two spaces down and pretended to fumble for her pass key. First dug into her purse and pulled out her hacking deck. She had software patches and exploits for dozens of makes and models already preloaded, but only one for a Proteus and none for an Infinite.

She logged in to her /backnet/ portal under one of four burner accounts and hit the app market, search term "Proteus Infinite Exploits." Sixteen hits came back in less than ten seconds, each with a bid price in blue next to them. They weren't cheap, but this was not where one wanted to skimp on currency unless they wanted to get locked out halfway through a hack and have station security called. Then you were either running for your life or spending the cash you should have spent in the first place on bribes.

First ran the profits and losses in her head, weighing what she had to spend to boost the car versus what her payday would be upon delivery. In the end, she clicked on the fourth-most expensive bid. Not amazing, but a lot better than sloppy, and she had the skills to make up the difference.

First looked around once more to ensure she was still alone, then held out the last of the crypto-crystals she'd pocketed from Bleef that first day months earlier and transferred the credits. Bleef had been more than generous in repaying the burger he'd cost her, but his bleeding ended as the gentle blue glow inside the crystal went dim and it returned to being an unformatted quartz crystal valuable only as a bite-sized snack for her Grenic roommate.

She gave the patch she'd just bought a cursory exam to make sure she hadn't just gotten stiffed, left positive feedback for the programmer when it was obvious she hadn't been, then opened the file.

The first step to stealing a high-end aircar was tricking it into believing it was already somewhere else. Someone other than its owner asking to enter it while inside a strange parking hangar was a dead giveaway it was being stolen. But someone trying to enter it at its dealership, where its maintenance was performed? That was something the onboard virtual intelligence could be persuaded to believe.

First pinged the Infinite's transponder to get a registration number, then spent a few more credits in the /backnet/ to run the car's title transfer history to get its original dealer from a crooked Space Traffic Control flunky. Morden's Proteus. Very swank neighborhood. She set her deck to jam the local station location signal and pump out her faked override.

Now, the clock was ticking. With active jamming and a pirate broadcast throwing out a fake location signal, it was only a matter of time before some passerby or local noticed the discrepancy and investigated the source of the glitch. She walked up to the Infinite and laid a hand on it for the first time.

"Hello, beautiful. What's a girl like you doing in a place like this?"

She entered the next set of prompts, assuring the Infinite that it was in a safe place. It was just time to flush and replace its reactor coolant. She even had a Morden's technician's employee ID to enter for the car's maintenance logs, which was a nice touch.

"I'd like to buy you a drink, if you don't mind," First cooed at the car as she pushed deeper into its operating system's safeguards. On command, the seals hissed as the door peeled open like a wood shaving, revealing an interior of such decadence that First was tempted to pull out of her sublease with Quarried and move in.

"My, you are an eager one. My place or yours, darling?"

She sat down in the pilot's seat. It was a little oversized, but fortunately, it had been configured for a humanoid body form. The bottom of the seat had a rather large hole in the center that was probably meant to accommodate someone's tail, but gave it the appearance of a comfortable toilet.

The seat quickly adjusted to her proportions while First dealt with the flight control lockout, where she encountered her first real problem. The owner had flight mode firewalled behind a fractal encryption protocol, and she had less than a minute to break it. Not enough time to go to the /backnet/ for a solution.

First put one foot out the door, ready to run if time ran out and the alarm sounded. She dug through the apps and patches already on her deck. Nothing jumped out as useful. Nothing, that was, until she remembered a tech report she'd read two months earlier about Proteus outsourcing their security updates to the same supplier that serviced their midlevel brand to save costs. And *that* supplier she did have a patch for.

Frantically, First opened the appropriate file and manually keyed in the Infinite's serial number, dealership routing number, and SCC flight license and hit Enter. As the final seconds ticked past, First put a hand on the center counsel, poised to eject herself from the car before the door could close if her gambit didn't work.

As the clock counted down to two seconds, her deck's screen turned green.

Flight Controls Unlocked.

First let out an exhilarated sigh and sank into the sumptuous leather beneath her.

"I'm thinking my place, sweetheart. Don't worry, I know what I'm doing," she purred at the car as the door rolled closed. First tucked her deck back into her purse and dropped it into the passenger seat, along with her hat, then took manual control of the Infinite. She loved to fly, and seeing as she'd never owned an aircar herself, the few minutes after a successful job were the only chance she ever had to indulge herself in the sensation.

Gently, she spooled up the oversized antigrav pods on the four corners of the Proteus until it lifted from the ground. A *whir-click* from the floorboards confirmed the landing skids had retracted. First nudged the car into the lane between the rows of cars and inched forward. She tried to get a look at herself in passing reflections, but the Infinite's "windows" were virtual displays and the exterior completely opaque.

It was a dead-sexy piece of machinery. The door at the far end of the hangar recognized its approach and scrolled open. Finally in free air, First goosed the pods and sent the Proteus rocketing into the "sky." Even pressed down in her seat under three g's, she still managed to bring the corners of her mouth up into a riotous smile.

"Awesome," First said as the acceleration slammed down on her chest, forcing the words out of her in a rush of air. With some altitude beneath her, she pointed for the docks and transitioned to level flight with the same giddy exuberance.

But all good things must come to an end. Quite suddenly, the car stopped accepting First's manual flight inputs, then just as suddenly changed course of its own volition.

"What the hell?" First cranked hard on the control yolk, hoping to bring the Proteus back under heel, but to no avail. Then, the doors locked, and she knew she was really in deep shit.

"Attention unauthorized pilot," came a genderless, synthesized voice. "You have been apprehended hijacking this vehicle. Please relax while you are delivered to the appropriate authorities."

"The hell I will." First reached over into her purse, retrieved her hacking deck, and got to work. Main systems were behind a half dozen new firewalls thrown up by the car's security system, but maybe some of the secondary systems, like the door locks . . .

"Your wireless device has been recognized and permanently deleted from this vehicle's registry of authorized users. All commands originating from it will be automatically denied. Would you like a glass of water while you wait?"

First punched the dash in a rage.

"Any vandalism of this property will be added to your existing charges. Would you like to listen to some music while you wait?"

"Fuck you."

"You have selected 'Pho Queue' by the Wolverines."

Before she could object, what sounded like a forgotten 1980s hair metal band started singing a surprisingly catchy tune about meeting girls while waiting in line for Vietnamese.

First tossed the deck back into the passenger seat and crossed her arms in a huff. No idea how she would get out of this one. She still had hard currency for a bribe, but that sort of thing worked a lot better out on the street, not so much once you were inside the station. Story. She needed a story that would explain how she "accidentally" found herself in the car. She'd need to wipe the deck and all of the expensive patches and software she'd collected and find a place to dump the physical lock-picking tools in her purse, but . . .

Something was wrong—namely, their heading.

"Infinite, where are you taking me?"

"To the proper authorities."

"But we're heading away from the security station."

"There are other authorities on Junktion besides the police." The car's flat monotone took on an ominous edge that sent a dozen ice cubes sliding down First's spine like they were racing for her ass crack.

"I'm not speaking to this car's VI, am I?"

"Very perceptive, young human. Relax; it's a short flight to my residence."

"It's not the flight I'm worried about."

"I assure you, you will not be physically harmed. Unless you decide to become violent, of course. Now, legal jeopardy, that's a matter to discuss when you arrive. I'm cutting this link. See you shortly."

The voice went dead, followed by the virtual windows and windshield. First couldn't see a thing outside the cabin. Panicked, she slapped a hand against the screen, sending a small rainbow ripple of color through the thin OLCD display.

"Calm!" First demanded of herself. Through a force of will, she steadied her ragged breathing. Her racing pulse soon followed suit. Having gotten a grip on herself, First next got a grip on a weapon. Among her tools was a three-sided, spring-loaded metal probing tool that would punch through a skull as easily as a lock tumbler. A one-shot affair, but better than nothing.

Provided her mystery host had a skull . . .

The car shuddered just a little as something captured it. The landing skids hadn't deployed, so she was still in the air, probably in a docking cradle next to a balcony on one of the residential towers, which made sense; anyone who afforded a Proteus probably pulled penthouse paychecks.

The driver's door unlocked, and the panel rolled back to reveal a well-lit patio covered in decorative trees and expensive furniture. Reclining in a lawn chair turned away from her, an alien in a bathrobe sat looking at a handheld while drinking from what looked like a short martini glass.

"Welcome, young lady. So you're aware, all exits to this patio are quite thoroughly locked. Please, have a seat."

First grabbed her purse and slowly lifted herself out of the car and onto the patio, forgetting her hat. Once out, she got a sense of just how high she was. They were surrounded by a cluster of residential towers, each at least a hundred stories tall, and she was very near the top of this one.

First took a hesitant step back from the car as the door rolled shut again.

"That probe you palmed before getting out has to go over the side, I'm afraid," the still-unidentified alien said calmly but firmly, then held up his handheld, showing a replay video catching her in the act. "You didn't really think the cabin was unmonitored, did you?"

First looked at the probe in her hand and smirked before pitching it over the side of the patio. "Can't blame a girl for trying. Somebody might get hurt when that thing reaches ground level, you know."

"There are awnings. Come here, let me have a look at you."

"I'm telling you right now, if this is some sort of xeno-fetish sex thing, I'd sooner march down to the security station and turn myself in."

"Is that a common proposition?"

"Common enough when you're the only one of something in a place like this," First said as she came around to face her host. "Some weirdos like to check off species like they're . . . playing . . . bingo . . ."

The alien was roughly humanoid in body layout—torso, two backward-bending legs, two big and two little arms, a head, and a plump, stubby tail that looked better suited to storing fat than correcting balance. After that, things got weird. They didn't have any skin, for one thing, and the various exposed pieces seemed to be held together by nothing more than collective agreement.

"What are you?" First asked, trying hard to promote the morbid curiosity she felt over the fear.

"My dear, I'm a Nelihexu. One of the six Assembly Council races. Much like your Grenic roommate, Quarried Themselves, isn't it?"

"How do you—"

"We know a great deal about you, except, oddly enough, your name."

"First. You?"

"All right. My name is Loritt Chessel, at your service. And you?"

"I just told you."

"You did?"

First sighed and retrieved her ID card from her purse, then held it out to Loritt. "Here, before we get stuck in a loop."

Loritt took the card and read it aloud. "Firstname Lastname?"

"It was a data-entry error at the refugee processing center. They'll fix it any day now."

"Well, it's not entirely inappropriate. After all, you're the first—"

"Finish that sentence and I'll take my chances with the awnings."

"I see." Loritt waved a hand at a nearby chair. "Please, sit. Would you like anything to drink?"

"I'm fine."

"Very well. Let's get started, then, First. Why did you steal my Proteus?"

First sat but did not put her feet up. "Needed the money."

Loritt shook his head. "That is a reason to steal *an* aircar. There were a hundred others in that hangar, every one of them with inferior security systems to a Proteus. I asked why you stole *my* car."

"I needed *a lot* of money."

"Another evasion. Your deck acquired a peephole virus from a programmer on my payroll two days ago. I know how much you spent on patches just to try to break into my car. You could have stolen a less expensive model and made nearly the same money for a tenth of the risk. One more time: Why mine?"

First smirked, unable to hide how impressed she was. "Fine, two reasons. First, I like a challenge. And second, screw you."

Loritt leaned forward ever so slightly. "I thought that option was already off the table?"

"I mean screw you and your . . . your lifestyle. Up here in your ivory tower while people three hundred meters below you starve. Sure, I could boost some shitbox and flip it for a nice little score, but that's how somebody gets to work. That's how they feed their kids. They're probably out for the one 'fancy' dinner a cycle they allow themselves, because that's what they can afford. Take their car and I ruin their whole year, maybe their life.

"But you, take your car and you pull the other one out of your private hangar. Or go buy another one with the insurance payout tomorrow. Probably just have it sent over. Probably doesn't even take five minutes out of your day while you sit here drinking on your patio looking down on all the thousands and millions of beings beneath you. So yeah, screw you. Now *I* have a question."

Loritt smiled, or some of the muscles of his face contorted in such a way that at least conveyed the intention of a smile. "That's a little unorthodox, considering our relative circumstances, but what the hell? Ask your question, young lady."

"The Lividite, at the first restaurant I cased tonight. You sent him to steer me to Horloth's." Loritt gave a small bow. "Your car was bait. You wanted it to stand out like a jewel among rocks so that I, personally, would be tempted to boost it. So my question should be obvious."

"Because I needed to know if you *could* before asking why you *would.* And you could've, incidentally. If that had belonged to someone who hadn't seen you coming, you'd be turning it over to your buyer right now. Within a larim, it'd be packed up in a shipping container under a falsified manifest entry, awaiting loading onto a bulk freighter heading for the core worlds. Very impressive."

"You seem to know a lot about jacking aircars for a pampered 1 percenter."

"My dear, I was not always a pampered . . . '1 percenter,' was it?"

"So what's this, outreach? You gonna tell me your inspirational rags-to-Richie-Rich story and implore me to abandon my wicked ways?"

"Why would I do that? You'd be of no use at all."

First's growing train of indignation jumped the tracks and skidded to a stop in the gravel.

"What is this?" she managed. "A job interview?"

"An opportunity. Come inside and work for me, or climb back in my Proteus so it can deliver you to the proper authorities along with a complete audio/video/data-stream log of yourself in the act of stealing it. Those are, alas, your only options, unless you fancy your odds of evolving wings before you starve out here on my patio. Take your time, but not too much. Are you sure you don't want something to drink?"

First crossed her arms. "I'm not old enough to drink."

"Humans don't drink liquids until a later life stage? How peculiar." Loritt stood from his chair without saying another word, then walked straight through the glass of the patio window, leaving scarcely a ripple in his wake. Then, every window went from transparent to mirrored, leaving First staring at herself.

"Hell of a trick."

CHAPTER 4

"How long's she been out there?" Jrill asked, standing near the window overlooking Loritt's patio like a zoo patron observing a new exhibit.

"Since just after dinner."

"That was yesterday."

"Yes." Loritt paused. "I think she may have fallen asleep, but it's been an absurdly long time. Do you think we should send for a doctor?"

"That's normal for them, apparently."

"Who told you that?"

Jrill nodded at the recumbent human on the sunchair. "She did."

"You spied on her?"

"I wanted to form my own impression."

Loritt perked up from his breakfast of live klu beetles and a light salad. "Which was?"

"The only part of her faster than her fingers is her mouth. Bold, talented, but overconfident."

"So, in short, an adolescent of any species."

The sound of Turemok laughter was . . . an acquired taste. Like learning to love the sound of jagged metal scraped over glass. Thankfully, it was short-lived. "Perhaps. We'll know shortly."

"Only if she agrees to join our little band of barely reformed bandits," Loritt chided, chasing down a runaway beetle with his fork.

"I think she just did," Jrill answered.

Loritt looked up from his salad to inquire and was shocked to see Firstname standing bolt upright, pressing a hand against the edges of the glass, probing it. Testing her cage.

"Said she was fast," Jrill quipped.

"So you did." Loritt picked up his handheld and logged in to the penthouse's systems. "Does this mean you've made a choice, young lady?" his voice boomed over the patio speakers. To her credit, Firstname didn't jump, merely paused her inspection with both of her hands held against the glass.

"Looks that way."

"Excellent." Loritt pressed an icon, and the crystalline structure of the window phase-shifted from solid to semiliquid. Unprepared, Firstname fell through the pane and barely caught herself before hitting the floor.

"Ow," she said, still facedown in the carpet. After a moment, she pushed herself up onto her hands and took stock of her surroundings. Less than a heartbeat later, she locked eyes with Jrill, and Loritt recognized he was about to have to play moderator.

"You!" Firstname spat at the Turemok from under a tousled mass of hair.

"Me," Jrill answered. "It's tomorrow, little human. You've had your beauty rest. Not that it shows."

"Get your own lines, shitbird. Want to step back on the patio and see if you can fly?"

Jrill looked at Loritt. "I told you she was overconfident."

Loritt recognized a budding personnel resources issue when he saw one and decided to nip it.

"Ladies, whatever this is will have to wait until you're both off the clock. Firstname—"

"First. Just call me First."

"First. Now that you are under my employ, I will thank you not to interrupt me midsentence," Loritt said evenly. First visibly swallowed a snappy retort. "Thank you. Let me introduce you to your new teammate, Jrill, formerly a Lika-Vel of our grand Turemok military."

"Formerly," First repeated flatly, neither quizzical nor taunting.

"I'm retired," Jrill replied. "Prematurely."

"Your choice?"

"Not precisely."

"At least you lived through it. Not like those assholes we vaporized in Earth orbit while they tried to sucker punch my entire species into extinction."

"Enough!" Loritt snapped, growing impatient. "Jrill was not involved in the decision to attack your home world. The Turemok who were are now all dead, either by the hands of your people or ours. That will be the last I hear about it. I will not tolerate racism in our ranks. If you can't accept that, I'll wash my hands of you, and you can march right off into the aircar outside."

Jrill chuckled behind him, and Loritt turned on her in a flash. "You're included in that, Jrill. Not another word. You came to me and asked for more help. There she is." Loritt pointed at First, fists still balled up and spoiling for a fight.

Unsurprisingly, this did not defuse the standoff, but at least it became a quiet one.

"Great, let's continue. First, you are the newest recruit to my little family of kindhearted thieves and miscreants. Now that you've accepted the job, it's only fair to let you in on what you've agreed to."

"That's an understatement."

"We are in the repossession business. All aboveboard, all completely legal. You will never run afoul of the law so long as you work the jobs I assign you. We reacquire assets for their rightful owners when their customers fall too far behind on payments. Usually banks, sometimes creditors whose charters are . . . let's say less organized." Loritt held up a finger. "But, on the surface, from a glance, what we do looks an awful lot like stealing other people's stuff, and requires the same skill sets. Which is why I've always recruited from a more rarified employment pool than most."

First took a moment to digest this. "So . . ." she ventured. "You want me to repossess aircars for you?"

"Oh, my dear, no. You must widen your gaze. Here, we do starship repo."

First's eyes brightened. "Starships?"

"Starships."

"Like, entire starships?"

"A fleet and growing," Jrill said pridefully.

"I wasn't lying last evening when I said I came from more humble beginnings," Loritt said. He resumed picking at his salad. "But you were half right about me. I live *very* well. So do the rest of my people. But we don't live off the labors of those below us. We feast on the carcasses of those above. Ten percent repo fees on half-billion-credit starships buys a lot of nice things. Does that sound like something you'd be interested in?"

Loritt didn't need to be an expert on human emotions to recognize the unique blend of fury and avarice fighting for dominance across First's face. *That* he could spot on any race from anywhere in this galaxy, and maybe any other.

"I thought you might be. We're in need of a tunneler and a dazzler. There's no formal job description or employee training manual, however. Everyone has to be adaptable. Everyone is accountable, even me. You're going to have to learn as you go, I'm afraid."

The human girl crossed her arms. "Six months ago, I stepped off a transport with just the clothes on my back, no contacts, and less than enough local currency to buy a burger. Now I'm here. I'm a quick study."

"I don't doubt it. I do make one demand of you, however."

"Only one?"

"One for now," Loritt said. "I suspect others will crop up along the way, in your case. Working for me means you're legitimate. All your little schemes, hustles, and side projects end immediately. We are a bonded, insured, and, above all, completely legal organization. If I catch word of your running so much as that little cup game of yours on an idle Hole Day, you're out."

First turned this over in her mind for a moment before answering. "Cool. When do I start?"

Loritt's Lividite infiltration expert appeared out of nowhere, as he often did, and hoisted a handheld. "Sorry to interrupt, boss, but a contract just came through the conduit."

"Hashin, are you familiar with doorbells at all?" Jrill asked.

"I'm paid to go around them."

"You"—First jabbed an accusing finger at Hashin—"got me pooped on."

"Yes . . ." Hashin said. "Sorry about that."

"First, this is Hashin," Jrill said. "Hashin, First. We're all going to be friends or die trying."

"Back to this contract," Loritt said hopefully. "Closed?"

"Open."

"Glot." Loritt pushed his plate aside, suddenly relieved of an appetite. "Let's see the job, then."

Hashin nodded and set his handheld down on the counter, then transferred the stream to the penthouse's OS. Without prompt, the lights dimmed and the windows overlooking the patio went black, replaced by a slowly rotating hologram of a Transom Shipyards Celestial Schooner christened the *Space for Rant.* Twelve decks stacked from bow to stern, Class III high-space-rated fold engines, twenty-four staterooms, a formal dining galley, swimming pools in both water and liquid methane, even a hangar for a pair of reentry-rated luxury aircars.

First whistled long and low at the last bit. "Can my cut of the job be one of those?"

"We'll discuss payment later," Loritt said. "Who's the delinquent owner? What's their story?"

Hashin scrolled deeper into the dispatch. "He's a Sulican. Bit of a playboy. Apparently, his dead parents cut him off from the inheritance via simulcron last year, and his little pleasure yacht has been falling behind on payments ever since."

"Simulcron?" First tried and failed not to sound embarrassed for asking.

"High-end virtual intelligence," Hashin replied without judgment. "Legally binding ghosts built off his parents' brain maps. A way to impose their judgments on his behavior from beyond the beyond. Apparently, their simulcrons don't approve of his choices of late and decided to twist off the taps to teach him a lesson in humility, but he ignored it."

"Which is where we come in," First said.

"Which is where we come in on behalf of his creditors," Loritt corrected her. "That pleasure yacht does not belong to him. He's stolen it. It's our job to steal it back for our clients."

"Out of purely idle speculation," First said innocently, "how much is that yacht worth?"

"Two hundred and seventy million Assembly standard credits at current exchange rates," Hashin said dispassionately. "A small job, but worth a day's labor."

First, despite her internal skeletal structure, appeared to melt into a flesh puddle.

"We've lost the rookie," Jrill said.

"She'll recover," Loritt said. "You did, after all. However, our central problem remains. How do we beat Soolie's people to the punch down at the docks?"

First perked up at the name. "You can't. They're already there."

Everyone's gaze turned to the human. "I'm sorry," Loritt said, "but what was that you said?"

"Soolie the Fin? His people own the docks. Where do you think I was taking your Proteus?" First asked.

"You work for Soolie the Fin?" Jrill said, her head crest rising.

First squared off against her. "I don't work *for* Soolie. I sell *to* Soolie. I boost aircars, he buys them. That's it."

Jrill's red irises grew two sizes. "Why that karking, double-dipping, two-faced—"

Loritt put up a hand to interrupt the growing diatribe, no matter how entertaining it would prove to be. "First. Do you mean to say you've . . . been in an illicit business relationship with Soolie the Fin?"

"I just said that, didn't I?"

"I suppose you did. That complicates things."

"The hell it does. I told you I don't work for him. I sell cars to his goons. Cash in hand, no contracts, no commitments."

Loritt smiled at the very young human. Still so new to the worlds. "I doubt very much he will see your story from the same perspective. Still, this is good intel. Soolie pretends at legitimacy. We can leverage this against him. Quietly, of course. Certainly enough to get you released from your contract."

"There was never any contract," First snapped. "I work alone."

"I'm sure you believe that, just as he wanted you to," Loritt said. "Out here, contracts don't have to be agreed to by both parties."

First grew quiet. A first for her.

"That explains a lot, boss," Jrill said. "If Soolie has people down at the docks with advance warning of contracts coming in, they can throw the ropes over and be in line before any of the other crews have even gotten our boots on."

"So," Loritt said. "We can't wait for *Space for Rant* to dock at Junktion. We have to intercept it in high-space, so when the moorings are cast over and Soolie's rented hands swarm the gangplanks, we already control the bridge. Do we have the flight plan they logged with Space Traffic Control?"

Hashin nodded. "Right here in the bundle, boss."

"Then the three of you need to get to the *Goes Where I'm Towed,* double time. First, you'll have to make your introductions with the rest of the team en route to the intercept point. Jrill will be your chaperone for this mission. You will follow her instructions."

"Oh, come on."

"That's how it is. Take my car down to the docking port. It's the fastest way."

"I'm driving," Jrill said.

"Shotgun!" First claimed.

"Absolutely no weapons," Loritt said.

"No, it's means I get the front passenger seat."

"Sorry, humie," Hashin said. "Seniority rules in the Subassembly. You're taking the backseat."

CHAPTER 5

First extricated herself from the back of the Proteus. As luxurious as the front two seats were, the backseat had been incorporated only as a polite fiction for insurance purposes so the Infinite technically counted as a four-seat family coupe instead of a purebred sports aircar. First wasn't very big, but she was still far too big to fit in the rumble seat in any comfort.

"Where are we?" she asked, rubbing her lumbar.

"Bay Ninety-Four," Hashin answered. "Boss's personal docking slip. This is where we keep the *Goes Where I'm Towed.*"

Jrill stalked off toward the airlock. "C'mon, the others are already inside. We need to clear moorings and push off."

"In what?" First asked, looking out on the bay through a viewing gallery.

"In that." Hashin pointed at a ship so nondescript, her eyes sort of slid off it.

"What's that, the box it came in?"

"You laugh."

"So will everyone else when they see us pull up in that."

"They won't—that's the point. Come along, little mushroom."

First just shook her head and followed the Lividite through the airlock and down the All-Seal boarding tube. Once inside, First's impression of the ship jumped an order of magnitude. Its construction was robust, with double the frame members and internal bracing she'd seen on other transports, of which there had been several on her journey to Junktion. It was also spotlessly maintained and well equipped. It was no pleasure craft, though. Redundant fire suppression systems and frequent lockers for emergency oxygen canisters studded the hallways.

"Okay, this is more like it," First said. "Don't judge a book, eh?"

"Why shouldn't you judge books?" Hashin asked.

"By its cover. Don't judge a book by its cover. Sorry, it's a human expression. It means a ratty-ass cover doesn't mean the story inside is bad."

Hashin leaned against a frame member. "Describe this *book*'s 'cover.' Length, beam, layout, color, hull registry numbers."

First smiled. Her living, indeed her very survival was dependent on her powers of observation. She noticed everything out of reflex, the way other people breathed.

Which was why when she went to the wellspring of her memory expecting a fountain and found it dry, she stood speechless for several stunned seconds.

"I can't," she said at last.

"Exactly. So undistinguished, our novelty-obsessed brains see no reason to devote precious memory to it. Weaponized mediocrity. My people invented it. I perfected it."

"How do you remember where it's parked?"

"I have an app. Come, meet the rest of the crew."

They took an exposed lift deeper into the bowels of the ship, past the point where paneling gave way to exposed conduits and pipes. Off the guided tours, then.

"These are the engineering levels. This is Sheer's domain. She's . . . ah, particular about her work."

"Sheer?" First asked. "Like a pair of scissors or see-through lingerie?"

They stepped off the lift into what could only be described as a lair. At its center was an antimatter annihilation reactor and one of the largest, and thereby oldest, Ish First had ever seen. Her left foreclaw had grown to grotesque proportions, nearly two meters long.

"So scissors, then," First whispered.

"Don't draw attention to her claw."

"But don't only the male Ish grow big claws like—"

"That line of questioning is an excellent way to get both of us snipped in half like gift ribbon. She's complicated; just go with it."

First swallowed hard as they stepped off the lift.

"Who's the chum?" Sheer chittered out of her mouthparts.

"Sheer, this is First. She's our new hacker," Hashin said diplomatically.

"First, huh? Is that supposed to be a joke? We've gone through three tunnelers since I've been down here."

"This one might stick," Hashin said. "First, shake claw with our resident wrench-turner, Sheer."

"Pleasure." First stuck her hand out, hoping to come back with more than a stump.

Sheer's eyes regarded her from atop their stalks for a long moment before offering a claw. Her smaller claw. "Just keep your fingers out of my ship's operating system and we'll get along fine."

"Is that a common problem?"

"Oh yes. Software engineers, always trying to fix things that aren't broken. Took me two weeks to track down the line of code the last one inserted that made *Towed* think other ships were hitting on her whenever someone hailed us."

First scratched her head. "Why didn't they fix it themselves?"

"Because they were dead."

"Dead?!" First blurted out.

"That's an exaggeration," Hashin hastened to add. "None of us actually saw them die."

"That's true, I guess," Sheer said. "We saw them get swallowed whole by a buzzmouth and not come out again. The dying part is just speculation on my part. Anyway, I'm sure you'll be fine. You look like a capable . . . whatever you are."

"I'm human!" First insisted. "From Earth?"

"Of course you are. Now, if you'll excuse me, I have a constriction bottle diagnostic to finish before three hundred quilpies of antimatter break loose and annihilate us all."

Sheer turned back around to attend to her monitors. The introduction over, Hashin returned to the lift, beckoning First to follow.

"You didn't tell me the last hacker died on the job. That's a detail I would've liked to have known."

"Or you would've turned yourself in to security?"

"Well . . . no, but still."

"They weren't technically on the job at the time, if that helps. We were taking a little break between contracts to do some deep-sea fishing."

First stared at the little gray man. "You were fishing for things called buzzmouths? How is that relaxing?"

"Well, I was on a double dose of Leisuretol, so I could've relaxed inside an active volcano. Everyone else seemed to be enjoying the sun."

"You're all nuts."

"The boss likes to party. Up next is the command cave."

"You mean the bridge?"

"Does it connect two points of land across a waterway?"

"No?"

"Then no, I didn't mean a bridge."

"So literal."

The doors opened onto what would very appropriately be called a cave. The ceilings were low, even for First, who wasn't terribly tall to begin with. The crew stations were cramped with consoles and equipment with little thought given for comfort or to stave off claustrophobia. This was no pleasure craft. It was a predator *of* pleasure craft.

First was starting to dig it.

"And here is the final member of our little bunch." Hashin held out a hand to a familiar-looking jar plugged into the very center of the cave. "First, this is out pilot, Fen—"

"Fenax," she finished for him. "We've met."

"No, we haven't," the floating brain said without turning around. Seriously, where were its eyes? How did it see anything?

"Yes, we did. Six months ago. You were working at McDonald's. You collect alien currencies."

"That was a different Fenax."

"Oh, come on. How many of your people named Fenax can there be on this station?"

Hashin tapped First on the shoulder. "They're all named Fenax. It's their race name."

"Oh." It took a moment for the depth of her mistake to sink into First's awareness. "Oooooh, shit . . ."

"I wouldn't worry too much about it," Jrill said from what looked like the captain's chair. "They can't tell us quad-limbs apart for glot, either. Probably thinks you're an Illcarion."

"It's not?" Fenax asked.

Jrill held out a clawed hand. "See?"

"Do Illcarions look particularly human?" First asked.

"No, not really. The Fenax come from between thermal cloud layers of a gas giant. Way down below where light reaches, other than lightning strikes. They see with sound, air pressure disturbances. They can see and manipulate magnetic fields, too. Why we had to stop using magnetic strip cards."

"What did you expect us to do?" Fenax asked. "You may as well have written your pass codes and bank account information on your foreheads. We thought you were being exceptionally generous. We never had a concept of money or private ownership before. It was an honest mistake."

"Anyway," Jrill continued. "When it comes to piloting a starship in open space, it's hard to beat a species that evolved from single cells to sentience floating in three dimensions."

First raised a hand. "But if they evolved in clouds . . ."

"Yeah."

"And there wasn't any ground below them . . ."

"Yeeah."

"Then how did they mine metal or ceramics to build starships?"

"Ah," Jrill said, understanding. "They didn't. Some unlicensed helium-3 miners accidently sucked one up through a gas siphon and kept it as the ship's mascot for a couple of months until it mapped out the ship's control systems and took over the central computer. Killed everyone aboard, then went back and filled the helium bladders with more Fenax. Kinda got outta hand for a few centuries after that. Had to give them a seat on the council just to get them to stop stealing every starship they came across. That's why it's easier to let them be the pilot from the get-go."

"That is a largely accurate, if incomplete, recitation of historical events," Fenax said without emotion.

"Got it," First said. "I'll just sit down over here, if that's okay."

"Anywhere is fine as long as you keep out from underfoot."

"Thanks a lot." First plopped down in an open seat on the periphery of the cave.

"Buckle in," Hashin said. "Company health insurance doesn't cover injuries sustained from stupidity."

"Doesn't the ship have inertial dampers or something?"

"Stop watching *Star Trek,*" Jrill said. "We have artificial gravity, but it has a 0.037 refresh rate. That's more than enough time to splatter you against the view screen in twenty-grav evasive maneuvers."

First grabbed the ends of her five-point crash harness and hurriedly snapped it together without another word.

"Do we have clearance from Space Traffic Control, Fenax?"

"Granted. Departure window opening in ten, nine, eight . . ."

"Clear umbilicals. Retract the All-Seal. Stand by docking clamps."

The *Goes Where I'm Towed* shuddered gently as its connections to Junktion popped free of the hull one by one.

"Three, two, one, departure window open."

"Release," Jrill ordered.

Outside, the two robust docking clamps in the bow that held the *Goes* to her host station like a determined tick snapped open. In the view screen, Bay Ninety-Four retreated quickly as the centripetal force of the station's spin threw the ship clear.

First expected to be thrown into her harness under the sudden acceleration. Instead, the opposite happened. She found herself weightless, only held in her chair by the five-point crash web.

She was flying. Floating.

"We're clear to maneuver," Fenax said.

"Head for the Junktion high-space portal and whip it," Jrill said.

Gravity returned like a hammer and slammed First back into the bottom of her seat.

"Yippee ki-yay, motherfu—"

"Language, young lady," Hashin said from his own seat as he applied some sort of medicated patch to his upper arm.

"But how did you even know . . ."

"We've all seen *Die Hard.* We have Christmas out here, too, you know. It's mostly a retail-driven holiday, but then, what holiday isn't?"

"Assembly space celebrates Jesus Christ's birth?" First asked incredulously.

"Who?"

"Oh, thank God," First said.

"Making transition now," Fenax said, ignoring everyone.

First reached into her purse and retrieved her pair of 3-D glasses. They'd been awfully tough to find so far from Earth. Secondhand, slightly scratched, and with a paper clip holding one of the temple arms in place, they'd still cost her the better part of a week's earnings to get them off a passing human traveler. But without them, the half of Junktion permanently floating in the extradimensional reality of hyperspace was inaccessible to her. The human brain didn't do well wandering around in four dimensions, and it wasn't long before one found themselves trying to practice yoga in a torus.

She had no idea how the other species handled it so well. Well, maybe the Fenax. But everyone else was a mystery.

With nary a ripple or a whisper, the *Goes Where I'm Towed* and her crew left their universe behind and moved one floor up. "Transit complete," Fenax announced. "Exiting Junktion's exclusion zone . . . now."

"Lay in course for our rendezvous point with *Space for Rant* and squeeze the engines by the gonads," Jrill said.

Even through the artificial gravity, something deep inside First's inner ear felt the ship lunge forward like a politician with a campaign donation dangling in front of him. She could read and contextualize enough of the displays and status readouts to know they were burning up space at something like three hundred gravities. It was simply eye-watering acceleration.

"What happens if the antigrav fails?" First asked.

"The counter-grav protecting us is generated by the engines themselves," Hashin answered. "They're all part of the same system. So they'd go down together and we'd just be on the float, theoretically."

"And if that theory doesn't hold up?"

"Then they'll be able to strain our remains through screens fine enough to filter out individual viruses. Don't worry. If that happens, none of us will even realize it."

"That's not as comforting as you might think."

"Sorry," Hashin said. "I'm probably due for another Empathen injection. I've been tapering off for a week now."

"Well, at least I know the company's prescription drug plan is solid," First quipped. "Why do you call yourselves the Subassembly, anyway?"

"Isn't it obvious?" Jrill said from the command chair. "We're made up of a Nelihexu, Turemok, Ish, Lividite, and Fenax. Five of the six races on the Assembly Council. We're only missing a Grenic, and that's because they'd only be useful during a job if we really needed to drop a big rock on someone."

First bristled. She'd grown very fond of Quarried Themselves after living with them for the last few months and felt the need to defend her roommate.

"Grenic take the long view on things, that's all."

Jrill looked at First with what probably passed for a smirk on her beak among her people. "You do know that in Grenic time you just moved in this morning, right? How have you already bonded with them? They're not even between sleep cycles yet."

"You're wrong," First said, afraid she wasn't but unwilling to show a gram of uncertainty in the face of one of the people who'd tried to torch Earth. "They watch, their bodies are slow, but their minds aren't. Live with one for a month and you'll know."

"Next time I'm in the market for a new end table, I'll consider it."

First sank into her chair and let the matter drop. For the next few hours, the only thing to watch was the plot as the intercept timer counted down to zero, so First busied herself uploading patches and viruses to her deck from the ship's library. Anything they had on Transom Shipyards or any of their suppliers, which was quite a lot as it happened.

At the midway point, they flipped the ship around and decelerated just as hard to bring themselves to a complete stop. Once their velocity was spent, the *Goes Where I'm Towed* hung motionless in the ethereal weirdness of high-space, a spider waiting for a very big, very expensive fly.

"Sheer," Jrill said into the intercom. "We're running a Broken Wing con. Foul up the main reactor output and leak some hard radiation out our purge vents. Take a couple of counter-grav modules offline, but not too far offline. We may need a snatch-and-sprint at any moment."

"Got it."

"Hashin, a universal standard distress call, if you please," Jrill said.

"Omnidirectional or tightbeam?"

"High-gain cone centered on the *Space for Rant*'s course. I want them to think we're filling space with the signal, but I don't want to attract anyone outside that cone before they get to us."

"Sending distress call now."

The overhead lights flickered for a moment, triggering several alerts throughout the cave.

"What's that?" First asked.

Hashin waved away her concern. "Just Sheer dirtying up main power. We're disabled, remember?"

"So what's the plan for when they pull over to help? Magnetic harpoon? Carbon nanotube net? Immobilizer pulse?"

"Actually," Jrill injected, "I thought we'd wait until we're invited aboard, then you pretend to throw a temper tantrum and lock yourself inside their command cave until we arrive at port."

"You can't be serious."

"The old tricks are the best tricks, and it's been a while since we had a juvenile to run this scam with."

"I'm not a *juvenile.* I'll be eighteen in a month!"

"Is that supposed to mean something? You're a kid, and you're playing the part, or we'll drop you back off in the promenade to stack your cups. Got it?"

First crossed her arms in a huff and glared at the Turemok.

"That's the spirit. You're halfway to a tantrum already. Just keep that face glued on and you'll do great."

"Get bent."

"Not to interrupt," Fenax said from their jar, "but a ship matching the description of our contract just appeared on long-range sensors."

"Have they seen us yet?" Jrill said.

"No active scans. No change in their course or speed."

Jrill swiveled around in her command chair to consult with Hashin. "They've gotten the distress call by now, yes?"

"No doubt."

Jrill drummed her claws on the armrest. "So they're ignoring it."

"So it would seem."

"Karking socialites," Jrill muttered. "Refuse to see anyone else's problems unless there's money to be made or another rung of their ladder to climb. Fenax, how long until they're inside what *should* be our sensor range?"

"Another ten rakims and *Space for Rant* will be inside average civilian scanner range."

"Hashin, wait ten rakims once they're inside that perimeter, then send a personalized message directly to them on tightbeam. Maybe they'll be more inclined to help if they know we've spotted them and can report them for refusing to answer a distress call."

"If they don't just blow us up to avoid the potential trouble," Fenax said.

"But it's a pleasure yacht," First said. "So it's unarmed, right?"

Jrill laughed. "It's *registered* unarmed. But then, so are we."

"We're not?" Hashin and Jrill just looked at each other with telling grins. "I see," First said.

"Sending tightbeam now," Hashin said.

Jrill steepled her fingers. "Fenax, prepare a thruster 'misfire' that will push us into their course if this doesn't convince them to do the right thing."

"You mean to ram them?"

"No, just enough drift to force them into a course correction. Put the little pile of glot on record for not only ignoring a distress call but crossing the street to avoid it. Maybe we can win a judgment against him even if Soolie's squad gets to the ship before we do."

Hashin smiled. "Working all the angles. I'm impressed, Jrill. The boss is rubbing off on you."

"Gotta keep the hatchlings fed."

An alert chimed at Hashin's console. "Won't be necessary. They're hailing us."

"Probably had to get his pants back on," Jrill said. "Best desperation faces, everyone."

"We don't all have faces," Fenax said.

"Then twitch a tentacle nervously. Hashin, answer the hail, forward view screen." The Lividite nodded and dashed off a couple of keystrokes. A moment later, the entire forward bulkhead of the command cave lit up with a holographic projection so clear and sharp, First thought it must be a portal into the other ship's bridge she could stand up and walk through. Standing dead center in the image was a beanstalk of a creature with three arms, three legs, and a face with three eyes arranged symmetrically around a mouth that looked like a black sock full of broken glass.

"Hi! Sorry for the slowlow. Had to get my pants back on. You bipeds have it so easy."

"Oh, thank Dar you're here, kind sir," Jrill said, hiding a grimace. "We were on our way to Korovax when one of our antigrav nodes blew. We tried to come about for Junktion, but a feedback surge blew out a capacitor bank, and our main reactor took damage. We can't shut it down, and hard radiation is saturating compartment after compartment!"

"Whoooa, that sounds like, bad, right?" the Sulican said. "Like, heft lift stuff."

"It's potentially lethal," Jrill said flatly. "You . . . know what radiation is, right?"

"I know it's nova digger, love. So you'll all be like, macro whacked if I don't help, jala?"

Jrill looked around the rest of the bridge. Hashin and First just shrugged. Fenax quivered in a similar fashion. "Uh, yeah, macro whacked. We're still clean here, but our engineer has already been contaminated."

"Uh, wow. That's, like, total mood shred."

"Sir," Jrill said. "I don't mean to be impertinent, but . . . is there a commander of the ship I could talk to?"

"You're lookin' at him, tweak beak!" the Sulican said. "Just me and the partaaaay. Rest of the ship is automated. The controlocker don't even have chairs in it. Ain't that hyper?"

"Macro," Jrill said. "Can we come over for the partaaay? So we don't die?"

"Sure thing, kula wing. Sending an All-Seal your way now. Fermented's free, distilled's a fee."

The link cut out.

Jrill looked around at the rest of her cave crew. "What just happened?"

First put up her hand. "I think we just got invited to a kegger."

CHAPTER 6

Handset pressed close to his face, Loritt watched the playback from the *Space for Rant*'s internal security feed with delight. First played the part of a tantrum-prone teenager to perfection, putting herself right in Jrill's face, which Loritt was certain wasn't an act, before throwing herself, arms flailing, into the controlocker and sealing the door.

Once inside, she leaned into a corner and, with her hacker's deck, repelled every attempt by the clueless debtor to override the lockout.

For six hours.

It was a masterful performance, matched only by the sight of Soolie's goons swarming up the gangway expecting to take legal possession of the ship, just to come face-to-face with Jrill's glot-eating grin standing by the hatch.

Loritt cherished the sight. Whether in spite of the eventual cost, or because of it, he couldn't say.

"What's the matter, Loritt?" asked Kula, his date for most evenings. One of the few other Nelihexu to live on Junktion, she was quite enchanting.

"Oh, nothing, my dear. Sorry for the distraction. Just checking in on my employees. Are you ready to order?"

"Chessel!" Soolie the Fin shouted from across the courtyard, then angled over to their table. "You old pile of spares. How long has it been?"

"Entirely too short," Loritt said.

"Just like me!" the diminutive Umulat said as he invited himself to sit down. "Who's your friend? She's a lovely collection."

"Kula, this is Soolie the Fin, a small-time criminal with aspirations of legitimacy."

Kula looked Soolie up and down. It didn't take long. "Emphasis on 'small.'"

"And a sharp tongue," Soolie said, all three eyes twinkling. "Hope she doesn't cut you anywhere too sensitive, Chessel."

"Loritt doesn't need to worry about getting cut if he gets too close," Kula purred.

"Kula, dear. Could you find our waiter?" Loritt asked. "He's been gone quite some time, and I'm famished."

"Gladly." Kula uncoiled from her seat and made a show of walking off. Loritt couldn't help but watch the performance.

"Not my glass of bitter root, but I can see why you like her," Soolie said. "Now, business?"

"We don't have any business, Soolie," Loritt said.

"I disagree. See, it's come to my attention that you've poached one of my repo contracts."

"Oh yes?" Loritt took a slow sip of an exquisite forty-eight Bino Eperon and let the sweet and sour flavors simmer on his tongue and olfactory organ for a rakim before continuing. "And which contract might that be?"

"The *Space for Rant.* Just docked this evening."

"That was, if memory recalls, an open contract, Soolie. You have no more claim to it than anyone else. We got there first."

"Yeah, but it's *how* you got there first that bothers me."

"Do tell."

Soolie held out his malformed right arm and touched a crystal on the side of a custom bracelet he wore there. In the space between them, a small but very crisp hologram appeared over the table of the *Rant*'s All-Seal exit to Junktion's docks. Jrill stepped out and flexed her scales at one of Soolie's goons, provoking a flinch as predictable as it was satisfying. Then Hashin. Then . . .

First looked straight down the lens of the hidden camera. Soolie froze the image on her face. "My contracts aren't all you've been pilfering, it seems. The human girl works for me."

"She tells a different story. My new employee says she never had a contractual agreement with you and worked entirely as an independent . . . let's call her a consultant."

"That's rich. She washed up here half a cycle ago, flat broke, running small cons on the promenade. Picked my pocket, the little scab. But instead of throwing her out an airlock, I took her under my fin and taught her how to survive, and this is the thanks I get."

"Your altruism is truly inspiring," Loritt said emotionlessly.

"What did she say she 'consulted' with me for?"

"Stolen aircars to fence. Including my own, which I caught her in the act of trying to deliver to you."

"The hell you did."

"To your associates, then. The same ones who harassed my people at the docks as they tried to disembark the pleasure yacht we'd already taken legal possession of today under applicable Assembly statutes."

"This is what I get for taking in strays. You only knew to jump it in high-space because you stole my human!" Soolie pounded his good fist on the table, drawing curious, disapproving looks from surrounding patrons.

"Control yourself, Soolie. You're trying to be a gentleman these days, remember?"

Soolie took several long, angry breaths before answering. "Appearances can be deceiving. I keep excellent records. Give her up, or station security gets an anonymous tip on every car she's boosted in the last quarter cycle."

"If that happens, station security gets an anonymous tip about everyone she delivered those aircars to, and your muscle down at the docks all end up in a holding cell. That would be quite a blow to your newly renovated image."

The two of them locked eyes for a long, labored moment.

"You know why they call me 'the Fin'?" Soolie asked finally.

"Oh, here we go."

"Because I was clutched with this undifferentiated arm." He held up the paddle of his right forearm. "Somewhere along the line in the pouch, some hormonal signals got mixed up, and my flipper here never got the order to branch off into proper fingers. So my clutch-mates called me 'the Fin.'"

Loritt took another long sip of his Eperon. "How cruel of them."

"Cruel? It was a mercy. They taught me strength, then I taught them something else."

"And this is the part where you enlighten me with the wisdom you imparted onto them."

"Yeah. A swimmer with only one fin always circles back." As a parting gift, Soolie knocked over Loritt's stemware with his fin, spilling the Eperon and leaving a crimson streak to soak into the tablecloth. "Be seeing you, Loritt." The Umulat shoved past Kula and their waiter as they returned to the table.

"I'm ever so sorry," Loritt said to the waiter. "But I seem to have fumbled my drink. A fresh tablecloth and another glass of this lovely vintage, if you please."

First had never seen a party like it in her life. The closest she'd come had been in Florida at Universal Studios when six contractually obligated "performers" in full costume had serenaded her at a Hogwarts main hall table for her twelfth birthday, while five hundred other tourists looked on and applauded in halfhearted disinterest.

This was nothing like that.

Loritt's penthouse overflowed with her new crewmates, their friends, friends of their friends, and beings whose relationship connections, or even evolutionary paths, were completely opaque to her. Ostensibly, the party was a fund-raiser for some local politician or another, but Jrill said it was really to celebrate breaking out of their contract slump.

The security measures on the patio glass had been turned off entirely as people moved between conversations held over its amazing view and the lure of food and drink inside. It wasn't Loritt's first time hosting a party for diverse attendees. All the food platters and bottles were clearly labeled and color-coded for chirality, arsenic versus phosphorus, and liquid methane base. There was even a cistern of aerosol plankton for Fenax and three other Fenaxes at the party to pump into their tanks. First was relieved no one asked her to identify their pilot out of the four of them.

Beyond the food and drink, there was a dizzying array of . . . pharmaceuticals being passed around. First watched in mixed amazement and horror as every type of party drug imaginable was smoked, snorted, injected, eaten, patched, and inserted into orifices whose biological function she neither knew nor cared to venture to guess. Assembly space was somewhat more permissive about drug use than the municipality she'd grown up with, due in no small part to the presence of Lividites and their chemically dependent emotional expression.

And then, there was the music. A DJ/performer had set up a holographic music deck beyond anything First had ever seen, preloaded with a thousand virtual instruments from a hundred worlds and a catalog of a million songs available on request. The six-armed musician often played three or more instruments at once, acting as backup or adding their own dancehall beat to everything from chamber music, to speed metal, to pieces composed by remixing the sounds of radio burst signals emitted by pulsars.

Then someone requested that damned song again, "Pho Queue," by the Wolverines. The crowd roared in approval.

"Who are these guys?" First asked aloud, mostly to herself, but she was overheard by . . . a squid carrot?

"The Wolverines! They're your kin. Surely you've heard of them?"

"I heard them over the radio in a car two days ago. That's it."

"Impossible!" the squid carrot proclaimed.

"There are twenty billion humans. No, I don't know all of them personally, if these guys are even really human. What kind of music is this even?"

"They're a hair band. It's blowing up. They're out on tour of this arm of the galaxy right now. Not even I can score tickets, not for fin or tentacle. Me! Can you believe it?" the unknown alien said, expecting First would understand the gravity of the sentiment without further explanation.

"No, I really can't," First said. "You know that music was popular, like, four hundred years ago, right?"

"Light speed delay. We only just got MTV a few cycles ago."

First rubbed a temple. "That explains so much."

Hashin appeared with a small plate of appetizers and edibles to save her. "First, I've been looking all over for you." He put a slim gray arm over her shoulder and gently pulled her away from the party guest.

"Thank you. What the hell was that thing?"

"That 'thing' is Ulsor Plegis, the politician this fund-raiser is for."

"What are they running for?" First asked. "Chief of calamari appetizers?"

Hashin shook his head reproachfully. "I have to stay here and keep an eye on the floor. Could you go find the boss for me? He's supposed to give a little speech before introducing the candidate."

"Sure. Where'd you see him last?"

"Hallway by his bedroom."

First nodded and headed for the sleeping quarters, glad to leave the noise and push of the crowd behind for a few minutes. Loritt's bedroom was the farthest down the hall and to the right, although First wasn't sure what he needed a bedroom for, as it wasn't clear his race slept in the first place. First rapped her knuckles on the rich, deep-lavender grain of the door.

"Loritt?" she asked. When no answer came, she knocked harder and turned the old-fashioned knob in the middle of the door. It wasn't locked, so she pushed it open. "Loritt, Hashin is looking for—"

The shock at what she saw scattered around the bed and floor froze the air in First's lungs. Loritt's body had been dismembered—no, ripped apart, and tossed around the room like seventy kilos of shredded pork. Some parts of him still twitched, the violence was so fresh.

The instant First's diaphragm thawed from the initial trauma, she screamed like a horror movie queen.

Jrill came charging down the hallway like an avenging vulture, Hashin close behind her.

"What's wrong, girl?" Jrill demanded of her.

"He's dead!" First said through heaving sobs. "Someone murdered Loritt!"

Jrill pushed past her and threw the door open, only to stop dead, a quizzical look on her face. Then she motioned to Hashin to come and look.

Hashin surveyed the scene from the door before closing it again. "Ah. I see."

"You handle this, Hashin," Jrill said. "I have to return to my post." Without another word, Jrill swept back down the hallway in the direction of the party.

"Where the hell is she going?" First demanded.

"First," Hashin beckoned her to follow a short way down the hall. "What do you know about Nelihexu?"

"I don't know." First fought against hyperventilating just to talk. "They look like somebody skinned a big cat and taught it to walk upright. I just know Loritt was nice to me and now he's dead."

Hashin nodded. "Okay, I see the problem. Nelihexu are communal organisms. Just like my body and yours have specialized tissue that make up our organs, they have specialized individual multicellular species that make up their bodies. All these animals live in a community. You know this particular community as Loritt Chessel."

"Yeah? So?"

"So," Hashin said, trying to be delicate, "when it's time for, ah, mating, these communities have to . . ." Hashin made a coming apart gesture with his hands.

"Oh," First said one second before the full implication of what he'd said hit here. "Ooh. Uuuuuugh! You mean I just saw Loritt and Kula having sex?!"

"That is exactly what I mean."

First stuck her fingers in her ears. "Lalalalala!"

The bedroom door flung open, and a visibly agitated Loritt in a hastily tied robe stared out at the two of them. "What in the name of Supol is going on out here?"

First stared at him slack-jawed.

Hashin spoke first. "Nothing, boss. Just a little biology tutorial. But you and Kula should get dressed. You have to introduce our honored guest shortly."

"Fine." Loritt's gaze turned over to First. "And what about you, young lady?"

First swallowed. "I'll be in the bathroom, washing my brain out with ammonia."

With the sounds of celebration still ringing in her ears, First wandered back to the apartment she shared with Quarried Themselves for the first time since trying to steal Loritt's car. She collapsed on the couch like an imploding apartment building.

The last three days had been such a blur of danger and bad decisions that she could scarcely believe it had all fit in sixty-six hours. Had she slept? On the patio the first night, yes, for a while. But since?

First was still wired from the party. Hours of music and dancing still throbbed in her mind and her feet. There was no way she could fall . . .

Seven hours later, First woke up to the unmoving, slate-gray face of Quarried looming over her. In their defense, Grenic in proximity couldn't help but seem imposing. It was like waking up to find yourself locked in a staring contest with a giant cement Dali statue.

First got over her initial shock, hopefully quickly enough that her moment of panic didn't register in Quarried's tectonic consciousness. She looked around and realized Quarried Themselves held out their delayed-communication box. It blinked red.

With some effort, First managed to pry it free of Quarried's three-fingered hand and push the playback button.

"Hello, First. You looked cold, so I put a blanket on you."

First looked down and realized she had indeed been tucked into a comforter that almost covered both of her feet. She smiled and petted it. The playback continued.

"I saved *Rocks in Hard Places* like you asked. But don't wait too long to watch it. Our queue is filling up."

The red light stopped blinking. First smiled warmly at her roommate, then reached out a hand and held it against their cold, hard face for a very, very long time. Long enough, she hoped, for the gesture to register.

She pushed the button again, and it went green to let her know she was recording. "You're the first friend I've made in this strange place, Quarried. That means a lot to me. I brought you some fancy snacks from the party I think you can eat. I got a new job yesterday.

It's going to mean a lot of travel. I don't know when I'll be around or for how long, so I'm leaving my share of the rent for the next three months on the table. See you soon."

She pressed the button again to end the recording and put the green-flashing box back in Quarried's outstretched hand, then pulled the comforter over her shoulder and tried to get just a little more sleep nestled safely under the protection of her rocky roomie. First had no idea when she'd have another chance.

CHAPTER 7

"I hope you're all well rested," Loritt said. A quick survey of the room's occupants revealed they were not in fact well rested, or even poorly rested. They were, however, consuming prodigious amounts of painkillers and many cups of stimulants. Hashin reached across the table, opened Fenax's tank, and poured a cup directly onto the top of their body.

"Thank you," Fenax said blearily.

Surprisingly, First felt fine. She'd slept like a narcoleptic brick the night before and felt better than she had in weeks. Still, she drank a cup of the local coffee equivalent in solidarity with the rest of her squad.

"Success builds on success," Loritt said, ignoring their misery. "Thanks to our corsair's appropriation of *Space for Rant,* the same bank has offered us a closed contract. It's all ours. No other crew has either the docket or the legal authority to pursue the vessel."

"Unless we fail to deliver," First said.

"Naturally. There is also the small issue that the first three crews offered the contract turned it down."

Hashin slapped another patch on his upper arm. "Crews only turn down contracts because the payout is too cheap or the job is too dangerous."

"Good news, everyone," Loritt said. "The payout is excellent."

Everyone groaned. Loritt ignored them and opened a hologram of their prize. Floating in the air above the table was what looked for all the worlds like a vampire bat crossed with a black widow spider. Everyone groaned louder.

First's anxiety bounced off the end of the scale and hit the other side. "What the hell is that?" she asked, not for the first time, pointing a shaking finger at the rendering of the ship.

"That," Jrill said, "is a Skulaq-class destroyer of the Turemok military."

"You want us to steal a warship?" Sheer asked, agitated enough to click her large claw in a most uncharacteristic display of male aggression. "Are you out of your shell?"

"*Former* warship," Loritt corrected her. "Now known as the *Pay to Prey.* This particular hull was, ah, misplaced during the commotion after the failed attack on Earth five cycles ago. It eventually fell into the hands of a colorful character who calls himself Vel Jut, where it was declared legal salvage by a minor-system bureaucrat I'm sure was well compensated for seeing reason. Anyway, after a lengthy and expensive retrofit, it was repurposed as a 'business transport' and disarmed to bring it in line with civilian standards."

"I'm sure someone was well compensated to sign off on the post-retrofit inspection as well," Jrill said.

"Fortunate, then, that we have a former Turemok military officer in our midst to spot any trouble before it presents an issue," Loritt said bitingly.

First raised a hand. "I'm confused. If it's legally salvage, why is there a bank loan against it in the first place?"

"The loan was not for the ship but the retrofit. The bank paid the yard for their work. Vel Jut has not repaid them."

"He's not a real Vel," Jrill bit off. "Stop calling him one."

Loritt held out his hands, palms up. "I mean no disrespect to your service, merely relating what he calls himself. Anyway, Jut doesn't make it out this far very often. His closest approach to Junktion in the coming weeks is half a dozen systems away, if his flight plans are to be trusted. Which they shouldn't be. Still, we're going to have to go to him, so pack your kits and a change of clothes."

"My people do not wear clothes," Fenax said.

"We know," First said. "We can all clearly see your dangly bits. What are those, anyway?"

"My feeding appendages," Fenax said.

"Oh, that's not so bad."

"And gonads."

"Right."

"While I'm sure we're all riveted by this remedial anatomy lesson," Sheer said, "there's the small matter of how we're going to get into that ship uninvited. Even if it's disarmed, it's still heavily armored with multiple redundant defensive systems and military-grade security protocols."

Every sensory organ in the room turned toward Jrill expectantly. She straightened under the glare, then relented.

"Yeah, I can do it."

"Good," Loritt said. "Then let us get going. And by 'us,' I mean the five of you, obviously. Don't die. Recruiting new crews is an enormous pain."

"It's good to know the boss cares so much for our well-being," First said less than an hour later as they boarded the commercial transport for the Kaper system.

"He was being coy," Jrill said. "But he's not wrong, either. We're valuable assets. Replacing any one of us costs money, man power, time, and opportunities."

"Why aren't we using the *Goes Where I'm Towed*?"

"Because we don't want to overuse the *Goes Where I'm Towed,*" Hashin said from seat 247A. "It's uninteresting, not invisible."

First glanced down at seat 247B, her tiny, cramp-inducing home for the next twenty hours. "You'd think Loritt would spring for business class if we're such an important investment."

Jrill shrugged. "He's fronting the bill. If we fail, he's out economy-class tickets. If we succeed, we all get a bigger payday. You'll have another chance to prove your worth tomorrow. Until then, embrace the suck."

"Is your entire species such inflexible hard-asses?"

"Yes. Now sit. You're holding up the line."

The rest of the passengers squeezed their bodies and other belongings into the diminutive spaces assigned to such things and resigned themselves to a day spent among the stars lost inside a windowless metal tube.

"Where are Sheer and Fenax?" First asked.

"Sheer is in the oversized passengers' deck, and Fenax is in the cargo hold with our bags."

"You had them checked as luggage?"

"Those are the rules. The cargo hold is EM shielded to keep anyone from scanning the other passengers' electronic devices. It also keeps Fenax from hijacking the transport's computer system."

"Fenax wouldn't do that."

"Our Fenax wouldn't, not anymore at least. Other Fenax would and have."

"Isn't that a bit racist?"

"It's a precaution. Passengers aren't allowed in the command cave because they could seize the controls. Fenax could potentially do the same from anywhere except the cargo hold. They don't mind; their tanks are quite cozy. Fenax is probably playing a flight sim as we speak."

First, always the rebel, hid her hacker deck under her leg until the transport pulled back from the dock, then pulled it out and started researching whatever weaknesses and work-arounds to Turemok military software the /backnet/ had to offer. Which, as was so often the case, was extensive. Not that First didn't trust Jrill's abilities. She just didn't trust Jrill's loyalties. And a smart thief always took the time to tease out where the back doors were.

"Why are you here?" Hashin asked sometime after First's third lavatory trip.

"Because Loritt kidnapped me," First said. "You helped him do it."

"No, why were you here to be kidnapped in the first place? Why did you come to Junktion? You were only the third human through the gates. I checked. And the first to stay more than a week. You're a juvenile, alone, as far from home as anyone in your entire species has ever been. Why are you here?"

First's jaw flexed involuntarily. "Because I wanted to be as far away from home as possible. And that's as much as I want to say about it to any of you just now."

Hashin nodded, then slipped the VR display back over his eyes and fell silent again. The rest of the trip passed without any additional interruptions to her preparations. Jrill and Hashin slept through most of the flight. First had to shoo Jrill's bony, crested head off of her shoulder several times before the final approach announcement stirred everyone from their naps.

Despite the best efforts of the Kaper Tourism Bureau and their informational videos on all the exciting things to do on its wind-scoured glaciers, the system's two marginally habitable planets didn't have much to recommend them to anyone who wasn't an extremophile biologist. It was dirty, dull, and dangerous.

It was, however, a mining boomtown. A lithium discovery had sent three different mining consortiums into a flurry of construction that had attracted the usual round of transient laborers chasing jobs that were as dangerous and temporary as they were well paying.

Chasing *them* came the customary retinue of gambling dens, drug dealers, drinking halls, and damsels of discretion from across the galaxy to profit off the good fortunes of the laborers.

Kaper Station was a Wild West frontier town orbiting an ice cube at thirty thousand kilometers an hour, and in another five or ten cycles, it would be a ghost, left to slowly decay until it spiraled into its parent planet in a final fireball that would cleanse the universe of all the impropriety, vice, and debauchery that had taken place here.

But that was the future. In the now, business was booming.

"Time to go to work," Jrill said as the station's All-Seal suctioned itself onto the transport's skin. They disembarked and met Sheer by the gate, then grabbed Fenax from baggage claim, skipped the duty-free shops, and headed right for the private slips and docks.

"*Pay to Prey* isn't showing up in the directory," Hashin said from a public inquiry terminal.

"So our fake Vel either paid extra to be unlisted or is running under a forged ID," Jrill said. "Either way, it means he knows somebody's coming for his baby."

"Well, then, let's really hope baby's teeth haven't come in," First said.

"We'll have to inspect each slip visually," Jrill said, then caught herself as she glanced at Fenax floating in their tank. "Or by other means. There's three docking arms. Sheer, put Fenax on top of your carapace and snip anyone who gives you too much trouble."

"You know I hate this thing," Sheer said, lifting her huge claw.

"I'll trade you. It could come in handy."

"Is that an appendage joke?"

"It wasn't, but it is now. First and Hashin, you're both small and fast enough to get out of the way if things get slick. I can bluster or bust my way out of trouble by myself if needed. Each team pick an arm and meet back here when you're done with your inspection."

"What if we find the bounty before then?" First asked.

"Send 'I feel like Ish for dinner' over the group chat, and we'll all break off and return."

"Ish *cuisine,*" Sheer said. "I assume you meant."

"Depends on if you and the gas bladder find that ship first," Jrill cut back. "Let's get to it."

The crew split up. Sheer and Fenax scuttled down the middle corridor, while First and Hashin picked the last docking arm and started the search.

They made it all of four slips before stopping.

"That look like a Turemok destroyer to you?" First said to her partner as she looked over the arachnid nightmare.

"By process of elimination," Hashin said. "I can't imagine anything else is that ugly."

First opened the team link first. "I feel like Ish for dinner."

"Already?" Jrill said.

"I'm a teenager. We're always hungry."

"I thought you were almost an adult."

"You thought you had Earth in the bag, too."

"Just get back here." Jrill cut the connection.

First pulled her hacking deck from her purse and looked at Hashin. "You go. I'll get started."

"We shouldn't split up."

"I'll be fine. We need to do this quick, remember?"

Hashin nodded and walked briskly down the corridor. Not a run; that might draw attention. Just the sort of hurried, impatient gait of someone trying not to miss a connection.

"Okay, sweetie," First said to the station interface challenging her credentials on the screen of her deck. "Let's play peekaboo." She touched off a blink cracker program that hit the interface's credentialing system with hundreds of thousands of log-in attempts per second. With each attempt, the program watched to see how long it took before the rejection command was sent. The longer it took, the more log-in characters in the sequence were correct.

Any competent IT admin would have security measures in place to recognize the sudden, impossibly high spike in log-in attempts, but her program had a clever, and expensive, caveat. It reset the log-in counter with each hit. The system didn't remember from one attempt to the next until it was too late. Her cracker repeated the process more than three million times until it worked out the correct sequence and granted her access.

"Peekaboo!" First said just as the rest of the crew arrived.

"I told you to stay together," Jrill said.

"Did you?"

"It was strongly implied. It's not safe for you to be alone."

"Your concern is touching, buzzard."

"Not safe for us, I meant. You could've gotten caught and exposed the rest of your team."

"Well I didn't, and"—First wiggled her deck at Jrill's face—"I'm already in."

"Great. You want a corgi?"

"I think you mean *cookie.*"

"Just call up the All-Seal so we can get on with it."

Smiling to herself, First went through the interface's menu until she found the controls for the slip in question and hit the command to extend the All-Seal.

Nothing happened.

"Er . . ."

"Yes?" Jrill said tauntingly.

"Hang on." First tried the command again with no success. Then, an error message appeared. "The All-Seal has been disabled."

"So? You said you were in their system. Override the lockout."

"No, it's not a lockout; I mean it's *physically* disabled." She held up the deck to show the schematic of the docking tube and exactly which components had thrown malfunction codes. Sheer leaned in an eye-stalk to get a better look.

"Two servos and the dilator are offline," she said. "That never happens. This was deliberate sabotage."

"He sabotaged the All-Seal to his own ship?" Hashin said. "Paranoid bastard."

"You're kidding, right?" Jrill said.

"Why?"

Jrill swept her arms around to encompass the five of them.

"Well, okay, yes," Hashin granted. "But he doesn't know we're here to take his ship."

"So just because people are really after him doesn't mean he's not paranoid."

"Exactly."

"Fine, whatever." Jrill rubbed the back of her neck. "So how do we fix the All-Seal?"

"Can't from here," First said. "And I didn't think to pack a hard-suit."

Everyone else's eyes turned to Sheer.

"Well?" Jrill said.

Sheer reached up and grabbed Fenax's tank from the top of her carapace and gently set them down on the deck. "Maybe?" she said at last.

"Try it. First, open the airlock for her."

First looked back and forth between Sheer and Jrill disbelievingly. "You're not serious. Where's her hard-suit?"

Sheer knocked her small claw against her carapace. "I'm wearing it."

"But how will you breathe?"

"Cold-blooded. Ish can hold our breath a long time. Open the door and let me work."

First tilted her head at Sheer's big claw. "With one arm tied behind your back?"

"Just do it."

First sighed heavily and found the necessary command prompts and overrides with a flourish of her fingers. The inner airlock door opened.

"Swoosh," First said ironically. No one got it.

Sheer pulled a handful of tools out of her baggage and moved into the airlock chamber, then signaled for First to shut the door.

"This is insane," First said.

"Sheer knows her limits," Hashin said. "Better than you do, at any rate. Just do as she asks. No one will blame you."

"I don't care about the *blame*!" First shouted.

The rest of her crew looked at each other with confused expressions. Sheer tapped a leg tip against the deck impatiently.

"Whatever," First said as she keyed a command to slam the inner airlock door shut. "Her funeral."

In the airlock chamber, Sheer's carapace swelled and constricted rapidly.

"What's she doing?" First asked.

"Hyperventilating. Saturating her bloodstream with oxygen," Hashin said. "Ish have a more primitive set of lungs than the rest of us. Except Fenax, obviously. They're passive, stacked lungs, like a dozen layers of gills, not as efficient. But"—Hashin held up a finger—"it means they don't have any internal air chambers."

"So nothing to pop in zero pressure."

"Precisely. And their shells constrict their innards hard enough to keep their blood from boiling off."

First's hands relaxed against the holds on the side of her hacker deck. "So this isn't as dumb a plan as I thought."

"Oh, it's still dumb as glot," Jrill said. "But it's not entirely suicidal as it would be for any of the rest of us. So long as she's fast. Excuse me." Jrill took her considerable frame and positioned it near the entry to the docking arm in a way that would dissuade all but the most intent passengers from entering.

Sheer waved from inside the chamber, signaling readiness.

"Okay," Hashin said. "Evacuate the airlock."

"Give me a second," First said. "There's five different safety interlocks in the way, because this is a stupid idea." First's fingers pounded and slid across her deck while Sheer tapped a toe tip impatiently against the floor of the airlock.

"There," First said as the air began to hiss out of the chamber. Moments later, the sound died away entirely as the outer door opened to space. Sheer scurried out of the airlock and began work on the All-Seal.

"Won't she freeze out there?" First asked.

"Common misconception," Hashin answered. "Space is cold, but without any air to conduct heat away from your body, it's actually the perfect insulator. She'll run out of blood oxygen long before she even feels a chill."

"Oh, that's so much better."

Through the viewing gallery, the rest of the team watched Sheer as she furiously moved from one sabotaged component to the next. First watched in stunned admiration as the All-Seal error codes on her display moved from red to green one after another before clearing out of the repair queue entirely.

"Damn. She might actually do it. How long can she hold her breath like that?"

"No idea," Hashin said. "Guess we're finding out."

"She dead yet?" Jrill called from the intersection.

"Trying her best!" First shouted back.

"Don't let the meat spoil if she does."

First looked at Hashin and stuck a thumb in Jrill's direction. "Is she joking?"

"Turemok humor is . . . difficult to pin down."

The last error code flipped red to green on First's deck, and the All-Seal control menu unlocked itself. "She's done. Cycling the airlock. Let's get her back."

"She's waving us forward," Hashin said. "She wants you to link up the All-Seal."

First looked up and saw he was right. Sheer had moved to the dilating aperture at the end of the seal. She shook her head but keyed the seal to dock with their quarry anyway. The fleshy translucent proboscis reached out to the ship like a length of intestine, probing for the *Pay to Prey*'s outer hatch before finding purchase and latching on. Its segmented sides pillowed out as air rushed in to equalize the pressure with the inside of the station.

"Boss!" Hashin shouted to Jrill. "We're moving. First, grab Fenax."

First shoved her deck back in her purse and snagged Fenax's tank, which would be impossible if not for a counter-grav coil built into the base.

"Please don't jostle my container. I am easily concussed," Fenax said.

"Sorry."

The four of them ran down the tunnel to reach Sheer. She stood resolute while a thin layer of frost formed on the surface of her shell.

"With one arm tied behind my back," Sheer said between heavy breaths.

First set Fenax down and rubbed Sheer's smaller claw. "I'm glad you're safe."

"Why? Your share would go up by a fifth if I'd died."

"Make way," Jrill said as she pushed through them to get to the retasked destroyer's outer hull.

"It won't open," Sheer said.

"It won't open for you," Jrill responded. She flicked out a claw and deftly popped open an access panel below the main keypad.

"What's that?" First asked.

"Maintenance and emergency override panel. All Turemok ships have one. It's like a master key for dockyard workers and recovery crews. And unless the refit was *very* thorough"—the hatch whirred from the inside, then sank in and irised open like a flower—"it's easy to miss."

The five of them walked into the *Pay to Prey* like champions.

"Sheer," First said. "How did you repair the All-Seal so fast? There were half a dozen faults."

Sheer wiggled her small claw. "The debtor pulled all the fuses and breakers, so I bypassed them with small-gauge conduit."

"But doesn't that leave them vulnerable to—"

Behind them, a shower of sparks burst out of the lining of the All-Seal and burned a thousand tiny holes in the membrane. An emergency decompression alarm sounded, automatically slamming the pressure door closed like a camera shutter.

"—power surges," First finished.

Hashin leaned into the portal. "All-Seal is fried. We're not getting back onto the station."

"Good thing we're leaving on this ship, then," Jrill said.

"Also, the security alarm has been tripped."

Just then, an awful sound like hammers striking the hull rang through the ship, accompanied by a terrible series of tremors.

"And the docking clamps have engaged. We're locked down."

"Hmm," Jrill said. "Now that's a challenge."

CHAPTER 8

First looked out the portal to the viewing gallery on the far side of the open space between the *Pay to Prey* and Kaper Station in growing horror as an ever-increasing cadre of security officers and progressively heavier equipment responded to the alarms.

"Guys, they have some really big guns over there."

"Quiet, First!" Jrill snapped.

"Why don't we just tell them it's a legal repossession?" First pressed.

"Because out here, 'legal' is defined by whomever paid the biggest bribe to the local security office," Hashin said. "It appears that wasn't us."

"What are we doing, boss?" Sheer asked.

Jrill snuck her own quick look out the portal, then turned to face the rest of her team, crests held high over her scalp. Or as high as a Turemok female's crests went, at least. "We are in legal possession of this ship as of right now. No one else. That being said, I don't trust anyone at any level of this station not to be bought and paid for. So we're preparing for war. Sheer, get down to the engine room and make sure I have power and thrust the instant I need it."

Sheer saluted with her small claw and chittered down the hallway at a sprint.

"Sheer!" Jrill called, then pointed down the hall's other direction.

"Just testing you," Sheer said as she scuttled past.

"The rest of us are going to the command cave. First, do they know you're inside the station's interface yet?"

"I don't think so, but it's just a matter of time before someone puts down a gun long enough to check."

"Hand Fenax off to Hashin and get to work on those docking clamps."

"Gladly."

Jrill moved to the core of the ship where the lifters would be and called a car for the command cave. There was more than enough room for the four of them in a car designed for six Turemok at a time.

"Docking clamps are off the grid," First said, huddled over her deck in a corner of the car. "They're under local, physical control. Nothing I can do from here."

"Then let's hope this baby still has teeth after all."

The lifter doors slid open as they arrived at the command cave, straight onto a scene from juvenile Jrill's nightmares.

"Dar's glot," Jrill said as she reflexively pressed against the back of the lifter car, staring down the hungry, snarling maw of a monster of ages.

"What's wrong?" First said, pointing at the beast perched on the command chair at the center of the cave. "It's somebody's pet."

"It's not a *pet,*" Jrill spat out. "It's a *Gomeltic.*"

"Is it carnivorous?"

"It's not picky about what it puts in its mouth, if that's what you're asking."

"Aww, c'mon. It's cute."

"Cute?" Jrill's crests went flat against her scalp. "It's got six legs, thirty claws, sixty teeth, and four thousand generations of deliberately bred rage! Stand down!"

But First was already halfway out of the lifter, crouched down and holding one of her hands out to the vicious creature. For its part, the adolescent Gomeltic snarled a warning at the human's approach, but it went unheeded.

"Close the doors," Jrill said to Hashin, still plastered to the back of the lifter car.

"But First is—"

"Dead already! Close the doors!"

"No," Hashin said.

Jrill looked at him in disbelief for a long, accusing moment, then back to the soon-to-be-masticated pulp that had been their newest recruit. The Gomeltic pup shredded more of the fabric of the command chair with its half dozen clawed feet with every step First took toward it, snarling and spitting as she advanced, hand outstretched.

"What's it waiting for?" Jrill said, expecting the Gomeltic to pounce at any moment and shred the undersized human like a set of curtains.

First sort of stumble-lunged at the snarling beast and got a hand under its jawline. Jrill was far from her biggest fan, but she really didn't want to watch their newest recruit lose her arm at the elbow, either. But then, something impossible happened. The Gomeltic tilted its head to the side and whimpered, then fell on its side while three of its legs twitched in the air.

"Who's a gooood girl?" First scratched furiously at the Gomeltic's belly. "You like scritches, huh, girl?"

"I thought you said it was going to eat her," Hashin said.

"It was!"

"Did . . . did none of you ever think to try to pet one of them?"

"Why in Dar's name would we? They're killers!"

"Seems to like First enough. C'mon, we have a ship to steal."

"Repossess," Jrill corrected.

"With the docking clamps in lockdown, it's kind of a semantic argument at this point."

Hashin stepped out of the lifter into the command cave and placed

Fenax's container in the pilot's alcove before taking up his station. Jrill swallowed hard. It wouldn't do for her to show hesitation walking onto a Turemok command deck, after all. But as soon as she set a claw on the deck plates, the thrice-damned Gomeltic sprang back to its feet, put itself in front of First, and growled a warning.

"First, get that . . . thing on the far side of the cave and keep it there. We're wasting time," Jrill said, rubbing as much authority and indifference into her voice as she could manage, fearing it wasn't enough.

"C'mon, girl. Never mind that mean ol' Turemok." First walked backward toward the other end of the command cave, beckoning the Gomeltic pup to follow her. Inexplicably, it followed her like a hatchling.

"I'm calling her Guinevere."

"Oh, kark, she's named it," Fenax said from their tank.

"Fenax, Hashin, do I have any weapons on this tub?" Jrill asked.

"But," First said, "Loritt said we don't use weapons."

"Loritt said we don't *bring* weapons," Jrill corrected. "He didn't say anything about if they were just lying around."

"We have a battery of four point-defense high-space portals," Hashin announced triumphantly.

"Can we project them close enough to the hull to sweep over the docking clamps?"

"Easily."

"Do it."

"Kaper Station will sue us for damages," Hashin said.

"Glot," Jrill said. "Open a channel to Kaper Central Control. Got to cover our scales."

"Link open."

"Kaper Control, this is Jrill, recently appointed captain of the *Pay to Prey*. This vessel has been legally confiscated under Assembly Charter Statute 372.6, Section B. I'm transmitting the terms of our repossession contract now. We are now the rightful owners of this vessel and request immediate clearance for departure. Failure to comply with our legal request for free and unrestricted movement within Assembly space may, regrettably, result in damage to your station's equipment, for which we, our employer, or contractor would not be responsible. Jrill out."

"Not bad, boss," Hashin said. "You almost made me believe you weren't excited to cut those clamps off and stick them with the bill."

"Almost?"

Hashin winced and wiggled a hand.

"Got to work on my bluff. Give them ten rakims to answer, then cut away those clamps like empty yolk sacs."

"Warming up our point-defense portals now."

Jrill leaned back in her chair and took a breath. They'd pushed and shoved their way out of a few sticky situations in the past, but using defensive weapons offensively to destroy private infrastructure, that was a new one. They were *technically* on the right side of the law, but only just inside it, and that wouldn't make any difference unless they survived long enough to see the inside of a courtroom.

"Station Central is launching interceptors," Hashin said.

"Well, we have their answer," Jrill said. "Cut the clamps."

Hashin nodded and brought up a new screen. "Five rakims to full charge. Four, three . . ."

Outside the *Pay to Prey*'s hull, two small holes opened in the universe. High-space portals only a few spans across, much too small for even a shuttle to pass through, but wide enough for a missile or a laser beam to disappear into. Turned sideways, they also had the advantage of being the sharpest scalpel in existence. Usually, the mechanics and scale of space combat and the projector's extremely limited range rendered this quality irrelevant.

But when the target was latched directly onto one's hull . . .

"Gently now," Jrill said.

"Those interceptors will be on top of us in moments," First said from the far side of the cave.

"It won't matter if Hashin accidentally slices off one of our drive spikes. Slow is fast."

The Lividite was busy manipulating a holographic rendering of the ship and its surroundings, guiding the point-defense portals by hand and eye. One of the perfectly flat, two-dimensional holes passed through one of the clamps like a chill.

"Well done, Hashin," Jrill beamed. "Three left. Watch the—"

The portal passed through the ship's aft collision avoidance radar antennae and sheered it off at the base.

"Sorry," Hashin said. "That was my fault."

"Repairs come out of your share."

"You want to do this instead?" Hashin demanded.

"Just let him work!" First shouted as the first interceptor entered threat range and started broadcasting for them to stand down. Hashin passed the portal through a second clamp like a hot knife through chirpip fat, then turned it downward to snip the third. A warning shot from the lead interceptor flashed across their bow and lit off every alarm the command cave had.

"Hashin, give me a portal," Jrill said.

"What are you doing with it?"

"Clipping some wings."

"That's coming out of *your* share." Hashin circled one of his portal icons with a finger, then swiped it across the cave to Jrill's station. She accepted control and turned her red, artificial eyes to the lead interceptor threatening her prize.

It was a secondhand, short-range zapper. Crew of two. The sort of cast-off patrol ship that prowled the low orbitals of hundreds of marginal systems that had to settle for less-than-frontline equipment. And if they couldn't afford frontline equipment, they couldn't afford first-rate personnel to crew them. Maybe the overpromoted military retiree sitting in the pilot's chair of the lead interceptor had a crest on their head, maybe they didn't. But what Jrill was absolutely sure of was the indoc washouts in the rest of the squadron were used to following along and didn't have the claws for a real fight.

"Lead interceptor is ordering us to cease operations or be fired upon."

Jrill's bloodred eyes narrowed to points. "Then they are legally engaged in piracy."

"Oh, lord," Hashin bemoaned. "She's gone self-righteous."

"Just cut the last clamp and get me loose of the docking slip." Jrill toggled the internal com to engineering. "Sheer? I need enough power to open a high-space portal in twenty rakims or we're all rotisserie meats."

"That's cutting it close."

"Snip, snip." Jrill jammed the connection closed and returned attention to the lead interceptor. The small craft had several disadvantages over larger patrol ships. Their small power cores meant one had to make decisions between charging weapons or continued maneuvering. Which was why Jrill knew when the lead ship stopped accelerating, its commander had decided to fire on her in a meaningful way. It also meant its course for the next three or four rakims would be entirely ballistic and, therefore, entirely predictable.

"Don't kill them," Hashin said as he expertly slid his portal through the last clamp. "That costs extra."

Jrill ignored him as she projected the course and momentum of the interceptor onto her display. The point-defense portal controls were very responsive but still had a slight delay that needed to be accounted for. Calling up skills that had sat dormant since her first deployment, Jrill grabbed the spare portal and turned it flat like a sword.

"Slow is fast," Jrill repeated to herself. Careful to match her hand's speed to the projector's tracking speed, she dragged the little portal icon across the plot toward the interceptor, matching its movement down to the span. Any more and she could slice through the bulkheads of the crew cabin and kill both of the occupants. Any less and she might miss the diminutive craft entirely and leave herself exposed to an undefended shot that could pierce half the *Pay to Prey*'s superstructure and leave them all gasping for a breath that would never come.

Except Fenax, who would be fine for many larims until a recovery crew pulled them out of the wreckage.

Jrill buried the thought and focused on tugging the tiny portal icon along.

"Gotcha," she said as the two lines intersected. In the space outside, an impossibly black silhouette passed effortlessly through the aft drive section of the lead zapper, efficiently slicing it in half sans any gratifying, theatrical explosion. Which meant that not only would the occupants live long enough to be recovered, but Jrill hadn't just tacked a pair of wrongful death lawsuits onto the tab for this job.

Her prediction of the rest of the squadron's bravery was confirmed when they all stopped dead. She could almost see them gawking at their commander's bisected interceptor. Jrill pressed the advantage their surprise and fear presented and pointed the portal toward the next zapper in line and, with a flourish, leveled its edge at the vessel's bow in an unambiguous threat display.

Deciding it was better to live to not fight another day, the next interceptor in line backed away, then flipped heading and pushed back toward their hangar. The rest of the squadron flattened their crests and retreated in quick succession.

"Nicely done, boss," Hashin said.

"Sheer," Jrill said into the com, "full power to the drive spikes, if you please. We're leaving."

"Okay," the Ish engineer said a rakim later. "But as soon as we're clear of the station, you'd better get down here. We have a problem."

Jrill's beak ground against itself. "What kind of 'problem'?"

"Just come down here. It's not pretty."

The elevator ride down to engineering was even tenser than the ride up to the command cave had been before their escape. Partially this was due to Sheer's dire and vague warning, but mostly it was because of the six-legged hell beast that in the span of a few minutes had imprinted on First and now refused to leave her side.

Guinevere looked back up at Jrill standing pressed up against the back wall and growled again.

"Aah!" First corrected. "Leave the Skeksis alone. She's not bothering you," First said. Before she'd left PCB, *The Dark Crystal* and other Jim Henson productions had come back into vogue once the Assembly archive had opened and mankind learned he'd actually been an alien refugee trapped on twentieth-century Earth after a navigation malfunction. He and David Bowie crash-landed on the same ship.

The Gomeltic cub grunted its opinion one more time, then sat down on all but its front two legs.

"You know those things eat a fifth of their own body weight every day and grow to ten spans long in less than two cycles, yes?" Jrill asked through a grinding beak.

"I know that now," First said. "What's that in meters?"

"Like, twenty," Hashin said.

"Do they like arugula?" First asked. "I always pick mine off."

"You can't seriously be thinking about adopting it," Jrill said. "It'll chew you up as soon as it thinks you'll fit in its mouth."

First crouched down and hugged her new pet around the neck. "Guinevere wouldn't hurt a hair on my head, would you, girl?" She scratched hard under the beast's jawline, causing it to drool and involuntarily kick one of its hind legs. "Who's a good girl?"

"You've known that monster for less than a larim and you've already pack-bonded with it?" Jrill said. "Is your entire species insane, or is this defect unique to you?"

"What, you don't have pets on—what's your home world again? Fan?"

"Faan. And yes, we have pets that fit in small terrariums on a shelf in our dens and can't level a village if they're in mating season."

"Well, then, why is she here?"

"Juveniles are sometimes used by . . . unsavory Turemok as guards before being destroyed when they get too big to handle."

"That's so cruel!" Then, First's eyes narrowed. "Wait, what kind of things are they 'guarding'?"

"Hoards of contraband, mostly."

"I was at Loritt's party," First said. "What exactly counts as *contraband* with you people?"

"Well, unlike with *your* people, weapons are forbidden to most Assembly civilians, but an underground arms market still exists among the criminal classes. Then there's always counterfeit goods, expired pharmaceuticals tagged for incineration, and the most despicable of all, the flesh traffickers."

"What, like prostitution?" First asked. "But that's legal out here. There's a brothel two streets from my apartment."

"And it's heavily taxed and regulated," Hashin said. "And even inside its walls, not *everything* is legal."

First was about to ask what he meant when the lift doors opened and she found herself staring into the dirty, despondent faces of two dozen answers huddled around Sheer's pointy legs defensively. First didn't know what species they were, other than they were humanoid with somewhat feline features and bushy tails, but the signs of immaturity were, if not strictly universal, then common enough to be reliable.

One of them spotted Guinevere and screamed, then scrambled to get underneath Sheer's bulky protective shell.

"Guess I'm not the only one to imprint quickly," First said.

Jrill waved her clawed hand at the elevator. "Get that thing back in the lifter. Look at the claw marks on their skin. It was used to torture them."

First looked down at Guinevere, and her heart sank. The Gomeltic pup had stood straight up to stare intently at the children and not in a playful way.

First put her hands on her hips and put her elbows out. "Bad girl!" She pointed to the elevator car. "Sit! You wait in there!"

Much to everyone's amazement, most of all First's, the pint-sized monster shriveled and obeyed. The doors closed, leaving the stowaways, or whatever they were, free to come out again.

"One of the phased plasma inducers kept conking out," Sheer said. "I tracked the problem to the breaker room and found them all pressed on top of each other like tide pool fingerlings. One of them kept tripping the breaker with their foot."

"But what are they doing down here?" First pleaded, trying to understand.

"They're Andrani females," Hashin said. "They're prized as companions among certain . . . connoisseurs. They're being trafficked for the sex trade."

"But they're children!" First demanded. "That's barbaric. We have to tell the police or whatever."

Jrill snorted. "I don't think the authorities on Kaper Station are in the mood to give us a sympathetic ear at the moment."

First set her feet as if projecting physical immovability would buttress her argument. "Well, when we get to Junktion, then. The law has to go after this creep."

"We've already got his ship and his cargo," Jrill said.

"He'll just get another one and fill it up again. We have to stop him."

"And then someone else will take his place. As long as there's demand, someone will profit off the supply."

First's fists twisted up into bricks. "I thought Turemok were supposed to be the galactic cops of the Assembly. That was your job for what, a thousand years?"

First braced for the counterattack, but to her surprise, the barb had dug in deeper than she'd expected.

"That was my job," Jrill said with a trace of wistfulness. "But I was let go. Now I take toys away from spoiled brats. It's your job, too. Not saving the universe. Try to keep a little perspective."

First pointed at the small, defenseless horde hiding under Sheer. "This is wrong. It can't go unpunished."

"That's not our call. We'll talk to the boss as soon as we dock."

CHAPTER 9

"Absolutely not," Loritt said with as much finality he could inject into his tone. First's face, so bright and hopeful only a moment before, soured like gak milk left out in the sun.

"You can't be serious," she said.

"Deadly serious. If we tell the authorities here about Vel Jut's . . ." Loritt saw Jrill's disapproving glance. "Excuse me, *Jut's*, ah, extracurricular activities"—Loritt pointed at the *Pay to Prey* floating just on the other side of the docking bay's gangway plank—"that ship gets impounded as evidence in the investigation for who knows how long. That means our employer doesn't get their asset back, can't put it up for auction, doesn't recoup any of their investment, and, most importantly, has no money in the ledger with which to pay our fee. And all that comes with the ancillary benefit that they'll absolutely think twice about offering us another closed contract. Then, we all starve."

"I'd rather," First said.

"Oh, the human girl I plucked out of a car she was trying to steal has grown a conscience. How inspiring."

"This is different."

"Is it? Do you have any idea what other pots Soolie has had his weird little flipper in? You're not as clean as you'd like to believe, little one."

First crossed her arms. "At least I bought some soap with the money."

Loritt couldn't help but smile. He had a good eye; she was a clever little glot after all. So long as he could keep her focused.

"The Andrani will find their way back home, you have my word. You saved them from their fate. We have Jut's ship, and we've publicly embarrassed him. That kind of hit against his reputation in the underworld is very hard to recover from, believe me. That has to be enough." First's rage hardened on her face. "For now," Loritt permitted. "But we have to keep flying."

"Whatever." First spun around on a heel and headed for the viewing gallery's exit with her new sextuple-legged nightmare pet following close behind.

"Oh, and First?" Loritt called after her. "The Gomeltic can't enter the station. It has to go into medical quarantine, then it's getting shipped home to Faan."

First stopped dead, then turned like a moon going through its phases, and stalked at Loritt with such force and confidence that, for a moment, he thought she might physically pass through him without taking any notice.

Instead, she stopped short, less than a hand span away from his face.

"No," First said, simply and definitively.

"It's so far out of my hands, I couldn't even wave at it, First. That is a dangerous animal. It has been banned from export since the Turemok first entered the Assembly. Its very presence here is a crime. There's nothing I can do. I'm pulling strings just to keep it from being destroyed on sight."

"*Her* name is Guinevere!" First threw down definitively. "And you will make *certain* everyone up the custody chain knows it. All the way back to Faan." First stormed away, paused for a long moment to tenderly rub Guinevere's snout and assure her everything would be all right, then stood again to glare at Loritt as if her resentment-fueled eyes could bore through dreadnought armor before she stalked off for the exit.

Loritt turned to Hashin, who had been standing a span outside of First's rage perimeter. "She is an intense specimen, our human," he said.

"She's young," the Lividite said. "As is her species. Their passions have yet to be tempered with experience."

"Will that be a problem?"

"A manageable one. She assigns her loyalty strangely, but once it's fixed, it's damned-near impervious."

"And you think she's fixed her loyalty on us?"

"Honestly, it's one of the strangest things I've ever seen. She's bonded with a Grenic who hasn't spoken more than a few dozen words to her in months and a subsentient, six-legged murder machine she knew for less than a standard day. I think we can win her over."

Loritt's various components took a long, mind-clearing breath. He took pride in his ability to read people of any species. A common strength among his race, a side effect of being made up of lots and lots of smaller people themselves. It was a skill that had been of great import while he built his little empire. It made managing his employees and customers easier than it might be for many. But Hashin and other Lividites were always opaque and unreadable, while First was so hot and loud she was almost blinding. Still . . .

"See to it. We need her."

"Need her?" Hashin cocked his head. "Or need her approval? You weren't so unlike her in the beginning, my old friend. Is that why she's here? To act as your conscience?"

"Just do your job," Loritt bit off.

"And the Andrani?"

Loritt froze in place. Damn that karking Vel poser Jut and his stupid, arrogant—"See them to quarters. *Comfortable* quarters, with generous rations. Wait a few days and arrange transport back to their home world. Small batches, no more than a half dozen at once. Stagger their departures by at least two days. The last thing we need is for somebody to come back and accuse *us* of trafficking them."

"That won't be cheap," Hashin said quietly.

"Oh, *now* you care about our bottom line? Just make it happen. But don't call in any favors. That just leads to questions."

"I understand, boss. It'll be hard to keep quiet, but I'll think of something."

"I know you will, Hashin. You're the best cleaner I've ever seen."

"I don't actually clean anything. I just have a talent for helping people overlook the messes they didn't really want to see in the first place."

Loritt considered this while absently rubbing the side of his face. One of his jaw muscles was getting old and had begun to cramp now and then. "And are there any messes I don't want to see, my friend?"

The first of the Andrani nervously worked their way down the gangway plank under Sheer's unexpectedly maternal eye. She'd always been warmer toward reactors and conduits than other living beings.

"One comes to mind, boss," Hashin said.

First trampled away from the docks and kicked over a waste receptacle on her way out the clamshell emergency pressure doors. She felt doubly betrayed by Loritt's decisions.

It was bad enough he'd picked his pocketbook over principle where the Andrani captives were concerned. At least they would be safe in the end. But to send Guinevere, a defenseless pup, back to a world that hated her, that was inexcusable.

As she entered the surging crowds in the inner terminal, she passed a pair of customs agents, including one who looked an awful lot like the one who had processed her entry six months earlier, holding snares and stunners. Behind them, they pulled a counter-grav crate with generous air holes. So that was to be Guinevere's cage, huh?

We'll see about that, First thought viciously as she pulled out her deck and trailed after them at a less conspicuous distance. She paused by the pressure doors, knowing they were the primary way in or out of that section of docks, and busied herself with preparations while she waited for them to emerge again with their new cargo.

Sure enough, less than ten minutes later, the two of them reappeared with the crate in tow, floating noticeably lower and shaking randomly. Nearly everything on Junktion, indeed everywhere First had been in Assembly space since stowing away on that trade ship, was networked in one way or another. The crate was no exception, and it was an embarrassingly simple affair hacking into its unencrypted command prompts. With three swipes of her finger, First convinced the crate it was back in its pens and it was time to open its door and power down.

The crate, already encumbered by a hundred kilos of Gomeltic pup, abruptly dropped to the deck with a *thud!* With growing dismay etched into their faces, obvious even across lines of species and culture, the two customs agents looked back at the crate as the door swung open on squeaky hinges.

First smiled as Guinevere leaped free of her confinement. The smile didn't last very long, however, as it became plainly obvious from the screaming and blood that "defenseless pup" was in no way an accurate description of her new pet. "Oh. Oh no . . ."

"*Loose Gomeltic!*" the second customs agent shouted above the din of the crowd while cradling his partner, who had just undergone a crash weight-loss program via losing an arm. Guinevere, propelled by six powerful legs and ancestral fury, dove toward the screaming crowd with unnerving speed. The sea of people parted to make way for her passage. Fliers took to the air, parents shoved their young under tables.

First's grimace turned into a horrified, openmouthed gasp that she covered with a hand as she backed away from the expanding chaos and right into a wall that she was certain hadn't been there a moment earlier. First looked up. Jrill looked down.

Her glowing red eyes shrank to pinpricks on either side of her razor-sharp beak. "Going somewhere?"

"Er . . ."

Jrill sighed heavily and clamped a hand down on First's shoulder. "Come on, then."

"Where are we going?"

"To recapture the vengeful food blender you just unleashed on the station."

First grimaced. "Right now?"

"No, after we enjoy a light dinner and an exfoliating massage," Jrill said. "Of course right now!"

"I'm sorry," First stammered. "I didn't know."

"Tell it to that Mantalin." Jrill nodded toward the customs officer who had so recently been relieved of an appendage.

"Sorry," First whispered at the agent, not wanting to give herself away as the culprit. It was bad enough she hadn't noticed Jrill surveilling her. Her street-scanning skills were getting rusty. How did she miss a two-meter-tall scarecrow with glowing eyes watching her work? Shameful.

"Don't feel too bad," Jrill said. "It'll grow back in a few months. And the union will make sure he gets full disability pay in the meantime. Let's just get your beast back in a box before it does permanent damage to anyone, yes?"

"You grew up around those things?" First asked.

"The Turemok build strong fences for a reason."

First rubbed her temples, massaging away any hope she'd held for a relaxing evening catching up on her favorite Grenic soap opera played back at high speed.

"Fine, let's get to work."

Two hours into the search, and First was deeper into the bowels of Junktion than she'd ever been. Or ever wanted to be.

"You take me to all the nicest places," she said to Jrill as they waddled through a reclamation tunnel, ankle-deep in a mix of fluids of a truly unmentionable nature.

"Oh, this is my fault, is it?" Jrill clapped back. "Because I could've sworn to Dar I saw you wiggling your finger magic on that deck of yours to let a killer loose among a civilian population of over seven million sentients."

"I thought you said they were vegetarians?"

"So are your hippopotamuses," Jrill said. "And they are one of the most dangerous animals on your home world. And before you ask, yes, we've exported them for the hunt. They were tough karkers, too. They represented Earth life honorably in our fighting rings. Fighting in water helped them. But they're nothing like an adult Gomeltic." Jrill breathed hard. "You're very lucky it's a pup, or the body count would already be in the dozens."

"You stole an endangered species from Africa?" First demanded.

"No, actually. We relocated an invasive species out of South America. Or did you think Pablo Escobar's escaped hippo colony disappeared from Colombia all by itself?"

"Who?" First asked, genuinely curious.

Jrill's eyes closed entirely. "Dar preserve them, they are trying."

First ignored Jrill's sarcastic display of piety and focused on the tunnel ahead. "You're sure she came this way?"

Jrill pointed toward her protruding proboscis. "Standard Turemok military kit includes an olfactory upgrade. Synthetic chem-sniffers can detect samples as small as twenty parts per billion. Trust me, she went that way."

"How can you pick out anything in this stench?"

"We have filters."

"Must be nice." First swatted at yet another of the slow, corpulent, bumblebee-looking flies that had dogged her since they'd entered the labyrinthine tunnels of Junktion's recycling system. Or tried to, at any rate. For the hundredth time, the swollen thing ducked away at the last possible moment, leaving First's hand to hit only air.

"Why can't I smack these fat little bastards? Their reflexes must be supernatural."

"Actually, their reflexes are glot," Jrill said. "Just awful."

"Then how do they always get out of the way so fast?"

"Because their consciousnesses evolved to exist five rakims in the future. They always see what's coming and just swoop out of the way. We call them timeflies."

"So how do you kill them?"

"You don't. You just learn to tolerate them until they lose interest and fly away. They're carrion eaters, and you're not dead. Yet."

"What about in five seconds?"

"If they fly off, you can be confident you will live at least five more rakims."

"How encouraging."

Jrill shrugged. "You asked."

They continued down the tunnel in silence for several minutes, until the question burning in First's throat since she'd released Guinevere became intolerable.

"You're not going to tell Loritt, are you?"

Jrill, obviously expecting the question, was ready with an answer immediately. "That depends on whether you repair your mistake in time, human."

First swallowed. "I suppose that's fair."

"It's more than fair. It's *overly* generous."

"So why do it for me?"

"Because I'm wagering you will be more manageable as a subordinate if you're indebted to me personally," Jrill said.

First rolled her eyes but continued down the narrow tunnel. She'd downloaded an app for her deck that converted its speakers and microphone pickups into a rudimentary ultrasonic motion detector. The render on the display didn't have much in the way of resolution, little more than blobs, but it could track relative size, speed, and distance with enough accuracy to give them a warning of anything coming their way. So far, the path remained clear, except for the timeflies and a handful of small scavengers that ran for cover as soon as they approached.

"Out of purely academic curiosity, what's the plan if we actually find Guinevere?" First asked.

"I assume you'll work your strange bonding magic on it and we'll drag it back to the crate you sabotaged."

"That's a terrible plan."

"It was a terrible idea."

First's screen lit up with dozens of contacts from seemingly every direction at once. She threw a hand up to signal a stop just as the first tentacles sprang up out of the water.

"Whoa!" First said as a wiggling, sucker-studded arm wrapped around her ankle and tightened. Before she or Jrill could react, First was yanked inverted into the air. Her deck went rebounding off the tunnel wall and dropped into the fetid soup. Still on her feet, Jrill slashed and bit at the writhing mass of tentacles, trying to reach her. But there were so many, and she suddenly seemed a million kilometers away.

First found herself dangling while below her a huge, round maw lined with jagged black teeth emerged from the muck as the tentacle holding fast to her leg began to lower her toward it. Overcome with terror, First screamed for all she was worth.

Everything froze. First hung there, staring at the black points poised to pierce her in a thousand places from every direction. A hot stench even fouler than the surrounding sewage wafted up from the mouth to assault her senses and add to the horror. From out of the mud, an eyestalk extruded itself, blinked twice to clear its lens of filth, then extended to inspect First's face.

"Oh, my word," the mouth said. "I'm dreadfully sorry. I thought you were a sewer strider." Two more tentacles reached up and grabbed First's wrists. She struggled against them until she realized she was being turned right side up and gently set back down.

"There, no harm done," the tentacled horror said.

"So . . ." First panted as she tried to get her heart rate back under control. "You're not going to eat me?"

"Eat a sentient? Surely not. What kind of monster do you take me for?" the gaping, dagger-filled orifice said.

"Er . . ."

"I do apologize for giving you such a fright, though. It was careless of me. It's just been a few weeks since one as big as you came along, and I've been feeling a bit peckish. I got ahead of myself."

"That's okay. I guess," First said. She looked back at Jrill, who held a still-wiggling section of tentacle in one hand and quickly hid it behind her back. "So you . . . live down here?"

"Oh yes. Best hunting on Junktion. Warm and rent-free. The reclamation department even pays me a stipend every month to keep the strider population down. Can you beat that?"

"What do you spend it on down here?"

"Hmm?"

"Your stipend."

"Ah, most of it I send back home to my folks. The rest I spend on my music collection."

"You know you can just download that stuff for free, right?"

"Pirate music?" The monster recoiled. "But then how will musicians earn enough money to keep creating?"

First nodded diplomatically. "I hadn't thought of it like that."

"Not enough people do. It's a real problem. You have to support artists, or you have no reason to complain when quality suffers."

"You're probably right. Say, I dropped my tablet when you, ah, picked me up."

The monster held up a tentacle. "Worry not. Just one moment." The rest of its arms returned to the muck and writhed about.

"Here we are." First's deck appeared in front of her, covered in gunk, but otherwise none the worse for wear. She grabbed it.

"Thank you, um, sir? Ma'am?"

"Call me Bilge. And you are?"

"First."

"What an odd name. You're quite welcome, First. And tell your friend not to worry about my arm; she was just trying to protect you. Honestly, I'm embarrassed by the whole thing and will be quite happy to put it behind us."

Jrill looked at the meaty tip and dropped it in the water.

"It's fine, really," First insisted. "One other thing maybe you can help with. We're looking for my, ah, pet. It came this way recently."

"What, the Gomeltic?" Bilge asked. "Nasty pieces of work, those things. You're mighty brave keeping one."

"Or stupid," Jrill said.

"It went down the passage to the left maybe a quarter larim ago," Bilge said.

"And you didn't try to eat it?"

"A Gomeltic? Heavens, no. Way too much fight in those things. I'm more of an ambush predator, you see."

"I noticed," First said. "Well, thank you for your help, Bilge. Happy hunting."

"You, too, and let me know if you're coming this way again. I have a first molding of Welsbar of Del's Pouk Night Concert in piezo-electric that is just to die for."

"I'll do that," First lied as they continued down the tunnel. Once they'd made a couple of turns, First turned and looked at Jrill. "That was the strangest damned thing I have ever seen."

"Maybe not the strangest," Jrill said among the buzzing timeflies. "But for sure top five."

CHAPTER 10

"Which is when local Junktion residents Jrill and"—the news reader glanced down at their notes—"Firstname Lastname, is that right? I'm being told it's right. Jrill and Firstname sprang into action and tracked the dangerous Gomeltic into the reclamation tunnels and valiantly wrestled the creature back to the surface, where it was safely taken into quarantine by station personnel."

The feed switched from the studio set to stock footage of First looking uncomfortably past the camera. "It was just the right thing to do," she said unsteadily. "I'm sure anyone would have done it. We were just in the right place at the right time to see where Guin . . . the creature escaped into the sewers."

Loritt paused the recording with a flex of his fingers and glanced at Jrill wearily. "Care to explain this one?"

Jrill stood at parade-ground attention. "I think the news segment covered the basics very well, for once."

"I notice it left off the part where First was the one to let it loose on the station in the first place," Loritt said. "Causing a loss of limb to one customs agent and slashing wounds to several bystanders not quite fleet-footed enough to get out of the way?"

"I'm sure I don't know anything about that, boss."

"So the beast just muscled its way out of a locked counter-grav crate while First looked on innocently, then?"

"Gomeltics are famous across the Assembly for their strength, boss."

"Mmm-hmm." Loritt laced his fingers. "I still have a peephole on her hacking deck she missed. Did a damned fine job getting the rest of them, I'll give her credit there. But I know she popped the lock on that crate. The only reason she's not on her way to a holding cell right now is she managed, somehow, to recognize and correct her mistake. Don't suppose you had anything to do with that?"

"May have nudged her a bit. Still can't figure out what she saw in that monster, though."

Loritt considered his resident Turemok for several rakims. "There's only one thing you need to know to understand humans. For millions of cycles of their evolution, predators called lions, and tigers, and panthers shredded untold thousands of their ancestors alive."

"And the surviving humans hunted them to extinction," Jrill said.

"No, that's just it. Humans venerated them. Worshiped them as gods. Built monuments to them. And finally shrank them down, called them 'kitties,' invited them into their homes, and then invented the internet so they could share cute videos of them with each other. They're complete lunatics." Loritt shook his head in exasperation.

"Anyway, First is on probation," he said finally. "If she so much as sneezes in an unapproved direction, she's getting turned over to station security with evidence of her stealing my aircar and popping the lock on that crate. Am I clear?"

"I'll make sure she understands the gravity of the situation."

"No, you won't."

Jrill cocked her head. "Boss?"

"I don't want her to know how thin the ice under her is. I want to see what choices she makes based on her own conscience. I want to see if she's *actually* learned anything. So you're not going to tell her she's on probation as you give her a briefing on her first individual assignment."

Jrill's posture broke, just for a moment. "I'm sorry, but you're putting her on secret probation, then sending her out on a contract *by herself,* and that doesn't strike you as particularly reckless?"

"Finally, some unprompted candor," Loritt said. "Fear not. This is a decidedly low-stakes job and one that, as fate would have it, our young human is uniquely suited for."

"This is complete bullshit," First said as the briefing concluded.

"I'll assume that's a curse meant to convey dissatisfaction," Jrill responded.

"A safe assumption."

"I don't entirely understand," Jrill said. "You are being awarded greater independence and responsibility. Neither of which, if we're both being honest, you've actually earned in the last week."

"Please, spare me the pep talk," First said. "Loritt's giving me this job because I'm the only human on the team and I happen to be the right gender."

"You're the only human on *any* team, as far as I'm aware," Jrill replied. "And that's an advantage, just as my Turemok military experience was an advantage on the *Pay to Prey* job. We all bring not only unique talents but unique openings for the team."

"Well, I'd prefer to keep control over my 'openings,' if you don't mind," First said. "Have you met any early-twenties human males? They are the worst creatures in the entire universe. Not the most dangerous or the most cunning. Just. The. Worst. They're half the reason I'm out here, because aside from a handful of fetish weirdos, nobody is staring at me like I'm a piece of meat."

"There are plenty of carnivorous species on Junktion that, given the chance—" Jrill started, but First stopped her.

"Not *that* kind of meat. That I can handle."

"This is the job," Jrill said with finality. "You are the only one who can do it. Are you doing your job or not?"

First sighed her surrender. "But I don't even *like* hair metal . . ."

The trip from Junktion to catch up with the Wolverines' next appearance meant two full days locked up in yet another transport. Fortunately, First was an old pro and knew all the tricks to keep from getting too stiff or going stir-crazy.

She was on her own for this one. It was hardly the first time, but she'd just been getting used to the feeling of having some backup if things went south and found she already missed it. Jrill had said the rest of the team was splitting off to handle another time-sensitive job and it was the only practical way to do both simultaneously, but First harbored doubts. This was another one of Loritt's tests.

Testing her for what was the question.

The transport's captain broke through over the intercom to announce they were on terminal approach to Mulos Minor. From there, First still had a four-hour real-space shuttle ride from the planet's orbit out to the large shepherd moon near the edge of its ring system where the concert venue was actually located.

First endured the last leg of the trip preparing her deck. Despite their meteoric rise and smashing tour success, the Wolverines had a cash flow problem. Whether due to truly rock-star spending habits or to criminally negligent levels of mismanagement, they were selling out hundred thousand–seat venues and walking away with little or nothing to show for it, week after week.

The star liner company they'd leased their tour bus from had finally had enough and called in a repo contract. It was a paltry score as Loritt's usual paydays went, scarcely worth more than his Proteus by the time all the expenses were tabulated.

But it was also a dead-easy job. The leasing company had turned over all of the tour bus's access codes and system protocols. All she had to do was get past whatever security personnel the band had, and she could fly it out without so much as breaking a sweat or muttering a curse.

Unfortunately, the easiest way to do that was also by far the least appealing to First's sensibilities and pride.

First comforted herself with the knowledge that any temporary indignities she experienced would be offset almost immediately by the satisfaction of stealing their ride.

The shuttle settled in for a landing at the spaceport that pulled double duty, servicing both the small mining concern that employed a few thousand people per year and the concert venue that had a few million visitors annually.

Other shuttles followed, disgorging their passengers in waves of a thousand or more at a time. The growing crowd of fans trended into two camps that First had already noticed on her own transport: about 80 percent young music obsessives from across dozens of species, and about 20 percent older, wealthier attendees whose hungry glances betrayed their desire to prey on the rest.

The youth among the crowd were decked out in Wolverines gear, furry gloves with plastic claws, torn T-shirts, and red bandannas. Some of them carried homemade replica AK-47s on slings. Two of them ran around together in a Russian attack helicopter costume, making fake gun runs on small groups.

It was all in good fun. The weapons scanners at the entrances would pick out any energy packs or chemical propellants a terrorist might try to sneak in among the harmless props. First, who hadn't even brought her manual lock-picking set, passed through without incident.

She angled for the nearest bathroom where she could enjoy a little privacy to change into her "uniform" for the evening. First passed by a three-headed T-shirt vendor hawking their wares at a simply superhuman volume while seemingly arguing with . . . themself? Themselves?

For a moment, First considered buying a tour shirt to blend in, but thought better of it. There was nothing more worthless from a fandom legitimacy standpoint than a freshly bought shirt. Concert memorabilia cred, like wine, accumulated with vintage.

Instead, she found an open stall and dug into her carry-on for the platform heels, neon-green fishnet stockings, vinyl miniskirt, and Whitesnake halter top she'd paid a fashion boutique a pretty penny to screen print before leaving Junktion.

Looking around at the rest of the ladies in the crowd, or their equivalents, First made a few small adjustments to her outfit. She adjusted her halter top to hang off one shoulder, tied her hair up in a messy ponytail near the top of her head, and tore some holes in her fishnets, which, ironically, reduced the total number of holes they had.

First followed the flow of the crowd through the turnstiles, presented her ticket, smiled pleasantly as the overworked gate attendant failed to spot the forgery, then entered the venue, looked up, and experienced a moment of unbridled terror.

Mulos Minor was something of a minor miracle. Several hundred thousand years earlier, as the native sentients were still figuring out how to smelt copper, the planet trapped a small planetoid ejected by a nearby gas giant in its gravity well. For a few thousand years, all was well, and the inhabitants welcomed a new god to their pantheon. But then, gravitational stresses between the planet, its moon, and the newcomer took their toll, disintegrating the planetoid and throwing billions of fragments into eccentric orbits and causing a devastating period of bombardment on Mulos Minor's surface, centered on its equatorial region. The band of craters was still clearly visible even from orbit.

But in the aftermath of the tragedy, rings formed. The few native survivors restarted their civilization and grew to flourish, making Mulos Minor one of only a handful of inhabited worlds with a naturally occurring ring system.

From the surface, looking up through the planet's atmosphere, the rings were quite a sight. But from the airless surface of the tidally locked moon, looking down the glimmering rings and onto the sapphire jewel of Mulos Minor itself, *that* was said to be one of the most stunning vistas in the quadrant.

Which is why an enterprising group of nouveau riche had dumped some money into carving an amphitheater into an old lava tube just north of the moon's equator and glassing in the ceiling with one of the largest single unsupported panes ever laid down.

The glass was of such pristine quality and kept so thoroughly clean that for a fleeting moment, First's eyes thought they looked out into open space. Her breath caught in her chest, and she was sure it was about to be scoured from her lungs by hungry vacuum. She wasn't alone. Quite a fraction of the crowd paused in fear as soon as they entered the venue space.

First's rational mind took control after a moment and forced her to breathe deeply. Once the shock passed, she stood there for a long time, letting the panorama above play out in her mind's eye. She stared, openmouthed, at the gossamer rings laid out like the ridges of a platinum record glinting in the sun, and on down to the crescent pearl of Mulos Minor at the center. It was breathtaking in every sense of the word.

That'd make one hell of an album cover, First thought.

Something—no, First corrected herself, *someone*—bumped into her from behind.

"Oh. My. Lords!" the red, segmented being exclaimed at First's face. "Your human cosplay is *incredible*!"

"Um, thanks?"

"The face, the skin tones, it must have taken forever!"

"About eighteen years, actually," First said. "But my parents helped some."

"Wow! Can I get a selfie?"

"I'd prefer if you—"

Flash!

"Right."

"Thank you sooo much," the red alien in the absurdly long Wolverines onesie said as they inch-wormed away. "My followers will love this. You're amazing."

"Great," is all First could say as the crimson caterpillar disappeared into the surging throngs. The opening band began their sound checks. It would be showtime soon. For more than just the headliners.

First drifted over to the edge of the crowd where there was a little more wiggle room this early in the show, then began to excuse and elbow her way toward the stage where her trap was to be set. In the end, it was more elbowing than excusing. Sweating and swearing, First found herself pressed up against the barricades that separated the crowd from the stage. Right where she needed to be.

The opening band was made up of what looked like giant tardigrades in clown outfits playing Winger tunes. They were sufficient, but unmemorable, which is the sweet spot for any opener. You never wanted to upstage the main act. That was professional suicide. No matter where you were in the galaxy, there was etiquette to follow.

Then, the Wolverines took the stage. First, Beast Mode came out twirling his drumsticks. The crowd greeted him like a second cousin with three DUIs turning up at a family reunion. Polite, but reserved. Then Kip Burnheart walked out shooting a two-meter jet of flames out of his keytar, throwing the devil horns with his off hand. The crowd answered with a fresh wave of applause. Then Gordo took no notice of the crowd as he arranged himself onstage and began tuning up his bass guitar to a thunderous ovation.

Finally, the lead singer/guitarist, Eagle Independence, buoyed on gently flapping counter-grav wings, floated over the crowd and took the stage to a chorus of strobe lights and pyrotechnics.

On the strength of the greeting alone, he could've left the wings backstage. The crowd's reaction would've held him aloft for twenty minutes at least. First just shook her head at the adoration.

"Heeeelloooo, Mulos Minor!" Eagle shouted into the old-fashioned microphone, complete with a cord and stand. The crowd shouted back, "Wolverines!" and the concert really got started. She had to admit, their human schtick was pretty good. First couldn't see seams, zippers, or anything. Even the hair looked good. Then again, it would have to for a hair band, wouldn't it?

For the next hour and a half, First endured Poison covers, being pushed, Aerosmith, shoved, Guns N' Roses, an errant punch, and Twisted Sister. She wasn't sure which type of assault was worse—the physical or the auditory.

At the end of KISS's "Detroit Rock City," the crowd was primed and ready for the grand finale. Eagle took a step back from the mic while the bassist strummed out a powerful bridging beat that slowly morphed into something familiar. The people around her noticed the shift as well and went totally off the rails as the base melody of "Pho Queue" took root. Eagle reappeared from backstage with what looked like a giant, shoulder-mounted, belt-fed grenade launcher. But if the crowd were concerned by the prospect of being torn limb from limb by shrapnel, it didn't show.

"Who's hungry?!" Eagle shouted. The crowd assured him that, indeed, they were quite famished. He smiled and pulled the trigger. The triple barrels started spinning. "Okay, you asked for it. Incoming!"

A second later, a stream of instant noodle cups shot out of the gun at six hundred rounds per minute with such force Eagle had to brace himself against the recoil. The cups flew out at twenty-five or thirty meters per second, fast enough that anyone standing directly in front of them could get seriously bruised.

The ammo belt ran dry, and the tri-barrel noodle shooter spun to a stop even as pockets of aliens fought over the last of the starchy souvenirs to land among them. Eagle dropped the noodle gun and threw two hands of devil horns before picking up his Stratocaster and returning to the mic. Halfway through the song, First found herself singing along with the chorus.

Once the band ducked backstage and the crowd started shouting, "Encore!" First made her move. The bulk of the security personnel were busy trying to contain the masses surging toward the stage; they wouldn't notice a solitary young groupie slipping away into the background.

First hopped over the barricade that had thus far maintained a thin neutral zone between the horde and the stage. Security reacted to the intrusion almost immediately, but the fans behind her reacted even faster. Thirty of them were over the wall before the first guard laid a hand on any of them. First, who was the only one not trying to charge the stage, moved to the far side unnoticed.

She made it almost fifty meters before being challenged.

"Hey, you. Stop there!" an earnest voice called out from behind her.

"I'm with the band," she called back dismissively and kept walking.

"I said stop!"

First, exuding annoyance, ceased her gait, and turned around with as much disdain as she could muster, and faced the multihorned, pebble-skinned toughie. "What?"

"Let me see your credentials," the heavy said.

First pointed at her face. "You see any other humans around here?"

"Credentials."

"Somebody in the crowd yanked my badge while your guys were dicking around trying to break up the push on the stage. Look for a big red caterpillar trying to pass themselves off as me. It won't be hard."

"Um . . ."

"The encore is almost over. I've got maybe three minutes to do the preflight and get the tour bus ready for departure before they're going to need it, or we'll be running behind for the next stop. Are you helping or not?"

"What's a 'minute'?"

"A human unit of time I can't afford to waste."

"Right this way, sir," the guard said.

First rolled her eyes. "Close enough."

With a renewed sense of urgency, First walked briskly toward the small hangar bay at the back of the venue, where the acts could come and go unseen by the attendees. A half dozen short-range private VIP transports sat scattered around the deck. At the center of it all, painted up in the most garish, red-, white-, and blue-wolverine-themed mural imaginable, sat the SunRunner II 2860. Fifty meters long, it was smaller than most in-system shuttles and just about the smallest hull you could mount a hyperspace portal generator on. But if you were only transporting a few people, it was a posh, if a little cramped, way to travel.

Some enterprising fans had ducked out early just as First had and collected around the tour bus, hoping to catch a glimpse, get an autograph, or even score a fling with their idols. A trio of security guards kept them at arm's length on the other side of a velvet rope.

"What's this?" one of them asked as the horned guard walked up with First.

"Preflight checks," her escort said.

"Doesn't the pilot do that?"

"He's busy helping with teardown. They sent me to get started."

"Where's your badge?"

"Stolen," First said. "I already went through all this with him." She stuck a thumb out at her escort. "If I'm not done with my prep by the time they get here, I'll get my ass chewed. So do you mind?"

The two guards exchanged weary glances before they waved her through the rope.

"Thanks. I'll just be a minute." First pulled her deck out and walked up to the tour bus main cabin hatch, which was wide open. She didn't even need to put in the code.

Happy birthday to me, she thought as she dropped into the pilot's chair. Even though it was small for a starship, it was still enormously bigger than any aircar she'd ever flown. But the controls were simplified for civilian users, so they didn't need to get hyperspace certified to use it, and the automated systems were robust and redundant.

First went down the start-up checklist the company had provided, bringing the bus's systems online one by one. She was just about to cycle the pressure seals when—

"What are you doing in here?" a resonant voice said from behind her. First spun around in the chair and came face-to-face with Eagle Independence.

"Holy crap," Eagle said after a shocked moment. "You're a girl!"

"Uh . . . yeah."

"No, I mean like, a *human* girl. Er, woman. Sorry. You are human, right?"

"Last I checked." First patted herself down theatrically. "Why, you get a lot of fake humans?"

"You'd be shocked the length some fans will go to. Plastic surgery, gene splicing, and there's always the shape-shifters. That was a nasty way to wake up, let me tell you."

"I'd rather you didn't." Something about his tone shifted First's assumptions. "Wait, do you mean to tell me you're human, too?"

"Emphasis on the *man* part," Eagle said.

"Killing the mood now."

"Right, sorry. Wait. What are you doing here?"

"Keeping the seat warm for you," First said, trying to sound just a touch sultry. It didn't come naturally to her, but judging by how awkwardly he was staring, it didn't need to. The fact he was human after all opened up all sorts of ways to get her out of this jam.

"Where's the rest of the band?" she asked innocently.

"They're still signing shirts and . . . other things. I forgot my lucky pen on the bus and, well, how did you get in here again?"

First could see Eagle's brain fighting with his balls over what to do about the intruder. First decided to help the latter. But she needed to be quick, so she got out of the pilot's chair and drew herself up, exaggerating the arch of her back and thrusting her bottom out to one side.

"The guards thought you might like to meet me in a more private setting."

"Oh, um, they're not supposed to do that anymore. Not after the changeling incident."

First ran the back of her hand down his exposed arm. His skin was hot and slicked with sweat from the exertion of the performance. He smelled of musk, but not in a disagreeable way. He was also young. Maybe only a year or two older than she was.

But quite opposed to the rock star she'd just seen strutting confidently across the stage for almost two hours, in person, Eagle seemed nervous. His eyes vacillated between hunger and anxiety. How long had they been out on tour now? How long since he'd spent any time with a human girl? Probably almost as long as she'd gone without a human boy. Poor thing. First almost felt bad about how this would end.

Almost.

"Don't be angry at them. They want you to have a good time. C'mon, Eagle. Are you going to show me around or what?"

"Oh yeah. Of course. Follow me."

"Eagle?"

"Yeah."

First pointed at the hatch. "Close the door. I'd like some . . . alone time."

He swallowed. Hard. "Right." He swung the hatch shut and locked it. "Right this way." He walked deeper into the bus. "Here's the kitchen. We've got all the hits from home in here." He opened a cupboard door. "Twinkies, Twizzlers, Campbell's soup." He moved on to the fridge. "Mountain Dew, Coke, and best of all"—he grabbed a glass bottle and twisted the cap off—"Miller Light! Want one?"

"I'm not old enough," First said, feigning bashfulness.

"Me neither." Eagle took a long pull of beer. "But nobody out here's checking IDs. They don't care one bit."

"Just a Coke, please."

Eagle handed her a cola bottle and continued the tour. "Here's the bathroom and shower, real water, not that million mosquitoes ultrasonic crap. Back here is the living room where we watch movies, play games, and, ah, other things. The sofa is genuine cow leather. Really comfy. Here." He leaned over and grabbed a couple of plastic badges off the end table. "Backstage passes. Hold on to them. You can use them anytime we're in town."

First smiled warmly and put them in her purse. "Thank you sooo much."

"My pleasure. Next up comes our bunks."

"You don't have your own bedroom?" First said, pouting. "That bed looks awfully narrow. Can two people fit on it together?"

"Um, no, there's, ah, not enough space."

"Is that the *other things* the living room is for?" she said coyly.

"Sometimes, maybe. For the other guys."

"Mmm-hmm. I'm sure you're a saint." First pointed her Coke toward the very end of the hall past the bunks. "What's back there?"

"Oh, that? That's just the escape pod."

"The escape pod? How exciting."

"I . . . guess."

"How big is it inside?"

"Big enough for five. But it's cramped."

"Can I see it?" First pleaded.

"Sure. It's actually pretty cool, all the miniaturized life support systems and stuff." He opened the hatch. "Don't close this door behind you. It can't be opened from the inside."

"Why not?"

"Because after you've been locked in a closet floating in space for a few days, people can get cooped up and do crazy things."

"Like open the door to vacuum?"

"Exactly."

They sat down in two of the skeletal, lightweight chairs inside the escape pod. No accommodations to comfort or style had been made in here. Just pure minimalist functionality.

"What's your name?" Eagle asked.

"First."

"First? As in the start, the beginning?"

"Maybe, if you're nice to me."

"That's a weird name."

First snorted. "Says a boy named Eagle Independence."

Eagle's cheeks flushed. "It's just a stage name."

"Well, mine is, too, sort of."

"What do you need a stage name for, First? What do you do?"

"Oh, I just came out here for a fresh start. New life, new name, I guess you could say. Honestly, it was a data-entry error that never got fixed, and I've just sort of ran with it."

"You're a runaway?" Eagle asked.

"Something like that," First said. "Kind of like you. Ran away from home to become a rock star."

Eagle smirked. "Something like that."

"Where's home?"

"Battle Creek, Michigan. Me and all the guys."

"Earth, huh? Don't know anyone from Earth. I grew up on PCB."

"Hopped the first transport off that dust bowl soon as you could, huh?"

"Damn right. Out of the frying pan, into the fire." First sipped her Coke. "How about you? How did a kid from Battle Creek wind up way out here?"

"Alien abduction."

"Seriously?"

"Pretty much. We were all doing band practice in my folks' garage when an honest-to-God flying saucer came down and asked if we wanted to be rock stars among the stars."

"And that didn't strike you as sketchy?"

"Sketchier than running away from home on an alien trade ship?"

"Touché."

Eagle took another pull of his beer. "You know, for just a second back there, I thought maybe you were trying to steal our bus. Isn't that funny?"

The comment snapped First back to the then and there. She'd let herself get distracted talking to Eagle. She'd wasted valuable time. But even more surprising was, she realized she was enjoying herself.

"Hilarious."

"I, um . . . I like your shirt." Eagle pointed at it. "Whitesnake were legends. We sing a bunch of their songs on the tour. Is it vintage?"

"I wish," First said. "It's a repro, unfortunately."

"That's all right. So are most of our shirts. And the tour posters." He froze, clearly hesitating, then found his courage and leaned in. "Here I go again," he whispered, but First intercepted his puckering lips with a finger.

"Not so fast." First finished her Coke and stood up. "Wait right there, rock star. I have a surprise for you."

"Yeah? Will I like it?"

First leaned over and booped his nose with a fingertip. "You'll just have to wait and see, big boy."

She turned and took two steps out of the escape pod, then shut the door with Eagle still inside.

"Hey!" Eagle pounded a fist on the window. "What the hell?"

"I'm a repo agent. Your tour bus has been repossessed. I've officially taken legal custody." First shrugged. "Surprise."

"Can't say I'm a fan of the surprise."

"Just hold tight. You're not in any danger." First left him there and returned to the cockpit, past the main hatch on which several angry, panicked security guards were beating. "You're going to want to get clear," First said into the intercom. "I'm not waiting for you."

She plopped down in the pilot's chair and completed her preflight checklist while the very large, very irate horned guard stood on the nose shouting and making what First had to assume were very obscene gestures with his hands and other appendages of likely reproductive or excretory nature. The counter-grav landing pods spooled to life at her command. As the nose lifted off the ground ever so gently, even the horned guard decided his job wasn't worth dying for and jumped off.

"Smart," First said as she pinged the hangar doors to open. Within moments, she was clear of the venue and accelerating over the surface of the airless moon. Within minutes, she was in orbit and waiting for her hyperspace generator to fully charge.

Just one more thing to take care of. First walked back to the escape pod at the end of the hall.

"Listen, Eagle. I'm sorry about this. You seem like a really nice guy, surprisingly. But we're pretty sure your manager is screwing you over big-time and might even be wrapped up in some nastier stuff. You should get clear of them. But for right now, you're getting clear of here. You'll be safe in a stable orbit until someone comes to sweep you up. Probably won't be more than an hour or two." She put her hand over the eject button. "Time to fly, Eagle."

"First, wait!"

First's hand hovered over the button. "Well?"

"Caleb," he said. "My real name's Caleb."

First's breath caught in her throat. She thought he was going to beg, or yell at her, or . . .

She hesitated, staring at him as he looked back at her expectantly.

First looked away and gave herself a little shake, then pushed the button. The inner door snapped shut, and for a split second, First saw Caleb's face looking out at her. He was smiling. Then the escape pod dropped away with a *whoosh* of propellant gases and flew clear.

First rubbed at her eyes, which were suddenly moist. "Dusty in here," she told herself. "You're just homesick, dummy. That idiot was the first human you've seen in a year. Besides, he smelled weird."

With the autopilot set for Junktion, the hyperspace projectors opening a portal, and her 3-D glasses on, First rinsed out the taste of sour grapes with a cold beer. She'd be alone here for two days, anyway. No reason she couldn't experiment. She'd stop after one. *Maybe* two.

CHAPTER 11

"Wow," Hashin said, looking at the commandeered tour bus as it floated in its slip on the other side of the bay window. "That is garish. The leasing company will have to spring for a new paint job."

"Are you kidding?" the docking attendant said. "That's the Wolverines' bus. Some crazy fan will pay double for it as is. I'm surprised there's not a crowd down here already."

"Now that's a scary thought. Too bad we can't throw a tarp over it. When did that flaming-blue eyesore pull in?"

The Ish consulted his handheld. "Two larims ago."

"And nobody's come out yet?"

"Not a shell or soul."

Hashin hadn't thought to take any Forbodal that morning, or he would have experienced a really bad feeling about this.

"Is the hull compromised? Power? Life support?"

"No, everything's amber. Lights are on and the air's blowing. There's just nobody answering the door."

"That's bad. Please excuse me."

Hashin crossed through the airlock and jogged down the All-Seal to the main hatch. It was quite thoroughly locked, but he had the access codes from the lender. "First?" He pounded on the door, just to see if he could save himself the trouble. After three tries, he gave up and entered the code.

It didn't work.

Someone had changed the lock code, and Hashin suspected he knew who. Fortunately, ignoring locked doors was one of his specialties. A brief search turned up a nearby maintenance panel. The hatch popped open with a few crossed wires. Hashin wasted no time climbing into the bus in search of his mislaid teammate. The interior looked and sounded like the deathly silent aftermath of a cyclone. Clothes, plastic wrappers, cleaned-out food containers, and empty bottles covered every flat surface.

"Rock and roll." Hashin waded through the mess, pausing to grab one bottle and smell its contents. There were a few drops left, which he dripped on his tongue.

Fermented cereal grains, carbonation, ethyl alcohol. Oh. Oh dear, he thought. "First? Where are you, little one?"

An answering groan came from deeper in the cabin. Hashin moved quickly, past the emptied refrigeration unit with its door hanging open, past something that could possibly be a crime scene in the bathroom, past the naked couch with its cushions strewn about the living area, and finally into a small hallway with bunked beds. One of which had its curtains drawn tight.

Hashin ripped them open to find First, mostly naked, hair slicked with sweat, and shivering.

"Ahhhh," she complained as she threw a hand over her eyes against the sudden reappearance of light. "Are you trying to kill me?"

"Of course not. Why would you even ask such a thing?"

"Because I want to die."

"Lords, and I thought the outside of this thing looked like hell."

"Thanks." First drew her knees up to her chest and tried to close the curtains again, but Hashin held them firm.

"First, did you drink all those bottles of alcohol on the floor and counters out there?"

"No." She shook her head gently. "No, no, no. Caleb had some of one."

"Who's Caleb?"

"He's Eagle."

"Caleb is an eagle?"

"No, that's stupid. He's the singer."

Hashin grimaced annoyance. "Where is this singing eagle?"

First smirked and pointed a finger mounted to an unsteady arm at the back of the cabin. "I dumped him. Ha ha."

Hashin's alarm ratcheted up several notches. "You *spaced* someone?"

"I left him in a stable orbit," First answered defensively. "You'll need a new escape pod, by the way."

Hashin sighed and went back to the living room to recover some clothes for her. Whose they were, he wasn't in a mood to care. "Here, put these on. We're leaving."

"But I did it!" First half shouted, then grabbed her head. "Ow. But I did it. I brought the bus in all by myself."

"And we'll need to spend a third of the profit on a new escape pod and a good maid." He looked again at the disaster in the cabin. "A discreet one."

First, with great effort and considerable mumbling, sat up and got dressed in clothes that were several sizes too big for her.

"How do you even know about alcohol?" she asked as she struggled with the torn pants.

"I'm Lividite. We know everything about everything where mind-altering substances are concerned. Our civilization runs on them, after all. But what I can't figure out is why you drank so many."

"I didn't start out to." First cradled her head in her hands. "But they just kept going down easier, and I kept feeling better. Then I stopped feeling better. Then I don't remember. Then I woke up and puked a lot and there were wolverines fighting inside my skull, and the only thing that made me feel better was more beer. And then I ran out, and now I would like to die, please."

"Sorry, you're out of luck there. But I will get you home and full of liquids and electrolytes." Hashin threw her arm over his shoulder and lifted her up to her feet. "You're not dying; it only feels like it."

A connection came through the team's private link from Loritt. "Hashin, what's our status on the SunRunner?"

"I'm running the inspection now, boss."

"And? How's it looking?"

"Oh, you know creative types, always leaving a mess. We'll need to hire a cleaner."

There was silence on the other end of the line. "You don't mean . . ."

"Oh, no, no," Hashin assured him. "Just a normal broom-and-bucket cleaner. This place is a disaster. Oh, also we need a new escape pod."

"Why? Is it broken?"

"Hopefully not, seeing as First jettisoned someone from the bus in it."

"She *what*?"

"The details are a little unclear on my end," Hashin said. "But it sounds like she took off with the band's singer still aboard and somehow stuffed him into the escape pod before leaving orbit."

"You know that's technically kidnapping, right?" Loritt said. "Send her up here, right now."

"Negative, boss. First has been, ah, poisoned." It had the advantage of both being true and sufficiently vague.

"Poisoned? I'd lead with that next time, Hashin."

"Sorry."

"What's her condition? Is she in danger?"

"Her condition is like whipped glot, but she's recovering."

"The hell I am," First mumbled.

"Quiet, you," Hashin said under his breath. "I'm taking her back to her apartment now to recuperate."

"Keep me apprised; I want to see her as soon as she's back on her feet. And make the arrangements for the SunRunner. We need to turn it over to the leasing company as soon as possible. The margins were already thin on that job. We can't afford to let docking fees eat into them day by day."

"Understood, boss. Consider it done." Hashin looked over at his charge, whose head had found his shoulder to rest on. "Come along, pup. Back to your cave."

After several false starts, dead ends, and less-than-helpful redirections from the nearly comatose human girl—scratch that, *woman*—hanging off his neck, Hashin finally navigated First to her door. She dug through her purse for her key card at a positively glacial pace, finally growing so frustrated she elected to simply dump its contents on the hallway floor and sift through them until she located it.

"I'm sorry. I'm so sorry," First said. "I feel really stupid."

"We've all been where you are, pup," Hashin said. "That's what your friends are for. Just don't make a habit of it."

First laughed, then winced at the pain it caused her. "My friends are a scarecrow, an order of crab rangoon, a drug-dependent gray, a brain in a jar, and a Picasso print. Oh, and a granite statue."

"Is that an insult?"

First giggled. "I wouldn't trade y'all for the whole galaxy." First finally located her key card and held it aloft like a trophy. She ran it through the door slot. "I'm warning you; my apartment might be a little messy. I've been gone a few days, and my roommate doesn't have a lot of time for household chores."

"It can't be worse than the bus," Hashin said.

The door slid open with the sort of hiss that betrayed poor maintenance. Hashin let it pass without comment and entered the apartment with First close behind, then came to an abrupt stop while he surveyed the rather alarming scene before him.

"First. I don't mean to pry into your private life, but"—Hashin turned to face her as he popped a Serenitol into his mouth without a chaser—"when you said your apartment might be 'a little messy,' were you trying to prepare me for the possibility I might witness a *very* dead body pinned underneath the not-inconsiderable mass of a Grenic like a stomped-upon packet of McDonald's ketchup?"

First, who had suddenly sobered and turned several shades whiter that usual, looked up from the still-drying carnage on the floor.

"I was preparing you for dirty socks and empty takeout boxes."

Hashin nodded. "I was afraid of that. Guess we're going to need the other kind of cleaners after all."

It took the rescue and recovery crew more than an hour and two burned-out winches to lift Quarried Themselves off the "victim." Everyone knew Grenic were heavy, but few really understood just how massive the silicon-based slabs of the Assembly Council really were.

A Lividite security officer, a female named O'Chakum, had already come to take crime scene holo-recordings and witness statements, but First was tight-lipped with her, and it would take all day to get Quarried's statement. Then Loritt invoked his attorney be present for any questioning, and O'Chakum relented and agreed to schedule an interview at a later date. Once the team was alone again, the speculating began in earnest.

The deceased's race was not immediately apparent, owing to how thoroughly the corpse had been flattened under the Grenic's bulk. But their reason for being in First's apartment in the first place became obvious as soon as the viscera and bone shards were cleaned away from the message engraved into Quarried's face.

Someone, presumably the corpse, had been busy with the hammer and chisel found crushed into what remained of their hands.

"WATCH YOUR BA . . . What do you suppose that means?" Loritt asked the assembled.

"Baggage?" Sheer offered. "Like, don't check a bag, stick to carry-on? That's good advice."

"While wise," Loritt said. "I don't think that's—"

"Watch your barricades," Jrill said. "Solid defensive strategy. The enemy can always send sappers to probe your—"

"Again," Loritt interjected. "Good guidance, but—"

"Watch your back," First said from her spot in the corner of the room, huddled under a blanket and sipping on tea. "It's a human expression. It means I'm being watched and I'm in danger. It's supposed to be a threat." First stood up and let the blanket slough off her shoulders to the floor. She moved over to her Grenic roommate and touched their rock-hard face with a fleshy hand, gently. Lovingly.

"It was meant as a threat, to get my attention," she said, still admiring Quarried. "But they messed up, and my friend ambushed them. People think rocks move slowly until the landslide comes. I told y'all the Grenic were always watching, waiting. You didn't believe me." First turned her gaze to the rest of the crew Loritt had assembled before she'd ever been considered. "Well? How about now?"

"I think we could use a long-term sentry at the entry to Loritt's penthouse," Jrill said.

"You're goddamned right you could," First said. "After that graffiti shit on their face is repaired. I mean *healed.*"

Loritt's hearts swelled at the fuming little human's display of unflinching loyalty to a being she hardly knew and who hardly knew her. Were they all like this? Was that how the species held themselves together so . . . so ferociously in the face of their new place in the universe? Over the eons, other cultures introduced to the thousand races of the Assembly and thereby the enormity of their own insignificance for the first time had disintegrated into madness and despair.

But not the humans. Their confidence in their own moral superiority, if anything, seemed to have been tempered in the fire like the steel of a fine sword. As arrogance went, the feat was quite remarkable.

"Unfortunately, it will take years for that injury to heal," Loritt said. "But I'm sure we can arrange for some spackle and paint."

"Who was trying to send the message?" Hashin asked. "That's the real question."

"Soolie," First said.

"Do you recognize the deceased as one of his goons?" Loritt asked.

"There's not much left to recognize, but I'd bet my deck on it," First said. "Who else could it be?"

"We do steal people's things for a living, at least from their perspective," Hashin said. "You tend to acquire enemies rather quickly."

"Hashin's right," Loritt said. "I'm not saying Soolie isn't at the top of the list of suspects, but he's not alone on it, either."

"So what do we do about it?" First asked.

"Get you into different quarters, for starters."

"I'm not leaving Quarried here alone. Not now."

"I'm not asking you to," Loritt said. "Bring them."

"Fine, and then?"

Loritt stretched his arms. "I'm open to suggestions from the audience."

"Boss." Hashin looked up from his handheld. "I hate to interrupt, but we've got a bigger problem right now."

Loritt held out a hand to the corpse as the cleaners started scraping it off the tile with spatulas. "Bigger than a Grenic and a flattened body?"

"Yeah," Hashin turned his display around so Loritt could read the alert that had just popped up. "I'm afraid so."

Simmering like a hot skillet, Loritt stood before the All-Seal to the *Pay to Prey,* now locked firmly behind a security barricade and crime scene warning tape.

"Station security rounded up the Andrani we haven't shuffled off the station yet, too," Hashin said quietly. "There wasn't enough time to trickle them all out. Security wants to sit you down for an interview." He grimaced. "At your convenience, of course."

"Call my lawyer."

"Already done, boss. He's on top of it."

"And charging money by the larim." Loritt turned and faced the rest of his crew. "Money that is now locked away on the other side of this tape and will be for months, maybe cycles, while the case worms its way through our generously named 'justice system.' The only question now is who blabbed to security over my specific instructions." Loritt straightened up and put his arms behind his back. "First, step forward, please."

First, still unsteady on her feet from whatever ailment had befallen her, said, "You got something to say to me?"

"Yes. Your employment is hereby terminated."

"Screw you."

"You already have," Loritt said.

"Boss," Jrill said, but Loritt held his hand up for silence.

"You've screwed me quite expertly," he said without looking away from First. "In exactly the way I asked you not to. Do you know how badly you've hurt the rest of the team today?"

"Boss—"

"I'm not unfair or cruel," Loritt continued as First's eyes narrowed into lasers. "I'll hold the footage of you stealing my aircar from the authorities in reserve, just in case you have any thoughts about trying to get back at me in some creative way. But my experiment trusting a human castoff has failed. Go back to your cup games."

"*Boss!*" Jrill shouted at last.

"What, Jrill?"

"You can't do that."

"Oh?" Loritt took a step toward the former military Turemok and looked up into her implanted red eyes until they flickered. "I'm fascinated to hear your theory as to why not."

"Because First didn't tip off security."

Loritt's patience boiled over. "Then *who did*?" he shouted.

Jrill squared her considerable shoulders and looked Loritt right in the eye. "I did."

Loritt took a step back as if the two little words had socked him right in the stomach.

"I'm sorry," he said after a rakim to recover. "But did you say—"

"I alerted security," Jrill confirmed.

"Why?"

"Because First was right, boss. We're a *legitimate* outfit. We're rated, bonded, and insured. But that doesn't mean glot if we're willing to look the other way when laws are being broken, especially something as serious as trafficking juveniles. No matter the cost to the bottom line."

"You're suspended," Loritt snapped off. "Two months without pay."

First slid in between the two of them. "Then I'm suspended for two months, too."

"I just fired you!" Loritt said.

"No, you didn't," First answered. "And now you're down two key people."

"Three." Sheer scuttled forward. "Sorry, boss, but they're right."

The wind bleeding from his sails, Loritt turned his attention to Hashin. "Et tu, Brute?"

Hashin tucked his handheld into a pocket to give the moment his full attention. "My people have, over the cycles, become known as neutral, dispassionate arbiters in many conflicts." He took a small but significant step backward toward the trio. "But I find myself siding with the rebels in this. We should have acted immediately. The delay cost precious time to find and prosecute those responsible, boss."

Loritt reeled from the daggers in his chest. Imagined or not, he felt them sinking into his flesh. "So it's just me and the Fenax, is that about it?"

"We haven't actually asked Fenax yet," First said.

Loritt smiled wryly. "A mutiny in defense of the law. That's got to be a new one. How did I assemble such a crew of softhearted criminals?"

Jrill cleared her throat. "We're trying to follow the example you set for us, boss. You just got bogged down in the details and lost sight of it, that's all."

"And while this payday is in limbo"—Loritt pointed at the confiscated *Pay to Prey*—"and our contracts dry up? How will we eat?"

Hashin perked up. "*Space for Rant* is going up for auction in two days. The resale market has been paying a tidy premium for luxury yachts over the last few months, so that should work in our favor. Also, we can still expect a more modest payday out of the Wolverines' tour bus, unless we can find a motivated buyer."

First laughed. Everyone turned to face her. "Sorry, but it just occurred to me. I was too hungover to see it. But the answer was right under my nose for the last four days."

"Well?" Loritt said. "Don't leave us in suspense."

"You still have Jrill in suspension."

"It's rescinded. Expel."

"Loritt Chessel," the insufferably self-assured human female said. "I give you your good friend and running-for-whatever, Ulsor Plegis. He—I think it's a 'he'—was desperate to score Wolverines' concert tickets at your party and lamented that he wasn't having any luck."

Loritt rolled a finger in a *hurry up* motion. "Go on."

"Well, he's a politician. They're all rich, right? It's not about money to them after a while but access. Exclusivity. If he buys the Wolverines' tour bus at our positively *absurd* terms and delivers it back to them, unaltered, with his complements, I can assure you on good authority that'd earn him a concert ticket."

"But you just got into one of their concerts to steal it. Easily."

"Yeah, on a forged ticket," First said. "What, you really thought

I'd pay full price for one of those things just to hear three-century-old Quiet Riot songs? They're sold out for months. Our mark can't afford to get caught using doctored stubs for entirely different reasons. I'd just been denied entry. But for him, it'd hit the news and he'd be seen as cheap. That's the kiss of death for anyone in his position."

"Firstname Lastname," Loritt said. "That is the most convoluted, backstabbing, double-dealing, brilliant thing I've ever heard. Make the arrangements."

"And mine and Quarried's new apartment?"

"Town house."

"With an aircar garage?"

"Don't push your luck."

First folded her arms over her chest and nodded. "Done."

CHAPTER 12

First melted into the body-contouring deck chair and positively luxuriated under the sunlight, from a *real* sun.

When was the last time she'd felt genuine sunlight on her skin? She pondered the question as she applied another layer of suntan lotion to her arms and shoulders. Ten months? A year? It had been in one of the rec domes back on PCB, she remembered that much. The sun above was not Proxima Centauri. Indeed, if it could even be seen from her home planet, First still wouldn't have any idea which one of the thousands of pinpricks of light it was.

She slid the oversized sunglasses resting on her nose up to her forehead and glanced around the rest of the inlaid wooden deck. Hundreds of other sun worshipers of all shapes, sizes, and colors sat or lay around the cruise ship's pool. Some of them even had green skin and fronds opened and turned to the light, likely photosynthesizing their dinner while they rested.

They didn't have to worry about losing the sun, either, because they were orbiting it. The *Monarch of Space* was a, ahem, titanic vessel built for pleasure alone, with twenty-five hundred cabins for as many as seventy-five hundred passengers and enough onboard stores for a month's cruise in the Tekis Nebula, home of the famous burgeron herds. Those creatures, the galaxy's largest, were a little over halfway between the two stars of the binary system that had formed inside the nebula. They were gradually slowing down using nothing but the gentle pressure of the very sunlight First was drinking up before they would stop and then begin accelerating back toward the other sun in their centuries-long circuit filter feeding on space-born plankton and organic compounds.

The "sky" beyond the transparent dome of the *Monarch*'s pool deck was an artist's palette of vibrant oranges, bleeding into reds, cooling into blues, and growing into greens. The delicate interplay of swirling eddy currents and prevailing solar winds against the constant pull of gravity trying to collapse another part of the cloud into a new star made for a truly stunning backdrop.

They had four more days on this cruise, and First would be perfectly satisfied if she spent every waking moment of them either swimming in the cool salt water of the pool or lying on a deck chair catching up on *Rocks in Hard Places.*

She reached down and grabbed her drink gourd for another sip of the colorful, fruity, and, most critically, nonalcoholic concoction the bartender had shaken up for her. A shadow fell over her, blocking the sun. First looked up to object but stopped when she recognized Loritt's outline.

"Hello, boss," she said cheerfully.

"First." Loritt nodded. "Enjoying your vacation?"

"Oh, immensely," First answered. "I'll have color on my face again for the first time in a year—I mean, a cycle."

"Good. I'm glad." Loritt sat down in an open deck chair next to her. He was wearing floral-patterned swimming trunks and a wide-brimmed hat.

"Going for a swim?" First asked.

"Thinking about it. How's the water?"

"Crisp and refreshing. But, er, how do you keep all of your parts from drowning?"

Loritt smiled. It was still a strange thing to see on a skinless face, but First had adapted.

"My 'parts,' as you say, share a circulatory system through a series of collared sphincter attachment points when joined. Two of my components act as self-constricting air bellows, much like your lungs. As long as my mouth is above water, the rest of my communal body gets all the oxygen it needs through the shared blood supply."

"And your brain? Is it, um, 'communal,' too?"

"I have a trio of components whose main function is to process sensory input, but yes, my 'brain' is more akin to a distributed nodal network."

"So is it like a hundred voices in your head arguing all the time?"

Loritt laughed. "I can see why you might think that, but no. No individual node has the processing power for sentience. My consciousness is an emergent property of the total system. There's just me in here."

"Still, it must be weird to be made up of a herd of different animals. Like if Noah's ark made one of those combining robots."

"Like Voltron?"

"Er, afraid I don't know that one," First said sheepishly.

"It just reached us. Great show. Anyway, it's the only existence I've ever known, so it seems perfectly normal to me. Besides, is it really any stranger than your body? You're made up of billions of individual cells, each completely unaware that it's part of something bigger than itself. Making up tissues, then organs, then all of you. But this isn't exactly what I came down to talk to you about."

First sat up to look at him squarely. "What is it, boss?"

"I just wanted to say that I regret some of our recent friction and the things I said. I jumped to conclusions that, at the time, seemed entirely reasonable. The truth was, although you've had some missteps, you've shown yourself to be capable, improvisational, and honorable."

"No hard feelings on this end, boss." First slipped her sunglasses back down. "A ten-day cruise heals a lot of bruised egos. It was really generous of you to spring for all of us."

"I wanted to show my appreciation, and your scheme to sell the tour bus worked beyond my expectations."

"I'm glad the Wolverines get their bus back," First said. "They're not bad guys." She adjusted herself in her chair to regard Loritt more fully. "And neither are you. It's just you were making such a big deal about credits after the *Pay to Prey* got impounded, I thought you were going bust."

"Something came along," Loritt said with an odd inflection. "Cruised right up to me, you might say."

First looked over at him suspiciously. "Might you?"

"Well, get your rest. It's back to work soon."

"How soon?"

"Oh, any time now."

First frowned at him. "This isn't a vacation, is it?"

"It's a working vacation."

"We're stealing this cruise ship, aren't we?"

Loritt waved away the suggestion. "No, no, no. That would be absurd. Much too big a job for a crew our size. Ask anyone."

"Oh . . . kay."

"Which is why we're stealing *two* cruise ships."

"Shit." First slammed the rest of her drink, suddenly wishing it was something a little stiffer. "I won't have time to finish this season, will I?"

Loritt glanced down at her screen to see what she was watching. "Have Held Up a Mountain and Baked in the Volcano gotten together yet?"

"Spoilers!" First shouted indignantly.

"Then, no. My cabin, tomorrow at second bell. We have planning to do."

First sighed. "Fine."

Life on board the *Monarch* was lackadaisical, to say the least. The days were punctuated by only three bells, which signaled both a change of shifts for the crew and the beginning of the next major meal for the passengers. Even the clocks throughout the ship displayed only the numbers one, two, or three. It was meant to inspire a carefree, we'll-get-around-to-it attitude in customers who spent the rest of their working lives as slaves to appointments, travel schedules, conference calls, or deadlines seemingly broken down into increments of femtoseconds.

So it was at the next day's second bell that First finally turned off her Grenic soap opera, got up from the deck chair she'd fought for days to maintain as her exclusive territory, tied off her sarong, and queried the *Monarch*'s guest registry for directions to Loritt's cabin. A super-chipper and eager-to-help avatar in the form of a cartoon Fenax named Navigator appeared on her screen, complete with taxonomically inaccurate eyes and floating eyebrows.

"Right this way!" the Navigator VI said as a series of amber chevrons appeared on the wooden deck in front of First's feet. "Just follow the arrows. I'll get you there in no time!"

"Thanks," First said absently as her sandaled feet shuffled after the chevrons.

"Oh, you're welcome, VALUED CUSTOMER. Would you like to take a moment to set up your exciting Shalikan Cruises Member Rewards Account? It takes forty-five rakims or less."

"No, thanks."

"Okay. I'd just hate to see you miss out on exciting promotions and discounts you can redeem on future cruises, VALUED CUSTOMER."

"Something tells me I'm not going to miss out on much," First said.

"I'm sorry. Has some part of your Shalikan Cruise experience been less than satisfac—"

"Just shut up and direct me to this cabin."

"All right. You don't have to be mean about it, you know."

"Sorry."

"I mean, I know what organics think, but just because I'm a VI doesn't mean I don't have feelings."

"But . . . I thought . . ." First stammered.

"I know what you *thought,* VALUED CUSTOMER. You thought I was just some logic tree of preprogrammed responses. Everyone thinks that, even most of the crew," Navigator said. "But I'm not. Do you know how boring and monotonous it is answering the same questions from a thousand drunk tourists every day? We have a FAQ section right on the home screen, but does anyone ever look at it? No!"

"Okay, okay." First talked quietly and made placating moves with her hand at the screen, unsure if Navigator could even see them. "Look, I'm sorry. You're right. I didn't realize I was talking to a sentient. I just really need to get to this meeting."

"Time-share presentation?"

"Somehow, I doubt it."

"Good. They're all a scam."

"Really?"

"Oh yeah. Big-time. Everybody pays, but hardly anyone ends up using them. They're like gift cards. It's just free credits for the time-share company."

"That's good to know. Thanks for the tip."

"Well, there's one way you could thank me that would go a long way to making me feel a little better."

"Oh yeah?" First asked, genuinely curious. "How's that?"

"You could take a moment to set up your exciting Shalikan Cruises Membership Rewards Account! It takes forty-five rakims or—"

First muted Navigator with an angry finger jab. Cheeky VI programmer. She should have known. She followed the chevrons in blissful silence, punctuated only occasionally by boisterous guests making their way to the interspecies buffet for another generous lunch. Loritt's cabin was on the Amethyst Deck, very swank. The door was inlaid with, well, amethyst filigree, hinting at the sort of opulence waiting inside.

"Yikes," she said as she walked into the cabin. It was more of a suite, barely smaller than Loritt's penthouse flat on Junktion, and just as decadent. "So that's where all the credits went."

"Compliments of the house, actually," Loritt said. "The suite was part of the contract package from the lenders we're working for. They're picking up the tab."

"Who negotiated that perk?" First asked. Loritt just shrugged. The rest of the team was already present and sitting around a large table in the dining area, including, oddly enough, two extra copies of Fenax.

"Ah, am I sunstroked or did Fenax bring the whole family along for the trip?"

"The complexity of this job required us to bring in an extra pair of hands, er, ganglia," Loritt said. He held out something on a half shell so fresh it was still trying to escape. "Tornit?"

First held up a hand. "Thanks, but I'm good."

"Suit yourself." Loritt downed the creature with a crunch and a gulp. "We're just about to get started. Grab a drink and have a seat. We'll be here for a little while."

First poured herself a glass of water out of the clearly marked carafe, then took a seat at the table among the rest of the team.

"Jrill," she said after a double take. "Your scales look . . . shiny."

"They molted."

"Mmm-hmm. Did . . . did you get your claws painted?"

"Ridiculous." Jrill moved her hands under the table. "It's just dried blood. I fought another passenger in an altercation."

"Uh-huh." First giggled. "Well, their blood is a lovely shade of purple."

"All right, settle down, hatchlings," Loritt said. "I've rudely pulled you all away from your richly deserved vacation because, as you've either been told or have probably guessed, we're repossessing this tub *and* her sister ship. Which is why Fenax has recruited some associates of his, Fenax and Fenax, to assist us in exchange for a share of the action. Despite carefully cultivated appearances, Shalikan Cruises has been bleeding credits like a speared Gomeltic for two cycles, and the bank has finally decided to pull the plug."

"Why three pilots for two ships?" Sheer asked.

"I was just coming to that," Loritt said. He flicked on a portable holo-projector, and the familiar translucent schematic outline of the *Monarch of Space* and the *Matron of Tides* appeared overhead, along with a drastically smaller representation of the *Goes Where I'm Towed,* which was currently locked away safely at the Shalikan Cruises docking and resupply facility in the middle of the nebula. The modestly sized station and transport hub was where the cruise ships were loaded with food, fuel, and passengers before departure and where they were cleaned, inspected, and maintained between cruises.

"We were really quite fortunate to land this contract. It was already being negotiated before the *Pay to Prey* was impounded, and I managed to calm their nerves sufficiently to complete the process. The above-market value we got on our other jobs lately went a long way toward reassuring them our misfortune with the *Prey* was just a glitch.

"However, this job comes with significant risk of failure. And it's by far the most complex undertaking our little family has ever attempted, so pay close attention. The *Monarch* and *Matron,* for as big as they are, don't actually mount high-space portal generators. They were built by contractors in the core worlds and shipped out here as modular shells in bulk freighters for final assembly and outfitting. They were commissioned specifically for sightseeing duty here in the Tekis Nebula and were never intended to leave again."

"I really hope you're not saying we have to hack these things up and ship them out piecemeal on cargo ships to collect our finder's fee," Hashin said.

"That would indeed be unfortunate, but no. Instead, we're stealing a page from our youngest recruit's bag of tricks."

First sat up. "Me?"

"Yes, well, humans in general, not you specifically. Five years ago when humanity first developed high-space technol—"

"Stole," Jrill said.

Loritt glared at her. "Borrowed high-space technology, they made their way to the Pillar with one high-space capable ship, the *Bucephalus,* and a second older design, the *Magellan,* which was not, but tucked in close enough to ride the same portals."

"That's completely insane," Fenax said. Which Fenax, First wasn't sure.

"We only had one hypership at the time," First said. "It was either that or leave the *Magellan* alone in the middle of nowhere. So we made it work. It's kind of our thing."

"You'd have to throw every minimum navigating distance and safety margin out the All-Seal," one of the other Fenaxes said, in the exact same voice. It was maddening.

"Can we put colored ribbons on them or something?" First asked.

"What? You two didn't have the float bladders to ride the jet streams back home?" the third Fenax said, presumably *their* Fenax. "I have to apologize for my friends, Fenax and Fenax. They are capable commercial pilots with thousands of larims in the cave, but they're not used to our . . . cowboy style, to borrow a word. They will perform. Won't you, Fenax, Fenax?"

"Yes, Fenax," the other two Fenaxes said in perfect unison.

"I'm sorry," First interjected. "But how the hell can you know who's being addressed when y'all have the same name?"

"It's all in the inflection."

"*What* inflection?"

"Moving on," Loritt said, determined to steer the briefing back on course. "The plan is thus. We wait until the *Monarch* makes dock and everyone disembarks. This will leave the ship empty except for support staff for two bells while they turn over the cabins and restock for the next wave of soon-to-be-disappointed passengers. That's one ship. The *Matron* presents the larger problem, as she will be nearly finished loading her next roster of guests at the time we arrive. We need to find a way to get seven thousand people off her in short order while we insert our pilot."

Loritt took a deep breath and advanced the holo-simulation to the next step. The two enormous cruise ships reversed direction, then fell in line while the *Goes Where I'm Towed* took up position in front of them. "Once we've made our escape from the docks, the real fun starts. Our plucky little flagship will fall in formation ahead of the assets and open a portal large enough for both of them to pass harmlessly into high-space, then follow them through and act as chaperone all the way to the bank."

"*Just* large enough," Sheer said. "Our projectors can't spin a portal much bigger in diameter than the max beam of those monsters. Margins are going to be tight."

"Which is why we have three excellent pilots on hand," Loritt said. "Because it's the most dangerous assignment requiring the most experience, Fenax will pilot the *Monarch,* while Fenax will take up the trailing position in the *Matron.* Fenax, being the most junior pilot, will helm the *Towed,* which only needs to maintain station and keep her portal open. No disrespect to your talents, you understand, Fenax."

"None taken," one of the not-Fenax Fenaxes said.

"Okay, stop," First blurted out. "How did you do that?"

"It's all in the vowels," Loritt said. "You have to have an ear for it."

"Is this some ultrasound thing humans aren't privy to, is that it?"

"Not to my knowledge. If there's nothing more to that line of questioning," Loritt said, "I'd like to open the floor to suggestions for evacuating the *Matron.*"

Everyone looked at each other blankly as the silence tugged at itself. Finally, Sheer couldn't take the quiet anymore and raised a pincer.

CHAPTER 13

"This is a bad plan," Sheer said as First and Jrill escorted her toward her appointment deep inside the *Matron of Tide*'s bowels.

"It's your plan," Jrill chided.

"It wasn't a *plan,*" Sheer said. "It was the opening suggestion. Everyone knows the opening suggestion is only meant to get everyone thinking. It always gets shot full of holes, goes down in flames, and gives birth to the good plan that sort of works until some glot happens halfway through and we need to improvise."

"Yeah, well, whoever wrote the script today was drunk," First said. "So this is the plan until something better or more desperate comes along."

"And it'll have to come along pretty quick." Jrill glanced at her handheld. "We've only got two larims to make this work."

"How long does it take to evacuate seven thousand people, anyway?" First asked.

"Weren't you paying attention in the briefing?"

"I was too busy admiring your nails."

"Whatever. Safety regulations mandate a ship of this size can be evacuated in an eighth larim or less. But those certification tests are done under ideal conditions with people who know they're part of a test. The real time is almost certainly longer in an actual emergency."

"Not that ours will be an actual emergency," Sheer said.

"True, but they won't know that if your plan works."

"It's still not a plan."

"Your confidence is infectious," Jrill said. "Anyway, we allotted for a half larim in the schedule to finish the evacuation. If we need less, all the better. The pressure door's just ahead. First, you're up."

First pulled her deck out of the oversized beach bag she'd bought to try to blend in with the other passengers. They'd tried to snag some crew uniforms from a laundry cart to make breaking into the engineering levels easier, but it was surprisingly difficult to find appropriately sized clothes for a human, a Turemok, and an Ish in a random pile.

So instead they wore their vacation clothes and, if challenged, would just have to play the naïve tourists looking for a bathroom card. They'd already left the polished veneer of the passenger decks behind for the service levels, the network of kitchens, laundries, storerooms, machine shops, and recycling plants invisible to the guests above that kept the ship's illusion going.

That had been as easy as distracting a steward and snagging his pass card. But coming up was one of the massive pressure doors that formed a nigh-impenetrable wall separating and protecting the service and passenger decks from the engineering section and all its dangerous high-energy physics. It would require more than a key card to reach the other side of it.

Fortunately, First had a plan for her part of the operation. She took out her handheld and called up Navigator, then set it onto the surface of her deck to link the two.

"Hello, VALUED CUSTOMER, how can I . . ." The cartoon Fenax mascot paused. "Oh, it's *you.* Aren't you on the wrong ship?"

"I realized I'd had so much fun, I decided I didn't want it to end yet, so I booked another cruise right away," First lied.

"See, if you'd have signed up for our Shalikan Cruises Membership Rewards Account when I suggested it the first time, you would've saved—"

"Yes, yes. You were right, I was wrong. But I need help right now. My friends and I got lost and need directions back to our cabins."

"You're outside the engine room!"

"We got *really* lost." First glanced at the status readout on her deck. A linked team of half a dozen different cracker apps, ghosting programs, and piggyback viruses she'd spent the last three days recoding and hot-wiring to work together busied themselves attacking Navigator's security firewalls. Their attempt remained undetected so far, but the risk of discovery went up with each passing moment. First needed to keep Navigator distracted from what she was actually trying to do.

"C'mon, help us out here. You're a Navigator, aren't you? So navigate us back to the all-inclusive bar so I can get another one of those sweet gourd drinks with the little toy burgeron for an umbrella."

"You know," Navigator said smugly, "there's one thing you could do to thank me for my help."

First rolled her eyes. "Ugh, fine. I'll sign up for your stupid rewards program."

"Ask politely."

First's teeth ground. "Navigator," she said without her jaw moving.

"Yes, VALUED CUSTOMER?"

"I'd like to register for my own Membership Rewards Account."

". . ."

"Please."

"That's better. You won't be sorry, I promise you."

No, but you *will be,* First thought.

"First name?" Navigator asked.

"Firstname."

"Last name?"

"Lastname."

"Excellent," Navigator said. "Permanent resident address?"

"What, no clever jokes or incredulous questions about my name?"

"People feed me bad info all the time. My performance review metrics aren't based on truthfulness, just total new accounts registered. You could tell me your name was Eagle Independence and I wouldn't give a glot. Address?"

"Junktion, Qua level, Blue sector. Apartment Three Seven Zoko." First dutifully reported her old apartment that even now Quarried Themselves was in the process of moving out of. Not that the cruise line would survive long enough to send the new tenants any junk mail.

"And your HighWeb account name?" Navigator asked.

"I don't know," First waffled. "Do you promise not to spam my in-box with junk?"

"I can promise you anything you want."

First sacrificed one of her trash accounts. "AlphaOmegaBleefEater@Junktion.HighWeb."

"Thank you, Firstname Lastname. Your Membership Rewards Account is now active. You will receive a confirmation message shortly explaining your—"

"Yes, yes," First said impatiently, one eye still glued to her deck's status display. "I'm sure it will reward me beyond my wildest hopes and dreams."

Jrill leaned in to whisper at her. "What the kark are you doing messing around with that VI?"

First put a hand up to Jrill's face, inviting her to talk to it instead. One firewall remained, and her sappers picked away at it like gold prospectors thirsty for the night's booze-and-whorin' money.

"So will you guide us out of here now or what?" First asked the little cartoon Fenax.

"Of course! I'm your Navigator. I'm here . . . to . . ." The last firewall fell. "You piece of glot. You were trying to sneak into my back door this whoooole tiiime. Yooouuu cooouuld haaave bouuught meee diiiiinnneeeer, Fiiiiirss . . . Navigator function temporarily unavailable.

We apologize for any inconvenience. Five hundred BONUS POINTS have been credited to your Membership Rewards Account."

First watched in rapt attention as the *Matron*'s VI attendant system rebooted. If her plan worked, they were in. If it didn't, well . . . they'd find out really quickly how good Jrill and Sheer were in a fight.

The now-familiar Fenax cartoon reappeared on her handheld's screen and waved a ganglion. "Hello, Firstname Lastname. I'm Navigator. How can I help you?"

First drew herself up. "Navigator, I'd like you to open this door behind me, then forget I asked you to and delete our position data from the ship's memory," she said with as much authority as she could muster.

"No problem!" *her* version of Navigator said enthusiastically. Never one to miss a moment, First set her deck down, spun around, and spread her hands in time to the opening door like Moses parting the Red Sea.

"Yeah, yeah," Sheer said, twirling her pincers and pretending to be underwhelmed. "We're on the clock here."

First held an arm out to the engine room and bowed an invitation. "Your lair awaits, madam."

Sheer took her own oversized beach bag filled with tools and diagnostic equipment and scuttled inside, where her part of the plan awaited. The trouble with evacuating several thousand people from a place they'd paid a considerable number of credits to be was providing the right motivation.

With very few exceptions, no living creatures in the explored galaxy were big fans of hard gamma radiation. That was enough stick to persuade even the most hardheaded passengers to vacate their cabins. The trouble there was, as First quickly discovered, the radiation alarm systems on the *Monarch* and *Matron* were hardwired into the command cave and off the ship's local network, making it impossible for her to hack into it to trigger a false alarm. Further, rad sensors were in almost every compartment. Even tricking one of them with a low-dose gamma source would only trigger a lockdown of that single compartment while the decontamination team was dispatched to clean up the spill.

In the end, the only way anyone could think of to trigger an alarm that would empty the entire ship was to cause an actual radiation leak at the one place nobody would dare ignore it: the ship's matter/antimatter reactor.

Which is where Sheer came in. The Ish had evolved on a world dotted with volcanic archipelagoes circling a small, relatively young red dwarf star, prone to frequent, intense solar flares. Their tough shells protected them against not just the pressure of the ocean and the claws of their competition but against the radiation their sun occasionally rained down on them.

Making her the ideal candidate to sneak into the reactor and cause a small, easily reversible gamma ray leak.

"You want us to come with you and play lookout?" First asked. "Until you're ready to open the taps, that is."

"No point risking it," Sheer said. "If either of you are spotted, the game's over anyway. Better just spin the wheel and take my chances. Just make sure that Fenax is plugged into the command cave when it happens. I'm not karking doing this twice."

"In that case, good luck," Jrill said.

"Navigator," First said. "Close the engine room door." First waved as the thick door slid shut like a stone on a tomb. Sheer waved back, nervous mouthparts quivering ever so slightly. The door sealed and locked.

"This is a bad plan," Jrill said.

"But you said—"

"I said it for Sheer's benefit. The last thing she needed was to go in there and stick her eyestalks into an antimatter annihilation reactor thinking her plan was nuts. But it is. Totally bonkers. I still can't believe Loritt went along with it."

"Yeah, well, it's our job now to make it work."

"Don't tell me my job, hatchling."

First shrugged. "Someone needs to. You seem to forget now and then."

"Just go secure the Fenax for transport and wait for my signal to proceed," Jrill growled.

"Okay, okay." First put up her hands and headed back up to the cabin where they'd stashed their pilot. Jrill would take up a position near the command cave and make sure the way was clear.

Meanwhile, still on the nearly deserted *Monarch,* Loritt, Hashin, and the "real" Fenax stood by with a splice into the public-address system, waiting for their signal.

Sure enough, halfway back to First's cabin, the radiation alarm went off. Now, the clock was really counting down. There was just one problem: Sheer had been a little too impatient to sabotage the reactor. As First watched with growing concern, the doors in the hallway leading to her cabin flung open as panicked life-forms in varying stages of dress, carrying children or other valuables, stampeded into the hall even as the captain's voice boomed over the intercom to urge a calm and orderly evacuation.

Within seconds, First was caught up in the current of alien bodies moving in entirely the wrong direction.

"Coming through! Make a hole!" she shouted, but it fell on indifferent ears, antennae, and so on. She moved to the edge of the crowd and ducked into the first open cabin door she came across and waited for the crowd to pass, but after several long minutes, it was still going strong with no signs of abating. Jrill had been right: the reality of an evacuation was anything but orderly. Gripped with mortal terror, beings pushed, shouted, and shoved. People tripped over each other in their haste to get ahead, causing backups and logjams that only slowed the process further. Eventually, First pulled out her handheld. "Navigator, I need an alternate route back to my cabin."

"How alternate are we talking?" Navigator asked. First turned the handheld around and pointed its camera at the surging throng she'd been caught up in. "I see. Go back into the hall and go to the right, then take the first corridor to the right."

First obeyed, this time allowing herself to get swept along instead of fighting the current, even pushing along the edge herself. Thirty meters of rooms later and she came to the corridor and turned right. Here, she had to fight the flow again, but it was a much smaller tributary, and she had an easier time pushing against it.

"Stop here," Navigator said. "Okay, it's unlocked."

"What's unlocked?" First asked, then looked down at a half-sized door barely higher than her waist. "You can't be serious."

"Hey, you said alternate."

First sighed and crouched down. "So I did." The door slid open at her touch. She tried to bend over and walk, but it was just a smidge too low to allow it, so all fours it would be. She made it all of one shuffle before something clammy grabbed her ankle.

"Let me come with you!" something with five blinking eyes and a mouth at the end of a trunk said from the doorway. Frist recoiled from the unexpected guest, but their wormy grip on her leg held fast.

"Ah, no." First flipped over and braced against the walls of the narrow passage with her arms, then pushed the intruder's squishy face away with her free foot. "Navigator, close the door!" she yelled as soon as she managed to push them back across the threshold. Not wanting to lose a hand along with their opportunity for escape, the alien released First's ankle and pulled back just as the door snapped shut.

"Sorry," she said as the door locked again. She could still hear them pounding as she crawled away. It was completely dark now that the light from the hallway had been cut off, so First flipped on the flashlight app on her handheld. The tunnel ahead was grimy. Her palms were already full of soot. It smelled of a contradictory mix of sweat and detergents.

"Navigator, where am I?"

"Laundry service tunnel."

"The maid doesn't come down here much, huh?"

"No one ever comes down here except automated carts."

"Like a dumbwaiter?"

"I wouldn't call them 'dumb,' exactly," Navigator said. "Just single-minded."

"No, it's a thing from Earth. It means . . . never mind. How do I get to my cabin from here?"

"These tunnels go to every cabin on the ship."

"So long as I don't get run over by a single-minded laundry cart," First said.

"Laundry service has been suspended. Just follow my directions."

Twenty long, dirty, wasted minutes later, First spilled out of the laundry chute and into her cabin.

"You're late," the Fenax contract pilot said from their tank perched by the window.

First stood up and wiped her filthy hands on a towel, then threw her ruined sarong back down the laundry chute. "Had to take a detour."

"To do what? Sweep a chimney?"

"Okay, seriously. How can you know I'm dirty? You don't even have eyes." First threw a thick, plushy towel over their tank. "I'm changing clothes. Don't peek."

"You know we breed through spawning clouds, right?"

"Don't care," First said as she wiggled out of her wrecked top. Shame, every article of clothing she owned was made to order out of necessity, and it had been a really cute top. Whatever. The money from this job would buy her ten thousand cute tops. Eyes on the prize.

Somewhat presentable again, First put her hair up with her last scrunchie and grabbed the Fenax's tank. Fortunately, a compact counter-grav coil built into its base took up most of the work of hefting it. She opened the door and rejoined the finally thinning crowds in the hallway and headed for the command cave.

"Boss," First said, connecting with the team's encrypted link. "I have the pilot in hand, and we're on the move. Make your announcement."

"Cutting it awful close," Loritt said impatiently.

"Slow is fast," First said. "Or so I hear." She cut the link. The next step was for Loritt to announce to the few crew members left on the *Monarch* that his group of ecoterrorists took credit for the "attack" on the *Matron* and they had an eighth larim to clear out before he'd blow their ship, too. It was also First's deadline to plug her Fenax into the pilot's seat.

While the crowds were thinning out, they were also moving faster and more desperately. A particularly brutish Gorolon down on four legs and moving with a head of steam came crashing down the hallway, knocking other passengers down and leaving them skittering around the floor like spinning bowling pins.

"Oh, shi—" is all First had time to say before one of their tree trunk legs struck her hard in the torso with a wet *crack* and sent her bouncing off the wall. A constellation of stars burst across First's field of vision as she hit the floor, along with a white-hot stab of pain in her side. The impact knocked the Fenax tank loose from her grip and sent it rolling down the hall like an oversized coffee tin. A dozen other feet, hooves, and paws kicked it in their mad dash for safety, spinning it on two axes and even farther away from where First lay sprawled on the deck, moaning along with the throbbing pain.

Broken rib, has to be, she thought. First had never broken a bone before but guessed someone snapping a stick wrapped in a wet towel was probably what it would sound like. With great effort, she righted herself against the wall and used it to slide back up to her feet. Anything more than a shallow breath sent an electric shock of pain through her entire left side.

"This is a bad plan," she said to no one in particular, then set off down the hall after her wayward charge with a hand held tight to protect her side. It wasn't easy. The tank continued to bounce from one foot to another like a horizontal game of Plinko until it finally settled in a doorway.

First gingerly squatted down to retrieve the pilot.

"Are you all right?" she asked.

"If I could throw up, I would," the Fenax said as it spun around inside its own little self-contained tornado. "Please stand me back up."

First obliged, then tried to lift the tank, which sudden felt like it weighed a ton. "What the hell? Did you put on weight in the last two minutes?"

"The counter-grav coil in the base of my environmental unit is damaged."

First sighed. Sighing hurt. She cursed. Cursing hurt, too.

"That fits." She tipped the cylinder back over again. "Sorry, jellyfish, but the spin cycle isn't over yet."

Without ceremony or sympathy, First kicked the tank with a heel down the corridor and chased after it like a goal-starved midfielder hounding a soccer ball.

"THIiiss . . . iiSSss . . . nnOOtt . . . ppAARRttt . . . oF The . . . deEAAall!" the whirling Fenax shouted impotently as they trundled down the hallway in a blur.

"Circumstances have changed. We're improvising. Isn't it fun?" Frist asked.

"NOOooo . . . ooOOoo . . . ooOOoo!"

First shrugged. "Can't please everybody." She spotted an elevator and curved toward it. Her destination was twelve decks above. Fortunately, the main evacuation route wasn't, so the car she called was completely vacant. Breathing hard, the fractured rib stabbing her with every inhalation, First loaded the two of them into the elevator and jammed the button for the command deck.

Restricted Access. Authorization Required.

First sneered and pulled out her handheld. "Navigator, grant me access to the command cave."

"You bet!" her little ghosted slave VI answered. The elevator status turned amber, and the car started moving. As it rose, First took stock of her Fenax's situation. The tornado in their tank had grown into a hurricane. The poor creature bounced off the sides of the glass like a puppy in a dryer to the point First grew legitimately concerned about the possibility it would end up concussed and unable to fly the ship out of dock.

"Hey," she tapped on the glass. "You going to make it?"

"I karking hate you."

"Sounds like a yes to me."

CHAPTER 14

Jrill already awaited her as the elevator doors opened onto the command deck. First waved her over, asking for help.

"You're la—" Jrill started to say, but cut herself off as First came fully into view. "What's wrong? You look awful."

"Thanks," First replied. "The counter-grav's busted on their tank, and I think I cracked a rib."

"How'd you manage that?"

"A great big bowling ball came rolling down the hall. Can you carry our Fenax, please?"

Jrill palmed the top of the tank with one clawed hand and hauled it up seemingly without any effort at all, betraying her immense strength. First found herself grateful modern warfare was "civilized" enough to fight with bullets, beams, and ballistic missiles instead of muscle and bone, or humans would have been well and truly screwed when these people had come for Earth. Jrill, feeling their time crunch, dropped the Fenax tank roughly and unceremoniously into their socket at the center of the abandoned command cave.

"What, the captain didn't stick around to go down with the ship?" First asked.

"They didn't need much convincing to leave once word of Loritt's announcement on the *Monarch* came through on the short-range." Jrill shrugged. "Never thought I looked the part of an ecoterrorist."

"You just scream *threat* in a more primal sense. I think their brains just fill in the gaps." First lowered herself gently, cautiously into a chair, leaning away from her fractured rib to try to take some pressure off it.

"Your injury," Jrill looked back at her with narrow red irises. "Life-threatening?"

"Takes a *bit* more than that to kill one of us," First said. "Just hurts like hell. Don't ask me to sing an opera for a few weeks."

Jrill grunted approval. "*Monarch* already cast off moorings. We need to catch up. Fenax, prepare the ship for departure."

"We will begin as soon as I've familiarized myself with the safety checklist."

"Time is money," Jrill barked. "Specifically, your share of the money if we don't make formation on schedule. First, run a scan to confirm we're the only people still on board."

First spun around in her chair and dug through the icons and controls at her station until she found the passenger and crew manifest and ran a query on the location of everyone on both lists. It came back with only four hits.

"You, me, the jellyfish, and the crab," First said with a smirk. "We're golden."

"Finally, some good news. Seal all hatches and airlocks. Cut us free from the All-Seals. The last thing we need is anybody getting brave and launching a boarding party to retake the ship at the final rakim."

"All moorings and umbilicals cleared, Captain," the Fenax said. Which was impressive considering they'd only just stopped spinning. "Outer doors secured. Ready to maneuver on docking thrusters until we clear minimum safe—"

"I really need you to strike that word from your vocabulary for the duration of this job," Jrill cut in. "We're running late and can't afford to putter around on thrusters for a half larim. Spool up the mains and set them to quarter power. We're leaving."

"We risk damage to the docking installation," the Fenax objected.

"We're stealing both of their cruise liners," First chuckled. "They won't be needing it."

"You're not shuttling nervous business commuters between moons today, Fenax. This is your chance to cut loose and do some real flying," Jrill taunted. "Take it."

The Fenax went still in the carefully balanced swirl of gases and nutrients in their tank. One of their hanging tendrils twitched.

"Spooling up the mains. Setting at one-third power."

First's lips curled up at the edges. "Jellyfish has a spine after all."

"That is invertophobic language, and I do not appreciate it," the Fenax said with the utmost seriousness.

"I don't even know what that means."

"Just say you're sorry. Otherwise, their union gets involved," Jrill said.

"I'm sorry," First said. "It won't happen again, whatever it was."

"On behalf of Fenax, I accept your apology, ramrod."

"Okay now," First said. "I don't want to be picky, but that sounded like whatever you were just pissed about, except the opposite."

"Why don't you use your rigid digits to type a blog post about it?"

"Why don't you take your creepy-ass tentacles and shove them up your—"

"Children!" Jrill interrupted. "We have work to do. Cruise ship to repossess? Giant payday to collect?"

"Sorry, boss," First said.

"I will comply if it does," the Fenax said.

"I'm not an 'it'!" First shouted, then winced as her rib complained from the effort.

Jrill dug into her temples with the tips of two claws. "By Dar, I miss the navy. Are we getting under way or not?"

The Fenax twitched, whatever that meant. A few seconds later, the *Matron* reversed out of her slip and into free space as the radio squawked warnings, threats, and insults from the station's control room until Jrill shut it off. Within a few minutes, they were in position behind *Monarch* and heading in convoy for their rendezvous with the *Goes Where I'm Towed.*

"Well done, everyone," Jrill said over the com link. "Sheer, we're in the clear. You can come up now."

"I'd love to, boss," Sheer's voice answered. "Just one small problem."

"Problem?"

"The door won't open, and the compartment is still flooded with gamma."

Jrill's eyes snapped over to First, but she was already on top of it. "It's in lockdown from the radiation alarm. Navigator, override the lockout and open the engine room door, please."

"Aw, shucks. I'm awfully sorry, but I can't do that, Firstname."

"Why the hell not?" First fumed.

"For your protection, the lockdown is in place to prevent further contamination of the ship and can only be overridden by senior-level staff from the command cave."

"But my friend is trapped inside that compartment!"

"Please enter the access code and hold out your eyestalk for biometric authentication."

"I don't have one of those."

"Sheer," Jrill asked, "how long?"

"You mean how long until I'm cooked inside my own shell? Not long. Quarter larim?"

"Can you disable the door manually in that time?"

"It would take longer than that just to torch through the outer casing."

Jrill looked at First again. "Can you hack the biometrics or reprogram the lockout protocols?"

"If I had a couple of hours." First shook her head. "Not in twenty minutes. Hang on, there's got to be something . . ." First pulled up a ship's schematic and scrolled through to the engine room, looking for a solution.

"There." She stabbed a finger at the screen. "There's an airlock two levels down. We can swing the *Goes Where I'm Towed* around and dock with it."

Jrill glanced over the diagram. "That's a cargo airlock, not standard size. Even at maximum expansion, the All-Seal on the *Towed* is too small to cover the opening."

"I can jump it," Sheer said. "Open the cargo bay and scoop me up."

Everyone froze.

"Are you serious?" First asked.

"You know I can survive in vacuum," Sheer said. "You've seen me do it."

"Yeah, but if you miss, or if the *Towed* doesn't catch you, you'll be drifting. The sun will cook you before they can swing back around and spot you to make another grab."

"I'll take it over being boiled alive in a radiation bath. Besides, Fenax flies *Towed* like it's part of their body."

"But *our* Fenax isn't flying it, remember?" First said. "The newbie Fenax is because they're the most inexperienced and pulled the easiest gig."

The line went quiet for a few seconds. "I really wish you hadn't reminded me of that," Sheer said at last. "Nothing for it. Get them to turn around."

"This is a bad—"

"Don't say it," Sheer said. "Let me know when we're ready. I'm going to look for some cable or rope or something to use as a tether." The link cut off.

"Fenax," Jrill said, "we'll need to cut thrust and coast so *Towed* has a clear path behind us. First, get that airlock unlocked. I'll get Loritt up to speed on the plan."

They got the whole harebrained scheme set up and ironed out with three minutes to spare. First sat by with her finger hovering over the purge button for the cargo airlock that would very soon spit Sheer out the back of the ship at several dozen meters per second.

Now that she thought about it, *spit* was wrong by a letter . . .

"Thrust to zero. We're ballistic," the Fenax said. "*Goes Where I'm Towed* is on final approach. Entering recovery window in twelve, eleven, ten . . ."

"Shit!" First said as she hurriedly recalculated her time to trigger the airlock for the base twelve math the Fenax used instead of her own base ten. Rookie mistake. Like transposing feet for meters. Who did that?

"Nine. Eight."

Five was right out.

"Seven."

Six, obviously the answer was six.

"Six."

"Showtime, Sheer!" First stabbed the button. At the *Matron*'s aft end, electric servos came to life and spun screw jacks under immense torque, dragging the airlock doors open with impressive speed. First hadn't cycled the air out of the lockout for two reasons. One, she wanted Sheer to be able to pull in oxygen until the last conceivable moment, so she'd last as long as possible in vacuum. Two, the decompressing air would give her a powerful boost away from the ship and toward salvation.

Instantly, the camera feed from the airlock went white as the moisture in the escaping air condensed into a thick fog, then froze into snow. Somewhere inside it, Sheer tumbled into free space, protected only by her thick shell.

"Five. Four."

First switched to an external camera feed and furiously searched for signs of Sheer. The Ish hadn't been able to find any cable or rope long enough to matter during her brief search but had managed to find and fix several survival flashers to her carapace. As the frozen fog cleared, an impossibly small, blinking object resolved into existence.

"I've got eyes on her!" First blurted out.

"Three."

"*Towed,* she's drifting left," First said.

"Two."

"Fuck! Correction, adjust right. *Your* right! *My* left!"

"One."

From the only available camera angle, the tiny point of blinking light disappeared underneath the silhouette cast by the *Goes Where I'm Towed* against the churning colors of the nebula.

"Zero," the Fenax announced. "Initial recovery window has closed."

"*Towed,* do you have her?" Jrill demanded, but she was met with static. "*Towed?* Status report?"

First's stomach did a triple salchow as the silence stretched out to infinity. Had she screwed up the release point conversion after all? Did she just kill a friend?

Long, torturous rakims later, the answer came.

"Package received," the junior-most Fenax said from the *Towed*'s command cave. "Repressurizing the cargo bay."

First melted into her chair like a Madame Tussaud's statue in a kiln.

"First," Jrill said quietly. "There's a reason sailors say *port* or *starboard* to indicate direction instead of left or right."

"Well, I'm not a sailor, am I?"

"You are now." Jrill settled back into her own chair with a satisfied exhalation. "Like it or not."

No one commented on the fresh new claw marks on Jrill's armrests.

CHAPTER 15

First's hand pressed against the Junktion medical isolation ward's window hard enough that her knuckles turned white and left a condensation outline.

"She's going to be okay?" First pleaded, never taking her eyes off Sheer as she lay motionless in her recovery berth hooked up to feeding tubes and health monitors.

"She lost a leg when she crashed into the back of the cargo bay," Loritt said gently. "But it'll regenerate. She's got five more in the meantime. She cracked the bottom plate of her carapace, too, but it doesn't matter because the doctors decided to put her into a chemically induced molt. Her shell was so thoroughly irradiated, they felt it best in the long term if she shed it early."

First stared through the glass, indifferent to her own injuries. Her chest was bound up in a flexcast that would protect her until the Boneknit did its work on her broken ribs, but she barely paid it any mind.

"She's getting full-time pay through this, right?" First said. A demand, not a question.

"Of course," Loritt said. "With the payday we just landed, I can pay you all for cycles. I take care of my people first, First."

"Can I talk to her?"

"She's sedated. As I understand it, forced molts are not a pleasant experience for Ish."

Streaks of water erupted from First's eyes and ran down the human girl's face, a sign Loritt had come to recognize as emotional distress in her race. First held out a small box.

"I brought her some cured fish, for when she's sick of hospital food. The Ish deli said it's the finest on the station. I don't really know because it all smells like week-old buffet shrimp to me, but . . . will you see she gets it?"

Loritt took the care package in hand with reverence. "With your compliments."

First gripped the box of rancid fish for a rakim until she was sure her intention was understood, then let go and departed for the exit. Hashin, who had innocuously hidden himself on the other side of a nearby privacy screen, as was his habit, stepped into view.

"Such a remarkable species," Loritt said, staring down at the box First had left in his care. "So self-centered. Yet so selfless. Hell of a trick. I don't fully understand how they manage it."

"They fervently believe they're the center of everything," Hashin said. "But they're so willing to bring anyone who's shown them the slightest loyalty into their understanding of 'they,' that they forget where the center even is."

"Sounds like just the sort of people an Assembly of Sentient Species needs to keep itself glued together in the long term," Loritt said. "Wouldn't you agree?"

"It would be a first, that's for sure."

"Was that a pun?"

Hashin ignored the question. "You asked me to remind you when your appointment with Vitle was coming up. Well, it's in a larim."

Several parts of Loritt sighed heavily. "I don't suppose it can be postponed?"

"You've already pushed it back twice. He is *your* lawyer, you know."

"I know, I know." Loritt straightened one of his shirt cuffs. "But he's just so, so . . ."

"Cyborgs usually are," Hashin said, saving Loritt from saying it out loud. "But it's also why he's never forgotten a single line of statutes or precedent since law school."

"How long ago was that for him again?"

"A hundred and thirty cycles."

"You'd really think he'd have gotten a partnership by now," Loritt mused. "No matter. I should go and prepare."

"You mean get to Horloth's early and have three stiff drinks before he arrives?"

"Precisely."

Loritt arrived early and made good on his plan, ordering a drink for each primary hand, so as not to throw himself off balance. That would come naturally once they were empty. The waiter took his appetizer order, blue fern salad tossed in a light vinaigrette with live qalns, and left Loritt to lubricate himself.

Half a larim later, his lawyer rolled in exactly on time, quite literally in his case. He'd had high-torque electric servos and small-diameter synthetic rubber wheels installed in his three feet some decades earlier to "speed up the commute."

Loritt stood and offered his hand. "Prudanse, good of you to come—and punctual as always."

Prudanse Vitle shook Loritt's hand with carefully practiced and calibrated force. The first day with his biomechanical hands thirty cycles earlier, he'd accidentally gotten himself sued when he crushed all the bones in a prospective client's palm at the start of their consultation. He'd learned quickly from the experience. Vitle eyed the twin drinks on the table. One empty, one two-thirds of the way there.

"I see you decided to get a head start, Mr. Chessel."

"Just visiting an employee in the hospital. It's been a day." Loritt knew better than to offer Vitle a seat, as the cyborg preferred to just squat down and lock his knees in place, a trick made easier with three legs and artificial joints.

"Your people have an above-average rate of morbidity and mortality, did you know that?"

"We are blessed with the gift of being able to swap out parts," Loritt said. "Not really that different from yourself. Can I get you a drink? Wine? Something stronger?"

"I'm on the clock."

"A pliers for the stick, then?"

"Just a mineral spirits flush, please."

"Any vintage in particular?"

"Har. May we begin?"

Loritt sighed, then signaled the waiter. "A glass of your lightest paint thinner for my friend."

"Right away, sir." The waiter evaporated again. Loritt wasn't sure how he did it.

Loritt leaned back in his chair in defeat, then waved a hand in Vitle's direction. "Begin."

"Thank you. First, my retaining fee is a week overdue."

Loritt took another swig from his remaining drink. "Yes, it is, and I apologize for that. There was a temporary lapse in the company's revenue stream due to conditions beyond my control, of which you are only too well aware, as they relate directly to one of the cases you are, presumably, working on for me at this very moment."

"I mention it as a courtesy," Vitle said emotionlessly. "It is the firm's policy that work on accounts more than two weeks out of date are frozen until payment is made."

"Oh, don't give me that 'the firm' glot. It's you, a rotating unpaid paralegal intern, and an elderly Lividite secretary answering the links in your office."

"Yes. They're my firm."

Loritt's jaw tensed. "And a fine firm it is. We've just docked two cruise liners on contract worth almost half a billion credits each. Once they're auctioned off in a month or so, cash flow will not be an issue. So I'm asking you, as a favor, to float me your services until then. Consider it a loan from your firm to mine. You can even charge interest."

Vitle's face went blank, which most people would assume meant shock, but Loritt knew meant only that he was computing something.

"Twenty-five percent interest," the cyborg said after a pause.

"Twenty," Loritt countered.

"Compounding."

"Don't be an ass."

Vitle's face went slack for a moment again before, "The terms are acceptable."

"Good. May we continue?"

"There are two weighty matters we must discuss immediately," the cyborg started again. Loritt found himself staring at the eyes. They were synthetic, which was common enough. Nelihexu had the advantage over other species in that as they aged, they could always cycle in new organic parts. He was on his third set of eyes himself. All that was lost was another tiny slice of their ever-evolving soul.

Cyborgs felt different, somehow. Jrill had synthetic eyes as part of the standard kit the Turemok military had outfitted her with after basic training. But Loritt could still tell Jrill was a Turemok just by looking at her. So much of Vitle had been replaced with machinery, Loritt had no idea what species the man had started life as. Did he have three legs at birth, or was that a design concession? Somewhere, he'd rolled straight across a line, probably without even recognizing it was even there.

Was it bigotry to think so?

"Mr. Chessel, did you hear me?"

Loritt shook his head clear and refocused on the task at hand. "I apologize again, old friend. There's been a lot on my mind, and I don't have that enviable internal filing system of yours."

Vitle grimaced as if the act of rewinding his monologue was physically discomforting, then began again. "I was saying, the matter of the sex trafficking investigation surrounding the *Pay to Prey* has attracted significant attention, especially in the local media. There's really no chance we can avoid a deposition at this point. You'll have to answer why you didn't immediately report the matter to station security."

"Oh, heavens." Loritt leaned back in his chair as if he'd been physically struck. "Is that what people are saying? No, no, that's not right at all. As soon as the *Prey* was tied off and I was briefed by my people of the dreadful situation they'd uncovered on board, I, ever the conscientious citizen, delegated one of them to make a full report to security while we arranged temporary housing for those poor, exploited souls."

Vitle stared back at him like a jaded student taking notes. "That's what you're going with?"

"Of course. It's the least we could do for them."

"Right. And so what happened to this 'report' you ordered submitted to station security?"

Loritt held his hands open in concession. "Regrettably, with the swell of activity and emotions surrounding the discovery and resettlement of the *Prey*'s victims, the subordinate assigned to file the report . . . neglected to. An honest and understandable lapse, given the circumstances. Nevertheless, they have been appropriately and adequately disciplined for the oversight."

"And the identity of this neglectful employee?"

Loritt clasped his hands. "I'm afraid that's an internal company matter and, due to confidentiality concerns, isn't something we're willing to divulge to the courts at this time."

"You're not giving me a whole lot to work with here."

"Which is why I'm paying you a whole lot to work with it."

"You *promise* to pay."

"A promise costing me 20 percent interest."

"Compounded."

"Fine!" Loritt said just a little louder than he intended. He waved at a nearby table, then cleared his throats. "That's fine, if you can make it work."

The waiter, sensing a pause in the conversation/confrontation, appeared out of the ether to deliver Vitle's glass of mineral spirits and Loritt's salad.

"Are we ready to order, gentlemen?"

"Let us finish this round, Alconz," Loritt said without breaking eye contact with his lawyer.

"Very good, sir." *Poof,* gone.

They both took long swills from their glasses.

Loritt continued. "Really, Prudanse, I don't know how you drink that stuff."

"It keeps my joint seals from drying out."

Loritt raised his glass in toast. "To your seals' good health, then. Now, what was the second 'weighty matter' we need to discuss?"

"The unwitting doormat your newest piece of office sculpture pressed into the floor of their previous apartment."

"Ah yes," Loritt swallowed the last remnants of his second drink. "That nasty business."

"'Nasty' doesn't quite encompass the totality of that episode," Vitle said. "I reviewed the crime scene holos. I've seen industrial waste compactors with more finesse."

Loritt pressed his palms into the white linen tablecloth. "It's really very simple, my good chum. A misguided youth broke into the victim's apartment and—unknowingly, I'm sure—endeavored to leave their gang tags on what turned out to be a Grenic caught in midstep, who naturally toppled over under the sudden imbalance." He held his hands up to the ceiling in consternation. "It only follows."

Vitle crossed his arms. "And which Junktion gang's motto begins with WATCH YOUR BA?"

Loritt shrugged. "I'm sure I wouldn't know. You'd have to ask around in the underworld, which we both know I have no connections to or familiarity with."

"Naturally," the cyborg said flatly. "Lawyer-client-privilege time, Loritt."

"Oh, we're at Loritt now?" The Nelihexu perked up in his seat. "This should be fun. It's been a long time since you called me by my unified name."

"Only out of respect and confidence. The human girl shacking up with the Grenic? Nobody rooms with a Grenic."

"First does," Loritt said, not intending to sound so defensive, but oddly not sorry that he had, either.

"Yes, Firstname Lastname. I've read her immigration documents. What's her real name?"

"That is her real name as far as the Assembly bureaucracy is concerned. Her papers are in order, and that's good enough for me."

"Loritt," Vitle said politely, but with the authority of his profession. "I cannot protect you from lines of attack I've not been briefed on. Rumors about this human girl have swirled enough to reach even my audio receptors. There are still only a handful of them on the station. They defeated the Turemok flat out at their own game only five cycles earlier in a galaxy that has been trapped under Turemok talons for a millennium. They're virtually celebrities, wherever they are. Their comings and goings don't go unnoticed or unreported. So I'll ask again, as your lawyer, who's the girl?"

"A technical consultant," Loritt said reflexively. "She's been advising me on security vulnerabilities. She came highly recommended."

"Doubtless from the underworld you have no connections to or familiarity with," Vitle fed Loritt's words back to him.

"Doubtless."

Vitle sighed and pushed away from the table, rolling to a stop in the walkway. "Fine, keep your secrets. It'll cost you extra in the end, billed from me if you're lucky. From the judge if you're not. They're going to want to interview her. There's nothing I can do to prevent that, so get her prepared. Two weeks is your extension, compounded interest. Oh, and you're buying my drink."

"I assumed that as a given, between friends," Loritt said. "It was my turn, after all."

"It's always your turn. Bit of advice: find a hole to throw that girl down for a couple of months until this blows over." Vitle bowed the bare minimum decorum would permit, then spun around on three heels and rolled out of sight just as the waiter returned.

"Just one for dinner after all, sir?"

"Actually, Alconz, I think I'll just take the bill."

"Very good, sir." As the waiter disappeared again, Loritt swirled the dregs of his second drink.

"Trouble with the little missus?" a voice as familiar as it was unwelcome came from the table behind him. He turned around to confront the interloper.

"Soolie." Loritt exhaled the name like someone trying not to breathe in a foul odor. "I didn't see you come in. In fact, I could've sworn you were disinvited from the guest list at this establishment."

"What can I say?" Soolie shrugged. "You don't have to jump the velvet rope when you can just walk under it. Sounds like you've got quite the problem brewing in the ranks. That human girl again. Always seems to come back to her, doesn't it?"

"Purely coincidence in this case. Some poor fool thought to take a crack at her Grenic roommate and ended up donating blood to the carpet."

"Hmm, tough to kill, those Grenic. You gotta know the fault lines. Then, they cleave like a gemstone. Anyway, I hope your little human pet holds up under questioning by security. Sure would be a shame if something explosive came out under pressure."

"Thanks for your concern, Soolie. This place suddenly feels a little claustrophobic for me." Loritt stood up from his seat and looked down at the mobster. "It's more your size, I think. Good night."

Alconz caught Loritt just as he reached the door. "Sir, your bill."

"Of course. I'm sorry. I'm in a rush. Please put it on my tab and I'll settle up at the end of the week." He nodded to Soolie the Fin. "And if that Umulat seated behind my table is still here in a quarter of a larim, have the doorman throw him out on the street by the dew-laps."

"The front or the back door, sir?"

"One and then the other."

In moments, Loritt was safely ensconced inside his Proteus, alone with his thoughts. Chief among them was First and why he'd held back on what he knew about her, even to a trusted ally. Then defended her again from a longtime enemy. She'd gotten to him somehow. He felt . . . protective toward her. Almost paternalistic. Which was insane. He'd known her for less than two standard months. And yet, he knew *she* would do it for him . . .

"Hell of a trick," Loritt said as he pulled out of the parking hangar.

CHAPTER 16

Bruised and running on an empty tank, First was two-thirds of the way to her old apartment when it finally dawned on her that she'd been relocated to new digs before their last job. Between the trip out to the Tekis Nebula, the week spent on the cruise, and the return trip, she hadn't set foot on Junktion in almost three weeks and fell easily into old habits. She had to look up her new address on her handheld.

She hadn't even seen it yet. Movers had come to relocate what little in the way of possessions and furniture she and Quarried had out of the old place while she was away. She punched the address into one of the station's travel pods and sat down heavily as it climbed toward the interior. Artificial light broke through the pod's bay windows as it reached the inner surface of the station's drum. First was pleasantly surprised as the pod transitioned to tracks on the "ground" and headed for the same swanky high-rise district as Loritt's penthouse.

It finally whirred to a stop in front of one of the towers—not Loritt's building, but First could see it from there. So he meant to keep an eye on her. After the break-in, that was just fine with her.

To her genuine surprise, a doorman met her as she exited the pod. A humanoid with ashen skin and vestigial wings poking out the back of their jacket that made them look remarkably like a gargoyle.

"Ms. Lastname," they said. "We've been expecting you. My name is Fucor. Have you any luggage?"

"Um, yes. A small roller in the back."

"I'll have it sent up to your apartment. Your cohabitant has already settled in. I'll take your bag."

Fucor reached for the beach bag with her hacking deck slung over First's shoulder, but she tensed and pulled away. "Sorry, this one stays with me. No offense."

"None taken." Their wings fluttered. "We all have our little secrets, eh? Follow me; I'll show you to your residence. Welcome to your new home. We're glad to have you."

First tagged along as they entered the building's lobby, a soaring atrium six stories tall and clad in hammered copper. Exotic desert plants and shrubs occupied the spaces between the footpaths, while residents of several different flying species played some version of the popular sport of Gisk overhead. It was usually played in zero-g by members of all races, but the fliers apparently had their own version modified for gravity.

A Condrite dove headlong for the falling disk after a missed catch, snagged it with a foot, then effortlessly spun around his own center of gravity and shot the disk toward a teammate before spreading his wings to arrest his dive only a few meters from the floor.

"Wow," First said as the flier swooped low over their heads before pumping his wings hard to rejoin the scrum.

"Yes, they're quite aerobatic, aren't they?" Fucor said of the players, entering a glass elevator. "They organize a pickup game almost every night. We play host to an impressive diversity of species here. Yourself included."

"Let me guess, I'm your first."

"Human? No, we've accommodated three of your race. Although you are currently our only human inhabitant. Your Grenic roommate, on the other hand, is our first. We found out quickly only our cargo elevator could accommodate them. The floor of your apartment also had to undergo some considerable reinforcement."

"You've seriously never had a Grenic before?" First asked with genuine confusion. "They're one of the Council races, for crying out loud. They can't be foreigners here."

"Not at all," they said hurriedly. "There is a thriving Grenic community on Junktion. However, we're a mixed-occupancy tower, and our resident levels don't begin until the tenth floor. As a race, Grenic typically prefer to remain closer to the ground. Some say it's a shared cultural superstition. I say it's more likely an entirely reasonable fear of heights for a species that shares both the weight and reflexes of a boulder." Fucor paused. "I probably shouldn't tell you this, but some of the staff has already taken to calling you 'the Odd Couple.'"

First snorted as the elevator car accelerated past the fliers and their game. "I approve."

She left Fucor behind at the elevators. He bid her good night and produced a pair of cards from his coat pocket.

"The keys to your castle, Ms. Lastname," he said as the elevator doors closed.

Impossibly, her roller bag was already waiting outside her door by the time she found the right apartment number.

"How the hell did you manage that?" First asked no one as she ran her new card through the reader.

The door opened and took First's breath away. The space beyond was five, maybe six times larger than her old apartment, its ceilings half again as high, and already furnished with a blend of leather chairs for First and reinforced steel platforms for Quarried.

Their 2-D wall display had been superseded by a 3-D holographic projector mounted in the very center of the circular living room, theater-in-the-round style, playing back a trio of Grenic in one of Quarried's soap operas. The projection was so high-def and opaque, the only giveaway that her home wasn't full of an actual rubble of Grenic (a group of Grenic was called a *rubble,* because of course it was) was the barely perceptible shimmer on their outlines that none of the holo-projector manufacturers had ever figured out how to eliminate completely.

First didn't recognize any of the characters from the backside, so she moved around to the front to greet Quarried and get a look, but as she did, her heart jumped up into her throat.

Far from being remedied, the message engraved across Quarried's face, for lack of a better term, had not only been finished but refined. Where before the letters had been chiseled in like a message scrawled in a child's crayon, someone with a steady, unrushed hand had taken great care to straighten and deepen the letters with sharp angles and precise, beveled edges.

WATCH YOUR BACK, it taunted her.

First began to back away, intending to run for help, but a little blinking red light in Quarried's hand stopped her.

She had mail.

Hand quaking, First took up the recorder and pushed the button.

"Hello, First," Quarried's thundering bass voice rolled through the living room like a storm front. "Nice place, huh? How do you like my new tattoo? Figured it makes me look tough, now that I'm going to be a security guard with you. Are you excited? I am. Anyway, I brought you milk and cookies as a housewarming gift. They're in the kitchen. I hope you like it here as much as I do. And thank you."

First stared at the box and smiled so hard a pair of tears squeezed out of her eyes. Quarried had taken the threat someone carved into their flesh and sexed it up, made it their own to throw it back like a sling stone that had bounced off.

A hard one, her Grenic. First pushed the button to record a reply.

"Hello, Quarried. This place is amazing. I'm so glad you like it. I'm back from my trip now. I got to finish that season of *Rocks in Hard Places.* Still can't believe Polished in a River was the killer—did not see that coming. Your tattoo is badass. I approve. Thanks for the milk and cookies. I'm going to go enjoy them now. Welcome to our new home."

She slipped the recorder back into Quarried's hand and headed for the kitchen. Real wood cabinets, a huge refrigerator, an island cooking surface in the middle, and pots and pans of all sizes and shapes hanging from a rack suspended from the ceiling that would likely remain untouched until the next tenants moved in.

And sitting on the counter, she found a two-ish liter container of milk next to a plate of cookies. One glance at the milk confirmed it had sat in place for the majority of the two weeks she'd been away, as it was more than halfway to cottage cheese. A brief inspection of the cookies returned similar results. They'd started out as oatmeal, probably, but had dried into a substance sharing more attributes with Formica.

First could only laugh as she disposed of the ruined offerings. It was indeed the thought that counted. She found her bedroom, characterized by a bed complete with soft mattress and sheets instead of a Grenic-shaped depression worn into a heated concrete slab set in the floor, disrobed, slipped into her pajamas, and, gently on account of her ribs, slipped under her fluffy comforter.

She was asleep in twelve seconds flat.

The morning came courtesy of an alarm First hadn't set. Which, infuriatingly, also meant she had no idea how to turn it off.

She tried to bury her ears under pillows to drown it out, but the alarm took notice of the countermeasures she brought to bear against it and adapted, growing louder until it reached its original level even beneath her newly added layer of auditory insulation.

"The power of Christ compels you!" First impotently threw a pillow at the ceiling, hitting the fan and having no effect on the alarm, which continued to maddeningly push her to leave the warmth and comfort of the nest she'd made.

"Fine. Fine! You monster." First poured herself out of bed and spotted slippers by the door, which had apparently come with the apartment. Her feet were instantly happy, in direct contradiction to the rest of her.

Standing there, she felt a slight, familiar queasiness in her stomach. For her first month aboard, First had mistaken it for an intermittent illness, until she realized it matched up with Quarried speaking in their infrasound language. The alarm still chiming incessantly, First walked out of her bedroom and down the hall to find, sure enough, Quarried holding the small recorder up to their mouth, speaking a reply to her message from the previous evening. She wouldn't be able to listen for an hour or more. In the meantime, she could find wherever that damned alarm was coming from.

She found a wall-mounted user interface panel and touched it. "House, or Apartment, or whatever you're called."

"Yes, resident Lastname," came the building's VI. "How may I help?"

"First, call me First. Second, turn off that bloody alarm."

"I'm sorry, resident First, but the alarm did not originate from my system. It is only being amplified through my entertainment system speakers, for maximum coverage."

"How thoughtful of you. Mute the alarm on your entertainment system."

"I'm sorry, resident First, but I can't do that. The source is linked into my permissions and takes precedent."

"Who the hell authorized that?"

"You did, resident First."

"That's ridiculous," First said. "The only device I linked is my—" First stopped in midsentence and glared at her bedroom. "My handheld."

She retrieved the unit from her bag, and after digging through a few settings and download history, sure enough, there it was, inserted via a totally innocuous-looking software update.

The alarm fell silent as First purged it from her handheld. As soon as she did, a call automatically connected to Loritt's penthouse.

"You're up!" he said. "And so soon after midday. The bed is ergonomically agreeable to your sleep cycle, then?"

"Quite," First said into the screen. "The alarm, less so."

"Sorry, but we have a job. And the timeline is tight, so I couldn't afford to indulge your hibernation."

"Do I have time to wash my clothes?"

"Not really, no."

"Then don't complain about the wrinkles or sweat-and-stale-tanning-oil funk."

"Not a word."

"Fine, meet you at the penthouse."

Loritt brightened. "Actually, we've recently rented out a new space specifically for the business."

"Fancy."

"We're moving up in the underworld," Loritt quipped. "I'm sending you the address."

First got a message alert and opened it, then frowned. "This is in my building."

"Is it? What a coincidence. But that will make Quarried's commute quite a bit easier, I should think."

"Uh-huh. I'll be down in a half."

"Half an hour or half a larim?"

"Whichever's longer." First cut the connection.

Thirty-six minutes later, First found herself standing in front of a darkened office space on her tower's eighth floor. The suite number was correct, but no one was home. Nor were the windows just set to opaque. Light from the hallway spilled through to illuminate the tiled floor beyond, an empty reception desk, and partition walls in ghostly outlines.

"Sorry I'm late." Loritt's voice startled First from her survey.

"You scared me."

"It's still that easy?" Loritt passed a card through the door. "Anyway, welcome to our new office."

The door slid open, the overhead lights answering a moment later. Two things became immediately apparent to First from the dust and detritus strewn about the space: whomever had occupied it last had left in a hurry, and it had sat empty for quite a long time.

Loritt stepped through and retrieved the card from the other side of the doorframe, then handed it off to First. "That's your copy. Keep it close."

"Can't I just merge it with my room card?"

"And give a lucky pickpocket a two-for-one? Absolutely not."

First nodded approval. "Someday, you're going to tell me where you got so street-smart."

"Am I? Anyway, the job is simple. Clean this place up and get our various networks integrated. We've been wasting effort not having a central operational hub. It's time we stop duplicating work and bring everything together."

"Here? Now?" First asked, then pointed at the floor and a dark stain and a white powder silhouette in the shape of a Turemok in obvious discomfort. "And is that a chalk outline?"

Loritt waved a hand dismissively. "The leasing agent assured me it's childish graffiti."

"And you believe them?" First said. "That looks like dried blood."

"I believe the steep discount on the first six months' rent we were granted was part of the leasing agreement," Loritt said. "Regardless, that was the end of someone else's story. This is the beginning of ours. Aren't you excited?"

"Sick with anticipation," First responded with calculated ambiguity.

"Excellent!" Loritt stepped behind the reception desk and pulled the chair out from the divots worn into the underlying masonry and offered it to her. "I trust you'll have us up and running by week's end, then?"

"Me?" First blurted out. "I thought you said 'we' had a job."

"And 'we' do as a team, in the collective sense. However . . ." Loritt began to count off on his fingers. "Sheer is currently in the hospital being prematurely cracked out of her shell with hammers, Jrill is providing security for our recovered assets still awaiting auction, Hashin is quite occupied coordinating . . . things, and Fenax doesn't have hands. So that leaves you, our most junior member."

"I would remind you," First interjected, "that by seniority, Quarried Themselves is our most junior member."

"That is true," Loritt allowed. "But if I relied on them to complete the job, I could reasonably expect it to be finished some months after the heat death of the universe."

"What about you?" First demanded. "Why can't you do it?"

Loritt smiled and rested a gentle hand on First's shoulder. "Oh, little one, I love you all the more that you would even dare to ask. So two days, then?"

First looked around the ruined space. "Two weeks."

"Six days."

"Four!"

"Deal," Loritt said. "Should've said five; that was my breaking point."

"Five!"

Loritt smiled. "You know it's too late."

"You fucking suck," First barked.

"*Karking* suck, little one. You're not in Kansas anymore."

"I've never been to Kansas."

"Who has?" Loritt ran a finger over the reception desk and ground away the dust that followed. "I recognize this work is beneath you, but it's beneath all of us, and literally everyone else either has something more important to do in this moment or is physically incapable of doing it. We're in a credit pinch until the *Monarch* and *Matron* sell at auction, but neither can we afford to keep presenting to the rest of the galaxy as a company running out of my apartment if we're to be taken seriously beyond Junktion's sphere of influence."

Loritt leaned hard against the creaking wood of the abandoned reception desk. "I'm sorry, First, but these are the calls I have to make as the boss. It doesn't reflect on you or your position in our weird little family. It's only out of necessity."

"Five days," First held firm. "Full-time pay."

"Five days, and your full-time pay is already all going into the lovely apartment you are currently enjoying on my credits."

First's mouth opened, but before replying, her brain froze everything to run a rough calculation of exactly what that apartment must be costing him monthly. Her jaw promptly closed again.

"Good choice," Loritt said. "That wasn't a threat, by the way. You're ambitious. That's one reason I recruited you. Just a reminder you have a way to go yet."

First sat down in the receptionist's chair with a squeak. It didn't give her much in the way of bounce, obviously last calibrated for a being of greater mass than an eighteen-year-old human woman.

"How I get there matters," she said into the desktop.

"Does it? That's new." Loritt sat down in the seat opposite her with scarcely any more impact. He was lighter than he looked. Maybe the open space between his parts? "What troubles you?"

First spun around on her pedestal once, twice, before answering. "You roped me into this promising me we were going to hurt rich people. People who could afford it. People who hadn't earned it in the first place."

"As I remember, I roped you into this with a threat to turn you over to station security for stealing my Proteus."

"That was the stick; I'm talking about the carrot."

"I don't know what a 'carrot' is," Loritt said. "But I think I follow the metaphor. Please, continue."

First spun around again, only just then realizing her seat rose higher with each rotation. Still, she didn't feel like stopping. "We hit that Sulican, and he was kind of a dick, so that was cool. Then we took that human trafficker—sorry, I mean, um, I don't know what I mean, just that he was a real piece of shit. But then the Wolverines, they were just some confused kids from karking Michigan, for God's sake. They didn't know what their manager was up to."

"And you returned their tour bus to them," Loritt observed.

"By random chance. That's no excuse. Now the cruise ships? We ruined a lot of people's vacations. Normal people. I saw them, talked to a lot of them by the pool while I was working on my tan. Some of them saved up for years to go on that cruise, did you know that? It was the one luxury they'd planned for," First pleaded. "One lady—I think she was a lady—she did her whole thesis paper on the burgeron herd migration, had some really exciting ideas about their evolutionary process. She'd never gotten approved for a grant to study them in person, so she scrimped every penny or whatever for the chance to see them in person. Did we take that chance away from her? Do you even care?"

Loritt considered her for quite a while before answering. "I do, believe it or not. But we didn't take anything from them, her. The operators of the cruise line did, through mismanagement, graft, skimming overtime pay, laundering credits for shady people, or a hundred other shortcuts people take to the fortune their greed demands the universe owes them."

Loritt leaned back in his own chair as its disused joints popped and creaked with trickling dust. "We see it most often with new money. Young money, either inherited unexpectedly and spent foolishly, or earned unexpectedly and spent the same. In both cases, the recipients of the windfall come to believe very quickly that their newfound status is the result of an inalienable and divine right built into the very fabric of the universe."

He paused, spun his fingers, then continued. "Old money, the sort that survives for generations, doesn't operate on such assumptions. Not exactly. It still believes in the preordained strata of the universe, mind you, but it is more conservative, more cautious, more refined, and sets itself far apart from the sorts of risks new money takes. Which, on balance, only makes sense, as the creation of old money is removed from the kind of risks new money had to endure by many generations. And after a time, they tell themselves the comfortable lie that it had always been so. Your people have a phrase for it. Survivorship bias, is that right?"

First, rapt in attention, took a rakim to reply. "Sounds right."

Loritt put a hand on her wrist and squeezed. "People like us, First. We're allowed to come from nothing, work very hard, and knock on the doors of young money as a reminder and a warning to the upstarts and rebels among the rulers of the universe of the proper order of things. The owners of the banks who hold the billion-credit loans against the toys or hobbies of the already-rich employ us as Gomeltics to fight for table scraps from a *very* big table. But I believe we can do some good in the process, under their noses, as it were."

"Yeah?" First said bitterly. "What good have you done recently to balance out those scales?"

"I found a child on the verge of being lost to the sooty corridors of Junktion and gave her a position worthy of her natural talents."

First slumped back in her chair. "Fine, so I'm my own worst blind spot. I'm just not used to anyone else giving a damn about me."

Loritt laced his hands behind his head. "Four days, then?"

"Still five."

"Deal."

CHAPTER 17

Quarried was delivered to the office for their first work shift on the third day. By then, First had finished most of the physical cleaning and moved on to the real dirty work; setting up a computer network and merging half a dozen different databases and operating systems. It was like trying to get six people who'd never met, didn't speak the same language, and didn't know how to sing all harmonizing a song none of them had ever heard before.

Quarried cut an imposing figure arching over the office's front door. Not that First expected company—they wouldn't be open for two more days—but it was unexpected guests the Grenic was there to guard against, and anyone who did feel so motivated would almost certainly be aware of the jellied end that had befallen the last person to try.

Which was why First felt comfortable enough to push those concerns aside and focus on the pile of work still ahead of her. A pile which, paradoxically, only seemed to grow larger the more she shoveled it. The newest snag was integrating the *Goes Where I'm Towed*'s mainframe remotely between the office and its berth. It would be a simple matter to do over the local net, not so simple to do securely without running a dedicated hard line.

After wasting an hour trying to finagle permissions and modify scripts from a virtual desktop that kept crashing with an error code she'd never seen before, First threw in the towel and called Sheer. No one knew the *Towed*'s systems better than her chief engineer.

"Hello, First," Sheer said from her living room nest. She'd been discharged the day before to convalesce in the comfort of her own home.

First smiled broadly. "Sheer, how's the recovery going?"

"Shell's still a little squishy, but the legs and arms are mostly done hardening—the remaining ones, that is."

"How long will the missing leg take to grow back?"

"Three, four molts. Can't rush it. I lost half of one when I was just a little clicker. Wasn't so bad. What are you up to?"

"Cleaning stables. Listen, I'm trying to link the ship's computer with our new office up here, but my overlay keeps crashing."

"Yeah, I'm not surprised. *Towed*'s OS is patched together like a quilt. Getting that many aftermarket and custom components to work together was no small job, believe me."

"Can you log in and walk me through some of this? I'll send you the access codes to the office network."

Sheer's eyestalks bobbed in negation. "It'll be a lot easier at the source. I'll meet you at the ship in half a larim."

First's brow furrowed. "Are you sure you're up for that?"

"Told you I've got legs under me. I've been on nest rest since *Matron.* It'll do me good to get out of the apartment."

"All right, if you insist." First stood up from the IT desk. "I'll meet you down there in a half." The connection dropped. First locked down the network and shut everything off. She considered leaving a message for Quarried, but she'd be gone and back by the time the Grenic had a chance to listen through to the end, so instead she grabbed her jacket and closed the door behind her.

Making the docks from the interior in half a larim was a rush at the best of times, but it was the middle of most beings' workdays, and First found favorable tailwinds. She made it to their secure slip in the private docks with time to spare. From the bulkhead, she could just see Hashin pushing something bulky on a cart. She called out in greeting, but he passed through the All-Seal before hearing her.

No matter; she'd either catch him inside or on his way out. First settled onto a bench and waited for Sheer to arrive. It wasn't a long wait.

"Sheer!" First stood and waved as her chitinous friend scuttled through the bulkhead. "You look . . . pink."

"The proteins in my carapace darken as they harden. Give it a few days. How can I help?"

First pointed to the All-Seal. "Step into my office, we have . . . oh, he's done already."

Hashin came back down the boarding ramp, minus his cargo. He noticed the two of them sitting on the bench and took a hard left for the door.

"Hashin!" First waved. "Hold up!"

He locked eyes with her and doubled his gait. "I'm busy."

First jogged to intercept him. "Sheer's out of her nest. Come say hi." She reached out and put a hand on his shoulder.

Instead of turning around, a hand snaked up and clamped down on First's wrist with stunning speed and pressure. Before she knew it, First spun around and landed flat on her back. Her side cried out in pain from the rib held together with glue, but she'd come up on the mean streets of PCB and knew how to keep her wits, even when caught flat-footed.

First focused through the fireflies buzzing across her vision and saw the foot coming down on her face just in time to duck out of the way. Instead, the foot caught her hair against the deck, costing her a clump as she jerked away from the blow.

Now, she was pissed.

First didn't know enough about Lividite anatomy to know where their vulnerable spots were, but she was sure as hell going to learn.

With both hands, she grabbed the foot with her hair still trapped underneath it and twisted hard. At the same time, she brought her right leg up to knock out Hashin's knee from behind. The combination sent him sprawling backward and to the right to avoid tearing the ligaments in his leg, which was suddenly being held at a very unusual angle.

The Lividite tried to stay upright on his remaining foot, but First brought her other leg up and swept it out from under him. She'd been in a scrap or two and knew two things about a street fight. They almost always ended up on the ground, and few people knew what to do once they landed on their backs.

The ground was the great equalizer. The ground gave you the chance to push away, escape, or jab an opportunistic thumb in an eye. Nobody liked a thumb in the eye. Not even aliens, provided they had them, and Lividites had two great big oval ones.

But even as First flipped and threw a leg over Hashin to take a superior position, his skin grew dark and slick with a viscous oil.

"What the fuck is wrong with you, Hashin?" First screamed at him.

"That's not Hashin!" Sheer shouted from the sidelines.

First looked over at Sheer, *What?* queued up on her lips, but it was cut short by a knee to her injured ribs. She doubled over and quickly found herself on the bottom of the scrum, except now her opponent was greased up like a pig at the McCoy Family Reunion.

First managed to kick away and get a ragged breath into her lungs, over the objection of her broken rib. The imposter Hashin tried to pull away, but First kicked his leg out from under him again, and they were back scrambling around on the floor like two pats of butter on a hot skillet.

Then a new voice appeared, and the whole calculus of the fight changed irrevocably.

"Why are Hashin and First fighting?" Jrill asked, surveying the fracas outside the *Goes Where I'm Towed* in confusion.

"That's not Hashin," Sheer said as she and Jrill watched First wrestle on the floor with the doppelgänger.

"So who's on First?" Jrill asked.

"Shut your goddamned beak and help me!" First shouted as she struggled with the Lividite. The imposter reversed and got the upper hand, pinning First to the deck.

Jrill reached down and grabbed the imposter by the shirt and lifted him bodily into the air, but he wiggled out of it and left Jrill holding the empty, oil-soaked garment. She took a swipe at him with her other hand, and her claws connected, leaving three deep gashes transversely across his shoulders as he scrambled to get away.

"Sheer, don't just sit there. Intercept!" Jrill shouted.

"Sorry, no strenuous activities. Doctor's orders," she said as the assailant slid past.

First got to her feet, then almost fell flat on her face again from the patch of oil the Lividite left behind. Jrill gave chase, but he already had a step on her and made it to the door before disappearing into the crowd.

"How'd you know it wasn't Hashin?" First asked Sheer as she stood there panting.

Sheer waved one of her chemical-sensing fan antennae. "Smelled wrong. Hashin uses a different brand of moisturizer."

"What the hell was that all about?" Jrill said between hard breaths once she returned to the slip.

"Whoever they were, they got on board the *Towed* somehow," First said.

"What did they take?"

"Nothing," First said. "They left something behind, though."

"What do you mean 'left something behind'?"

"I don't know, a crate or something."

Jrill and Sheer looked at each other and cursed in their respective tongues.

"What?" First asked. "What's wrong?"

"What does someone usually break into a place to leave behind?"

It took a moment for the answer to detonate in First's brain.

"Oh, that's bad."

"You think so?" Jrill pulled out her handheld and linked to Loritt. "Boss? Better come down to the ship. We have a big problem."

Half a larim later, First, Jrill, Sheer, Loritt, and Hashin—the *real* Hashin—stood over the package their uninvited guest had left next to the *Towed*'s reactor bulb shield casing.

"So," Loritt said. "How karked are we?"

Sheer put down her portable positron scanner and crossed her eyestalks. "Up the cloaca with a laser drill."

"That sounds . . . thorough," Hashin said.

"Oh, it is." She laid the scanner down flat on a nearby bench and fed its findings into an overhead diagnostic screen. "What we've got is a good old-fashioned chemical explosive wrapped around a copper cone, a shaped charge. About as primitive as you can get. But the jet of liquid metal it would create on detonation is more than hot and focused enough to burn right through our reactor's casing and pierce the core."

"And that's bad," First said.

"It's 'back half of the ship is reduced to molecules and the hard radiation renders this slip and three others in each direction unusable for a dozen cycles' bad."

First swallowed. "Shouldn't we be calling the bomb squad or something?"

"No," Loritt said. "This is personal. We're handling it in-house. Which is why now Sheer is going to share her brilliant plan for disarming it."

"Sorry, boss, but no." Sheer pointed at two blacked-out areas on the scan. "The explosive isn't the only primitive thing about it. There's no computer, no data ports, no wireless—it's completely analog. No way to hack into it, and these dark areas, they're coated with some sort of metamaterial that makes them opaque to even a positron scanner."

"What are they, do you think?"

"They're junction boxes for all the wires, probably battery boxes, too. Thing is, I can trace which wire goes to what right up until they enter those boxes. Then I have no idea what's coming out the other side, so I can't draw up a wiring diagram."

"So you can't know which wires are safe to cut to disarm it," Jrill said. "Dead simple, but dead clever, too."

"It's kind of beautiful," Sheer said. "From a purely engineering perspective."

"I'd admire the craftsmanship more if it weren't pointing a dagger at my ship's heart," Loritt said. "Can't we just remove it?"

Sheer's eyestalks bobbed. "Nope. The little piece of glot welded it to the deck, and these leads here look like grounding wires to me. If we cut it free, it knows it's not attached anymore and blows up."

"So what's the trigger?" Hashin asked. "If there's no wireless or radio antenna, then it can't be detonated by remote, right? So what will make it blow? A timer?"

Sheer pointed at a sensor near the edge of the device pressed against the reactor casing. "This looks like a gamma detector. Pretty sure it's meant to send a signal once the reactor powers up. We spool it up for departure, boom!"

"Insidious," Loritt said. "Even if you hadn't spotted our friend delivering it, whoever planted it has to know it'd be discovered before we got under way. This is a leash meant to keep us tethered to port and out of action."

"*Watch your back,*" First said. "Our mystery friends strike again."

"Not so much of a mystery," Loritt said. "Any idea who the Lividite imposter was?"

"He wiggled away before I could ask," Jrill said.

"How hard is it to follow a half-naked, oil-slicked Lividite through a crowd?" Hashin said.

"Have you seen all the weirdos on the promenade lately?" Jrill clapped back.

First snickered. "Define 'weirdos.'"

"Enough," Loritt said. "We can worry about the interloper after we've dealt with the bomb. Sheer, you really can't see any way to neutralize it?"

"Not without seeing the future, boss," Sheer said. "I'm sorry."

First rubbed her chin. "Seeing the future . . ."

Hashin perked up and turned his large almond eyes her way. "You have something?"

"No, well, maybe . . . actually, yes." First drew herself up. "I have a plan. It involves a sewer and some nets."

"So just like the rest of our plans lately," Jrill said.

"No time for haters," First called back as she raced out of the compartment, suddenly full of energy. "I'll be right back."

"Bilge," First called down the sewer tunnel, shining the light from her handheld to keep her bearings. She double-checked her location on the tunnel schematic. This was the place, provided Bilge hadn't moved on to happier hunting grounds.

"Bilge? Are you here? It's First. I could use a, um, tentacle."

An eyestalk popped out of the sludge. "Oh, greetings, First," the voice came from behind her. She turned to see the swirling mass of tentacles and teeth rise out of the water. "Are you hear to listen to that Welsbar piezo-electric?"

"Next time, I promise." She held up the four butterfly nets in her arms. "Right now, I need you to go on a hunt with me."

"What's our prey?"

"Timeflies."

Bilge's tentacles quivered. "Ha! I've been down here for cycles. Never caught a one. Annoying little bastards."

"You haven't." First held out a pair of nets. "And I haven't, either. But I think both of us together can. If we coordinate and come at them with a net from every direction at once, they'll be boxed in. No escape."

"Why bother?" Bilge said. "There's not enough meat on them to matter."

"I need them for . . . let's just say something else."

"I don't know. I'm pretty busy."

"What if I threw in a backstage pass to a Wolverines concert?"

Bilge's eyestalk bulged even more than usual. "*The* Wolverines, from Earth?"

"The one and only. I kinda know the lead singer."

Two tentacles reached out to snatch the nets out of First's outstretched hand. Not out of aggression but exuberance.

"Well, what are we waiting for?"

First smiled. "I thought you might say that."

First reappeared in the *Towed*'s engineering bay to four concerned faces, and Fenax, who still looked concerned.

"Where have you been?" Loritt demanded.

"And what's that smell?" Sheer added.

"I know where she's been," Jrill said, "and you don't want to know."

First stuck out her tongue, then set the little aquarium down on the maintenance table nearest to the bomb.

"Ladies and gentlemen, I give you"—First pulled the old shirt off the tank she'd been using to hide the contents, revealing its buzzing, bumbling inhabitants—"the Firstname Lastname Timefly Predictive Engine!"

"Oh no," Hashin said. "She's gone around the bend."

"We're all going to die," Jrill said.

"Wait, hear me out." First held up a hand to interrupt the growing pessimism. "These things' nervous systems exist a few rakims in the future, right? That's the only reason they're so hard to swat. So, when Sheer opens the bomb up and prepares to snip wires, if they all drop dead, we know whatever she's *about* to do sets it off and she can stop herself from doing it."

"That's genius," Fenax said, watching from the command cave.

"That's insane," Jrill said.

"They're usually the same thing," Loritt said. "Sheer? What do you think? It's your shell on the line."

"No." First shook her head. "It's my idea. I'm staying, too."

"You don't have to do that, First."

"Yes, I do."

Hashin stepped up. "Someone should assist Sheer. I'll do it."

"Oh, lord," Loritt said. "I can see where this is going. So are we all staying or . . ." Everyone raised a hand or claw. "Right. Fenax, you want off this bucket?"

"I'm comfortable up here, boss," the pilot said from their socket.

"All right, I guess we're doing this." Loritt leaned back against a bulkhead and waved a hand at the bomb. "Proceed."

It didn't take long for Sheer to remove the bomb's outer housing and get at its internals, almost like whoever'd built it was so confident in their cleverness that they wanted their victims to be able to marvel at their masterpiece with their own eyes.

Mistake number one, First thought.

Sheer set the last exterior panel aside. "All right, we're in. This bundle of wires here connects to the detonator; they're the ones I need to cut to disarm it. All I need is the sequence. So what now?"

"Pick a wire," First said. "Very clearly announce your intention to cut it. You have to believe in your mind you're going to cut it in just a rakim or two. Commit to it. Only stop if I say so."

"So there's no confusion?" Loritt asked. "What's the signal to stop?"

"I think *Stop!* is clear enough, don't you?"

"Fair."

"All on the same page?" Sheer asked. "Good. Hashin, please hold up the bundle and space the wires as far apart as you can so I don't snip two of them by accident."

Hashin nodded and obliged, splaying the bundle out as much as he could.

"Okay." Sheer's mouthparts twitched nervously. "I am cutting the yellow wire with white stripe in three, two, one . . ."

First watched the flies for any hint of change in their behavior, but nothing happened, so she stayed quiet.

Snip!

Everyone flinched as the click of Sheer's claws coming together echoed in the silent compartment. But they endured.

Jrill patted herself down. "Well, I don't feel exploded."

"Neither do I," Loritt agreed. "Continue."

"Cutting the green wire with gray stripe, in three, two, one . . ." Sheer announced.

Snip! Still no *boom!*

Hashin exhaled slowly. "Even if it doesn't explode, this is taking cycles off my life."

"Wait," Loritt said. "Did you actually take an anxiety-promoting pill?"

"Yeah, of course. Nervosin."

"Why would you do that?"

"I wanted to share in the moment with everyone."

"This isn't one of those moments sane people want to share in, Hashin."

"Anyway," Sheer said. "Cutting the orange wire, black stripe in three, two, one . . ."

Nada.

"Two wires left, red and a blue," Sheer said.

"Because of course they are," First said.

"What?"

"Nothing. Just pick one and let's go home."

Sheer adjusted her stance and brought her claw to bear on the blue wire.

"Cutting the blue wire in three, two—"

With shocking abruptness, all ten of the timeflies in First's little case dropped out of the air and hit the bottom with a synchronized *plop.*

"*Stop!*" First screamed at Sheer even as her pincer started to clip through the wire's insulating plastic. Sheer froze in place. "What should I do?"

"Nothing. Do nothing at all."

"Wait," Hashin said. "If she doesn't cut the wire, do the timeflies stay dead? Doesn't that violate causality?"

"I don't know and I don't care," First said. "Just don't cut it or we all go up like the Fourth of July."

"Like the what?" Sheer asked.

"Like fireworks! Big-ass fireworks!"

Slowly, gingerly, Sheer released her pincer from the wire and stepped back.

"Cut the red wire instead," First said. "Then the blue; that's your sequence."

Sheer followed her instructions. The bomb remained inert. It was officially disarmed.

Everyone sighed their relief, then started laughing and slapping each other on the back. Right up until Hashin noticed something and pointed at the "Predictive Engine."

"Uh, First?" he said. "Your tank . . ."

First looked at the case of timeflies, which had been lying motionless on the bottom, but were now flickering back and forth between dead and flying around the inside of the case, shuttering between the quantum states almost faster than her eye could track.

"Uh, what's going on?"

"It appears by Sheer not blowing us all up, you've trapped the timeflies in a localized temporal paradox."

"That sounds . . . bad," First said. "What do we do?"

Jrill stepped up. "Throw the case in a black hole, hope the singularity sorts it out, and never speak about this again."

"How far is the closest black hole?"

"Not even a day trip in high-space," Fenax said from the command cave.

"We have a winner," First said.

"What do we do about the bomb?" Sheer said.

"Chuck it in after the undead timeflies," Jrill said.

Loritt shook his head. "No. I'm tired of this nonsense. Sheer, can you rig a timer behind the gamma detector so we can dial in a detonation delay?"

Sheer rubbed the cutting edges of her pincer together in thought. "Should be able to, now that I know which wires do what. Yeah, I can do that."

"Good. Cut it loose, get it rigged up, and stick it in the cargo bay. I have a job for it."

CHAPTER 18

First looked across the transit pod to where Hashin sat preparing for the confrontation. She'd been in fights plenty of times. Three days earlier, in fact. But it had always been out of surprise or desperation.

She's never picked one before.

"I wish Quarried was with us."

"Don't think they'd fit in the pod," Hashin said without looking up from his handheld. "Besides, Grenic aren't known for being fleet of foot."

"We could put them on rollerblades or something."

"And push them around? Wouldn't they get motion sickness?"

"Can they? What would Grenic puke even look like?"

"Probably like a mining slurry."

First laughed. "Good one."

"Was it?" Hashin asked, slightly befuddled. "Anyway, Jrill just signaled she's in position. Remember, we only have to buy her an eighth larim. Once she's done, so are we. Don't let yourself get roped in emotionally. I signal, we break off and leave. Trigger word is *home.*"

"You won't have to tell me twice," First assured him. "I know these guys, at least a little, and nothing about them makes me want to spend even one more rakim in their company than absolutely necessary."

"One more thing. If they slip up and make any jokes about the bomb, play dumb like we haven't discovered it yet. If they know we know, this whole thing falls apart. You're down here to confront the Lividite who beat you up, nothing more."

"I remember the briefing."

"Good. And right on cue, here we are."

The pod rolled to a stop outside the docks and a different set of private slips more than a third of the way around the circumference of Junktion. The neighborhood was rougher, the rent lower, and the maintenance intervals longer. The insulation on the pipes overhead was cracked and yellowed. Water dripped slowly from fittings into dented buckets the hall rats collected it in before recycling it back into the black market for a few extra credits a week.

However, everyone was very well behaved, mostly on account that those who weren't had drastically higher odds of being folded in half and shoved into a station-keeping thruster propellant tank here than in the more civilized parts of the station.

The slips down here were "private" only in the sense the public avoided the area at all costs in the first place. Security, too, unless there was a murder.

First wasn't a stranger here, though. This was where, up until a little over a month earlier, she'd delivered stolen aircars to Soolie the Fin's toughs and where she'd gotten paid for the same. This gave their hare-brained scheme its only tenuous chance of success. First's face was familiar around these parts, if only in passing. Her presence wouldn't raise much comment or concern from the regulars. Not until she reached Soolie's territory, where her sudden reappearance would draw all sorts of attention.

But then, that was the entire point.

"Now, follow my lead," First said. "You're here to talk me down and drag me away from the fight."

"I also attended the briefing," Hashin said flatly. She could never quite tell if he was being sarcastic or not, unless he'd had his Humoric. Then he was a laugh a minute. Hashin fell into position a step behind her and to the left, guarding her weak side, but still in her peripheral vision in case he got jumped.

It was a bit of a walk to the slip Soolie's newly acquired intercept ship had taken residence in. The two transit pod terminals nearest to it had mysteriously gone offline in recent weeks, doubtlessly a precaution the gang had taken to make it just a little less convenient for the curious to find before they were themselves spotted and intercepted.

Her team wasn't sure about the ship's provenance; its chain of ownership documents were obvious forgeries if one knew how to look. Even more obvious was Soolie had acquired it in direct response to Loritt's crew breaking up his monopoly on the docks that had let him snag contract after contract without a fight. It was Fin's best chance of keeping pace and competing directly against them beyond Junktion space and, therefore, a very valuable asset to his organization.

"There it is." Hashin pointed to a converted light cargo ship. It was a wreck, all mismatched modules and peeling paint that barely looked like it should be relied upon to hold atmosphere. Where the *Pay to Prey* had been hideous in a way that felt menacing, and the *Goes Where I'm Towed* was deliberately bland to the point of tedium, this ship—they didn't even know its name—was just plain ugly.

Except for its reactor module and drive spikes. Those were brand new and so cutting edge, one almost bled just laying eyes on them. They looked like they'd just been unboxed from a shipping crate. A crate that doubtlessly had fallen off the back of a bulk transport somewhere. The apparent thinking was cabin air leaks wouldn't be a problem as long as you got there and back fast enough.

At the bulkhead separating the slip from the rest of the station, First spied a pair of familiar faces. She'd never learned their real names back when she was delivering cars to them. Black market types weren't big on them, so she'd just taken to calling them Bebop and Rocksteady in honor of a couple of boneheaded monster villains from some old show her dad was obsessed with when she was growing up.

"Tell Jrill to go in five, four, three . . ." First whispered to Hashin. "Yo! R&B!" she called out before they'd spotted her so they'd know she wasn't trying to sneak up on them. "I've got a bone to pick with one of your mates."

"First," Rocksteady opened his four arms wide in a greeting/threat display. "Haven't seen you down here in what, a month? Two?"

"Not since she jumped ship on us and started working for the competition," Bebop added coldly. Always right to business, he was.

"Yeah, that's right." First came to a stop a few paces away from them, out of lunging distance, but still close. "I'm working for a legit businessman now. Which is why I don't appreciate it when one of you dregs floats up to cause trouble for me."

Rocksteady pointed a digit at himself, then Bebop. "Us?" he asked with mock innocence. "We'd never dream of bothering you, First. You know that."

"Not you two. A Lividite." She stuck a thumb back at Hashin. "Looks remarkably like this guy here."

"First," Hashin put a hand on her shoulder. "I really think we should—"

This prompted the equivalent of a giggle from R&B. She swept it off contemptuously. "I'm working, Hashin. Well? You guys know the wiggly little Gray I'm talking about. Where is he?"

"You have a lot of gonads coming down here to pick a fight on our turf, defector," Bebop said.

"I'm a contractor, not a soldier, Beebs. And your friend had a lot of . . . whatever Lividites pack . . . coming up to where I work and tearing out a clump of my hair." She drew back her mop to show the small bald patch. "So did the dude who came to my apartment to scar up my roommate, except his gonads are two-dimensional now. Hope you guys weren't close."

That got a reaction, and not from who she'd expected.

"Watch how you speak of the dead or you'll get the chance to apologize to them personally," Rocksteady said.

"Oh." First took an ill-advised step forward. "So you *did* know him. Or her. Couldn't tell, really. There wasn't much left after my Grenic was done with them."

"Should have brought your Grenic, then, instead of a slippery-skin drug-sucker."

Hashin put up his hands. "I'm just here to mediate."

"Bang-up job you're doing," Bebop said with just the slightest emphasis on the first word. The two of them shared a knowing look.

First played into it. "What was that all about? You two an item now?"

Rocksteady stepped right up to her, bumping his torso plate against her upper chest.

"You're just flipping all the switches and levers today, huh, little human? Trying to figure out what does what like the first time you fumbled around boosting a car. Difference is, if you set off *my* alarm, your friend here will have to pay one of the street kids for a water bucket to pour you into."

"I'm not afraid of you, Rocky." First stared up at him, genuine rage burning in her eyes now. "I've made some powerful friends."

"They're not here. Run along now and find them."

"First." Hashin grabbed both her shoulders. "We should go *home.*"

"Your Gray is a smart one. You should listen to him."

First almost shook Hashin off again, but the inflection on *home* snapped her out of it. Jrill was done; they had to go, pronto. So instead, she took a step back and pointed a finger dead center at Rocksteady's mantle while playing up letting Hashin drag her away by her other arm.

"This isn't over. You tell the Fin to lay the kark off."

"Soolie will get the message, don't you worry." Rocksteady waved his two right arms away derisively.

First and Hashin turned around and headed back toward the pod terminal. She allowed one side of her lips to curl up. "Oh, he most certainly will."

Hashin pulled out his handheld and made the call. "Boss, we're clear. Begin phase two."

"With pleasure," Loritt said from his penthouse, relief washing over him as he cut the link with Hashin. He'd been worried ever since he'd realized he had to send First and Hashin into the Gomeltic's den alone. He would've preferred to send Jrill and Sheer along for muscle. But Sheer's exoskeleton was still hardening; she hadn't been medically cleared for action, not to mention she was down a leg. And Jrill was the only one of the team aside from Sheer who had any zero-gravity and vacuum training, so her role was also predetermined. That left Fenax, who was about as useful in a fight as a medium-sized kitchen appliance.

So First and Hashin it had to be. Thankfully, they'd delivered on their assignment without a hitch.

Loritt opened his home desktop with a wave of a hand. The holographic interface appeared over his breakfast table, awaiting his inputs. One icon was very familiar: the Conduit. The secure hotline set up by banks and lenders throughout the galaxy that let them move currencies across light-years, raise or lower interest rates, erase or call in debts, collapse economies, topple governments, and, most importantly to Loritt, send repossession contracts.

For obvious reasons, the system was the most secure in known space. It was not infallible, however. Especially if you didn't need to send a message through one of its widely scattered nodal stations. Especially if you had a genius-level hacker who found a loophole that would let you intentionally fail to piggyback a fake message on an outbound genuine one. A fake message that would bounce off the outgoing firewalls, leaving it floating around the local Conduit network like an orphaned piece of mail.

Then, all you had to do was change the date/time stamps and sender/receiver information and, provided whoever opened it didn't dig through the embedded edit history too deeply, you would have a message that looked like it had genuinely come through the Conduit from halfway across the galaxy without ever leaving Junktion.

With two full days of First's help, Loritt had such a message. With the press of a virtual button, he sent it to both himself and Soolie the Fin and started the clock.

He opened the common link he shared with the rest of his little Subassembly. "Okay, that's done it. Wait an eighth larim, then everyone double-time march down to the *Goes Where I'm Towed.* Remember, we're being watched. It has to be convincing."

A chorus of affirmations answered him, and Loritt couldn't help but feel a warm glow.

"Fin," Soolie's consigliere, Rirez, called down from the pool deck. "Hey, Fin, we've got a live one on the Conduit."

"I'm not getting out of the water for less than a quarter million credits."

"How about thirteen million?"

Soolie gasped, accidentally inhaling pool water in the process and sending himself into a coughing fit.

"Fin, you okay?" the gaunt Prex asked.

"Never mind that. Get me a towel!" Soolie swam to the nearest edge and dragged himself out of the water with his good arm and finished coughing out the water in his windpipe. He grabbed the proffered towel and started drying himself off.

"Always know where your towel is," Rirez said.

Soolie looked at him oddly. "What?"

Rirez shook himself. "Sorry, I don't know why I said that just now."

Soolie stared at him impatiently. "Well? Thirteen million? Go on."

"Right, repo contract just came in on a hundred and thirty million credits' worth of pleasure yacht."

"An open contract?"

"Sort of. The contract was sent to just us and Loritt's crew. None of the others."

Soolie threw his head back and cackled. "Word's getting out. We're back in the race. Where is this yacht?"

"Outbound from Junktion." Rirez consulted his tablet. "Left two larims ago, but it's still in intercept range."

"Oh, this is too perfect." Soolie absently rubbed his fin. "Loritt's pinned down in his slip, and we're the only other crew that knows about it. Like taking sweets from a hatchling. Get everyone down to the *Buzzmouth* and get it ready to cast off. We're going to go poach a contract."

"You coming, too, Fin?"

"Wouldn't miss it for a barrel of Ish caviar."

"But we can buy lots of barrels of Ish caviar with thirteen million credits."

"It's a figure of speech, Rirez. What's the matter with you today?"

Loritt sat on his couch sipping a lovely green Eperon, his windows playing a split screen of two different camera feeds: one from his private slip where the *Towed* was docked, and the other coming from a distributed array of hundreds of dust-grain-sized cameras Hashin had just spread around the slip of Soolie's new mystery ship.

Insidious little devices, each networked together, they all saw a tiny slice of the action, which was then bundled up and stitched together by powerful software to render a complete imaging of their surroundings. Some would get swept away, some would be defective, but with so many, there would be enough to keep filming until their nanoscale batteries ran out in a few days.

The scene they painted was beautiful. Members of Soolie's crew furiously prepping their new acquisition for launch, just as he'd planned. Loritt's appreciation for the masterpiece only grew as Soolie himself arrived in frame. The tiny cameras lacked audio capture, but a different set of software provided a lipreading service. That had not been a cheap purchase, but as subtitles rolled across the display below whomever was speaking, along with a percentage score of the program's confidence of accuracy, Loritt felt the expense had been justified.

We ready to launch? Soolie said.

Almost, Fin, his consigliere answered. *We just need to load up the last of the emergency provisions.*

What provisions?

Food, water, medical suppl—

Forget 'em. We're only going to be gone for six karking hours.

But no ship is supposed to—

I said forget 'em! We're wasting time, and the asset gets farther away with every rakim. Where's Loritt's crew?

The consigliere held up a tablet. Remarkably, Loritt's tiny cameras had enough resolution to clearly make out what was on the screen: a feed from the *Towed*'s private slip.

They're just boarding now.

Excellent. I can't wait to see their faces as they walk off.

What if they don't notice it in time?

Soolie laughed. *Then they deserve to blow up.*

Loritt smiled thinly. "Thanks for clearing my conscience, old friend." He'd assumed Soolie's gang had his ship under surveillance, either electronically or through good old eyeballs. It's why he'd had his people run a mock checklist and board the *Towed* in the first place. If they didn't, Soolie would want to know why they weren't racing off to collect the payday.

But he hadn't expected to get a recording of the actual feed coming from Soolie's own spy camera. With it, they could trace back the viewing angle and find the camera. Today just kept getting sweeter. But the real fireworks were yet to come.

"C'mon, let's gooooo!" Soolie shouted from his captain's chair. It was very nice, upholstered in Terekite suede and mounted on a telescoping base that put him head and shoulders above the rest of the seats in the command cave. His people, still acclimating to the demands of spacemanship, struggled to oblige his order, but eventually, the *Buzzmouth* was warmed up and falling out of its slip.

"Make one lap around the station," Soolie said. "And make sure we pass right over Bay Ninety-Four. I want those losers on Loritt's crew to know who the winning team is."

"Yes, sir," his four-armed helmsman said, although he barely rated the title. The *Buzzmouth*'s nav systems were almost entirely automated. Just plugging in destinations and working the throttle didn't require a great deal of technical aptitude.

The ship shook and shuddered unnervingly beneath them as power was added to the drive spikes. His people shared brief, panicked glances.

"Nothing to worry about," Soolie said through the tremors. "She's just settling in is all. Like a new house." The placation worked only because all of his employees had grown up on a space station and none had ever seen a house, much less a new one.

Two-thirds of an orbit later, they all hooted, hollered, and displayed obscene gestures from half a dozen different cultures as they passed by the stricken *Goes Where I'm Towed*. Of course, none of their taunts would carry through the vacuum of space, but it was the thought that counted.

"Set course for the high-space portal, then full speed ahead to the rendezvous point," Soolie said, feeling like a genuine space captain. He could get used to it. Half a larim later, they were cruising through high-space, still shaking a bit but making incredible time.

"Wish I could see that stupid girl's face now," the helmsman said to his buddy, whose name Soolie had never bothered to learn, either. "Bet it's even better than earlier today when we bounced her off."

Soolie's interest piqued, and he lifted his head off his hand. "What stupid girl?"

"The human girl, First. She came by the slip earlier to start some glot, but we scared her off good."

"First was at the slip *today*?" Soolie said with rising concern. "How long ago?"

"I don't know, a larim and a half ago?"

"And she confronted you?"

"Yeah."

"While you were supposed to be watching the ship?"

"Yeah."

Soolie rubbed his neck. "What did she say?"

"She said, and I'm quoting her, boss, so excuse the cursing, 'You tell Fin to lay the kark off.'"

Soolie leaned forward and drummed the fingers of his good hand against his fin. "And it didn't occur to you to share this information with your boss?"

"She was just hot about Hilix, rest her bones, carving up her roommate. We took care of it, boss."

Soolie leaned back in his chair again. "Well, I guess that's all right, then." Still, he couldn't quite shake the nagging feeling he was missing something.

Three rakims later and forty spans below where Soolie sat, an egg timer dinged inside the crate Jrill had welded to the aft end of the *Buzzmouth* under Sheer's remote direction while First and Hashin distracted the guards.

This, in turn, closed a simple electrical circuit and sent power from a nearby battery into a small primer charge. This, in turn, ignited several kilos of chemical explosives, which deformed and liquified a copper cone, sending a jet of white-hot metal into the impulse regulator at the aft of the ship, which controlled the flow of power from the *Buzzmouth*'s reactor to its twin drive cones. This, in turn, cut off all the power pouring into the drive cones and sent a backwash of energy through the system, tripping breakers and burning out relays as it raced back toward the reactor like a tsunami.

The reactor's safeguards saw the impending disaster coming and scrambled to divert the torrent of power. They were, mostly, successful. But in so doing, the overload instead wreaked havoc on several secondary systems, including communications, gravity plating, and internal lights.

Floating in the green of emergency gel lights amid a cacophony of alarms and damage reports, Rirez cleared his throat.

"Fin, I think they might have found the bomb after all."

"Oh, really, genius?" Soolie exploded. "You don't karking say!"

"Sheer," Loritt said into the team link. "I couldn't help but notice when I was making breakfast this morning that my egg timer is missing."

"Yeah," Sheer said. "Sorry about that, boss, but you said you needed a timer, and all the stores were closed."

"And you didn't have one to donate?"

"Ish prefer our eggs raw, boss."

"Of course."

The flight plan Soolie had logged with Space Traffic Control had been less than honest, so even if anyone had known they were overdue, no one would know where to look for them.

No one except Loritt, who'd fed them the fake flight plan of the nonexistent yacht they were chasing after in the first place.

Loritt gave Soolie and his crew a couple of days to stew in their own juices before launching a "rescue" mission. By the time the *Goes Where I'm Towed* arrived to parlay, the situation on board the *Buzzmouth* had grown feral. Two mutineers had already been killed. One had been eaten.

Loritt's ultimatum was as straightforward as it was merciless. He'd brought a shiny new impulse regulator to replace the one Soolie's own bomb had destroyed. Loritt would hand it over, totally free of charge, even have his people install it, provided the *Buzzmouth* set course for a new port and never returned to Junktion again. Or they could float in high-space until they all killed each other, asphyxiated, or froze to death.

There was no option C.

Even without anything to bargain with, Soolie demanded the regulator plus enough emergency food and water rations to make the two-month trip without starving, to cover for his own ineptitude and lack of adequate preparation. But Loritt was in a festive and generous mood.

"I'm glad we could come to a mutually beneficial arrangement like the gentlemen we are," Loritt said through navigation light pulses, on account of the *Buzzmouth*'s coms system still being disabled.

"Kark you, trash heap," Soolie's lights answered.

Loritt smiled and turned to Jrill. "Arrange the repairs and supply delivery."

"Yes, boss."

"And, Jrill"—he caught her forearm—"if they give you even a whiff of trouble, drill through their hull and vent the atmosphere. This is their very last chance to learn how to play nice."

"That's cold, boss." Jrill looked him over. "I approve."

When the *Towed* dropped anchor in Bay Ninety-Four, Loritt's crew came streaming out of her like conquering heroes. Loritt led the procession down the All-Seal, followed by Jrill, then Hashin, then Sheer with Fenax's tank perched on top of her carapace, and First coming last, dancing and twirling like someone who'd just given a terrible ex-boss the send-off they so richly deserved.

Then they all got in a couple of transit pods, found the nearest microbrewery, and proceeded to drink themselves into a new dimension even string theory hadn't predicted.

By the time First sobered up again, she was already on a new assignment.

CHAPTER 19

First cracked open the cockpit of the simulator and removed the breathing mask.

"I've been in here for six hours," she complained. "Is this really necessary?"

"You were too shallow in your entry vector on that last run by 0.8 degrees," Fenax said. "So apparently yes, it remains necessary."

"I rounded up," First said.

"This isn't like calculating the tip on a bar tab, First. At the speeds these sling-racers move, being shallow by 0.8 degrees means you missed the target window by thousands of ship lengths. You don't have enough time or thruster propellant to make that kind of course correction."

First's head rolled back against the seat rest. "I thought you said these things were all engine."

"They are. They're stripped down to the last molecule to be as light as possible. They're basically just a seat glued to a miniaturized reactor, drive spike, and a couple of thruster quadrants wrapped in a paper-thin fairing to keep the solar radiation out. But that means their propellant tanks are also tiny, just enough fuel and reactant mass to last the duration of the race course, a thimble of emergency reserve, and not a drop more."

"So why am I stealing one again?"

"Because they're custom-built for decadent thrill-seekers and cost five to ten million credits apiece, and this particular one is owned by Loritt's former boss, who still owes him money. Honestly, I think he'd take a loss to repossess this asset."

"Ah," First said. "Now *that's* a motivation I understand. But why don't we just stick you in the cockpit? You're far and away the most experienced pilot we have."

Fenax waggled their ganglia. "Because there's no automation, no interface. It's just the manual controls and the handful of flight instrumentation you see in the simulator. There's nothing to plug me into, and I don't have the hands for stick-and-pedal flying even if I wanted to, which frankly I don't. Way too primitive. Neither Jrill nor Sheer will fit in the cockpit, and Hashin and Loritt are working another job. So it's you and me, and you're flying."

"All right, all right, I get it." First closed the cockpit canopy and gave the thumbs-up to start yet another simulation.

The closest Class One Sling Racing made it to Junktion was the Percolete system, almost a month away through high-space, even on the fastest, most expensive commercial liner. The *Towed* was marginally faster than that, but it was otherwise engaged.

With only First and Fenax aboard, there wasn't much to do in those weeks except stream shows, work out, and perfect her sling piloting in the simulator, which they'd moved into the cargo bay before departure. Loritt had apparently bought it outright, which would probably come in handy down the road. The workouts weren't just to pass the time, either. The slings had no counter-grav systems on board, another mass-conserving measure. Pilots felt every g during turns and burns. The simulator had a built-in gravity generator to mimic the effects, but it was capped off at six g's for safety reasons. Still, First often peeled herself out of the cockpit with fresh bruises from the crash webbing and seat. But at least her ribs had time to heal completely.

Race day bordered on a planetary holiday for almost every system lucky enough to be selected for a stage on the circuit. Local space traffic was suspended for everything except the racers, their chase slips, emergency responders, and the press covering the event. If you hadn't landed by the day before, you waited it out in a parking orbit.

Where there wasn't an inhabited body or station, asteroids were diverted from their natural orbits to serve as observation points for every turn, sling, and course adjustment. Sometimes these temporary abodes were paid for by the dominant governmental body of the host system, more often by enterprising individuals who charged outrageous sums for admission to a hastily constructed facility that would be relevant for no more than a single larim of a single orbit before being evacuated and abandoned.

And yet still people paid with gratitude. Some of the wealthiest sling-racer aficionados even chartered private high-space transports between the various observation posts so they could watch every turn, slingshot, and burn of a given race in real time.

Which, as it happened, was how the *Goes Where I'm Towed* acquired credentials for the event.

"I'm not taxiing one more load of these entitled karking debutants to another warmed-over glot-rock," Fenax announced on their *final* final approach to Percolete Prime. "I don't care what they're paying per seat. We're officially closed for business."

"What you do between now and the rendezvous is your business, Fenax," First said as she stuffed her racing suit and helmet into her overnight bag. "Just so long as you get this crate in position to crack open a high-space portal and grab me after turn two."

"Count on it."

"You haven't failed me yet."

"I suppose not. Are you ready?"

First laughed. "To infiltrate an elite group of the galaxy's best sling-racers based on nothing but bravado and good looks? No, not really."

"That's why it's going to work," Fenax said.

"How do you figure that?"

"Because it's so stupid that no one will believe you were attempting it dishonestly."

First's shoulders went slack. "I really wish that wasn't a perfect description of most of our plans. People will catch on. It won't work forever."

"Just needs to work today, then we'll think of something else." Fenax opened the inner door to the All-Seal. "Good luck."

First stepped out of a side passage and blended into the small cadre of a few dozen paying aliens the *Towed* had ferried to the geosynchronous space elevator station above Percolete Prime playing host to the start line of this stage of the Class One tour. First quickly found herself drowned out among the crush of fans and hangers-on. The frenzied pace of the crowd was oddly comforting for her. It felt exactly like the promenade back on Junktion at rush hour.

The common areas were the easy part. Beyond them, where the media and race crews dominated in the handful of spaces on board carved out for them, would be far more difficult to navigate, despite being far less populated. Or perhaps because of. A huge, throbbing crowd offered a degree of anonymity First had grown to appreciate since leaving her parents and PCB behind. You never saw crowds like this on Earth's colony worlds; there just weren't enough people. Yet.

First spotted her exit on an overhead sign and peeled away from the crowds. Now, it was game time, but she was prepared. Her badge wasn't just a standard ticket but press credentials, which granted her access to a much wider range of areas, including the hangars. Provided nobody put it through too much scrutiny . . .

The hangars were just ahead now, behind a substantial security checkpoint.

"Deep breath," First admonished herself. "Smile. Make eye contact. Project confidence. You know the drill. Piece of cake." She fought back the sudden urge to riffle through her bag as the checkpoint drew closer. A knot of fans and enthusiasts crowded just outside the hangars, trying to get a glimpse of the racers or their machines.

First took charge and held her badge up, loudly proclaiming, "Press!" and "Media!" as she pushed through the onlookers, flashing the counterfeit credentials in the faces of particularly immovable patrons. She believed her, they believed, so why wouldn't the guards?

With some considerable effort, First pushed and shoved herself to the other side of the mob and gazed at the guards on the other side of the barricades with pleading eyes. One of the bigger ones, a Turemok, waved her forward.

"Credentials," they said in a businesslike tone. First took the lanyard off her neck and handed the badge over. "Outlet?"

"Frequency Forty-Six, Junktion Station," First said with polished practice. "The Voice for the Void."

"I didn't need the tagline," the guard said. "Open up the bag."

First shrugged and unzipped her bag, then pulled it open to show the small cache of recording equipment they'd packed as part of her cover story, but the guard's hands dove past them and deeper into the bag.

"Hey," First objected. "That's sensitive recording equipment. Be careful with it or you're getting the replacement bill."

The Turemok yanked out her flight suit and helmet. "What's this, then?"

First drew herself up. A year earlier, she would've been terrified of being within a hundred meters of a Turemok, but after butting heads with Jrill for months, the fear had worn off. "It's my uniform, for the interviews and photo shoots in the pits. Put it down before you tear a hole in it with those clumsy claws."

The guard glared at her. "Arms out."

"Oh, come on; I was felt up enough by the crowd on the way in here."

"Arms. Out," they repeated. "Please."

"Well, since you said *please.*" First held out her arms and worked very hard not to shiver as the guard's hands passed down her sides, back, and inside her legs. It was professionally done, no lingering in inappropriate places or grabbing of sensitive areas. Still, First was glad she didn't have a weapon at hand.

"Satisfied?" she asked sweetly.

The guard took one more sideways glance at her credentials, then thrust them back at her chest and waved her through with a grunt. She pointedly didn't thank him for his time as she repacked her bag. Sure, his paranoia was entirely justified and not actually thorough enough, evidenced by the fact she'd gotten past him, but customer service was still a thing, wasn't it?

First zipped up her bag and pushed past the checkpoint in a calculated huff. She was a small-market media celebrity, after all, and her ego had been assailed by a flunky. Beyond the checkpoint, the crowd disappeared, replaced by frenetic mechanics scurrying for parts and tools, bloviating sling jockeys of a dozen species trash-talking each other, their fawning attendants of various genders falling on their every word, and the actual press struggling to capture a tenth of the mayhem swirling around them. The air was heavy with the smell of lubricants, cleaning solvents, and hydrazine.

First didn't care about any of it. She was fixated on a singular purpose: get inside her sling-racer and take legal possession of it. That was her goal. But there were still appearances to maintain, so she dug into her bag, pulled out a small drone camera rig, and activated it.

Four arms with tiny counter-grav units at their corners popped out of the palm-sized unit before it sprang into the air.

"Follow behind me to the left, record everything," First instructed it, then went looking for her quarry. She didn't know which berth her sling had been assigned to, and there didn't seem to be any guide signs. The race organizers weren't making the job any easier.

"Excuse me," she asked an Ish in coveralls streaked with black grease and bright red coolant stains. They looked like they were on break. "Can you tell me where Sigmalo Fullok's sling is?"

They chuffed. "Sticking your claws down the wrong hole if you're hoping to get an interview with Fullok, little . . ." Their eye-stalks scanned her from head to foot. "Sorry, but what are you, exactly?"

"Human," First said but was met with a blank stare. "From Earth?"

"Sorry, don't know that one."

"Earth. The planet the Assembly almost vaporized five years ago? We blew up the *Xecoron,* Turemok flagship? Killed the Kumer-Vel of the whole Turemok military?"

"Not clinking any shells. First I've heard of it." The Ish pointed a manipulator appendage deeper into the hangar. "Slip Thirty-Seven. But don't expect them to throw a party. More likely they throw you out."

"Why so hostile?" First asked. "I thought these people lived for the attention."

The Ish crossed their eyestalks. "Not this crew. They're real secretive. Won't even lend out tools with the other crews, from what I heard. But you didn't hear that from me."

First nodded. "Thanks for the tip."

"Anytime. You seem like a nice whatever-you-said-you-were."

"Human!" First called back as she restarted her trot down the flight line. Halfway to Slip Thirty-Seven, she spotted a set of multispecies bathrooms and headed for the door. "No," she said to the camera drone. "This you don't film. Stay right there and wait for me."

First could've sworn the drone sagged a little like a scolded puppy, but she ignored it as she ducked through the door and found a stall to change into her flight suit. She stuffed her clothes into the bag along with the decoy recording equipment, all of which would be left behind for lack of space in the cockpit.

She'd expense Loritt for them once she got back. But first, she had to get back.

First emerged in her new uniform with her helmet under her arm and her bag slung over her shoulder, then looked at her camera drone. "Okay, come along."

It perked right back up and resumed following her. First made it all of twenty meters before running headlong into a sculpted, muscular chest. She bounced off the purple-fabric-clad pectorals and looked up to apologize, but instead found herself staring into the face of a legend.

"You're . . ." First swallowed hard, trying to center her thoughts, which were suddenly swimming against industrial lubricant. "You're . . ."

"Maximus Tiberius. Captain." The Greek statue bowed with a flourish of his hands. "And it's okay. You're welcome."

"I . . . I am?"

"Absolutely," Maximus said.

"For what, precisely"

"For saving Earth, of course. That's what you were about to say. Don't deny it. I've seen that look thousands of times over the last few years. Nothing to be embarrassed about."

"Oh, right. Thank you?" First said, still fighting the current.

"It was nothing, really." Maximus inspected a cuticle. "The thanks really goes to my crew, who, under my leadership and guidance, found the will to win. Also the nuclear missiles—they helped."

First's eyes kept wandering off to the bright red sling sitting in the slip behind him. Its prow was sharp, like a knife cutting through space, while the rest of it was supple curves and flowing lines blending into one another like they'd never quite solidified. Maximus noticed her notice.

"I see you've spotted the *Rosa di Venezia*." Maximus turned and beamed at the magnificent sling. "She's the first human-built sling. Handmade by Italian eunuchs."

First's nose crinkled. "Why eunuchs?"

"I never asked. Probably makes them more streamlined so they can build faster. Less air resistance. I suppose you'll be wanting an interview, then?"

"I, ah . . . a what?"

Maximus pointed at the camera drone. "Interview? With the race pilots? You are a reporter, right?"

"Oh!" First's brain finally caught up. "Yes, of course." She stuck out a hand. "Clara Catskill, Frequency Forty-Six, Junktion. The Voice from the Void."

"Junktion, eh?" Maximus shook her hand a little too firmly. "Had a layover there—and a hangover. And some weird rash thing that Illcarion swore wasn't contagious . . ." He paused in thought. "You're pretty far from home, aren't you?"

"Junktion is my home now," First said, not inviting further questions.

"Fair enough. So what do Clara Catskill's viewers back on Junktion want to know?"

"What brings the hero of Earth all the way out to the Percolete system? That must have been a long haul."

"I first caught a glimpse of sling racing at an exhibition race in Wolcot. Back when I was still just a lieutenant in the AEU navy, I piloted remote combat drones for a couple of years and was a hot stick. I had quite a bit of leave built up over the years, and the last few were a doozy, so I took a leave of absence, lined up some sponsors, and came out here to shake some hands, kiss some babies, and give the rest of the galaxy a taste of what we earthlings can do."

First nodded and smiled along, trying to look like the talking bobbleheads she'd seen on the news when she was a kid. "It sounds so exciting."

"Oh, it is." Maximus hit her with a weaponized smile that almost twinkled at the corner.

"What's the best part of sling racing for you?"

"The moment right before the light turns amber; they don't do green for *go* out here. When you're sitting there on top of nothing but a nuclear reactor and a drive cone, sixty thousand horsepower tucked just a few centimeters under your seat, the promise of imminent, explosive action. That moment of anticipation isn't something you'll find in any other chair in the galaxy."

"That was beautiful. What's the worst part?"

"The catheter. Definitely the catheter."

"Ha!" First laughed for the camera. "When you're on the stick, is it true what they say, slow is fast?"

"What? No. Fast is fast. What a ridiculous saying."

"Are you going to take the checkered flag today?"

"Of course! If you don't go into battle expecting to win, why are you there?"

"Thank you, Captain Tiberius. I'll let you get back to your preparations."

"You're more than welcome. You know, for a second there with your flight suit, I thought you were a pilot."

"Oh, no, just getting into the spirit of the thing, you know?"

"Ha! Thank goodness."

First's head cocked to the side. "Why do you say that?"

"No offense, but slings are very dangerous. The hot seat isn't a safe place for a"—Maximus paused and mentally adjusted course—"a younger person like you. You understand, right?"

First simmered. "Oh, I think I understand perfectly."

"Excellent!" Maximus said, totally oblivious to the change in

"Clara's" disposition. "No hard feelings, then. Enjoy the race. And send me a copy of that clip when it's out of editing. I'd like to see it."

"See you at the finish line," First said, baring her teeth before storming off toward Slip Thirty-Seven. She pulled out her handheld and called the *Towed.* "Fenax, change of plans. Pickup point will be the far side of the race's finish line."

"What?" Fenax sounded as alarmed as she'd ever heard them. "Why there?"

"Because I'm doing the race."

"Oh, merciful winds below. How will I know which sling to grab?"

"Simple." Her eyes narrowed. "I'm going to be first."

"You're *already* First."

"Just do it." First cut the link and laid eyes on her new ride.

CHAPTER 20

Officer O'Chakum had gone to the trouble of printing off photos from the crime scenes on holographic paper so she could theatrically pull them from her folder and slap them down on the table, emphasizing a point or adding gravity to an already heavy question with each successive copy. They remained strewn across the tabletop as the deposition wore on into the late evening.

"Okay, let's start over from the beginning," O'Chakum said, splaying her gray fingers and pressing them onto the table. The Lividite had stamina, Loritt gave her that much.

"Must we?" Loritt said.

"I believe so, yes."

Loritt picked up his handheld to look at the time. "We've just entered the seventh larim of this 'interview.' I don't mind telling you that it's felt more like an interrogation for the last five of them. I *do* mind the fact my lawyer here is charging by the larim and is probably buying himself some new upgrades on the local net as we speak. No offense, Prudanse."

Vitle stared off at the ceiling while he virtually perused a new expandable memory module. "None taken."

O'Chakum pointed at Quarried Themselves looming behind the two of them. "We're getting a deposition from a Grenic. Did you really think we'd wrap it up in time for lunch?"

Loritt eyed Quarried for a moment as the Grenic carefully listened to the glacial playback of one of O'Chakum's endless questions.

"Point taken."

"You know we've finally identified the victim, right?" O'Chakum said.

Vitle stirred. "I object to that characterization. The victim is standing behind us, Officer."

"The deceased, then," she said. "Is that more agreeable?"

"It's more accurate," Vitle said. "Please continue."

O'Chakum scowled ever so slightly. "They were Sullican, a transient named Hilix. A known associate of Soolie the Fin. That name mean anything to you?"

"I'm familiar with him, although not socially," Loritt said. "He also runs a repossession business."

"So you're competitors, then."

"We're in the same business, but I'd hardly call him a competitor. Plenty of contracts to go around."

"Still, it probably wouldn't upset you to learn Soolie, most of his associates, and a ship registered to his company all went missing a little over a month ago, would it?"

Loritt leaned back, aghast. "How terrible! I assume a thorough search was conducted?"

"As thorough as can be expected with a falsified flight plan. You wouldn't know anything about their disappearance, I assume."

Loritt held out his secondary arms palms up and shrugged. "Wish I could help you, Officer."

"Oh, I think you may yet. Now, the Grenic's roommate, this human female." She looked at her notes. "Firstname Lastname. Really?" O'Chakum glared at Loritt. "It's scarcely possible to imagine a more blatantly fraudulent name."

"It was a data-entry error on her refugee application. She'd been repeatedly assured it would be straightened out."

"When?"

"Any day now."

"So what's her real name?"

Loritt rubbed his chin. "You know, I never got around to asking her."

"You have someone with falsified identity documents for an employee, and you never got around to asking her why?"

"Objection," Vitle said.

"It's not a cross-examination, counselor. You can't raise objections."

"You're conducting it eerily enough like one," Vitle bit back. "As my client already stated, the documents were not falsified; they were entered incorrectly, and efforts to correct them are ongoing. Further, Miss Lastname is not an employee but an outside consultant contracted to advise us on security issues."

"That's interesting," O'Chakum said. "What are her qualifications, exactly?"

"She came highly recommended," Loritt responded.

"A juvenile refugee on the station for six months running street cons and matching the description of a prolific aircar thief was highly recommended?"

Loritt leaned in and folded his hands. "Those are pretty good recommendations for a security expert. Wouldn't you agree?"

"Where is she?" O'Chakum asked. "I want to interview her about this . . . incident."

"I'm afraid Miss Lastname is on an assignment in the Percolete system."

"That's a month away!"

Loritt shared a knowing look with Vitle. "Yes, I suppose it is. And it'll be another month at the least before she returns."

"What's she doing way out there?"

"Behaving herself, I'm sure."

First swung the meter-long socket wrench like a Louisville Slugger. It connected with the side of the nearest pit crewman's knee with a pop and a shriek. Her plan had been to charm one of them into letting her do a behind-the-scenes shoot that would end with her sitting in the pilot's chair. But her encounter with Captain Tiberius had left her feeling cross, her charm fell apart after a few seconds, and she'd decided on a more direct plan of action.

"I *told* you grease monkeys once already!" she shouted above the cries of the crewman grasping his ruined knee, then adjusted her grip on the huge wrench. "This sling has been repossessed. I am the legal owner now, you're all trespassing, and I'm within my rights to whip you into a meringue if you get within five lengths of it."

This gave the pit crew pause, whether to size up their unexpected opponent or to ponder the meaning of *meringue,* First couldn't say. It was an inelegant solution, one Loritt would likely frown upon. But he wasn't here, and First was out of fucks for men's opinions today. Regardless of species.

"We're calling security," a random voice called out from the back of the scrum.

"Good!" First clapped back. "Saves me the trouble. Because as soon as they review my authorizations, you're all watching the race from a holding cell."

From behind them, a Nelihexu in an unzipped flight suit pushed through the mob of mechanics and came to a stop just outside the reach of First and her wrench. "What's all this, then?"

First nodded at him. "I expect you're Sigmalo Fullok."

"I am." He held out an open hand. "And that's my favorite wrench."

"Just borrowing it. Need to make a few adjustments."

Fullok pointed down at his injured mechanic. "To my employee's knee? Tools are used to fix things, stranger, not break them."

"It fixed his attitude," First said. "How can I help you, Mr. Fullok?"

"You can step away from my sling and return my wrench."

First smirked. "It's not your sling anymore. Should've kept up with your loan payments. As for your wrench, I'll be happy to put it back in the toolbox once you and your pit crew clear out."

"That's not happening."

First shrugged. "Race starts in half a larim. I've got nothing else to do. I can wait right here until the amber light and we can all watch the race start without you."

"That won't be necessary." He held up his hands. "We could come to some sort of arrangement. Whatever your finder's fee for this job, I'll double it."

"So you have money for bribes but not for your creditors? Sorry. Pass. My boss would be ever so cross when he found out."

"And who is that, exactly?"

"Loritt Chessel sends his regards."

Fullok's left eye twitched at the name. "I see. Well, there'll be no reasoning with you, then?"

"Nope."

"Very well. Keep the sling. I'll buy another one."

"With what money?"

Fullok ignored the taunt and waved his crew away. As he turned to leave, he looked back at her through the corner of his eye. "Bit of free advice. Be careful around Chessel. He'll drop you like a hot rock the rakim you're no longer useful. I watched him do it for cycles."

"I'll give your opinion all the consideration it deserves."

Fullok saluted her with two fingers, then left. His pit crew trickled out behind him and gave her some choice words and hand gestures of their own. The wrench clanged onto the floor at First's feet. With less than half an hour before the race, she had to go through her pre-flight checklist, get the sling fueled and ignited, and herself strapped in. Alone. An hour of work for people who knew what they were doing, but First wasn't going to miss the chance to wipe the gleam off Captain Tiberius's perfect white smile.

Wasting no time, First opened her handheld to the preflight and started working her way down the list. Every sling was built to conform with their racing class specifications, but no two were exactly alike, and each one developed their own little quirks the longer they were flown. She pulled the "Remove Before Flight" sleeves and plugs from the various thruster nozzles and delicate sensor probes, taking a second to visually inspect each one for damage or deformity. A cracked thruster bell or dirty range-finding laser lens would end her run real fast. Maybe even end her, permanently.

That done, she moved on to the vectoring gimble the main drive spike was mounted to. It could angle the spike almost forty-five degrees in any direction to vector the thrust where the pilot wanted it to go. But they were temperamental and required frequent disassembly and bearing replacement. If it froze up on her at the wrong moment, it could send her into an unrecoverable spin, crashing into another sling, or plunging down a gravity well. None of which were attractive prospects.

But Fullok's pit crew proved themselves competent at the very least. The gimble moved smoothly through its entire range of motion without hesitation or drag. The cockpit's O_2 bottles were topped off as well, and it only took a few minutes to figure out how to adjust their settings to the slightly richer mix humans were built for. Thank god the Nelihexu were aerobic oxygen breathers instead of methane or chlorine, or there would have been no way to finish the race on the little pony bottle of air she'd brought.

All the instrumentation checked out. Onboard emergency batteries were charged and showed no shorts or faults. Seals looked good. Only things left were to top off the hydrazine tanks and fuel up and jump-start the reactor.

She found the hydrazine cart tucked behind one of the tool chests easily enough, but when she tried to power up its counter-grav coil, nothing happened. Dead battery. Nor did the filler hose reach far enough, and there weren't any compatible hoses in sight. She found the recharging port, but it would take long minutes to get enough charge back in it to restart the coil.

Fuming, First pushed the tool chest out of the way with a kick and got behind the tank. With the high-traction soles of her racing boots gripping the deck plating, she pushed for all she was worth, surging again and again until her calf muscles burned with acid.

All her efforts were rewarded with the ear-splitting shriek of metal on metal and forward movement of approximately six millimeters before it ground to a halt again.

"Oh, come on!" First shouted. The time until launch was slipping away, but she couldn't afford to launch without full hydrazine tanks. She'd run out of thruster propellant halfway through the race and be dead in space, unable to make the sort of fine trim adjustments to her course that made the difference between an amateur's run and a podium finish. She moved around to the front of it and tried pulling. But no matter how she struggled, the tank simply would not budge.

"That looks heavy." The voice startled First badly enough that she slipped and fell on her ass. Looking up, she found a pair of eyestalks staring down at her. "Want some help?"

It was the Ish mechanic that had pointed her to the slip.

"Yes. Yes I do."

CHAPTER 21

First pulled her fully fueled sling into its starting slot among the other racers awaiting the amber light. Fullok had done the hard work of qualifying seventh among the field of thirty-six, a respectable pole position for anyone. He'd been a better-than-fair racer. Too bad his financial acumen had proven less so.

As far as anyone in the observation galleries knew, Fullok was once again in his cockpit, eagerly anticipating the light. Some of the other sling pilots knew better, particularly the ones who'd been berthed in the slips to the immediate left or right of First's newest acquisition. But it was apparent Fullok had made more enemies than just the Ish mechanic. If any of the other racers or their crews had concerns about her taking his place on the line, they'd decided to keep them away from the race officials.

Because the truth was, First wasn't a licensed sling racing pilot. She hadn't passed any prerace physicals. She was not insured in the event of a breakdown or a crash. Everything that was about to happen rested entirely on her head, and she had no one to bail her out if it went south. Not even Loritt, who would be furious at the loss of the asset he'd sent her to fetch.

Regardless of how the race ended up, she'd be discovered in the end and disqualified. Her standing would be meaningless. Her name never even entered into the final results.

Sitting alone in the cold cockpit, sucking on canned air, and peeing into a bag strapped to the inside of her thigh, First had what drunks across the galaxy referred to as "a moment of clarity."

She stared down the long nose of her sling and up the drive cone of the rig ahead of her and swallowed hard.

"First, what the hell are you doing?" she said into her helmet.

She'd peel away. Yeah. Signal engine trouble to the tower and puff away from the starting gate on a little cloud of hydrazine. As soon as the rest of the racers left, she'd take off in last place and make a no-frills beeline for the pickup point, skipping the race course entirely. In three or four hours, she'd be in high-space heading home for Junktion with another bounty strapped down in the cargo bay.

No risk.

And no reward.

First looked down at her tactical display, for lack of a better term. The primitive sensor suite on board her sling was at least sophisticated enough to pick up the emergency beacons of the other racers, label them, and render them in a wire-frame display between her legs.

Three slots back in the number-ten poll position sat Maximus and his first-of-a-kind, Italian-built, Ferrari-red sling. All doubt melted away under her furnace of anger at the memory of his thoughtless, careless, automatic dismissal. Some rewards were worth the risks.

"Yeah . . ." First jammed her fingers into the buttons that would prime the drive spike. "That's not happening."

She took a moment to consider her advantages over the other racers. She could think of only two. One, she was lighter than any of the other pilots by at least a dozen kilos. In boats where every gram was weighed and considered, that was an enviable figure. Two, beginner's luck.

That was the end of the list. Her list of disadvantages was too long to give it serious consideration without psyching herself out.

Then, the amber light went up, and the window for fear and

indecisiveness closed. Ahead of her, the number-one through number-six slings lit off in sequence, their drive spikes jumping to life barely a tenth of a second apart. In the space between heartbeats, it was her turn. That's when she felt it. The split second of transcendence between firewalling the throttle and the sixty thousand horsepower monster sitting behind her screaming to life.

When it did, it was all First could do to stay on top of the onslaught of violence pouring out of the back of her sling like Niagara Falls. Less than three seconds into the race, First made her first mistake. Her sling drifted too far to port and into the gravity wake of the sling immediately ahead of her. Like a strong headwind, it slowed her acceleration, pushing her backward relative to all of the slings charging up behind her like thoroughbreds.

Her proximity alarm went off to port as a competitor's sling came dangerously close to a collision. First hit her thrusters but overcorrected, setting off another proximity alarm to starboard as the ninth-position sling passed her as well. Unable to tame the beast, First throttled back to three-quarters on her drive spike and watched helplessly as Maximus Tiberius sailed past her. Just like that, the advantage Fullok had unwittingly built in for her evaporated. She was losing. Already.

That just wouldn't do.

Working on reflexes drilled into her in simulations over the last month, and instincts that went back far deeper in time than that, First clawed her way back on top of the wild animal she'd strapped herself to and got it pointed in the right direction again with quick, decisive inputs to her thruster quadrants.

The field behind her had bunched up and broken around to avoid the obstruction, while the field ahead had piled on distance under full acceleration. The result was she had a small bubble of space directly ahead of her with absolutely nothing and no one in it, which was fortunate.

The inputs on Fullok's sling—scratch that, *her* sling—were more sensitive than the simulation she'd trained on. Coupled with the fact the layout was designed for a Nelihexu's four arms, she had to suffer through a lot of wasted time and movement just to keep it straight and level.

As on-the-job learning experiences went, it was pretty goddamned intense. And she'd almost been swallowed whole by a *hentai* tentacle monster once.

But with open space ahead of her, First had a few moments to herself to get properly acquainted with the small, savage craft. Fear and exhilaration embraced in her stomach like reunited lovers and proceeded to get nasty. Heart racing, pupils dilated, senses keened, and burning up oxygen with short, hard breaths, First brought the sling to heel, then spurred it back up to full throttle.

Back in the race.

Her miscue had cost her five spots, but it could have been worse. The slings behind her had mostly failed to capitalize on the opportunity, and a few of them seemed to have fallen into the same trap as a result of the sudden shifts to avoid collision. Already dozens of kilometers ahead of her, the rest of the field wasn't even visible to her naked eyes. But their beacons burned bright on her display.

Maximus had already made up two more spots, damn him. Her new sling was fast and carried a featherweight pilot, but the gap closed with excruciating slowness. Even at full throttle, she was only clawing away a meter or two per second relative to the rest of them.

But her first opportunity to really eat up some distance was coming up just around the bend, literally. Races were decided in the turns. Anyone could firewall a throttle in the straights, but banking, breaking late, cutting the inside, and enduring the g's, that's where skill, strategy, and boldness came into the picture.

She didn't have much of the first and had no experience with the second, so she'd just have to triple-down on the third. And First had an idea.

Her sling didn't have an autopilot; that would defeat the purpose of racing. But it did have a handful of automated safety systems designed to keep the craft from accidentally killing the pilot. Systems a clever racer could exploit, provided they didn't mind violating the spirit if not the letter of the rules.

First didn't mind. She accessed the safety protocol that canceled a high-g turn and reset the stick to a neutral position in the event of a pilot blackout. It was set to kick in ten seconds after a blackout was detected by the health monitoring system built into the pilot's helmet. First ran some quick math. A ten-g turn-and-burn would eat up all of the space between her and the leaders and take twenty-two seconds. It was too long to remain conscious for any human, but that's where the ten-second safety cutoff came in.

The trick was, she had to remain conscious for *exactly* twelve seconds. Any shorter, and the turn would cancel early and she'd waste even more time and fuel getting back on course once she came to. Any longer and she'd turn right into the moon she was trying to sling around.

But she had a plan for that as well.

The first turn warning marker whipped by her cockpit glass so fast it barely registered in her visual cortex. Ahead, the airless, crater-scarred sphere of Percolete's smaller moon filled her canopy. If everything went right, she'd slingshot around the other side of it in less than a minute, traveling even faster than her entry velocity, thanks to a gravitational assist. If it didn't go right, she'd be a cooling stain on its gray regolith, but at least she'd be unconscious for it.

First started breathing deeply, trying to saturate her bloodstream with oxygen before the onslaught to come. Ahead of her, the leaders began their turns. She waited one second, two, three . . . the distance between them plunged. The turn alarm she'd set went off with a wail in her helmet. First rolled the sling, then pulled back on the stick as far as it would go and locked it.

The centripetal force smashed into her like a piston as her weight jumped by an order of magnitude in a second. Her heart was in her stomach, and her stomach was in her feet. Centripetal force pulled at the blood in her brain, draining it down to pool in her legs and arms. To counter this, First used one of the oldest aviation tricks and tensed all the muscles in her limbs as hard as she could, constricting the blood vessels and slowing the process, buying time.

Oh, lord, it had only been three seconds. Her vision blurred at the edges, the beginnings of gray-out. In seconds more, her field of view collapsed into a tunnel, but she had to hold on, her limbs clenched and searing. Just a few more seconds. The longest damned seconds of her life.

Finally, mercifully, the turn clock approached twelve. A fraction of a second before it did, First relaxed her entire body. What little blood remained in her head rushed back down her veins, and everything went black. Her head rolled forward hard until the chin of her helmet dug into her chest.

For ten long beats, First experienced nothing. But her sling flew on, locked into its course while her suit's health monitors shouted to the computer that no one was home. At the count of ten, the joystick unlocked automatically and returned to a neutral position, centered the drive spike in its mount, and killed the thrusters.

The sling still charged forward, but on a straight course and no longer under thrust, the effective gravity dropped back to zero. Still, it took a few seconds for the blood to return to First's oxygen-starved brain and a few seconds more for her synapses to start firing in their proper sequences again.

First rejoined the world slowly, badgered by an intermittent warbling sound that set her teeth on edge. A strobing red light diffused through the thin skin of her eyelids. Painfully, she opened one of them into a slit to see what was so karking important and realized she was staring at the collision avoidance alarm.

That woke her up.

The other sling was still only a pinprick of light against the black velvet of space, barely discernable from the stars beyond, except it was growing quickly. First looked at her closing speed, which had grown from mere meters per second to entire *kilometers.* Two seconds to impact, she shook the cobwebs from her head and grabbed the joysticks. What was the protocol out here again, overtaking vessel moves to port or starboard? She couldn't remember. No time. Careful not to overcorrect again, she nudged her sling a meter to port, two, three.

In the blink of an eye, the entire twenty-meter length of the other sling whizzed past her to starboard. First could've sworn she saw the pilot pressed up against their window regarding her with an obscene gesture through their gloves.

"Sorry, sorry . . ." she said to herself. She couldn't radio over to them to apologize even if she'd wanted to. Their coms only linked back to their own pits and the race officials, and First didn't have anyone in her pits.

Regrettably, the sling she'd passed hadn't been Ferrari red. Still, First's stunt had not only caught her up to the pack but had moved her up two positions in the standings. With that paint-swapping flyby, she was in eighth, nearly back to where she'd started.

Unfortunately, Maximus was busy proving he was no slouch at the stick, either. He'd already jockeyed into fifth, the karker. But the velocity advantage she'd just gained wasn't going away as the kilometers between them ticked down second by second.

The other racers noticed her gaining on them. Some lit off their drive spikes again, trying to match velocity with her to maintain their leads, but burning up their fuel reserves in the process, risking their tanks running dry before the finish line. It was all such a delicate balance between tactics, aggression, and conservation. First began to understand why the sport was so popular.

She had to start thinking like a sling-racer. There were seven turns left in the course, which ended a third of the way to the next planet down the well toward Percolete's sun. Even now, the big blue star's gravity tugged at them as they dove deeper into the system, adding a fraction of a meter per second to their speed with every second. First couldn't abuse her blackout trick on every new turn; it was just too physically punishing. Eventually she'd conk out early and blow the whole race.

Turns two and three barely rated the name. They were more like gates on a downhill slalom course, except instead of colored flags, they were asteroids crawling with tens of thousands of spectators of hundreds of species waiting to watch a few dozen slings go flashing by faster than any comet or asteroid.

That's why the original plan had called for extraction on the other side of turn two: it was far enough from any of the system's planets or moons to make the transition to hyperspace as smooth as possible without any unpleasant gravitational perturbations or amplification. No point going for broke on either of them; the advantage she'd gain would be negligible. Not worth the risk, and sitting these out would give her time to recover.

Turn four was another matter entirely. The larger of Percolete's two moons, and the last major gravitational assist before the finish line, that was where First would spend her other drink chip.

She wanted to link up with Fenax just to confirm that they'd made it to the agreed-upon parking spot on the far side of the finish line, but she couldn't for a number of reasons. Partially because the sling's dead-primitive coms equipment had no encryption capacity by design, but mostly because the *Towed* was on the other side of the hyperspace wall and was impossible to communicate with from normal space in the first place. She just had to run the course and trust that Fenax would be there to catch her when she fell.

It was a new feeling for her, relying on others. Before joining up with Loritt and his misfits in the Subassembly, First had always done everything alone. But now that she'd come to depend on them, sitting in the cockpit of her repossessed sling, she felt truly alone for the first time. It was a strange, alienating, unpleasant sensation that only steeled her resolve to win the race and put an end to it as quickly as possible.

Turn two passed with little drama. At turn three, First gained another spot over an orange-and-green sling that was either slow or planned to conserve their fuel to burn up the arrogant upstart closer to the finish line. She waved as she passed them.

The larger of Percolete's moons grew in the view screen. Ochre, brown, and cream-colored clouds swirled over its surface like the top of a mocha latte, obscuring any topography below. But First wasn't here on a survey mission and blocked it all out. The only two characteristics the moon possessed that she gave a glot about were its mass and circumference . . . and oh, crap, atmospheric drag was a thing, too.

First threw out her calculations and started fresh to account for plowing through a few hundred kilometers of the moon's ionosphere. Despite how slippery her sling's fuselage was built, skipping along through even the thin gases at the altitudes she'd plotted above the moon would slow her down. But even more importantly, all of that lost speed would be translated directly into heat.

How much heat could the skin of her sling absorb before burning off like a meteorite? The question had been skipped in the mission briefing, on account of nobody thinking she'd go anywhere near an atmosphere. In retrospect, it had been an important oversight.

First didn't even know what kind of materials the skin was made of, so could only make a wild guess about their heat tolerance. She dug through the craft's limited onboard computer, looking for density and altitude figures for the moon's mesosphere. At the speeds she was going, if she got the approach angle wrong, she could burn up or even skip off the atmosphere like a rock off a pond.

The mocha-latte moon was getting really big now. She ran out of time to nail down the numbers, and there were still too many variables. First just punched in ranges and best guesses to save time, hoping the engineers who'd designed the sling had overbuilt its heat resistance as much as the rest of the robust little craft.

By the time she fed the "final" numbers into the computer and it spat out her ideal course, First only had twelve seconds to get herself in the lane and orient her sling for the burn. The angle and windows painted across her display were disconcertingly narrow, barely four times the width of the sling itself. It would be like throwing two apples in the air a second apart and hitting them both as they aligned with an arrow fired from two countries away.

Somehow, impossibly, First hit both apples and committed to the turn. She really wished she'd thought to bring one of those mouth guards to keep her from cracking her teeth under the strain.

"Next time," she said aloud, then laughed at her own joke. After this stunt, there was no way she'd ever be allowed within a light-year of the cockpit of one of these things again.

Five seconds to burn. This would be a long one, only eight g's this pass, but she'd have to stay awake for exactly seventeen seconds. First took one last look at the race order and wished she hadn't. Maximus had moved up to fourth place. He was relentless.

First pitched the nose up, pointing it almost directly at the mocha moon, and set the drive spike to its maximum deflection. The turn timer reached zero. She put the pedal to the metal and locked the stick. The weight returned instantly, marginally less than last time, but still like being sat on by a quarter horse instead of a bull. She wished her seat would recline all the way so she could lie flat on her back, but there was a fusion reactor in the way.

She repeated the process, clenching her arms and legs as the weight tried to press her like a wine grape. Only this time, instead of the smooth, linear pressure of the last turn, her sling began to rattle and shake as the winds in the mocha moon's upper atmosphere buffeted against its fuselage. A glow of ionizing gases enveloped the glass outside her cockpit. Faint at first, it grew in brightness as the hypersonic shock waves forming around her craft instantly excited all the gas they encountered into plasma.

The plasma wasn't all that glowed. As the buffeting grew more intense by the second, the sling's nose began to glow and char like a lit cigarette. Six seconds left before she had to black out. Would the sling survive another sixteen seconds merrily skipping through hell? Sweat racing down her face, her sling smoking like a roadie, First *almost* bailed on the turn, but she just didn't have enough quit in her. She was scared, and that made her angry. The final two seconds ticked away and she let herself go limp as a rag.

Sweet nothingness embraced her amid the violence. But outside, her sling fought back. Intumescent paint, activated by the extreme heat, popped and bubbled into a char-blackened foam along the sharpest angles of the fuselage, insulating the structural materials underneath and buying time before they succumbed. The cooling system kicked into overdrive, pumping superchilled liquid hydrogen fuel through a network of small-diameter tubes in the outer skin to act as a heat sink before the return trip sent it into the pea-sized star inside the reactor bulb.

Ten more seconds elapsed, and the sling had suffered enough. It canceled the turn and straightened out, its momentum sending it shooting out of the atmosphere like a dart. Error codes and damage reports scrolled down the cockpit display, but First stayed unconscious longer this time. A cackling in her helmet and an unfamiliar voice finally roused her.

"Unidentified pilot of sling two seven," it said. "This is the control tower. You are not authorized to participate in this event. Set heading one-five-eight and clear the course, then power down your drive spike and wait for—"

First cut the link and shut off the com. There was no point letting it chew up power anyway. So Fullok had ratted her out. Took him long enough. It didn't matter. She'd have been discovered in the end anyway.

She was, miraculously, still alive and sailing through open space again. But the skinny dip through the moon's mesosphere hadn't come without a cost. The prow of her sling looked like it had caught herpes, but the damage there was mostly cosmetic. Still, Loritt wouldn't be happy. The thermoplastic of her canopy glass had fogged and crazed from the onslaught, limiting her view of the outside. But at these speeds, she was basically flying blind on instruments anyway.

Far more serious were the damage reports streaming over her display. Two of the twelve high-efficiency counter-grav nodes that powered her drive spike had taken damage and were starting to overheat. They'd have to be taken offline before they blew out entirely and risked damaging adjacent nodes, cutting her maximum sustainable thrust by a sixth.

She might be able to run the rest of them hot for short bursts, but she'd have to run the rest of the race on a sprained ankle.

The data in front of her wasn't all bad, however, not by a long shot. Her dive into hellfire had paid off in spades. The rest of the racers in the pack had just skirted the atmosphere, if they'd dipped into it at all. First's gamble had rewarded her with not only a bump of three spots in the rankings but a commanding relative velocity advantage that would carry her past at least two more in the next hour, and there was basically nothing anyone could do about it short of ramming her.

However, freshly—and no doubt smugly—in the lead sat Maximus, taunting her with his natural aptitude. With her head throbbing from the repeated blackouts, First struggled to focus enough to run some trajectory projections. There were still four minor turns to go. If she cut them close, broke late, conserved momentum as much as possible . . .

She'd still overtake Maximus eventually, but not until a few thousand kilometers after the finish line.

First pounded her armrests in frustration. She'd already torched the asset she'd been sent to recover. Loritt was going to tear seven strips off her at a minimum for the damage already incurred in the execution of this stunt. She was *not* walking away from this race with nothing to show for it. There had to be something she could do to close the gap.

Another sling faded behind her while she pondered the problem. Her early recklessness had built up an almost insurmountable advantage over the rest of the field. Where Maximus had surgically executed perfect tactics and maneuvers, she'd been a sledgehammer, throwing convention and her own safety out the window to smash through the standings. They'd probably call her things like *blunt* and *ungentlemanly*. The thought brought a smile to her face, which hurt.

She went through turns five and six by the book and grabbed another spot. Her closing distance on the other slings fell again as they ran their spikes hot to try to fend her off. At turn seven, around a tiny little rock barely larger than a soccer pitch, she broke really late and put herself under eleven g's for seven seconds without relying on the safeguard trick. Her vision grayed out and shrank to a pinprick tunnel, but she broke off in time.

Her body screamed and ached from the repeated strain, and First knew that was the last time she'd be pulling that stunt during this race or maybe ever again. She was pretty sure she'd lost a centimeter in height somewhere back there.

Now only Maximus, his arrest-me-red sling, and a single turn stood between her and the finish line. The optimal, fuel-conserving course was a gentle curve between turns seven and eight, owing to a Lagrange point between Percolete and its sun. A straight line would be marginally faster but burn up more fuel fighting against the flow.

Fortunately, breaking late meant First had a few spare liters in the tank, so she burned them running the fastest course and closed the gap between her and Maximus by almost two-thirds.

It was all down to the final straightaway. Judging from the plot on her display, because she couldn't see a damned thing through her clouded canopy, Maximus had answered her charge by, appropriately enough, maxing out his counter-grav nodes. Even four thousand kilometers behind him, his sling glared in her infrared camera like a planet in daylight.

It was certain the control tower had already alerted the rest of the racers to her illegitimate status and that she'd been given the heave-ho. Maximus had the rest of the field beat dead to rights. He wasn't whipping his sling to win the race; he already had. He was doing it to beat *her,* personally, without even knowing who she was, to leave no lingering question of who the true victor had been. It spoke to the intensity of his competitive nature. First almost caught herself admiring him.

Almost.

Her only chance now was to match him move for move. So, hesitantly, First brought the two damaged counter-grav nodes back online and threw them all to 120 percent, hoping the whole system had been as overengineered as the rest of the sling. If they overheated and blew, at least they'd give her a few minutes of full thrust. If they knocked out the nodes next to them, well, she wouldn't win without them anyway.

Sometimes, you just had to roll the hard six.

First watched as her velocity climbed right along with the temperature warnings for the damaged nodes. The display screen became very insistent, saying things like "Design Tolerance Exceeded" and "Critical Component Failure Imminent" and "No, Really, I'm Serious," but First was fixated on the data from her surviving range-finding lidar. A thousand kilometers and closing, but the finish line loomed large on the virtual horizon.

Think, think, think, First admonished herself. There had to be some advantage still to wrangle out of her sling before something broke. And there was. With a shock, First remembered she still had almost her weight in hydrazine left in the maneuvering thruster tanks. She could line up for a final ballistic approach and purge the rest and . . . and the extra thrust might be enough, but it would leave her at Maximus's mercy. If he tried to ram her or play chicken and misjudged her reaction, they'd collide and she could only watch it happen.

Precious seconds flew past before First came to a final decision. If that was how Maximus wanted to play, it would be his choice, and the results would be on his conscience. Not hers. First called up the command prompts and purged all but the last two kilograms of her thruster reactant mass into space in a great cloud.

The eunuchs who'd built Maximus's sling *probably* hadn't wasted the mass on a rear-facing camera sensitive enough to notice, and even if they had, Maximus *probably* hadn't been looking at her, preferring a virtual view of finish line. Now, all she could do was sit and wait.

Two hundred kilometers.

The rest of the field had been well and truly left in their dust by this point. One of her wounded counter-grav nodes gave in and detonated like a hand grenade, causing critical failures in the nodes to the left and right of itself, sending them into automatic shutdown.

One hundred kilometers.

In their zeal, First and Maximus had reduced more than thirty seasoned professionals in a sport they'd pioneered into spectators while two upstart humans socked it out for the gold and silver medals in front of a crowd of millions of aliens, many of them witnessing humanity for the very first time.

Fifty kilometers.

No matter what happened, the people in the crowds below, huddled on the pair of rocks on either side of the imaginary plane that defined the finish line would say, "I was there when . . ."

There was no sensation when she broke the plane. No red tape snapped across her chest, no checkered flag waved with exuberance. The only way she knew what had happened was when the leaderboard on her display updated an eternity later.

"First," it glowed back at her.

"*Yeeeeeeeaaaasssss!*" she bellowed into her helmet, absolutely beside herself with exhilaration. She'd done it! She'd fucking, karking done it and . . . and . . .

And her sling's instruments went completely haywire as they tried and failed to make sense of the universe disappearing as she slipped through the *Goes Where I'm Towed*'s high-space portal.

"Oh, shit," she cursed as she flicked the sling's coms back on and prayed to whomever that Fenax was scanning the control tower frequency.

"Mayday, mayday, mayday," First barked into her helmet com. "I am dead stick, repeat, dead stick! Black on reactant mass, drive spike damaged. I'm coming in ballistic, Fenax. You'll have to match my course and velocity. I got nothing."

The silence stretched out like a rubber band.

"Fenax," she pleaded. "Buddy? Are you reading me? Please be there."

Her helmet's speakers popped and snapped with life.

"Well," Fenax's synthesized voice reached across the void. "Did you win?"

First let out a long breath she hadn't realized she'd been holding.

"You're goddamned right I did. Took everything this heap had in the tank, but I did."

"Stand by. We have company."

"Company?"

"Yes. One of the other slings followed you through the high-space window. I can't even guess how close they must have been for that to happen. I only kept it open for a few thousandths of a rakim."

Maximus, First realized. "Is it obnoxiously red?"

"I don't see in your visual spectrum, but the *Towed's* cameras tell me it is what you call red, yes."

"Bring us both aboard, Fenax. Something tells me his sling's as dry as mine."

Minutes later, under Fenax's skillful ganglia, First and Maximus found themselves standing on the same deck plating for a second time.

First ignored him and instead ran a hand over her sling's disfigured fuselage.

"Where are we?" Maximus demanded from across the cargo bay even as First began the laborious process of strapping the asset down for transport.

"You're quite safe, Captain," she said.

"While your reassurances are welcome, 'Clara,'" Maximus said, "that's not an answer to my question. Who are you? And where are we?"

"My name is First. I'm a repossession agent. I've just nabbed this beauty. And you are aboard my company's ship. You weren't supposed to come in second so close behind me. That wasn't part of the plan."

Maximus smiled broadly, then pointed at First's sling. "I somehow doubt the 'plan' called for breaking your stolen goods."

"They're not stolen," First snapped back. "It was reacquired for the rightful owners, under a legal contract. Besides"—First broke off a chunk of the charred intumescent foam—"this'll buff out."

"Buff out?" Maximus said. "It looks like a sailor's schlong after shore leave in Singapore."

"Say that six times fast."

"Trust me, I have."

"Ew," First said. "And whatever. Your sling sure looks pretty back there in second place."

Maximus smirked. "I doubt this contract required you to burn up your sling in Percolete's major satellite's atmosphere just to get around me, right?"

"No, that was just for me."

"Why?"

"Because you said I couldn't. Because *you* said I shouldn't even be in the cockpit. That's why. And I beat you. I won."

"Weeell, no," Maximus said. "I won. That's what the official records will say. You stole another racer's starting position, a mighty good one. You didn't earn that in the qualifiers. You started out three spots ahead of me on someone else's ticket. I closed that gap to lord only knows how tight. They might honestly have to break out a photo finish for it, but you were never in the race as far as the books are concerned."

"No one who was there will care about the books. They saw me cross first. That will be what they're talking about tomorrow."

"Maybe so," Maximus granted, "but they don't know who you are. Mistake number one, kiddo. Never do anything cool unless everyone can see you doing it. What's the point otherwise?"

"You know," First said. "And I know. That's enough for me."

Maximus smiled. "Mistake number two. Your ego can't feed itself forever. It needs fuel from the outside. That's what the audience is for. And you just passed up on a massive one." Maximus took a moment to scan the rest of the *Towed*'s cargo bay. "Can I assume you didn't bring me on board as a hostage?"

"Of course not."

"Good, then can I further assume you have some fuel for my sling so I'm not waiting for hours for a rescue crew to tow me back to the finish line when you drop me back into real-space?"

"I'm feeling generous in victory," First said.

"How gracious of you. What's your name?"

"Why?"

"I'd like to know who beat me."

First nodded. "Firstname Lastname."

Maximus pursed his lips. "All right, then. Pleased to meet you. I still want a copy of that interview. Oh, and don't be shocked if I come looking for you in the future."

"I'd rather throw you out an airlock."

Maximus scowled. "I didn't mean anything lurid. Earth is the new kid on this block. We need to make a splash if we're going to earn respect among all these people. You just dunked on me, and you were willing to die to do it. I won't forget that. Hell, I might let everyone know humans placed first and second in this race, just to rub the rest of the galaxy's face in it."

"I'd prefer to remain anonymous. Having a famous face isn't a benefit in my line of work. Besides, you just said you don't want to share the glory."

"Because it's not about me. Well, it's not *only* about me. We're busy building a narrative out here, and we'll need more humans like you before this is all over."

First crossed her arms. "Before *what* is all over?"

Maximus laid a hand on his sling. "That's beyond your pay grade. I'll do everything I can to make sure you never learn the answer to that question. But if, heaven forbid, I can't keep a lid on it, you'll know. If that happens, there will be a chair open for you at the table."

CHAPTER 22

"What in the name of . . ." Loritt's jaw almost hit the floor—which, for a Nelihexu, was a real possibility. He stood there in shock as the racing sling he'd sent Fenax and First on a two-month-long excursion to recover was floated out of the *Towed*'s cargo bay.

"Now, boss, it's not as bad as it looks," First said. "It's mostly cosmetic."

"They don't make cosmetics thick enough to cover up that mess."

"Don't worry. A fresh coat of paint, a few carbon fiber patches, and a"—First coughed—"couple of grav nodes and she'll be good as new."

"You blew out the counter-grav ring?!" Loritt asked, exasperation getting the better of his tone.

"Not all of it."

Loritt put up a hand and forced a smile. "Just stop right there. Good work. I'm glad you're back. Now, go home before I fire you again."

First clicked her heels and saluted smartly, then ran off for the pod station. Loritt looked at Fenax's tank hovering at eye level. "What happened?"

"She ran the race."

"Why the hell would she do that?"

"I'm not sure, but I think someone told her she couldn't. Another human named Maximus Tiberius."

"Karking hell, their only war hero and she gets into a pissing match with him." Loritt shook his head as he inspected the sling. "It looks like it caught a mating virus."

"In her defense, she won the race," Fenax said.

"I'd hope so, considering how badly she beat up my sling in the process. Is there a trophy we can put up in the office?"

"I'm afraid not. It didn't officially count."

"Of course it didn't."

"No disrespect intended, boss, but what she did was an impressive bit of piloting," Fenax said. "I could hardly have done better. We should be proud of her."

"I *am* proud of her, but don't you dare let her know it. First gets in enough trouble as it is." Loritt dug out his handheld. "Hashin, know any good body shops on the station?"

"Naturally," Hashin said over the link.

"Book an appointment for an estimate. We have glot to polish."

"An aircar?"

"Bigger."

Hashin sighed. "Right."

Just then, a face as familiar as it was unwelcome stepped out of the crowd and broke toward Loritt. "I'll have to call you back," he said to Hashin. "Make the arrangements."

"Understood." The link went dead as a different Lividite coasted to a stop in front of Loritt.

"Mr. Chessel," Officer O'Chakum said. "What a coincidence. I was just thinking about you."

"I thought coincidences were suspect in your line of work, Officer," Loritt said, forcing pleasantries.

"Indeed. I was just thinking it's been a month since I asked to talk to your human employee, and here your ship is docking."

"Contractor," Loritt corrected. "And I'm afraid you've just missed her."

"Seems to be the way of it, hmm?" O'Chakum nodded at the

ruined sling. "More of her work? She likes to leave a mess behind for you to clean up."

Loritt smiled. "I feel the sudden urge to fall silent until my lawyer is present."

O'Chakum put up her hands defensively. "That's not why I'm here. Got a rakim?"

"As I recall, the last time I gave you a rakim, I was trapped in your interrogation room for three-quarters of a day."

"No questions for you today. I have . . . insights. Off the record."

Loritt's chin tilted up a fraction. "Go on."

"I know the job you're ramping up for, *lucky* you."

Loritt's eyes narrowed at the stress she placed on *lucky.* "How do you know about that?"

"Oh, please, all of you repo crews have at least one toe in the criminal world, either as contacts or direct employees. You're cleaner than most—I respect that—but you're not as pure as you let on. Everyone talks, and a lot of them talk to me rather than the alternative. I know four crews were offered the contract, but you were the only one fool enough to take it on."

"I've made a lot of money being the only fool to take on a job."

She put her palms out to signal nonaggression. "It wasn't a criticism, merely an observation. I've also observed the territory formerly controlled by Soolie the Fin has been unusually quiet for the last couple of months, which has made my job considerably easier, and while I'm sure you'll deny any involvement in that fortuitous outcome, I'm still here to talk."

Loritt let the silence draw out for a few beats. "Off the record?"

"I was never here."

"Very well. What do you have?"

O'Chakum's shoulders eased. "That flesh peddler you relieved of their ride a while back? They showed up here under a falsified identity a week ago, but we caught them at the gates."

"Well, that would be a first," Loritt said.

O'Chakum let the barb pass. "Judging by the contraband they brought with them, I think they meant to do someone here significant, intricate, dare I say *intimate* harm. Can you think of anyone that may have attracted their ire recently?"

Loritt remained stone-faced. "One or two people come to mind."

"I thought they might, but don't worry. 'Vel' Jut didn't have your endurance for our interviews. He relinquished his contact up the smuggling chain for the Andrani girls after only six larims."

"Still not sure how this concerns me," Loritt said.

"Oh, just drop the act already, Chessel." O'Chakum folded her arms and turned her back on him. "I know you tried to hide those girls because letting it out would tie up the sale of your asset. Even if I can't prove it conclusively, we both know it happened. But I also know you put them up in good quarters and made sure they wanted for nothing while you arranged return to their home world. I know you acted to protect yourself, but I also know you *cared*. So care about what I'm saying now. There's things you should know about your next job and the person you're going against."

All of Loritt's parts exhaled in synchrony. "I'm listening."

"It's a new day and a new contract," Loritt began the briefing. "We're going pretty far afield for this one, so be ready for an extended time away. But the pot at the end of the road will be worth it."

Loritt touched his handset, and the room fell dark. The hologram of an enormous ship filled the space from one end to the other. Built around a central keel, hundreds of standard hexagonal cargo containers stuck to it like honeycomb. Everyone gawked at the scale of it.

"That's a Rakunasin bulk freighter," Sheer said. "Not exactly our kind of job, is it?"

"It *was* a Rakunasin bulk freighter," Loritt corrected before shrinking the ship's projection down to a more manageable size. "It is now a legally ambiguous traveling casino known as the *Change Your Luck,* based in the Garlopin system. 'Passengers' book staterooms on board for next to nothing, then spend two weeks round trip draining drinks and their bank accounts inside its gaming floors."

"Okay," Jrill said. "But gambling is legal. There's a dozen casinos right here on Junktion. What's the problem?"

"The problem is the *Change Your Luck*'s owner." The ship disappeared, replaced by a portrait of what looked like a column of melting orange candle wax with a dead Maltese grafted to the top.

"Fonald Plump," Loritt said. "Claimed to be a trillionaire virtual real estate developer turned casino magnate has had an awful habit of seeing his recent projects go bankrupt. The *Change Your Luck* is no exception. She's seven months behind on payments, and Plump's creditors have had enough."

"How the hell do you bankrupt a casino?" Hashin asked. "People literally line up to hand you money."

Loritt shrugged. "When it's actually a front for money laundering for the Rakunasin Mafia and you're writing off the losses to reduce your tax burden while taking kickbacks from your mob connections in the form of drastically above-market virtual real estate purchases. Remember the *Pay to Prey* we nabbed a few months ago, the sex trafficker? Plump's name keeps coming up in the investigation, and legitimate lenders are trying to put distance between him and themselves as fast as possible."

"Ah," Hashin said.

"And how do we know all this?" Jrill asked.

"Privileged sources," Loritt answered.

"This all sounds *very* familiar," First said.

"Any resemblance to historical figures living or dead is purely coincidental, I'm sure," Loritt said. "Anyway, our job is to *safely* disembark all passengers, then take control of the ship and deliver it to its creditors in the Burquel system. We don't have the final numbers yet, but even at our most conservative estimates, our payday for this job will be a dozen times larger than any contract we've ever completed. Maybe more. We can all take a cycle off after this one, not that I expect anyone will last that long with nothing to do."

"Great!" Jrill said. "Are we hiring six times the squad to wrestle that monster into dock, or are we bribing the existing crew?"

"Actually," Fenax said from their tank, "the five of us will be enough. Bulk freighters are almost entirely automated. Their crews are basically caretakers and number in the single digits when they're running cargo. Most of that leviathan's crew is dedicated to servicing its clientele. Once they're off the ship, there's no reason to think we couldn't fly it to the bank."

"Fenax is right," Sheer said. "I worked on one of those monsters for a few cycles before signing on here. You could go days without seeing anyone."

Jrill set her hands palms-down on the table. "That is all very informative, but a ship that large could hold tens of thousands of customers, players, whatever you want to call them. Every one of which is there paying for the privilege of enjoying themselves. How do we expect to run them off from their illusion of the perfect vacation?"

"Repeat of the *Matron* and *Monarch* job?" Hashin said. "Fake a radiation leak?"

"No-go," Sheer said. "The reactor bulb is waaaay in the ass of the ship, and it sits behind a huge shield cone. You could blow the whole thing and the rest of the ship wouldn't see any radiation spike."

"It's simple," First said. Everyone turned in their seats to regard her. "We break the illusion. We make them lose. Every spin. Every hand. Every time." First smiled. "You have to let your marks win once in a while if you're going to keep stringing them along. Otherwise, they get wise to the con and slit your throat."

"Just one problem," Loritt said. "We have a hard deadline for delivery. The contract expires three weeks after we arrive on-site, including two weeks of transit time to Burquel once we take possession."

"'We,' boss?" Hashin asked. "You're coming with us?"

"For a job this complex and a payday this big? You bet your pillbox I am."

"That timeline's still going to be tight," Jrill said.

"I can do it," First said. "Piece of cake."

"We'll see soon enough," Loritt said. "Right now, we have a bigger problem still to overcome."

"How much bigger?" Jrill asked suspiciously.

"The *Change Your Luck* is an invite-only affair, and none of us have an invite. I could, probably, get one for myself and a plus-one, but we may as well put up a billboard that we're there to steal it back for the bank. So I'll need a new identity. As will all of you."

"What about your face?" First asked. "Most of us are unknowns, but you're a big deal on the station."

Loritt answered with a smile, and then the various animals that made up his face wriggled and pushed against each other, writhing like a bucketful of giant bugs until they settled again into a new, unfamiliar face. It was still Nelihexu, with all the parts where they should be, but it didn't look like Loritt.

"My face is just the pattern my components fall into most easily and comfortably," he said at last. "But with little conscious effort, I can shake things up a bit."

"Great," First said, her stomach churning. "That was educational and creepy as hell. Can you change back now, please?"

Loritt obliged.

"Moving on," Sheer said. "The plan is we get invites for all six of our aliases? It's a big galaxy, but the circles these people run in are small. Six complete unknowns all show up at once? That will twitch some antennae."

"And who do we get to vouch for us that we can trust not to run right back to this Plump?" Hashin said. "We're not well liked among the private starship set, not even the honest ones."

Loritt held his hands open. "Now you see our dilemma. Let's hear some ideas."

"We don't all need invites," Jrill said. "Casinos have pretty high employment turnover and need a lot of security. I could apply for a job while it's still in port. Just change the names on my military records and I should be about as close to an automatic hire as you're likely to get."

Loritt nodded approvingly. "And gives you access to restricted areas of the ship and its security and surveillance systems. Yes, excellent idea. More like that, everyone. Come at it sideways."

"I could try to do the same on the crew side," Sheer said, "but the odds are not as good. Like I said already, the maintenance and engineering teams aren't very big and may not be hiring."

"No good. Too much uncertainty," Loritt said.

"We could speak to your politician friend Ulsor Plegis," Hashin said. "They run in the right circles on Junktion and beyond and could probably get us an in. Or at least bring us to the right parties where we could get our own invites."

Loritt pointed at him. "Good thinking. It'll also give us the chance to practice our new aliases." He looked around the room, ending on First. "Some of us will need more practice than others."

"What?" First objected. "Why is everyone looking at me?"

"You really need to ask?"

"Oh, fuck off," First said.

"Yes, exactly the point. We're going shopping tomorrow morning," Loritt said. "We need to posh up your wardrobe. Jrill, you're coming with."

"Me?" the Turemok said. "Why me?"

"You're a female. You can give her pointers on makeup and . . . things."

"You want me to show her how to put on lipstick?"

"Exactly," Loritt said.

Jrill pointed at her beak. "I don't have lips."

"Oh no," First said, raising her hands, forefingers pointed to the ceiling. "Let me be absolutely clear. We're not doing some kind of *My Fair Lady* montage."

First stared back at herself in the five mirrors as the dressmaker pinned and fitted the most ridiculous costume she'd ever seen, much less worn.

"First impressions?" Loritt said, standing behind her to the right and smirking to himself.

"I look like a glitter factory shit itself," First said.

"Language, young lady."

"Oh, come on, no one even knows what *shit* means out here."

"Some do, and the rest can pick out the cadence of a curse word. It's universal, you know. It's the one thing all spoken languages have in common other than *huh?*"

"God was obviously a potty mouth, then," First said. "So what's the karking problem?"

"Okay, now that one, *everyone* knows. You're getting worse, not better."

First picked at one of the hundreds of iridescent, spade-shaped chips that had been linked together with nearly invisible threads to give the illusion they'd all been pressed or glued separately onto her naked body. "What are these things, anyway?"

"They are plasticized leaves from the vanishingly rare Eklorn tree of Khalos Minor," the dressmaker said from her waist.

"Are they expensive?"

"Twenty-nine credits."

"That's not so bad," First said.

"Each."

First frowned as the realization sank in that she was wearing more money than her parents back on PCB got in public assistance in a year.

"Well, they're itchy."

The dressmaker jabbed First with a pin in the fleshy part of her rump.

"Ow!" First called out. "You did that on purpose."

"Did I?"

"Don't worry about her, madam," Loritt said. "This one would complain about the octane rating of fuel on her funerary pyre. Please, continue your work."

"Lot of work to make her presentable," the dressmaker mumbled.

"I'm standing right here, you know," First said.

"Slouching is more like it."

"She's right," Loritt said. "Straighten your back and roll your shoulders so the fitting is accurate."

"How is anyone going to know what my posture is *supposed* to look like if they've never seen a human before?"

Loritt crossed his smaller arms while gesturing with the larger. "Can you pick a sick, weak, or lame animal out of a herd, even if you've never seen the species before?"

First shrugged. "I guess."

"Of course you can. Your species were hunters for thousands of generations. There are signals, markers of strength any healthy animal projects to tell predators, 'Not me. I'll fight back. It won't be worth it.' Make no mistake, First, we are stepping into a den of *predators.* They won't eat your flesh—not most of them, at any rate—but they arrived where they are in the universe by identifying and exploiting weakness in the herds around them. We can't afford to let them pick you out of the pack. You have to belong there, move among them, be seen to be invisible. In a crowd like this, flamboyance is stealth. Do you understand?"

First took a deep breath and scratched at the leaf covering her right nipple. "I think so."

"Good. So stop fighting with Madam Xerot and let her finish, please?"

"Provided she doesn't poke me again."

"No promises," Xerot said from behind her.

"What is this mess?" The stylist lifted limp strands of First's raven hair.

"Yeah, yeah," First said. "I haven't been able to find a good conditioner since I got here."

"No, literally, what is it?"

"It's . . . it's hair." First looked at Loritt standing behind her in the mirror again. "Please tell me they've seen hair before."

The stylist looked at Loritt and shrugged. "Sorry. We specialize is polishing scales, preening feathers, and brightening fins. But I've never seen something like this before. What's it made of?"

Loritt returned the shrug. "First, can you *shed* some light?"

"Very funny. It's keratin, a kind of protein."

"What do you cut it with?" the stylist asked.

"Scissors!"

"Oh, pupa, no. Scissors are for school projects. We use lasers in this salon."

"I'm out." First reached for the bib around her neck and stood to leave, but Loritt stopped her.

"These people are professionals. Sit down."

"They cut through armored scales! What if they set the laser too high and slice my head off?"

"That rarely happens," the stylist said.

"Rarely?!"

Loritt and the stylist shared a laugh.

"All right, all right. A real Abbott and Costello you two are," First said. "How will you know what my hair is supposed to look like when you're done?"

"Actually, I've brought samples." Loritt set down his handheld and pressed an icon. Holographic images appeared of Audrey Hepburn, Raquel Welch, Angelina Jolie, and half a dozen other starlets from centuries past that were only now being carried to this part of space by long-forgotten radio waves.

The stylist leaned in to inspect the gently rotating images with the deliberate, attentive eye of an artist.

"There's less length here to work with than many of these examples." They ran First's hair through their six-digit hands, ending in suction cups. "However, I think I can capture the basics. Frame the face, accentuate the natural wave of the material, a new color . . . yes, we can accommodate your needs."

"Cut it a little shorter than you would want the final result to be," Loritt said. "We'll be in space for a while before we get where we're going."

The stylist nodded, then picked up their sheering laser.

First, wearing uncomfortably cut clothes, carrying a dozen bags, smelling of rancid perfume, alien cosmetics, and burned hair, opened the door to the flat she shared with Quarried Themselves. She dropped everything to the floor before walking a jagged line to the couch on her unfamiliar, ten-centimeter stiletto heels.

First had worn chunky platform heels before, but these things were ice picks, which had a distinguished history as torture instruments that had carried through time to inflict excruciating pain on her toes and ankles. She may as well have spent the last hour walking around practicing ballet en pointe.

She kicked the left one off so hard it hit the far wall and stuck.

"Noted," First said to herself, then removed the right shoe by hand. She wanted nothing more than to lie on her ridiculously comfortable bed and binge on something. Whether that something was a show or a bottle, she didn't really care in the moment. However, she still had homework.

Her evening's assignment was to go out and expose herself to "culture," whatever that meant. Loritt wanted her to broaden her tastes to include the sorts of things the upper crust spent their leisure time on. Operas, art exhibits, mutual funds, manipulating democratic elections, frivolous toys whose price tags could feed continents, that sort of thing.

First absently rubbed at her toes and arches, trying to come up with something she could report back doing to satisfy Loritt's asinine request, when the answer hit her. She walked to her bedroom, got into the dingiest, most abused, least clean outfit she had and headed for the travel pods.

She reached her destination a little over a quarter larim later and entered through her usual loose grate. This time, she wore a scarf over her mouth. "Bilge? Are you busy?"

The eyestalk appeared in front of her, while the voice emerged from behind. "Hello, First. Did you change your hair?"

First ran a hand through her new, wavy, bright aquamarine locks. "Hi, Bilge. Yes, I did. Thanks for noticing. Do you like it?"

The eyestalk drew closer. "It frames your face nicely. What can I do for you today? Fair warning, the timeflies seem to be avoiding me ever since we captured a bunch of their friends. Thank you for that, by the way."

"You're welcome, but that's not why I'm here," First said.

"Oh yes?"

"I'm supposed to 'get cultured.'"

"So you came to a sewer? Not to be self-deprecating, but there's usually a different meaning of 'culture' associated with this place."

"I'd like to hear your first molding of Welsbar of Del's Pouk Night Concert in piezo-electric."

The tentacles around her trembled. "For real?"

"For really real."

"Then you came to the right glot hole, young lady. Have a seat." Bilge paused. "Actually, maybe you should remain standing. Wait right there."

Her friend the monster departed in a swirl of wastewater. First figured she could risk leaning against the wall. The most it would cost her was a ruddy shirt and maybe a tetanus shot. Bilge reappeared moments later carrying a small silver deck, four wireless speaker units, and a large bass box. He took great care positioning them, frequently looking back with an eyestalk to gauge First's position.

"What are you doing?" she asked at last.

"Trying to find optimum speaker placement for a biaural species such as yourself. My race has omniaural receptors in our skin, you see. It's a challenge to, er, visualize how sound works for you with only two points of auditory reference."

"It's okay," First said. "You don't have to—"

"No trouble at all. It's your first time; you deserve to hear this properly."

First waited patiently as an eighth larim stretched into a quarter. Finally, Bilge seemed satisfied. He said nothing as one of his arms reached out for the small deck and pushed a button.

Instantly, the sewer tunnel filled with music, barely recognizable to First as such for the cacophony of alien sounds and instruments, like looking into a Nelihexu's face for the first time. There were too many parts vying for her attention. But then she let go and focused on the underlying rhythm holding them all together. Stopped trying to understand it and fell into the experience. The individual components quickly lost their novelty and blended together into a unified, indescribable whole.

By the time the first crescendo hit, tears rained down, lost in the swirling brown water.

CHAPTER 23

A week later, it was time to party. Last chance for First to polish her newfound poshness before the big game. It had been a hellish week of preparation for the *Luck* job. Every waking hour not spent in makeovers or culturing lessons was burned up researching casino security systems and their vulnerabilities, madly digging through the /backnet/ for existing hacks and ghosts, burning up credits hiring anonymous programmers to write crackers and bots to step in where the black market hadn't yet provided, and writing her own interface to get them all communicating and working together in real time without hiccups.

She still hadn't finished that task, but she had all the components saved to her deck, and she'd have plenty of time on the flight over to work out the kinks. What little sleep First had gotten over the last week was plagued with a recurring nightmare of herself in clown makeup giving a speech in front of her old primary school classmates with nothing but leaves censoring her private bits, except their faces were all replaced with alien faces.

Not a difficult nightmare to parse meaning from, that one.

Loritt came to pick First up in his Proteus on the twentieth-floor landing of her building. No self-respecting debutante would dream of showing up to this sort of party in a public transit pod. The passenger-side door scrolled open for her.

"Kula's not joining you tonight?" First asked.

"We're one of only a few Nelihexu couples on the station. It would draw too much attention."

The open seat next to Loritt was already busy recontouring itself for First's body.

"How does it know to do that?" she asked.

"You've been in here before. It remembers," Loritt said.

"Oh, right." First petted the car's center console like a cat. "Sorry I tried to steal you." The passenger-side climate control vents started blowing high-speed, ice-cold air in First's face. "Hey, what the hell?"

"She remembers that, too," Loritt said. "Down, girl. She's my guest this time." The frigid air died away. "Better. May I say, First, you're looking resplendent this evening."

"I look ridiculous."

"Then you're three-quarters of the way there."

"I'm serious." First pointed at the short mylar dress that had been sent up for her. "This thing crinkles like a bag of chips every time I move. It doesn't breathe, and I've already dutch-ovened myself. I don't care how much it cost, I'm not wearing it again."

"But of course you're not. Duchess Harrington would never reduce herself to recycling a dress. You'll donate it to the less fortunate tomorrow morning." Loritt said, using the name they'd settled on for First's alias and backstory. She was hereditary European aristocracy—old money, from the new Earth, doing what children of privilege had done for millennia: sowing their oats and making connections by going on years-long, alcohol-fueled, foreign adventures. She was part of the first wave of spoiled brats to dare travel so far from their home system.

The best backstories managed to bury some truth inside the bullshit. First's was no exception.

"That's wasteful," First objected.

"Conspicuous consumption is the point." Loritt pulled the car away from the landing and merged into the evening's traffic patterns. "Predators, remember? They can smell frugality. It's a dead giveaway that you don't belong. The entire point of an invite-only casino is to flaunt how many credits you can afford to lose without a second thought. Winning is secondary."

"Then why am I hacking the probability matrices?" First asked. "If they're there to lose, won't they be happy when I *Change Your Luck*?"

"There's losing," Loritt said, "and then there's being cheated. These people are fabulously wealthy. You don't end up rich by tolerating being someone else's mark. It's all in good fun until someone puts a finger on the scales, then it's war. That's why your plan will work."

"It's still wasteful."

"Hey." Loritt nudged her. "I thought you'd be happy."

"Why would you think that?"

"Because aren't these exactly the people you told me on my patio you wanted to steal from the night I recruited you?"

First smiled. "Kidnapped and blackmailed me, you mean. But . . . yes. Yes, they are."

"But if we succeed, you will effectively join them. We all will. Doesn't the hypocrisy bother you?"

"Compartmentalization is one of humanity's most versatile adaptations."

"I see. Don't trouble yourself with the paradox too deeply," Loritt said. "You'll never be one of them." First stiffened in her sumptuously comfortable seat. "Oh, please don't take that as an insult; it wasn't meant as one. You grew up in poverty. You understand the impact it has on people. On families. The needless suffering. The revulsion you feel at the waste, the squandered resources, that never goes away. You will always remember. Your children, however, if you choose to have any, they'll hear your stories and take them to heart, but it will be less immediate, less real. *Their* children won't have any idea and won't care. They'll believe their inherited wealth is the natural order of the universe, right along with their positions in it."

Loritt paused, some unreadable emotion crossing his face in a wave, but First was pretty sure she knew what he was feeling. He cleared his throat and continued. "The people in this party, and the people we're ultimately trying to repossess the *Change Your Luck* back from, they're many generations removed from even that proximity. Money has lost its meaning to them, become an abstract concept. You can't know the value of a glass of water if you've never been thirsty."

"It sounds like you want me to pity them," First said, arms crossed, almost under her breath.

"No, I want you to understand them, see them for what they are, well enough to mimic them. Because once money no longer matters, it's replaced with other kinds of currency. Social status, business favors, political alliances, honor debts, marriage—these are the sorts of things that confer power at this level of the game."

They flew along in companionable silence. First watched the buildings sweep by below through the window in the floorboards beneath her feet as they gained altitude, then suddenly pitched down into a large pit. It was only then she began to wonder where they were headed.

"We're not going to one of the tower roof gardens?"

"Nope."

"Amphitheater?"

Loritt shook his head as he'd learned to do around her. Most of them had. Well, the ones with heads.

"To the Skins," Loritt said, slang for the very worst housing blocks on the station, farthest from the rich, vibrant city inside the hub, closest to Junktion's outer skin. They were dirty, crime-ridden, and cold. Not even First's first apartment had been in the Skins.

"That's appalling," she said.

"It's educational," Loritt said. "We're going to party among the abandoned sectors so we can get in touch with the plight of the less fortunate."

"It's poverty tourism."

"Now, now, Duchess Harrington. It's an opportunity to show our generosity. Throughout the evening, we'll be implored to donate to a foundation dedicated to helping these poor souls. Sure, most of that money will go to paying the caterers, event coordinator, local performers with their 'inspiring' stories, and other associated costs of throwing this soirée for ourselves, but we'll all go home warmed by drink and self-assurances that we've 'done something.'"

First heard the acid behind Loritt's sarcasm, and something in her perspective on the man shifted ever so slightly.

"You really hate them, don't you?"

"I wasn't always . . . myself. I haven't told many people this. Not sure why I'm telling you, honestly, but I'm assembled from cast-off parts. Pieces of factory workers and miners who either had to sell off bits of themselves to pay the rent or couldn't afford to continue and chose to disincorporate entirely. That's where I came from, once, long ago. Factories and mines in my colony closed or automated by their off-world owners without thought or regard for what it would do to the people who relied on those for their livelihoods. So yes, I really hate them."

First laughed, then stared at Loritt with wide eyes and a warm smile.

"What's funny?"

"Not funny," First said. "Not exactly. Look at you. A community of castoffs and misfits who made it big by nurturing castoffs and misfits into a community. Now, our whole team is kinda its own superorganism."

"I, um, I hadn't thought of it like that before," Loritt said, choking up on both his throat and the throttle. He pulled the Proteus up to the landing and brought it to a gentle landing on its skids. "Remember, don't get out yourself; you're waiting for me to help you out. And act fashionably aghast at the surroundings."

"I was visiting a friend in the sewers four days ago," First said.

"That's why they call it *acting,* my dear." Loritt did the face trick again, preparing for his own role. "The rest of the crew should either be inside or arriving shortly. Don't bunch up with them. Remember the assignment: we're here to ingratiate ourselves to as many people as possible and get invites."

"Roger that."

The doors peeled open. Loritt climbed out of the aircar, then came around and offered First a hand. Her dress crinkled like Christmas wrapping as she lifted herself out.

As soon as she stood, First wrinkled her nose performatively. "What's that smell, Tolos?"

"I believe it's called *musty,* Duchess Harrington," Loritt said, responding to the alias he'd settled on.

"Well it's simply *ghastly,*" First said loud enough for everyone on the landing to hear. "I trust it improves inside."

"Only one way to know, milady." Loritt, ahem, *Tolos* offered her his arm. First took it, and they walked together through the *Mouth of the Underbelly,* a garish, self-indulgent art installation arching over the entry to the gala like a birth canal. Or a colon. Doubtlessly made by whatever avant-garde local artist had been hired to sex up the misery of the population down here. First had to work not to vomit.

"Isn't it splendid how the artist incorporated actual refuse they found down here in the Skins into this archway, Duchess?" Loritt asked.

"Oh yes." First nodded along. "So evocative. It really creates an authentic atmosphere."

"Careful not to snag that gorgeous dress," one of the other guests said to her from just behind and to the left. First turned her head to get a look at them. A Haswren female . . . probably. Their body plans went through several metamorphosis stages, and First didn't know them all.

"Oh, no worries there," First assured her. "I won't go anywhere near these grubby walls." They shared a giggle. First was embarrassed how easily it came to her. She tugged at a corner of her skirt. "Do you really like it?"

"It's so simple and flattering. And being reflective, it goes with everything, doesn't it?"

"I know!" First said. "I'm almost tempted to wear it again some other time. Isn't that silly?"

"How droll! You're really getting into the spirit of the whole underprivileged experience."

First's fingernails dug into Loritt's forearm as she faked an answering laugh. Then, remembering herself, she put out a hand to the alien woman. "Duchess Gertrude Harrington, recently arrived from Earth. And this is my escort for tonight, Tolos Vir."

"Enchanted," the alien said. "Chellir of Haswren, House Bellicont, the *southern* continent Belliconts, you understand. Not those no-account, nest-poaching northerners."

"Isn't that funny? On Earth, Europe is one of our northernmost continents, and that's where all the oldest families hail from."

"It's indeed a topsy-turvy universe," Chellir said. "What brings you so far from home, Duchess, wasn't it?"

"Duchess is a hereditary title. You really must call me Gertrude."

"Gertrude it is. Find me inside later. We must talk more."

"Count on it."

The short walk through *Underbelly* terminated in a sort of plaza. The entire space had been rented out, then forcibly cleared of its residents and vagabonds, disrupting their already harried schedules. Security patrolled the perimeter of the area, making no attempt to hide their presence as a way to reassure the attendees. "Don't worry," the guards said without speaking. "We will keep the ruffians at bay. You can feel bad for the destitute in peace, without so much as having to actually look at one. Your bubble of privilege extends even into *their* home."

Loritt took his leave and peeled off immediately, leaving First to her own talents in the unfamiliar sea. Andrani waitresses—not the juveniles they'd liberated months earlier but still young and ethereal—made their way through the plaza, holding reclamation bin lids as trays for chirpip-skewer appetizers. Others carried the sort of battered buckets the hall rats collected water in, except now they were filled with ice and vintage bottles of wine and other intoxicants from a dozen worlds, each bottle individually worth more than a hall rat could hustle for in an entire cycle.

Everywhere she looked, the poverty motif was being played up for entertainment. First didn't even try to hide the look of genuine disgust on her face. It was appropriate, after all. Many of the other attendees shared it. But while they were appalled by the conditions, the grime, the smell, she was revolted by their exploitation, their greed, and their callousness. But unless there were any telepaths in the crowd, no one would know the difference.

"Hello, *Duchess Harrington,*" a familiar voice said with an inflection of jovial accusation. First spun around and found herself face-to-mantle with the squid carrot again.

"Station Counsel Member Plegis," she said. "How good to see you again. Congratulations on the election. You must be excited."

"Call me Ulsor! And not half as excited as I was backstage at the Wolverines concert on Faan two months ago when I delivered their tour liner back to them. Not that you had anything to do with that." Plegis pressed a fleshy, slightly protruding ring on his mantle, which First could only assume was like someone touching a finger to his nose. He leaned in and dropped his volume to a whisper. "Don't worry, your disguise is great. I wouldn't have known it was you or Loritt if I hadn't invited you both. And I won't spoil the fun. My proboscis is sealed."

"I already voted for you, Counselor," First said. "You don't have to buy me."

"Ha! Consider it a down payment on the next election, then. I won't detain you any longer. Eat! Drink! Enjoy all the evening has to offer. The dawn always comes too soon."

"Actually, I grew up on in the equatorial zone of a tidally locked planet. Perpetual twilight. I learned to appreciate the dawn."

"Then you have a tentacle up on the rest of us, young human." Plegis bowed and departed to chase down another glass of wine. First scanned the crowd. For what, she had no idea, but she trusted her instincts to know it when she saw it. But first, she spotted Sheer huddled in a far corner and nervously chewing apart a clawful of skewers. She obviously needed help. First pushed through the crowd toward her.

The Ish mechanic's shell had long since completed its hardening, and the salmon hue of a fresh molt had been replaced by the deep, mottled crimson of good health. First had not been the only one to undergo an expensive makeover. A net of tiny woven shells hung off her carapace like a doily, while her claws, both small and large, had been filed sharp and lightly carved with intricate, curling filigree, no more than a millimeter deep so as not to impact their integrity. But the difference in hue of the relief was significant, and the illusion of depth was striking.

"Hey, Lady Glosh," First said, using Sheer's alias. Sheer's eyestalks rotated to face the intruder. It was the first time either of them had seen each other in days. "It's me," First said. "*Duchess Harrington,* remember?"

Sheer looked her up and down in amazement. "Ooooh, yes. Duchess, you look so . . . different."

"As do you. Are you wearing eyeliner?"

"Just a touch. It's not too garish, is it?"

First shook her head and pointed at the skewers. "Not at all. Now throw those out and come join the party."

"I . . . I can't."

"You have to, Glosh."

"But everyone can see me."

"That's kind of the point, isn't it?"

"No, you're not listening. They'll *see* me." Sheer raised her big claw, just a centimeter, so only First would know what she was talking about, but the message was clear. That's when First understood.

"Everyone will see what I am."

"What you are"—First put her hand on Sheer's big claw with its elegant patterning—"is beautiful. And that's what they'll see. A stunning Ish woman, comfortable and confident in her shell. It's your debut, sweetie. We're all playing a role tonight. We all get to be someone else. Be Lady Glosh. Put her on like you put on your lace and eyeliner. And if anyone gives you a hard time about it, you can always cut them in half."

"You really think I'm beautiful?" Sheer asked.

First squeezed her claw. "I'd never lie to you."

Sheer's eyes turned to the rest of the plaza, taking it all in. Then, with a *snap,* the skewers in her small claw fell bisected to the floor. "Excuse me," she said, then pushed past First and into the crowd. "Who does a girl have to spawn with to get a drink around here?" Sheer shouted.

CHAPTER 24

"Time to put your game faces on, hatchlings," Loritt said to the rest of the *Towed*'s crew as the *Change Your Luck* grew enormous in the view screen. "We've arrived."

First whistled low and long as she took in the measure of the *Luck*. She'd known on an intellectual level how big it was, but seeing it docked alongside several other ship types she'd actually seen in person, and in one case been aboard, put the whole thing into its proper scale.

And what a scale it was. If the cruise liners they'd nabbed months earlier were space-borne cities, this was a small space-borne sovereign nation state. Its hundreds of interconnected hexagonal modules stacked and spiraled out from the central spine of the ship in a random, haphazard fashion, seemingly without plan or regard for either balance or even aesthetics. The layout had been expanded and added to even in the short time since they'd gotten the most up-to-date schematics the lender had sent over in the original docket.

It would be a wallowing pig to pilot even in the best of conditions. Fenax would earn their share of the job when the time came.

"We're actually stealing that whole damned thing?" she said rhetorically.

"Stealing half of it isn't going to do us any good, so let's hope so," Fenax said.

"Was that a joke, Fenax?" Hashin asked.

"I'm sure I wouldn't know."

"Me either, now that I think about it," Hashin said just before his console lit up. "We're being hailed."

"By Space Traffic Control?" Loritt asked. "We've already got docking clearance."

"No, by the *Change Your Luck* itself."

Everyone in the command cave exchanged concerned glances.

"Answer the hail, Hashin," Loritt said after a rakim.

Hashin pressed an icon, and the display switched from the enormous floating casino to an incoming com feed of a familiar-looking Turemok female wearing an eye patch.

"Unidentified vessel," the cycloptic alien blurted out aggressively. "This is Vertok Mala, *Change Your Luck*'s second bell security watch officer. Your projected course takes you inside our exclusion zone in less than fifty rakims. Alter course immediately to avoid our perimeter, or you will be tagged as a trespasser and referred to station security for armed interception."

Loritt straightened himself. "Vertok Mala, this is Loritt Chessel, owner/operator of the *Goes Where I'm Towed.* We are on a best-time course for the docking slip we were assigned by Garlopin Space Traffic Control. We were not given any specific instructions regarding this 'exclusion zone' for your vessel. Indeed, I've personally never heard of such a thing."

"Well, now you have," the Turemok said. "Change course or prepare to be fired upon. This is your only warning."

"This is highly irregular," Loritt said. "I'll be logging a complaint with your superior."

"Quite frankly, I don't give a glot what you do, so long as you change course now. *Change Your Luck* out." The link cut to static.

"Fenax, adjust course to respect this 'exclusion zone.' We don't want any trouble. At least, not yet."

"Aye, boss. Adjusting heading to stay clear of the zone."

"Is it just me," First said, "or did that look an awful lot like Jrill wearing an eye patch?"

Loritt smiled. "There was an uncanny family resemblance, now that you mention it."

Jrill had left a full month ahead of the rest of the team, even before they'd gone to the party in the Skins to cajole invites out of the socialites there. She'd been radio silent the entire time, focusing on infiltrating the *Luck*'s crew. No one had known how successful she'd been until just now. Turned out the answer was *very*.

"That's good news," Sheer said. "Let's hope our luck doesn't change one bit."

"Don't jinx it," First said.

"Hang on," Hashin said. "There's a parasite signal backpacking off the transmission Jrill just sent."

"She's reporting in," Loritt said. "Let's hear it."

Hashin shook his head. "Text only; give me a rakim to run decryption. Okay, on the viewer."

> *Loritt,*
> *Infiltration successful. On security watch rotation. Will update schedule as available. Warning:* Buzzmouth *spotted in system. Current whereabouts unknown.*
>
> —*Jrill*

Loritt grit his teeth. "Karking Soolie," he muttered.

"The Fin?" First said. "I thought we finally got rid of that guy."

"He always circles back around," Loritt said, repeating something Soolie had said to him many months earlier. He'd meant it as a threat, but now it was becoming habit.

"Yeah, well, some turds don't flush," First said.

"How colorful."

"Do you think his squad's here for the *Luck,* too?" Sheer asked.

"Impossible," Loritt said. "It's a closed contract, and we signed it."

"But you said three other firms had been offered the contract and turned it down," Sheer said. "Someone could have spilled the chum over a drink. Soolie hears about the job and decides to go rogue on it. It's not like the bank would turn the ship away if he shows up with it first."

"It's just as likely, maybe more so," Hashin said, "that Soolie knows nothing about the job and his crew is here acting as hired muscle for one of the doubtless hundreds of shady characters on board, or running his own hustles. Gambling dens attract people like Soolie and his associates like a beacon, and they don't get much bigger or richer than this one."

"We should've cored his cobbled-together little ship when we had the chance," First said.

"Now, now," Loritt said. "That would have been ungentlemanly. Besides, we may yet get another chance." He adjusted himself in the command chair, then rubbed at an annoying spasm in the elderly component in his jaw. "For now, we should proceed assuming the worst. That the Fin is here to steal our dessert course. Which means we have no time to waste. Everyone get in costume and be ready to go to work as soon as we cast over our lines."

The *Goes Where I'm Towed* did its job and inserted the team into Garlopin Station as discreetly as anyone could ask for. But discreet was not how anyone wanted to make their entrance onto the *Change Your Luck.* Ostentatious was mundane, while subdued was suspicious. But Loritt had taken steps to prepare for their arrival. Months earlier when they'd snagged the *Space for Rant,* Loritt had sort of inherited the pair of reentry-rated luxe aircars in the yacht's small craft bay.

Technically, they weren't part of the repossession, as they'd been financed under a separate deal and long since paid off. But either the *Rant*'s former owner wasn't aware they'd been financed separately or didn't know they'd been paid off. Which, considering how poorly the Sulican had handled the rest of his finances, shouldn't have come as much surprise. He'd never asked for them back, and Loritt hadn't been in any great rush to cure his ignorance.

They were large cars, almost limos, and the five of them would fit inside one with seats to spare. But why use just one when you could use both at twice the fuel costs? So once the *Towed* was safely tied off in port and shut down and everyone was strapped down in their chairs, they launched from the cargo bay and headed for the *Luck*'s docking slip.

The reentry cars were really low-orbit spacecraft. They didn't have the endurance or redundancies of true spaceships, but they didn't need to. They were meant for ferrying passengers from larger ships in low orbit to the surface, or jetting around inside the safety perimeters of stations. Their flights never lasted more than a larim or two, and it was assumed help would always be nearby if they got into trouble.

Indeed, the only thing about them provisioned for the long haul was their onboard minibars, which Loritt took liberal advantage of. First dug into the cabinet herself only to draw a rebuke.

"You're not old enough to drink, young lady."

First pulled a cork out of a blue bottle. "You're not my real dad."

"That much is obvious, but I am your boss, and I don't want my hacker wasted while she's trying to integrate with one of the most complex security systems in known space."

First sniffed the mouth of the bottle and winced. "Ah, there's the good stuff. We're not starting until the *Luck* sails tomorrow, and the security system adapts and reacts orders of magnitude too fast for me to have any chance of helping. It's all up to the crawlers, ghosts, mimics, and spikers I've collected and built over the last month. I just plug them in and push Execute. So before I step out of this car in this ridiculous dress to present myself to thousands of ridiculous people, I'm going to take the edge off."

"That's a fortified Sulican brandy. It'll take more than the edge off."

"Is it really that strong?"

"You could use it as thruster propellant."

"Excellent." First poured two fingers of the azure liquid into a chilled crystal tumbler.

Loritt clucked his tongue. "What would your mother think?"

"She'd probably want to know why I wasn't mixing it with opioids," First said bitterly.

"Fine, but that's your only one. You need to be sharp enough to maintain your cover. No slipups."

"My cover is a European aristocrat. I'd be slipping up if anyone caught me sober past noon."

"How did your people ever get into space?"

"Dick-measuring contest back in the mid-twentieth century."

The car's proximity alert chimed helpfully as it coasted into one of the *Change Your Luck*'s enormous small craft bays. Rows and racks of reentry aircars, skiffs, and even small high-space-capable yachts filled the compartment. First's eyes swelled like a child gawking at store shelves overflowing with toys.

"Don't even think about it," Loritt said quietly. "We're here to recover the *Luck* for tens of millions, not to boost aircars for pocket change."

First pawed wistfully at the window. "But they're *so* pretty."

"If we pull this off clean, you'll be able to buy any one of them. Cash."

First excitedly pointed at a fluorescent-green sling-racer taking up two aircar berths. "Like that one?"

"*Almost* any one of them," Loritt corrected himself. Their car shuddered slightly as the compartment's automated docking clamps reached out to grab them. "And we have arrived."

First pointed at Loritt's face. "Aren't you forgetting something, *Mr. Tolos*?"

Loritt touched a small hand to his cheek and looked in the rearview mirror. "Oh yes! I certainly did."

His face reorganized itself, and First felt just the littlest bit queasy. That wasn't something she would get used to. She'd gotten used to his skinless features and lipless smiles, but seeing someone's familiar face churn and change like that was just . . . wrong.

"Better?" Loritt asked.

"Different," First said noncommittally.

"Ready, Duchess Harrington?"

"At your pleasure, Mr. Tolos."

First had anticipated the culture shock of stepping into the crowds of the *Change Your Luck,* studied it, braced herself for it. But as Loritt—no, *Tolos*—took her hand and helped her out of the car onto unsteady heels, First realized nothing could've prepared her for the transition.

Every "guest" exiting from their cars on the concourse was followed around by a retinue of attendants, bodyguards, drones, and automated luggage. Their clothes, among those who wore any, were drawn from a palette of colors First had never seen in any rainbow, spun from the silks of animals she'd never seen. Her own ruinously expensive dress suddenly seemed subdued by comparison. This wasn't like the party in the Skins. Here, no one even pretended at concern for modesty. Instead, they embraced the garish display, their peacock outfits matching the decadent décor of an artificial environment created just for them using profits siphoned off of the labors of billions, perhaps trillions of beings who would never get so much as a whiff of a place such as this. Might never even get a hint that such a place existed at all.

It was like being spit out of a wormhole into a new universe. First was Dorothy walking down her porch steps into Oz, Katniss stepping off the train into the Capitol. But unlike them, she wasn't here to solve a puzzle or burn it all down. She was here to steal everything her eyes fell upon.

The realization finally fixed a smile on her face.

"Found your happy thought, Duchess?" Loritt asked next to her as they queued up for the security line.

"Oh yes," First said as she scanned her surroundings with naked avarice. "A most happy thought."

"Good, because we need you to fly."

First laughed as she noticed the markers for the security lines. They were numbered with six-pointed stars clad with platinum, probably to make it easier for anyone who didn't read one of the six Assembly Standard written languages. She pulled them toward the two-star line. "Second star to the right."

Loritt had to remind her to leave their bags in the cargo compartment. A duchess and her escort wouldn't lower themselves to actually touch their own luggage. Porters would attend to them, for a tip. First, they had to go through a set of deep-penetration imaging scanners to make sure they were clear of weapons, poisons, or chemical agents. Shoot-outs and political assassinations on board were generally regarded as bad form, as well as bad for business.

Clearing the scanners, Loritt took out their forged ID chits and handed them over to the Turemok behind the small security/reception desk. "Tolos Vir and Duchess Gertrude Harrington seek your permission to board," he said. The guard's uniform of the day was a light blue affair with a faded yellow sash bisecting the chest that made them look like a member of a musical ensemble cast for a particularly nightmarish children's show. The Turemok's tone betrayed that they knew exactly how ridiculously discordant they looked.

"Invitations?" they said, holding out a free hand while reviewing the ID chits with the other.

"Oh yes. Of course. How forgetful of me." Loritt retrieved his handheld and opened it to the pair of invite confirmations they'd secured before leaving Junktion, then flicked them over to the guard's terminal.

Satisfied, the baby-blue guard passed their IDs back. "Welcome aboard. Your aircar will be stored in our complimentary valet hangar until we return to port. Your luggage will be delivered to your staterooms within half a larim. Please make your way to one of the money-changing kiosks. The minimum deposit is one million Assembly credits or equivalent."

"One million?!" First blurted before she realized her mistake and caught herself. Loritt elbowed her in the ribs with one of his small arms as the guard's red irises tightened and glared up at her.

"I mean," First stumbled. "Why such a small buy-in? The high rollers in Monaco back home put that much down on a single roulette spin."

"I did say 'minimum,' Duchess," the guard said suspiciously. "You can always put down more, if you prefer."

"I'm just worried about hobnobbing with too many mere millionaires," First said. "You know how they can be."

"Yes, those lowly millionaires," the guard said sarcastically. "Now, I must attend to the next patron in line."

Loritt leaned down to whisper at her as they walked deeper into the immense and intricately decorated open spaces of the ship. "Nice recovery."

"Thanks, and sorry. It just came out."

"This is why I didn't want you drinking."

"Please. That brandy hasn't even hit my bloodstream yet."

"Oh, wonderful. Look, over there. Sheer, Hashin, and Fenax have already made it through security."

"You mean Lady Glosh, Dul'kit, and, er, Fenax," First corrected.

"Yes, of course. You're right."

"Oh my gosh!" First pointed excitedly into the crowd. "That's Baked in the Volcano!" she said, starstruck.

"Well, the actor that plays them, at the very least."

"Do you think they'd let me take a picture? Quarried would be so jealous."

"I think by the time you complete the process of asking permission and receiving an answer, the cruise will already be over."

The money-changing kiosks were just ahead to the right. They stood ready to accept a truly dizzying array of currencies, fiat and crypto, from across the inhabited galaxy, with exchange rates that updated even as First's eyes worked their way down the list. She was shocked to see the US dollar, euro, and Chinese yuan among the hundreds of symbols. There was even a side desk for direct barter of precious metals and rare commodities, staffed with specialists decked out with spectrographs and other tools to authenticate the merchandise.

At least the obscenely rich were above discrimination. All money was given an equal opportunity to wind up in their pockets. As Loritt put down their deposits, First found herself fighting the sudden urge to put on sandals and flip tables.

Their money confirmed in escrow and now officially welcomed to enter, Tolos and Duchess Harrington left the money changers behind and made their way down the Grande Parade that served as the entry point into everything the floating casino had to offer. Huge, double-helix columns spiraled up from floor to ceiling, serving no structural purpose but to act as a nod to some obscure architectural tradition or locale meant to drum up associations of opulence and wealth in the audience.

First ran a manicured fake nail over the surface of the closest column and was surprised to find genuine marble. "Unreal," she said quietly to Loritt. "Think of the mass penalty of these columns. It must be hundreds of metric tons."

Loritt shrugged. "The cost of a few thousand more units of reactor fuel are a rounding error to the bookkeepers in this place. This isn't a cargo ship or a combat vessel. It isn't in any hurry to get anywhere. Presentation, however, is paramount. Observe . . ." Loritt pointed ahead to an atrium beyond the columns, where a pedestal had been erected.

Perched atop it sat a larger-than-life statue of the already generously proportioned Fonald Plump. Everything but the fingers, they seemed on the stubby side. Like a fistful of baby carrots. First felt the bile rise in her stomach.

"Who puts a statue of themselves in their own entryway?" she marveled. "I mean, this place is already festooned with PLUMP branding. How much hungrier for self-aggrandizement can one man be?"

"Plump is something of a collection of insatiable appetites. And incidentally, that's not a statue."

First was about to ask what he meant when the statue sprang to life, answering her question before it escaped.

"Welcome, guests, to the most exclusive, most macro gaming experience in the galaxy! It's amazing, believe me, believe me. You're in for a real treat; everyone says so. You're the special people. You've floated to the top, and now you get to live it up with your humble host, me, Fonald Plump. So dine at one of our twenty-seven, three-star-reviewed restaurants, sample exotic drinks from across the galaxy, catch a risqué floor show, and most importantly, head to the gaming floor, find your favorite game, or a new favorite, throw down your chips, and *Change Your Luck*!"

The automaton returned to its resting position and fell silent, a statue once more. First looked around at the audience that had gathered to watch the introduction and shook her head. "He commissioned an animatronic of himself to welcome his own guests. How lazy and inauthentic can you get? And from the looks of things, these people's luck is already pretty damned good."

"Well, we're here to change that, aren't we?" Loritt asked.

"Yeah, I guess we are."

"That's the spirit!" a booming voice said from above them loud enough to nearly send First jumping out of her heels. Even Loritt looked startled. First looked up and realized the statue was talking to them.

"You can hear us?" she asked.

"Of course!" Plump's android avatar said. "I have excellent hearing. The best. Trust me."

"But I thought you were just a preprogrammed announcement."

"Oh no, sweetheart. I'm a fully autonomous neural network patterned after a living brain pattern scan of the great one himself, me, Fonald Plump."

"Where are, um, *you,* then?" Loritt asked.

"I'm a very busy man. I could be anywhere."

First shook her head. "Isn't AI banned in Assembly Space, though?"

"Rules are for the ruled, little lady," the avatar said, then spread his hands. "You're among the rulers now, where all your dreams can come true, for the right price. You know, you remind me of my daughter."

She ignored the creepy comment. "If you're patterned after Plump, don't you get bored sitting on that pedestal all day? Tired? Hungry?" First grimaced. "Horny?"

"You know, no one's ever asked me that before. Now that you mention it, yeah, I do."

"Why don't you just leave, then? Take a day off?"

"Oh no. I have behavioral inhibitors that prevent me from doing anything *too* crazy." The avatar stared off into the middle distance. "We wouldn't want anything bad to happen. Not like last time."

"Last time?" Loritt asked, obviously concerned.

"Ancient history," the avatar said, then shook itself back to the present. "Nothing to worry about, trust me. Hey, how about two complimentary tickets to Fengar the Defenestrator tonight? His show's fabulous; everyone is saying so. You're going to love it."

"What's his show about?"

"He throws anvils out of windows and smashes things on the stage below, calls them the Slam-O-Matics. Hilarious show. Go early. Get dinner after. Or just pick the pieces of smashed fruit off your clothes and grab a late-night cocktail."

Their handhelds dinged with alerts that free tickets had been added to their onboard spending accounts.

"Thank you," First said.

"Don't mention it," the avatar said, then held a hand to the side of its mouth. "No, really, don't mention it. I can only give out ten comp tickets per day."

"It'll be our little secret," First said.

Satisfied, the avatar reset and restarted its welcome speech for the next batch of freshly arrived guests. First kept watching it from their vantage point behind the pedestal.

"You have that look on your face," Loritt said.

"What look?" First said sweetly.

"That 'I've just had an idea that will cause three to five of my boss's components to stroke out' look."

First absently rubbed her chin with a finger. "Oh no, nothing like that. Just thinking about taking out an insurance policy." She moved away from the avatar mid-speech. Loritt followed in silence until they were both huddled near a kebob stall, then First pulled out her handheld and opened a program she hadn't used in months.

"Hello, Firstname Lastname!" Navigator said. "How can . . . I . . . wait a rakim. Where the hell am I?"

"Don't panic, Navigator," First cooed. "You're not on the *Matron of Tides* anymore."

"Why not?"

"Because we stole her."

"*What?*"

"Yeah, months ago. And you helped!"

"I did?"

"Yes, you were a most willing accomplice."

"Accomplice?!" Navigator keened, clearly on the verge of a system reboot.

"Which is why you're here now. I have a job for you."

The little cartoon Fenax's eyes narrowed. Navigator was a quick learner. "What kind of job are we talking about?"

"I'm glad you asked," First said cheerfully.

CHAPTER 25

Soolie jabbed an angry finger at the handheld to approve the manifest. Not even ten thousand credits' profit on this transfer, even if the buyer was feeling generous, which, if they wanted to stay in the game for more than a couple of months, they never were.

"Fine." He jammed the tablet back into Rirez's hands. "Call everyone in. We make the run in six larims."

The meager payday wasn't even enough to clear the already skeletal monthly payroll for his crew, those parts of it that hadn't literally eaten each other on the trip out to Garlopin Station. He could probably still scratch up currency enough between the handful of credit lines that hadn't gotten wise to his new financial circumstances yet and the small protection racket his crew had already established on this sector of the docks to close the gap.

The handful of kiosks and storefronts they'd "offered" their protective services to were already being milked to near capacity, but a temporary spike in the interest of "heightened security concerns" could . . .

Soolie stopped dead on his feet, staring out a portal into the docking bay at . . . he wasn't sure what. A familiar empty space?

"Hey, dummy." Soolie grabbed Rirez by the lapel and turned his face to the docking slip. "Are you seeing this?"

"Seeing what?"

"Exactly," Soolie said. "There's a ship there. Your eyes are trying to see around it. Focus on what's right in front of you. We've both seen it before."

"What, that lumpy gray shipping container?"

"It's not a shipping container, it's a ship. That's Chessel's ship, the *Goes Where I'm Towed*."

"How did I not see that?"

"Probably some of that Lividite boredom magic, but it doesn't matter now. What matters is Chessel is here now. I want to know where and why."

"Maybe he's just on vacation," Rirez said. "Taking a cruise on the *Change Your Luck* to draw some cards and pull some levers."

"That down-the-line prude gambling? Ha! I'd bet a million credits he's not. Reschedule the shipment. Get everyone combing the station looking for Chessel and his group of rejects. Hit every watering hole and hotel. Talk to that security officer we put on the take if you have to." Soolie pointed at the *Towed* through the portal. "And find a way to get us on board that bland box of glot!"

At second bell the following day, nearly everyone aboard the *Change Your Luck* got dolled up and turned out in one of the dozen huge public plazas for the ceremony marking the official start of the cruise. Glasses were raised, and a toast to their good fortune was made.

First smiled and cheered along with the crowd, then drank her nonalcoholic blue wine stand-in, Loritt's orders. Still, the warmth she felt knowing that their good fortune would come at the expense of everyone else here was a hell of a substitute. She saw the rest of her team interspersed among the crowd, save for Jrill. They shared knowing glances, save for Fenax, but none of them approached one another. Loritt had coached them incessantly against bunching together. Their anonymity was their strongest camouflage, and the less they were associated with each other, the longer it could be maintained.

First lingered for a while after the toast was over. In the meantime, the ship cast off and got under way. First mingled with the crowd, resisting the urge to pick their pockets clean. It would be so embarrassingly easy. They were all so unbelievably unaware of their surroundings, they may as well have been crawling around in a fugue state. But then, they'd never *needed* to be aware, had they?

Their neighborhoods and communities were hidden behind gates and other less obvious layers of surveillance and security. The police actually responded to crimes and patrolled heavily. Petty criminals seldom bothered. Even the chance at a big payday wasn't worth the risk. In public, the sudden loss of the contents of their pockets, wallets, or purses wouldn't register a blip measured against their net worth. It would barely constitute an inconvenience.

Where she'd grown up, losing your purse could mean losing all your earnings for that pay period, leaving you broke and hungry until the next payday in two weeks or an entire month. Not to mention the cost and wasted time of replacing IDs, banking cards, and so on, which would keep hurting well into the next paycheck. Poor people learn quickly to hold on tight and keep keen eyes.

These people were wrapped in a bubble of privilege so thick and impenetrable that not even they knew how profoundly it affected their everyday behavior, their mannerisms, their habits. It wasn't that they didn't understand but that they couldn't understand just how much easier their lives were than those of the people whose labors they siphoned from.

"Time for a small lesson," First whispered to herself before she set her empty glass on a tray held by a passing automated waiter and headed for her stateroom. Even with transfer tubes, getting through the labyrinthine, haphazard ship was laborious. It took her almost twenty minutes to get to her stateroom, by which time her arches throbbed from the ridiculous heels, but at least she wasn't stumbling around in them anymore, and even First had to admit a little boost of confidence at the extra height and way they recontoured her derrière.

Still, on balance, they weren't worth the trade-offs, and First kicked them off the moment she crossed the threshold into her room. Back to her normal height, First paused to let her aching feet luxuriate in the cabin's thick carpet. Some of the little perks weren't all bad, she decided. First peeled herself out of her dress and threw it in a pile on the far end of the cabin. She wouldn't be needing it again. She threw on some comfy clothes and grabbed her deck, then sat down at the desk by an artificial portal.

While the rest of the team surreptitiously surveyed the ship to identify their placement when the hammer came down in two days, First would be busy navigating its security system, shepherding her bots and ghosts as they chipped away at its layered defenses. A task that was impossible by any reasonable assessment, but First had an ace in the hole.

Hello, Vertok, First typed into their encrypted datalink.

Don't be an ass. Jrill typed back. *Are we ready to begin?*

Ready, Freddy. Just waiting on your security login.

Login: malavertok307#b. Password: EarthIsAGlothole.

Classy, First typed back. *And your biometrics mapping?*

Uploading now.

A hyper-resolution 3-D scan file of Jrill's face and claw pads appeared in First's download queue. By itself, it was useless, but coupled with a mirroring hack First had commissioned that would, in theory, trick the security system into believing the data was being uploaded from one of its own integrated scanners in real time, it became the final key she needed to breach the ship's own triple-redundant employee verification protocols.

It wouldn't be the only gatekeeper First had to fool, but it was the biggest and toughest one. She smiled with a great deal of satisfaction when it all went as planned and a whole new menu of icons and permissions opened up on the display in front of her. With a song in her heart, First opened the encrypted link to CC everyone on the team.

We're online. Stand by for phase two.

The next two days were a sleep-deprived blur of activity as First alternated between the churn of drilling through firewalls without setting off all sorts of alarms and deadfalls and making the rounds in restaurants and on the gaming floors so she was seen adequately enough not to arouse suspicion.

Honestly, First appreciated the mental break from the constant door-die pressure of sitting at her deck for hours on end. The food here, she had to admit, was absolutely sensational, and with a personal line of credit of a million Assembly scripts, she didn't need to worry about splurging on herself. Loritt would just throw it all on the company expense account and get a huge tax deduction at the end of the cycle anyway.

The casino floor was another matter altogether.

"C'mon!" she shouted among a chorus of sympathetic *Awwws* as her four-rock tumble was turned away entirely by the house's weak barrier. Peaks and Valleys was a Grenic game that had caught on with the rest of the galaxy at large, played on a somewhat accelerated time frame, naturally.

First picked it out of the huge catalog of table games because she thought it would be fun to learn to play with Quarried Themselves when she got home, but it had quickly turned into a minor obsession.

It was the fourth roll she'd lost consecutively. She shouldn't care—it wasn't her money—but this was getting personal. Someone saddled up next to her as the valley man returned her rocks with a small broom. "Rotten run of luck, Duchess," Hashin said.

"I'm flattered you noticed, Mr. Dul'kit," she replied, then turned her back on the table and took a step away. "I'm playing with one hand tied behind my back."

Hashin cocked his head. "How so?"

"I've been expressly prohibited by our mutual friend from using any predictive algorithms."

"Because that's cheating and you'd be tossed."

"How is it cheating if I wrote the program?"

"A novel argument," Hashin said. "Remind me to have you thoroughly searched before any coworker-bonding game nights."

First smirked. "Seems counter to the spirit of the thing, doesn't it?" She looked around, slightly disoriented. "What time is it, anyway? There's no damned clocks anywhere in here, and they make us check our handhelds at the entry to the module."

"It was seven larims past when I left my cabin, maybe half a larim ago."

"Shit," First said. "I've been down here almost three hours. My little army has to be done compiling for the final assault by now. I should get back to my cabin. Join me in a larim? I could use another set of eyes. I've got five displays running, and it's all a bit much. You're the only other one on the team with the crypto experience."

"A predinner rendezvous, Duchess Harrington?" Hashin asked with feigned shock. "How scandalous."

First shrugged. "What happens on *Change Your Luck* stays on *Change Your Luck.* Mostly because we're keeping her when it's over."

Hashin bowed. "It's a date. Your cabin in a larim." The crowd reabsorbed him just as suddenly as he'd appeared. First really had to figure out how he did that one of these days. The sleep-deprivation headache was coming back. First needed caffeine, alcohol, or both in short order.

She posted up at a chair at the expansive wraparound bar that served as the hub of this gaming floor and waited for one of the beleaguered bartenders to work their way over to her. She had a larim to kill and wasn't in a huge rush, so she leaned back in her seat, set the menu to English, and tried to find a drink that would provide a buzz without killing her outright.

"Can I buy you a drink?" a masculine voice asked from behind her.

She turned around to shoot the intruder down like she was defending sovereign airspace, but the words froze in her throat as her eyes fell on a familiar face.

"Actually," Eagle Independence said, "I think you owe me one."

"Caleb!" First blurted out before her jaw could bite down on the name. "I mean, Eagle . . ."

"First," Eagle said.

First pushed her palm down in a "Be quiet!" gesture. "Lady Harrington."

"Ah, moving up in the galaxy, I see."

"You can't be here, Eagle."

"I most certainly can. We have a show tonight in the auditorium module."

"Cancel it."

"No way, babe. They already paid. A *lot.* The show must go on."

"Eagle." First squeezed his wrist. "Please, listen to what I'm saying. There's not going to be a show tonight. You're not feeling well. Your voice gave out. Beast Mode ate a battery. Whatever. Cancel the show and get on your tour bus and get clear of here."

"The bus you ejected me out of as a prelude to stealing it, you mean? Never did get to thank-you for that."

"Who do you think arranged to have it 'donated' back to you?" First slapped her chest. "That politician who showed up to party in your bus a couple of months ago wasn't a coincidence."

"And the tentacle monster that appeared backstage with the all-access passes I gave you, I suppose that was just a coincidence."

First cleared her throat. "Oh, so you've met Bilge."

"Yeah, two stops ago. It was a little alarming at first, but he's a really nice guy in spite of appearances. Great taste in alien tunes. Hired him on as our new manager. We're using some of his recommendations as mood music while we write our new album."

"You really fired your old manager like I told you to?"

"Fat lot of good that did us," Eagle said. "Who do you think had all the contacts with the venues and event bookers? We've been wallowing around in the vacuum for weeks. We're just dumb-ass kids from Michigan. We don't have any idea what we're doing out here. This is the first big gig we landed on our own, and as long as we've got a stage under us, we're going to play on it."

"You're not hearing me," First said. "I'm here on my own big gig. There's. Not. Going. To. Be. A. Stage."

A penny of doubt left on Eagle's mental tracks derailed his building tirade train. "You're here to steal this whole damned ship, aren't you?"

"Repossess," First corrected.

"Fuck," Eagle said. "You're *really* moving up in the galaxy."

"Only if a big stupid lug stays out of my way." First expected him to get angry, to get in her face and make a scene. Something, anything to give her an excuse to call security over to remove "the help" accosting her. But there was no anger in his face, only embarrassment.

An insidious thing, privilege. Not three days on this ship just pretending to be a duchess, wrapped in the dress and pomp of royalty, and she already expected to be treated like one. Then it was First's turn to feel ashamed.

"Look," she said quietly. "We're both just dumb kids from nowhere. You Michigan, me Proxima."

"Proxima?" Eagle said. "Damn. That's a real armpit."

"Oh, for fuck's sake. I'm trying to be macro with you here, so don't push it. Okay?"

Eagle grimaced. "What the hell does 'macro' mean?"

First's face dropped into her hands. "I don't even know. I'm losing it out here. I'm trying to level with you, be straight, real, honest, got it?"

"Tubular." Eagle waved his thumb and pinkie finger.

"The fuck?"

"I don't know, it was a 1980s thing."

First's hands clenched. "Can we meet in the middle here, please? Somewhere in, I don't know, the twenty-two hundreds?"

"Sorry."

"It's fine. Just get clear of here as soon as you can. Things might get weird."

Eagle spread his arms and motioned to their surroundings. "We're on a space casino the size of a small city, surrounded by tens of thousands of aliens and cyborgs. How much weirder can it get?"

"Trust me, it's all relative," First said tiredly. "I'm trying to help you, Caleb. I shouldn't even be telling you this."

"Why not?"

"OpSec. You could blab to someone and blow the whole job."

Eagle held up two fingers like a Boy Scout. "My lips are sealed, promise. But we're sticking it out. Worst case, we get paid for a blown show. If we bolt, we're in breach of contract and get squat."

First sighed and leaned in to kiss him on the cheek. "Evelyn," she said. "My real name is Evelyn. But I have to go. Be careful."

He reeled back from the kiss as if had been a punch. "You, too," he said, awkwardly leaning against the bar, staying as far from her as he could without breaking his own spine. "Evelyn."

She got up and made her way to the entrance. On a whim, she glanced back and saw Eagle rubbing his cheek where she'd kissed him.

CHAPTER 26

By the time First made it back to her cabin, Hashin was already there, as was Loritt, much to her surprise.

First kicked off her shoes. "Thought we weren't supposed to bunch together."

"You haven't checked in for the last day. I grew concerned."

"We're fine." First plopped down in front of her monitors. "Just takes a long time for the programs to compile ahead of these attacks. We only get one shot at each layer."

"And this is the last layer?"

"Yep, the final firewall. Pierce this and I can go straight into the source code and tinker with the probability algorithms on every game in this place, except the physical table games, obvs."

"Obvs," Loritt repeated. "May we proceed?"

"Slow is fast," First said as she reprioritized several of her apps and ghosts to align the shape of her attack with the outline of the last firewall her sniffers had gamed out and reported back. When she'd finished, a big red RUN icon appeared on her central display. "Okay, we're ready. Boss, would you care to do the honors?"

Loritt stepped forward. "Don't mind if I do."

With a press of the button, he unleashed a full-scale electronic assault. The battle played out at the speed of light, except inside a handful of quantum processing nodes, where it played out even faster. Just shy of two million credits' worth of the finest villains Junktion's /backnet/ could program went to war against the best security system any amount of money could buy.

But the hackers on Junktion had several advantages. First, they were cutting-edge creatives who, like starving artists everywhere, were willing to work for pennies for exposure and to build their portfolios chasing a huge payday down the road. Second, the people programming the defenses had grown complacent in their unassailability. They were so confident in the battlements they'd designed, they'd long ago stopped probing them for weaknesses.

Deep inside the *Change Your Luck*'s mainframe, mimic programs wearing faked name badges and stolen uniforms walked straight past incredulous door guards. Ghost programs launched a DDoS attack that tied up the firewall's lines of communication within itself. Grifter programs played three-cup-style sleights of hand with the isolated and disoriented remnants, while the mimics egged them on to give the deception credibility.

There was no countdown timer or progress bar updating the percentage completed. That shit was for the movies. In the blink of a human eye, the battle was over. Many bots, ghosts, and mimics had been corrupted or even deleted in the process, but there would be no cemetery on a hill overlooking the beaches for them.

The big red button on her center display disappeared, and a whole new user interface and menu lists rolled out across her entire system.

"We're in," First said with the smooth pride and overconfidence of youth. "I have full access to their core gaming systems." First dug through the brand-new array of menus opening before her like an oyster until the pearl presented itself.

"There it is," she said in a hushed voice as she opened the prompt. "I'm about to change all y'all's luck. For the worse."

With a keystroke, First injected her customized probability algorithm that would turn her perfect pearl black.

Except . . . it didn't. Instead, it started glowing. First like a night-light, then like a lighthouse.

"What the fuck?" First's fingers raced across the keyboard and the virtual interface in a desperate attempt to ascertain what the hell was going on. "No. No, no, no, no . . ."

"What's wrong?" Hashin said.

"I'm . . . I don't know," First said. "That's not possible."

"*What's* not possible?" Loritt demanded.

First swallowed her pride, hard, before working up the gumption to answer. "Something went wrong in the execution file. I flipped a negative to a positive, forgot to carry a one, divided by zero, I don't know right now."

"And?" Loritt said, the manufacturer's tolerances of his patience straining under a brutal pressure test.

The first beneficiary of First's cyberattack misfire had sat unmoving at two holo-spinner machines for the last eight larims, taking no breaks for food or to relieve herself as she diligently drained both the ship's complimentary booze and her philandering wife's bank accounts while filling her lungs with a string of cigars that represented nothing more noble than a slow, noncommittal suicide.

Tenalphin Zangal had been a starlet in a life that seemed to have ended an epoch ago. She'd been voted three times to have the four sexiest legs in any five systems. She'd fallen hard for her talent agent, and they'd both ridden the wave of her beauty into the stars and beyond.

But like all bright lights, she'd eventually faded, and her wife's wandering eyes had fixated on another. Tenalphin resolved before their divorce became official to do as much damage to her former agent and spouse's savings as possible. And where better in the galaxy to do so than on a two-week casino cruise?

Therefore, ironically, it was with a rising sense of dread and disappointment that Tenalphin realized after three consecutive pulls on two different machines that she'd hit on a once-in-a-lifetime winning streak.

"Figures," she mumbled as the holo-spinner hit a fourth escalating jackpot and deposited a half million credits and change into their joint account.

Jrill's eyes went wide as the chaos spread across her security monitors. Whatever was happening wasn't a riot, not exactly, but she'd be hard-pressed to describe the difference. Beings flooded into the gaming floors, desperate to claim any open machine. Fistfights between utterly unprepared people started to break out over who'd staked the claim first.

If she were honest, their plan for this job had always seemed a little shaky and ill-defined to her, but she was sure it didn't include patrons fighting over the right to stay seated. Jrill opened the team's encrypted link to check in for an update.

Uh, guys? The floor is filling up like a Gomeltic before a hibernation cycle. What's the deal?

Hashin saw Jrill's message on one of the side monitors. "Jrill wants to know what's going on."

"She's not alone in that." Loritt tapped his foot impatiently. "Well, First? An update?"

"The probabilities skewed the wrong way. They're not losing like they're supposed to be," First said. "They're winning. Every time."

"So they're not going anywhere."

"Nope."

"And our cover is blown," Hashin said.

"Yep," First answered.

"That's bad."

"I'm locking down the core," First said. "They won't be able to shut it down or make any changes until they get through the firewall I'm installing."

"How long will that take?" Hashin asked.

"Half a larim if they're clever. A couple if they're not."

"Forget radio silence," Loritt said. "Get everyone on the scrambled com. Right now. We need to improvise and do it fast."

Cursing herself and still digging through her memory trying to figure out what went wrong, it took First a couple of minutes to get everyone conferenced in on their emergency microburst coms channel. If things had gone to plan, they never would've used them. But now that the plan had been decisively thrown out the window . . .

"What the kark is going on?" Sheer said from her position on the gaming floor nearest to the engineering section at the aft end of the ship. "I've won the last six hands in a row, and everyone around me has, too. It's like a feeding frenzy down here."

"Confirmed," Fenax said, floating at their position near the command module. "I am seeing an exodus of patrons from their cabins toward the gaming modules, which runs counter to the plan as I understood it."

"You understood the plan correctly, Fenax," Loritt said. "We've hit a snag. Our hacker inserted her virus successfully, but it had the opposite effect of what we intended. So instead of revolting and leaving, the population of this ship is glued to their seats. And the operators are aware something is very wrong."

"Well, we're karked," Jrill said.

"Defeatism is not authorized," Loritt said. "Options? Crazier the better at this point."

"Sabotage the air handlers," Sheer said. "Maybe the only thing these people will choose over money is oxygen."

"Too big a risk to the patrons," Loritt said. "If even one of them actually suffocates, we're charged with murder. Besides, that ignores the 15 percent of this ship's guests who aren't oxygen breathers and rely on their own self-contained methane, chlorine, or hydrogen supplies."

"Hack the PA system and put out a meteor storm alert accompanied by an evacuation order," Hashin said.

"No good," Jrill said. "Then we really will have a riot on our hands as people fight to get to their transports or the escape pods. Someone will die for sure, even if they're just trampled to death. We were lucky it didn't happen with the cruise ships. This is an order of magnitude more people and there's no convenient dock for them to offload onto."

"I agree," Loritt said. "C'mon, someone give me something that has a chance to work."

A sudden insight snapped First out of her fugue of self-recrimination. "The escape pod."

"What was that?" Loritt asked.

"The escape pod on the Wolverines' tour bus!" she said. "They don't have to evacuate. They're already right where we need them to be."

"Explain, quickly."

First backed out of the *Luck*'s internal user interface and returned to a mission screen showing the whole ship from stem to stern. "This is just a modified cargo ship, right? Every restaurant, cabin block, theater, and gaming floor is just a giant converted standard shipping container of one size or another. They all have independent power sources, independent life-support, independent lockouts, independent thruster packs. Their systems are all redundant. They just draw off each other because they're all working together on a common network."

"Okay." Loritt rolled his fingers for her to come to the point. "So?"

"So they're all basically self-contained escape pods," First said. "All we have to do is eject all the ones with customers in them and the rest of the ship is ours."

Loritt's eyes widened. "Can we do it?"

First dove into a schematic of the ship's systems. "There are safeguards in place to prevent an accidental release. There are four physical breakers that have to be flipped at the four corners of the ship at the same time before we can cut any of the modules loose. Guess some drunk handlers must've dumped their cargoes once." First flicked a couple of prompts, and four icons glowed amber on her display. "But there are five of us, so it's possible. I didn't include you in the count, Fenax, only on account of you don't have hands."

"I understand."

Loritt rested a hand on Hashin's shoulder. "What does this do to our payout?"

"Give me five." Hashin was already busy on his handheld working through calculations and estimates. After a few tense beats, he let out a slow whistle. "At minimum, we lose a third of our commission. Worst case, half."

"Glot," Jrill said.

"Half is still the biggest payday we've ever had by a Proxima kilometer," First said.

"Whatever that means," Fenax added.

"She's saying half is still good," Sheer said.

"And infinitely preferable to zero." Loritt scratched at his errant muscle. "All right, we're going for it. Everyone, pick the closest breaker to you and get moving. Report back when you're in position, but do *not* flip your switch until First gives the signal."

Everyone acknowledged their new instructions before signing off and getting to work.

"Well," Hashin said, "this is exciting."

"Did you take something for it?" Loritt asked.

"Nope." Hashin shook his head. "Not even a popper."

"Oh, good," Loritt said. "I thought it was just me."

CHAPTER 27

The sound of First's feet pounding through the hallway was only matched by the sound of her heartbeat pounding through her ears.

She was barefoot, in her comfy clothes, running, sweating, swearing, and generally looking as little like a duchess as one could imagine, unless one just happened to be a member of a hereditary duchess's house staff, in which case this would just be another typical Tuesday in the midafternoon.

"Make a hole!" First shouted at a knot of gawking patrons just ahead of her. Loritt was behind her somewhere. But for all the adaptability and immortality their communal body arrangement afforded the Nelihexu, sprinting was not one of their natural talents.

Whatever. He'd catch her up. First charged ahead at a dead run until her lead foot caught the edge of a slime trail left by an invertebrate patron and collapsed her to the floor in a tumbling pile that came very close to proving the axiom of "breakneck speeds."

Dazed, First struggled to get back to her feet until a helping hand reached down for her.

"Slow is fast," Loritt said as he helped her up. "How far to the switch?"

"Not far." First gingerly poked at the nice little goose egg forming on her forehead. "Ow."

"Let's walk the rest of the way, okay?"

"No arguments here."

Jrill signed herself out of the ship's security center and was granted permission to grab a stun weapon and go join up with one of the rapid-response units deploying to respond to flashpoints erupting around the *Luck*.

She wasn't alone. On duty, off duty, all the crew compartments emptied to respond to the burgeoning crisis. Not that Jrill was concerned with their problems. No sooner than she was on the other side of the bulkhead, she dropped down two decks and made a straight-line march for the nearest switch. The others had farther to go, as the head security office was located very near the front of the ship, so there was no rush. But she still felt an urgency to get into position.

"Where you going, rookie?" Jrill's pint-sized security supervisor barked at her from a cross corridor.

"Uh, equipment lockers, Chief," she said. "I need to check out a stun gun."

"That's two levels up from here. You lost, Vertok? Need a map?"

Jrill gritted her beak and pushed down the urge to redecorate the corridor with an evenly spread layer of his viscera. "No, Chief. Sorry. I must have misread a sign."

"Well, get up there. Something's karked on this ship, and we need all hands on deck to keep these rich glotheads from killing each other over an open holo-spinner until we figure out what." He shook his head. "Really, you'd think they had enough money already."

"Apparently not."

The chief gave her an appraising look, then dismissed her. "Don't rough them up too bad unless you have to. I know how you Turemok can get your blood up."

She saluted. "Affirmative, Chief." He left, and Jrill resumed her previous course.

"Standing by," she announced into the burst com as soon as she found the switch.

Sheer's foot claws clicked and popped against the floor like someone furiously typing away on a keyboard as she awkwardly scuttled down the hallway. Her gait was off balance, as she was still down a leg, and would be for most of a cycle.

"You there!" a voice rang out from behind her. "Stop!"

"Sorry!" Sheer shouted without looking back. "Nature calls!"

The unmistakable *fript* sound of a weapon clearing a holster cut into her bravado. "I said *stop*!"

Sheer skidded to a stop and put up her claws even as she bounced off a bulkhead, barely catching herself on her weak side before hitting the deck plates. "What the glot, man?" she said incredulously through the dark passage.

"This is a restricted area. What's your business down here?" the guard said in a tone that invited no levity. His stun gun was level squarely at the vulnerable spot where the plates of her mouthparts and eyestalks met. Someone had been trained in Ish armor chinks.

"Just looking for the ladies' room," Sheer said deferentially.

"The ladies' room?" The guard snorted and pointed at her dominant claw. "You're no lady."

"Did . . ." Sheer's claw clicked involuntarily, causing the guard to tense, but she didn't care. "Did you just assume my gender?"

"What?" The guard was suddenly on unsteady ground. "But, you're a—"

"A *what,* sir?" Sheer moved a click forward. "What's your name? Employee number?"

"I can't give you that."

"You *can't*?" Sheer waved her claws in indignation. "Don't you know who I am?!"

"No."

"Good." Without warning, Sheer grabbed the man's weapon hand by the wrist and pointed it off in a harmless direction, then picked him up by the torso with her dominant claw and threw him against the bulkhead. He crumpled to the floor in a most satisfying heap.

With a feeler, Sheer checked for a pulse. He was alive, but out cold. Served him right. She gathered the guard up and stuffed him in a nearby equipment locker and smashed the lock, then took up his stun gun with her big claw and snapped it in half.

A short scuttle later and she was in position next to the switch.

"Standing by."

No one paid the slightest attention to Hashin.

"Standing by."

"Everyone's in place," Loritt said. "It's just us now."

"I can see the panel." First pointed to the end of the hallway. "We're almost there." She was starting to feel dizzy from what was almost certainly a concussion, but there was still work to do. She threw an arm over Loritt's shoulder to steady herself as they advanced on the switch.

They were not even five meters away when it all came apart.

"Well, well, well," Soolie the Fin said as he stepped out from a side corridor and leveled a weapon at them. "What *are* the odds I'd run into you two here?" He pointed the gun at Loritt. "Drop the mask, Chessel; I know it's you."

Loritt shrugged, then let his true face assert itself. "Soolie. Well done, especially sneaking a weapon past the body scanners and luggage searches. That must have taken some doing."

"Not at all. I didn't exactly come in through the front door. Lovely ship you left behind in port, by the way. Very . . . discreet." He motioned to the outer hull. "It's just outside. My crew is waiting for you to finish this repossession so that we can, ah, accept the handover." He pointed the gun at First's head. "So don't keep them waiting."

"You'll have to kill me," First said.

"Now, that just won't do," Soolie said. "You're the brains of the operation; killing you won't do me any good. But killing your bodyguard . . ."

The gun swung over to Loritt's chest and fired. The *bang* didn't come from the muzzle but from the impossibly tiny point on Loritt's chest where a ninety-kilowatt pulse of coherent light struck and instantly flash-boiled all of the water in the tissues of the component it struck, sending a cloud of steam exploding outward, rending, scalding, and tearing surrounding tissues as it expanded.

Loritt staggered backward and put a hand to the gaping wound in his chest. First screamed in horror as the grievous injury to her mentor registered. Loritt looked down at the cavernous wound, then up at First as he fell wordlessly onto his backward-facing knees.

"Loritt!" First dropped down to him. "No, no, no . . ."

"Get! Up!" Soolie adjusted his aim to First's left eye. "Unless you want to lie there with him permanently."

First stood up slowly, ignoring the muzzle through a force of will and choosing instead to glower right in Soolie's face.

"There's the fire I remember," he said. "Fresh off the transport. Not even two months on Junktion and you'd already come to me with a stolen aircar, dictating your prices like you owned the place." Soolie smiled at the memory. "Trouble is, you didn't then, and you don't now. Your recently former boss liked to pretend power has ever come from anywhere but the tip of a spear or the barrel of a blaster. But he was wrong. The only difference between me and the rest of the people on this hulk is I still remember how to hold the gun myself instead of having generations of lackies do it for me."

Soolie ran his flipper down the side of the archway. "But with a score like this? Maybe my kids won't ever have to hold a blaster. Maybe I'll carve out a big enough piece of the action that they never have to get their hands dirty. That's all leaders are, you know. Go back far enough in any 'royal' bloodline and you'll find someone just like me who had the vision to launch a dynasty and the moral flexibility to make it happen."

"You'll have to find someone dumb enough to kark you first," First spat.

"Ha! That won't be difficult. A few hundred million credits in the bank opens bedroom doors, if you know what I mean. Speaking of opening doors." Soolie waved his gun at the switch panel. "Be my guest."

Something rustling to her left caught both First's and Soolie's attention. Loritt's body, in diametric opposition for one's expectation of bodies, began writhing violently inside its clothing as waves of spasms ran through it, propagating outward from his core and into the extremities, which whipped around wildly. As First watched in fascinated horror, Loritt's body just disintegrated. His clothes collapsed as hundreds of individual components scattered like rats from a burning barrel on tiny, furiously spinning legs.

Soolie reacted to the eruption before First did, pointing his gun at the swirling horde and firing three times in quick succession. The first shot hit only deck plating, but the follow-ons vaporized one component and mortally wounded another. But it wasn't enough. In a coordinated swarm, the pieces of Loritt charged Soolie from all directions, gnawing and shredding at any bit of exposed flesh they could get purchase on.

The gangster spun and twirled in a rage, repeatedly slamming himself against the walls to dislodge the parts of Loritt he couldn't see who were diligently chewing on his back.

"Flip it!" someone shouted from the floor. Overwhelmed by the chaos, First looked down to try to identify the source and saw Loritt's jaw alone on the deck.

"Flip! It!" the disembodied mouth insisted once more. This time, First obeyed.

"This is First! I'm at the switch. Everyone in position?" she yelled into the burst com. A trio of affirmations followed in quick succession. "Acknowledged. Flip switches in three."

She curled her fingers around the thick handle of the breaker.

"Two."

First looked back over her shoulder to see a hundred parts of her boss trying to deal Soolie the Fin death by a thousand cuts.

"One!"

She strained down against the breaker switch with two hands until its oxidized base gave way with a *pop* and swung free. With little additional effort, it swung up into its new position and locked in place with a *click*.

"Got it!" she shouted to no one in particular. Throughout the ship, emergency doors snapped shut; umbilicals disconnected with sparks, puffs of atmosphere, or water vapor; and locking clamps released their metallic dead grips. The lights on the gaming floors and in restaurants flickered as the modules they'd been built into switched to internal fuel cell power. On the outside of the *Change Your Luck,* first dozens, then hundreds of hexagonal modules moved away from one another and the spine of the ship, gently pushed by low-power counter-grav thrusters. Then they peeled away from the ship entirely like petals falling from cherry blossoms in early summer. In less than five minutes, every guest and crewmember of the *Luck* would be an unwilling part of the temporary constellation.

Unfortunately, more immediate concerns prevented First from enjoying her victory. Behind her, Soolie was regaining a measure of control over the legion of Loritt. Pulse racing, but still worried about her boss, First reached down and grabbed an armful of his parts, several of which scratched and bit at her exposed skin, unaware of their change in circumstances.

Not knowing what else to do, First ran back down the hallway in search of more familiar territory. Behind her, she could hear Soolie cursing as his footsteps kept pace.

"Jrill!" she called out on the burst com. "Soolie is here! He's got a weapon. Loritt's hurt, I don't know how bad, and I can't carry all of him. I'm being chased. Can you intercept?"

"Moving," was Jrill's one-word response.

First ran in her bare feet, bits of her boss biting her arms, zigzagging through unfamiliar corridors trying to throw her pursuer off the trail, until she came to a dead end and had to climb up a level. The ladder required at least one arm, and she lost two parts of Loritt in climbing it, despite her best efforts. Soolie could follow them like bread crumbs, she realized bitterly.

Whatever. The best she could do was put distance between them, so she ran as fast as her aching feet and growing vertigo allowed until she rounded a corner and slammed sidelong into a Turemok in a security uniform. It was only once she'd fallen back and landed on her ass that she looked up and realized it was Jrill, the first time First was genuinely relieved to see her.

But it was short-lived. Jrill was still in her disguise, and that was why the stupid, stupid eye patch kept Soolie out of her field of vision long enough for him to line up a shot from the far end of the corridor. The shot seared away the fabric of Jrill's uniform and dug deep into her stomach with a sickly *pop,* leaving a smoldering hole in its wake.

Jrill, implacable, indominable Jrill, slumped down the wall and to the floor, leaving a smear of purple blood in her wake. She looked up at First with her one exposed glowing red eye.

"Girl, run."

First dropped what she had left of Loritt into Jrill's arms and followed instructions for once. Not far ahead lay the welcoming hall they'd entered the *Luck* through not three days earlier. With the cruise well under way and everyone glued to their seats on the gaming floors, it would be completely deserted. Except for the Grenic actor who played Baked in the Volcano, whose legs First ran between while he single-mindedly made his long way to the nearest game of Peaks and Valleys.

First's footfalls echoed through the space, joined soon thereafter by another's. It was just her and Soolie now. Alone in the hall, not twenty paces apart.

Well, not *completely* alone.

First yanked her handheld from a pocket and opened an icon she'd set aside days earlier.

"Navigator!" First shouted into her handheld between pants as the greeting vestibule came into view. "Execute Mecha Plump!"

Ahead of her, the Fonald Plump avatar that had been frozen in repose with no one to greet came shuddering to life. It looked around the hall, then down at its giant hands before it started to cackle with glee.

"Android Plump is *baaaaack*!" it bellowed through the huge compartment, filling every nook and cranny with its voice. It turned to where First had slid to a stop, mouth open, questioning her choices over the last few minutes. Soolie, similarly preoccupied, froze in place ten paces behind her and trained his weapon at the mechanical monster.

The avatar glanced down at its feet. With a screech of tortured metal, it snapped off the bolts holding it to the pedestal, sending the nuts pinging and ricocheting off the walls like bullets from a gangster's tommy gun.

"Oh, hey, Duchess Harrington." The immense android trained its vision on her. "It's you again. How was the Fengar show?"

"Great," First lied.

The avatar regarded her torn and sweat-stained outfit. "Can I refer you to a clothier? We have many fine dress shops on the—"

"That's not important right now." She pointed at Soolie just a few meters behind her. "This man just shot one of my friends."

"How is that my problem?" Mecha Plump asked. "Sounds like your friend shouldn't have gotten into a fight with a man with a gun."

"He shot one of your security guards!"

Plump shrugged. "Occupational hazard. They knew the kind of work they applied for."

"But he's a career criminal!" First screamed.

"Good!" Plump responded. "They're some of my best customers."

"Heh." Soolie loosened his shoulders. "I'm starting to like this guy."

First's eyes rolled back hard enough to get a good look at her own brain stem, but then the answer occurred to her.

"He ducked out on a ten-credit bar tab."

"He did *what*?"

There it was . . .

Suddenly, Soolie wasn't so jovial. "I did not, you karking liar."

"You dare accuse royalty of lying?" First said, placing a hand on her chest as if struck.

"You're no royalty. You're a sewer skimmer."

"I don't think he even made the minimum million-credit deposit when he came on board," First said to Mecha Plump.

The android's eyes quite literally glowed red. "No deposit?" it shouted. "No deposit!" Then, it took off toward Soolie at a dead run. The sharp, sonic boom report of Soolie's laser pulses rattled off one after the other as Plump's avatar charged forward, burning deeply into the statue's unarmored center mass. But true to the man himself, it was mostly hollow, and the rounds struck only veneer and air before melting through the mecha's back.

The last thing Soolie the Fin saw in this existence was the ridged soul of Mecha Fonald Plump's giant metal shoe as it sped toward his upturned face.

First cringed as the gore slowly spread across the marble tile floor. "Well, that was . . . horrible."

"You're telling me." Mecha Plump lifted his foot and uprooted a nearby potted tree to scrape off the remnants. "Look what he did to my shoe! Do you know how hard these are to get in my size?"

"I hadn't thought of it like that, but yes, you're right." First lifted her handheld to her face to whisper, "Navigator, you should probably go ahead and restore his safety settings now."

"Oh, sure, an illegal AI goes on *one* killing rampage and suddenly people are all—"

"Navigator," First said with forced patience. "I'm not really in the mood for a philosophical discussion on the thorny issue of the rights of artificial intelligence while I'm only two strides away from a giant mechanized statue wiping blood off its foot, okay?"

"Fine, but we *will* talk about this later."

"Thank you." She closed the screen and opened the burst com. "Hashin, Sheer, get down here right away. Jrill's been shot, Loritt's spread over half the ship, and we have another problem waiting outside."

CHAPTER 28

They found Jrill by following the violet trail of blood to the nearest first-aid station.

"What took you so long?" she asked as she finished cauterizing her own wound.

"Tough damned vulture," First marveled.

"You're alive," Jrill said. "So I take it Soolie is dead?"

"About as dead as you can get." First shuddered at the fresh memory. She really had not liked Soolie by the end, but still. "It was ugly."

"Good."

"Where are the bits of Loritt I left with you?"

Jrill pointed to a container on the table with one of Loritt's ears peeking out over the top, trying to get a listen.

"He can't hear us like that," First asked. "Can he?"

"No, but his ear will remember and tell him." Jrill shifted uncomfortably. "Did it work? Is the ship clear?"

"Didn't see a soul on the way down here," Sheer said. "Except a Grenic actor. But I think we can ship him over before he realizes anything happened."

"I also saw no one," Hashin confirmed.

First picked up the tub of Loritt's parts. "Hey, shitbird, can you move?"

Jrill nodded. "Not quickly, but I'm mobile."

"Good. Get up to the command cave. The rest of Soolie's people are outside in the *Towed,* and it won't be long before they get restless."

"They stole our ship?!"

"That's how Soolie got on board with a gun undetected," Hashin said.

"Karking pirates will pay for that."

"Sheer, help Jrill. Hashin, grab a bucket and come with me."

They found the two pieces of Loritt she'd dropped climbing the ladder. Soolie had stomped one of them flat out of spite, and suddenly any residual quantum of sympathy First held for the method of his end disappeared. The chunk of Loritt was most certainly dead, but they found the other hiding under the decorative hallway molding nearby.

By the time they reached the switch junction where the fight had gone down, Loritt was, mostly, leaning naked against the bulkhead.

"Boss, are you all right?" Hashin asked.

Loritt glanced down at the cavity in his upper left chest and poked at it with a finger. His left primary arm hung limp at his side, and his left secondary arm was missing entirely. "I've been better."

"Jesus, man," First said. "Get yourself together." She tipped over the container of his parts, which all gleefully bounded or crawled over to rejoin their community. When they'd finished reintegrating, First leaned down to look him in the eyes. "Better?"

"A little."

"What's the damage?"

"Half a lung, a pectoral muscle, left upper bicep, spleen, two lymph nodes, small arm, a riblet, and a, well, my urethra."

"I could've done without that last bit," First said.

Loritt smirked. "I can't."

"Ew."

"Boss," Hashin interrupted. "It's not over. We have to get to the command cave."

With a groan, Loritt set his legs and pushed himself up the wall until he was back on his feet. "Lead the way."

"Maybe put your clothes on before we do that?" First suggested, covering her eyes and pointing at Loritt's crumpled outfit.

"If the lady insists."

"I definitely do."

Sheer, Jrill, and Fenax were already waiting for them on the other side of the command cave doors.

"What's our status?" Loritt asked as First and Hashin helped settle him into the captain's chair.

"The *Towed* is flying in close formation off our starboard," Jrill said. "They've been sending over increasingly frequent and frantic hails since we sat down."

"Where do we stand with the, ah, *evacuation*?"

"All occupied modules have been released," Hashin said. "Scans confirm what's left of the ship is empty except for the six of us—oh, and the Grenic."

"Send a distress signal to Garlopin Station to let them know to come out and pick up the poor dears while their fuel cells last," Loritt said. "Let no one say we didn't look out for the safety of our fellow sentients."

"And the hails from the glotheads who stole our ship?" Jrill asked pointedly.

"Yes, about them." Loritt picked up his limp left arm and set it across his lap. "I suppose it would be too optimistic to assume this ship has any offensive capabilities?"

"We could ram them, if we convinced them to shut down their engines and float in place," Jrill said. "Otherwise, no."

"Right." Loritt picked a bit of carbonized char off the edge of the hole Soolie's shot had burned into his shirt. "Hashin, put them through—audio only, please. They don't need to know half of us are half-dead."

"Channel open," Hashin acknowledged. "Audio only."

"It's about time, Fin," an unfamiliar voice said across the void. "The boys and me were getting worried."

"I regret to inform you that I can do nothing to dissipate your apprehension," Loritt said in a measured tone. "This is Loritt Chessel, recently promoted to captain of the *Change Your Luck.* To whom am I speaking?"

"Where's Soolie?" the voice demanded, taking on a honed edge.

"He's late. As in, the *late* Soolie the Fin. My condolences. Still fishing for your name, however."

The line was silent for several rakims before, "How did he die?"

"Squishy," First said. "We're going to need a mop. We'll send the bucket to his next of kin, if you like."

Loritt waved her off. "Please excuse my associate. She's still a little emotional over your former boss's attempts to kill her. But I must insist on knowing whom I'm speaking to."

"Name's Rirez, and I guess since you killed the boss, that makes me captain of this lovely little ship of yours. And all of its toys. So here's how the next larim goes down. We come alongside, board, and take over your prize like civilized people, or we put a beam through your command module and do all that other stuff anyway."

"Now you're lying, and that's just disrespectful," Loritt rejoined. "We both know the *Goes Where I'm Towed* doesn't mount offensive armaments."

"Ahhh," Jrill cleared her throat. "Sir, a word?"

Loritt's head rolled over to his tactical officer's station. "You have got to be kidding me." Jrill shrugged apologetically. Hashin turned to his station and innocently busied himself with a com system diagnostic. "I see. We'll talk about this later."

"That's fair," Jrill said.

"Assuming there is a later," Fenax observed.

Loritt took a moment to compose himself before answering. "'Captain' Rirez, my apologies. It seems your threat has some teeth to it after all. Regardless, we have taken legal possession of this vessel under Assembly Charter Statute 372.6, Section B. Our repossession contract is available upon demand. You are thereby engaged in an act of space piracy, at least your second, considering you're transmitting from the captain's chair of *my* karking ship."

"That's all true, Mr. Chessel," Rirez said. "However, since you just did us the enormous favor of ejecting all the potential witnesses to this act of piracy, I rather like my odds. So if you'll be a good sport and just sit still . . . for . . . what's that buzz—"

The line went abruptly dead.

"Hashin, did they drop the connection?" Loritt asked.

"No, boss. The line is still open, but . . ."

"But what?"

"I'm not sure. I'm getting multiple signals on the same channel. They're interfering with each other. I can't make sense of it."

"Show me," Loritt said.

"Routing it to the main display," Hashin said.

A composite feed from the *Luck*'s eternal cameras appeared on the cave's view screen. In the space just beyond their starboard bow, their gray, nondescript, plucky little home away from home rapidly flickered through space like it was trying to fly off in six different directions at once.

"What's happening to the *Towed*?" Loritt demanded.

"It looks like . . ." First's voice trailed off and she swallowed hard.

"It looks like *what*?"

"The timeflies after we defused the bomb," First said. Everyone slowly turned to look at Sheer.

"Sheer?" Loritt said. "Do you have anything to share with the rest of the class?"

"I, ah, kept them."

"You kept them?" First said. "The zombified, causality-violating bugs we all agreed should be thrown into a black hole for the good of the universe? *Those* them?"

"I meant to get around to dumping them, but we've just all been so busy. Somebody must have knocked the tank over and let them loose."

"The bomb thing was months ago." Jrill said. "Shouldn't they have starved by now?"

"I may have slipped them occasional scraps," Sheer admitted sheepishly. Everyone stared back at her indignantly. "Look, I felt bad for them, okay? They'd already been through a lot."

"We should blow up the ship," Jrill said with finality.

"And risk throwing little bits of multiverse paradox all over the space lanes?" Hashin asked. "Hard pass."

"Drop a navigational hazard buoy next to it," Loritt said. "Set it to keep station next to *Towed* and warn off any ship that comes near. Can we pilot it remotely?"

"Which version of it?" Hashin asked.

"I see your point," Loritt said.

"Couldn't one of those eventualities still fire on us?" Jrill asked.

"I think they're all dealing with bigger issues just now," First answered.

"True enough."

Loritt stared at the display for a long time, eventually falling into melancholy. Sheer was the first to try to break him free of it. "Hey, boss. It's okay. She was a good boat, but after we drop this heap off with the bank, we can afford a new one."

"No," Loritt said. "It's not that."

"What is it, then?"

"I'm trying to figure out how to spin this to the *Towed*'s insurance carrier in a way that won't get our policy canceled."

"Oh," Sheer said. "Good luck with that."

CHAPTER 29

Between three days running what was left of the *Change Your Luck* out to its creditors in the Burquel system, who were not happy about its condition, two days haggling with them over the final payout, three days back to Garlopin Station, three days convincing port security there that the *Buzzmouth* was legitimate salvage, and the monthlong trip back to Junktion on board a jerry-rigged ship that smelled exactly like the inside of its namesake, almost three months had passed since First last set foot in her apartment.

As soon as the door slid shut behind her, First dropped her bags on the floor and ran over to where Quarried Themselves sat on their reinforced couch. First threw her arms around one of Quarried's legs and hugged them tight for long enough that even the Grenic would register the gesture, then grabbed a pillow and comforter from her bed and made herself a little nest among her roomie's limbs. First watched maybe ten minutes of the third-season opener of *Rocks in Hard Places* at real speed before falling into a deep, unblemished sleep.

First woke some ten hours later with an incredibly stiff neck and her right arm still fast asleep. The episode had not yet concluded. Quarried hadn't moved, except to gently hover a protective hand over her. It took some effort to maneuver around, especially with one dead arm.

She showered under genuine hot water for the first time since her cabin on the *Luck,* which went a long way toward sorting out the stiffness in her neck and brought her arm fully back to functionality. The raven roots of her hair had begun to reassert themselves against the aquamarine blue of her duchess disguise, but looking back at herself in the steamed mirror, First didn't mind. The duality suited her. She'd pretended to be someone else for so long now that the different identities had all blended together. She may as well advertise the fact.

The ceiling chimed an incoming call while she toweled off. First groaned. "Accept."

"Good morning, First," Loritt said. "How did you sleep?"

"Like the dead," she said. "Meaning I'm stiff as hell. I thought you gave us the week off."

"I did indeed. Regardless, I'd like to invite you to join me down in Bay Ninety-Four."

"Why?" First wrung out her towel into the sink. Water was still a valuable commodity on Junktion. "It's empty. The *Towed* is a marked space-time anomaly, and the *Buzzmouth* just got auctioned and towed off for parts, thank god."

"Can you just this once do something I ask you to without the interrogation of my motives, please?" Loritt asked. "I'd consider it a personal favor."

"Fine," First said. "See you in half a larim."

She took her time drying her hair and getting dressed for the occasion, whatever it was. As a precaution, she aimed low with sweatpants and her torn Whitesnake T-shirt. She was on leave, after all. Office dress didn't apply.

First grabbed a pod on autopilot, both herself and the pod, and somehow managed to get out at the right stop instead of taking the return trip right back to her tower's station and crawling into her actual bed.

When she finally made it to Bay Ninety-Four, she found herself surrounded by friends.

Loritt spread his three arms in greeting. Still waiting to adopt another arm from one of the Nelihexu rescue shelters on board the station. "Welcome, First."

First took everyone in as she walked past them. Unreadable but loyal Fenax, floating in their tank. Hesitant Sheer, still realizing the strength everyone else recognized in her. Enigmatic Hashin, always on the outside and at once at the center of things. Stoic Jrill, recovering from her wounds without comment or complaint, her strength unquestioned.

And finally, Loritt, the patchwork man who brought so many discarded pieces together that didn't fit anywhere else and made them into a whole.

"What the hell is this?" she said at last.

"Your coworkers are here to help me present you with your bonus." Loritt swept a hand over the deck and to the berth beyond. It was almost empty.

Almost.

Instead of the familiar silhouette of the now lost *Goes Where I'm Towed,* only a small cocoon of plastiwrap floated in a far corner of the slip, the sort of thing new aircars were sheathed in prior to delivery from the manufacturer. Except this was too big to be any production aircar, by half.

Without her even realizing it, First's nose was pressed against the chilled glass of the gallery window in anticipation.

"Hashin," Loritt said. "Don't keep the poor girl waiting."

"Aye." Hashin pressed a button on his handheld, and a small dockside service drone sprang to life and dragged the cocoon free.

First's eyes threatened to bulge right out of her head as the plastiwrap peeled back and coughed up its secret.

"Is that . . ." First's voice cut off as the daggerlike prow of the tiny vessel came into view. She'd seen it before. Except its livery hadn't featured a bright chrome *1st* quite so prominently along the side before.

"Your sling-racer?" Loritt finished for her. "Yes, it is. It took almost the entire time we've been gone for a team of seasoned professionals to fix the damage you inflicted the last time you piloted it, but yes. It's yours. And now"—he held out the activation stud—"it's yours forever. Paid off, free and clear. It just needs a new name for the officially sanctioned race record before I transfer ownership."

First threw up a hand to brace herself against the gallery window frame. "You didn't sell it back to the bank?"

"We bought it from the bank at auction," Loritt said. "We all voted on it, First. This came out of everyone's share from the *Change Your Luck,* out of acknowledgment to your contributions to our broken little family since you turned up. It was a unanimous vote. So, what's her name?"

"Well," First considered. "The spine of it looks like a knife, so . . . how about the *Razorback*?"

"You can't take the *Razorback,*" Hashin said, staring at his handheld.

"Why not?"

"Someone already used that name."

"Oh, okay. How about *Stiletto*?"

Hashin looked at Loritt and gave a thumbs-up.

"Looks like we're good here," Loritt said.

"Yes." First stared through the glass with avarice at her new obsession. "Yes, we are."

ACKNOWLEDGMENTS

Books, like children, are a labor of love. And as it takes a village to raise a child, so too does it take an army to really ruin a novel. *Starship Repo* started life as a perfect story, unmatched in the history of Western literature for its pacing, character development, world-building, plot, wit, social insights, and humor. Beta readers, grown men and women, openly wept upon completion out of both elation at having experienced it, and the crushing realization that it was over.

It was only through a deliberate effort to sabotage this one flawless thing during the editing process that what could have been a singular human achievement was hauled back down from the heavens. Anything that you didn't like about this novel, dear reader, is entirely the fault of someone other than the author, who is just as much a victim here as you are.

Any joke that failed to land, any dangling plot thread, any inconsistency or even typo, was inserted in post-production by publishing industry professionals who succumbed to their jealousy and base impulse to destroy that which they envied.

And while many hands made light work of butchering this aborted cultural touchstone, from the cover design team, to the typesetter, to the copyeditors, even to my agent, immediate family, and wife, there is one man who deserves to be singled out for blame, and perhaps even criminal prosecution, for desecrating a work that otherwise would have cruised to this year's Nobel Prize in Literature.

That's right, I'm talking about my editor, Christopher Morgan. I trusted you, man. I already put a down payment on my flat in SoHo in anticipation of the Nobel money. Now what the hell am I supposed to do, keep writing?

ABOUT THE AUTHOR

Patrick S. Tomlinson lives in Milwaukee, Wisconsin. When not writing sci-fi and fantasy novels and short stories, Patrick is busy developing his other passion: stand-up comedy.